72 Hours to Graceland

By David W. Hensley

Dead Man's Run: Book 2

Three Ravens Publishing

Chickamauga, GA USA

Welcome to the world of the ***Car Warriors: Autoduel Chronicles*** — Tales from the freeways of the future, where the right of way goes to the biggest guns and death sports rule the airwaves. From clandestine highway battles to prime-time arena combat, jump behind the wheel, follow the fast-paced action, and never forget to Drive Offensively!

Car Warriors: The Autoduel Chronicles is set in the world of ***Car Wars*** by permission of Steve Jackson Games Incorporated.

72 HOURS TO GRACELAND By David W. Hensley
Published by Three Ravens Publishing
threeravenspublishing@gmail.com
P O Box 851, Chickamauga, Ga 30707
https://www.threeravenspublishing.com
Copyright © 2023 by Steve Jackson Games

All rights reserved. No part of this publication may be reproduced, distributed, or transmitted in any form or by any means, including photocopying, recording, or other electronic or mechanical methods, without the prior written permission of the publisher, except in the case of brief quotations embodied in critical reviews and certain other noncommercial uses permitted by copyright law.

For permission requests, contact the publisher listed above, addressed "Attention: Permissions".

Publisher's Note: This is a work of fiction. Names, characters, places, and incidents are a product of the author's imagination. Locales and public names are sometimes used for atmospheric purposes. Any resemblance to actual people, living or dead, or to businesses, companies, events, institutions, or locales is completely coincidental.

Credits:
72 Hours to Graceland was written by David W. Hensley
Cover art by: oldmanlogan

Ebook ISBN: 978-1-951768-94-2
Paperback ISBN: 978-1-951768-95-9
Audiobook ISBN: 978-1-951768-96-6

Thank you, to all of our backers of the Car Warriors Kickstarter project!

Jessie D. Foster
Kevin A Davis
David Hankins
Alyssa Casto
Jeffrey Riggs
Jorge Markin
Randal Dilday
Julian W. Thompson
Jeff Dodge
Rich Neves
Cursed Dragon Ship Publishing
Stace Johnson
Val Cassotta
Jef Farnsworth
Jeffery Sergent
Jason Walters
Mark Wagner
Keith Unger
Jonathan Hurley
Jim Tullis
Mark Strahm
Karl J. Smith
John Pieper
Dustin "TinyMonster" Rhoades
Jedikiah Springfield
Larry Southard
Jeff Johnson
James Emil Conason
Aaron Spriggs
Scott Long
Reed Snyder
K.C. L'Roy
Tee Stoney
Todd DeWolfe

Brian Thacker
Caleb Pittman
David A. Jepson
Tad K
David Glover
Ramón Terrell
Eric Stuyvesant
Gavin Inglis
Mark Stallings
Brooks Moses
Brian Healy
KB Carlisle
Andrew Franklin
Stephen Dedman
Rolf Laun
Wild Card
Marc Alan Edelheit
Rob Kamm
Peter J. Jansen
Nicholas D Miller
Danny White
Jordan C
Kenta Washington
Robert Gilson
Marcus Evenstar
Sammy
Kim the Troublemaker
Jonathan Bowen
Brian John Skillen
Jim Davenport

Monty Rasmussen
Alex Rath
Ch. N. Heinzl
Bart Kemper
Jim Tetrick
Jason Lankford
Glitz & Blam
Eric Moorefield
Jerry 'Archer' Schaefer
Milton Fernandez
Jim McLaughlin

Table of Contents

Dedication:

There have been a fair number of people in my life to whom I owe a debt of gratitude. This book is dedicated to the four most important and influential of those people. The first two of the four have passed beyond the veil, and I can only hope they know how much I loved them and wish they were here to see a novel with the name Hensley on the cover. This book is dedicated to my grandma Fern Hensley, who taught me to read and helped me fall in love with tales of daring-do. To my mom, Sandra Walters, who encouraged my love of books and telling stories. To my dad, Dennis Hensley, who "rubbed some tough on me" and pressed me to read more than just fiction. Finally, to my best friend and partner in crime for the past thirty years, my wife Nichole. Without her, none of this would have been possible.

Acknowledgements:

I am learning that no story makes it into publication without a lot of brain-sweat, dummy-tax, hard work, and encouragement. Without further ado I would like to say thank you to some of the folks who did those things. Don and Matt for early reading and feedback, Ron for helping me with the question of cannibalism, and Nichole for listening to me jabber incessantly about everything from biodiesel made from human fat to magnetohydrodynamic power plants. I would like to say thank you to the one and only Steve Jackson for keeping me on the straight and narrow as it pertains to the *CarWars* Universe and for providing the opportunity to play in his sandbox. Finally I would like to thank Benjamin Tyler Smith, Hillbilly, the Word Witch and everyone else at Three Ravens for being so damned great to work with.

A word from Steve

The **Car Wars** game has been around for a while now. It's practically a tradition. We've been driving offensively since 1980 . . . six editions now. Design your car, set up a few ground rules (but not very many!), load 'em up, and go. The right of way belongs to the biggest guns.

When Scott Tackett told me he'd like to do some **Car Wars** fiction, I listened. Scott's Three Ravens Publishing has a great stable of new authors plus some friends who have been writing for a long time now. Good combo. And he's got big plans. If the Dead Man's Run series goes as planned, there will be more than a dozen novels and at least one volume of short stories. So, if you like it . . . we'll be back.

If you'd like to see the game that spawned all this, check the back of the book. Just like the old paperback days, there's an ad. Tradition is important!

And I hope you enjoy this story. I sure did.

– Steve Jackson

Chapter 1

Robert hated mornings. Not because he had trouble waking up. Most days, he woke several minutes ahead of his alarm and lay in the predawn silence expecting to feel her warmth, hear her gentle snore. Today was no different, and neither was the disappointment. So, Robert Fulton Henry hated mornings. He got out of bed all the same.

This morning, like most mornings, he dropped his scuffed boots at the door before stepping into the kitchen. He measured a full pot's worth of coffee into the filter, poured the water, and clicked the switch. It was too much coffee for him to drink. He'd been a one-cup guy for a long time. She was the one who drank the stuff by the gallon.

He turned to the stove and set to making breakfast, two eggs fried hard for her and three over easy for him with a slice of toast for each on "the good bread." Her words, not his. They hadn't eaten bread made from wheat flour since the second blight. But the stuff they were making from algae flour wasn't half bad. The eggs were an extravagance, and she wasn't going to eat hers. He made them anyway. The coffee was made by the time he had finished slipping the two breakfasts onto plates. He poured two cups, one with milk and sugar and the other with heavy cream and honey. He never could figure out what she found appealing about milk and sugar.

"Breakfast's ready." He slid the plates and cups onto the small square table near the galley-style window. She'd laughed at him when he told her the window made the trailer's tiny kitchen feel like a pirate ship.

Robert ate his breakfast in silence. If he were honest, the thing he hated most about mornings these days was the silence. Not the absence of all sound. Just the lack of the sounds the other half of life brings to the equation. No banter, no annoying jokes, no ass chewings about the placement of his dirty socks.

Silence.

He finished his eggs and coffee, rinsed out both cups, dumped her uneaten food into the trash, emptied the coffeemaker, washed both sets of dishes, and dried them before returning them to the cupboard. One of these days, he was going to stop making her breakfast. Just not today.

"Well, guess it's time." He stepped into the single-wide living room.

Robert pulled the battered monocrys jacket from the horseshoe coat hook by the door and shrugged into it. He checked the battery charge and load on his Chrysler .45 before shoving it back into the gun belt and aligning it around his hips.

He grabbed the M310 carbine from beneath the coat hook and checked the battery charge and ammo counter. Battery life on a weapon modified for caseless ammo was just as important as the ammo itself.

The security monitor flickered to life; the motion sensor mounted on the front corner of his trailer tripped. Robert glanced over at the video feed and stopped. The security lights gleamed from a sleek new Luxford Drummond Cormorant parked behind his old deuce and a half.

"What in the hell does this guy think he's doing?" Robert rechecked the load on the carbine, glanced around the living room, and over the bar into the kitchen. All of the armored shutters were battened down tight.

Both of the Cormorant's front doors swung open. Two figures stepped out of the armored interior, heads turning, eyes scanning the shadowy bulk of trailers, cars, and rusty chain link fencing that comprised Meadow Lake Estates Mobile Home Community. The rear door opened, and a tall, broad-shouldered figure stepped out into the predawn gloom.

"Damn." Robert disarmed the security alarms and locks on the armored front door.

He shoved the heavy door of his trailer open and stepped out onto the covered porch, carbine held at low ready. Down the street to his right, strains of neopunk metal competed with the screeching howl of an angle grinder hard at work. It sounded like his neighbor Mabel was hard at it in her shop. She was most mornings.

"You look a touch lost," Robert called from the waist-high armored railing of the front porch. All three heads swiveled in his direction. The driver's hand dipped toward his waistline.

"I wouldn't if I were you." The driver's hand stopped just shy of the open suit jacket. Robert kept the carbine at low ready, the barrel not quite aimed at the driver. "Can I help you, fellas?"

"Looking for Bobby Hank." The guy at the rear stepped away from the armored safety of the car. He squinted at Robert, trying to see past the bright security lights.

"No one lives here by that name." Robert kept his carbine at the ready. These three had the look of corporate types. Tailored suits, sleek, well-armed, and armored transportation. The driver and the front passenger moved with that smooth confidence you get from years of experience and training. Certainly corporate security, probably former military if Robert was any judge. The rear passenger was an odd fit, but the three-thousand-dollar designer suit tagged him as the corporate representative.

"Mind if I come on up and set a spell?" The Company Man asked. He may have looked corporate, but he sure didn't sound that way.

"You, yes." Robert unlatched the screen door. "Your company goons, no." Something about the Company Man's voice nagged Robert. He knew that voice.

The Company Man shrugged and made his way to the white picket gate, leaving the driver to handle closing the car door. He looked young for a company man. Then again, Gold Cross was a standard perk at most big corporations, so perpetual youth was an option if you were far enough up the corporate ladder.

"Like I said. I'm looking for an old friend, Bobby Hank." The Company Man stepped through the gate, pausing to close and latch it before making his way up the long ramp to the screen door. The way he said "Bobby Hank" was definitely familiar. Robert had heard that voice say those words hundreds of times. Sometimes across a table and a couple of cold beers, other times through the speakers in his driver's helmet in the arena.

"Gordon?" Robert asked.

"Bobby?" The Company Man looked Robert up and down.

"Gordo!" Robert let the M-310F dangle and pushed open the screen door. "You're looking pretty damned good for an old fart."

"New meat." Gordon stepped through the screen door. "You look— "

"Old Gordo," Robert said. "I look old."

"Still wearing your original meat, huh?"

"Yep. Still wearing the original." Robert grinned. "Well, the original I mustered out of the service with."

"I ain't seen you since…must have been Chicago '63."

"Nope." Robert shook his head. "Carter Stadium back in '62. Won the division championship that year."

"That's right." Gordon nodded. "You put me and Tommy Gates on the slab. That was some fancy shooting."

"Hell no." Robert shook his head. "Kat pulling that Ivan's what did it. Was like shootin' fish in a barrel."

"You're telling me that any old gunner could have punched both Tommy and my tickets from a moving platform at that distance?"

"Well, OK, maybe not any gunner," Robert said. "You gotta admit Kat pulling that Ivan is what set up the shot."

"Yeah, maybe."

"Maybe? You don't want to admit that you were just plain outclassed."

"You might have a point." Gordon laughed. "Hey, didn't you and Kat win the National Championship that year by pulling off a Josie Wales?"

"Yep." Robert nodded.

"Ballsiest thing I've ever seen in an autoduel." Gordon shook his head. "That girl could drive."

"She sure could." Robert sighed. "She sure could."

"How is Kat these days?"

"Dead."

"What? What about her Gold Cross?"

"CDRS." Robert stared at the tightly woven rug, at the patio chairs he'd pulled out of that fancy neighborhood down in Norfolk.

"What?"

"Clone Download Rejection Syndrome." Robert wasn't smiling anymore.

"Meat shakes," Gordon shuddered. "She'd downloaded before, right?"

"A couple times, yeah." Robert nodded.

"What happened?"

"Poughkeepsie."

"What the hell were you two doing up there?" Gordon asked.

"Was a private gig." Robert stepped back out of the doorway. "Big payday, enough to get out of the game for good."

"What happened? Radiation?"

"Nah, radiation levels are fine if you don't stay very long." Robert shook his head. "There's more than radiation wrong with Poughkeepsie. The Ruskies must have hit it with some kind of bioweapon after they nuked it. Or maybe the radiation mutated something that was already hanging around. Who the hell knows. Either way, it did something to Kat's DNA."

"Just hers?" Gordon asked.

"Probably not, but I'm still wearing original meat," Robert said. "On the way back, we got hit by a cycle gang. They took the package and left us for dead. I woke up in a hospital bed, Kat woke up in an incubation tube. Three days later, the tremors started. A week after that, she was half out of her head with hallucinations; a week later, she was dead."

"How the hell did a cycle gang get the drop on you and Kat?" Gordon asked.

"We got sloppy. Too busy celebrating, not busy watching our six."

"Shit."

"Yeah." Robert pulled open the durasteel door of his trailer. "You didn't come all this way in your shiny new Cormorant with your boy scouts and designer suits to pay a social call."

"No, I guess not," Gordon said.

"You want something."

"I do."

"Well, come on in, I'll put on some coffee, and you can tell me what your bosses want."

Chapter 2

Gordon sipped his coffee and grimaced. "Pete's balls, Bobby."

"Too strong for you?" Robert poured himself a fresh cup, dragged out the other chair, and sat. The kitchen felt much smaller with Gordon's bulk crammed into the corner by the galley window.

"You could remove paint with this stuff."

"Probably. I get it from a place down in Norfolk."

"Norfolk?" Gordon asked. "That's deep in the dead zone."

"So."

"So, you drive all the way into the Hampton Roads Dead Zone to scavenge coffee?"

"Among other things." Robert drank. "Best way I know to make money outside the arena."

"Clearly." Gordon gestured at the small kitchen with his mug. "Real palace you got here."

"It's home enough." Rob shrugged.

"Didn't you and Kat buy that big spread out in Colorado?"

"K&B Ranch." Robert nodded. "Two thousand acres with a proper manor. Blast doors and windows, weapons turrets, automated defense systems, and a full armory in the basement."

"Why aren't y'all there?" Gordon took another drink.

"Sold it." Robert drained his cup and stood.

"What the hell for?"

"After that first bout of the shakes, we figured it was a fluke." Robert walked to the coffee maker and refilled his cup. "You know what the odds are on anyone having CDRS?"

"A million to one, at least."

"I can tell you. The chances of any individual having it in their first download are .0000001. That's one in ten million." Rob raised the half-empty carafe in silent question. "Do you know what the chances are on your second or third, or fourth download?"

"No." Gordon shook his head and held out his half-empty cup.

"It jumps up to one in three hundred eighty-six million." Robert leaned against the stainless-steel countertop. Kat liked things clean and industrial; God only knew why.

"So basically, zero chance of having CDRS after your first successful download."

"Yep. That's what all the labcoats say." Robert walked back over to the chair and sat. "Do you know what kind of treatment there is for the shakes?"

"No." Gordon shook his head.

"None. Zero. It happens so damned infrequently that there are no therapeutics, no treatments, no cure."

"What's that got to do with you selling your ranch?"

"Plenty." Robert sat his cup down on the table and stared hard at Gordon. "When the love of your life, your best friend, keeps dying and dying hard, you do anything to find a cure."

"Anything?"

"We used up all of her Gold Cross insurance, then mine on new bodies, new downloads, hoping that with each one something would change, would be different."

"It wasn't?" Gordon asked.

"Nope."

"Gold Cross didn't have any answers?"

"None." Robert shook his head. "I started digging, looking into CDRS, cloning, and consciousness download."

"Oh?"

"I didn't understand most of what I found, so I went looking for researchers. Turns out you can't download a consciousness into a body that's not genetically identical to the original."

"Hell, Bobby, everyone knows that."

"You know why?" Robert asked.

"No."

"Neither do the big brains in white coats." Robert shrugged. "Best they can figure is something's tied up between DNA and consciousness. That consciousness takes up more bandwidth than just the brain. Like the brain is spreading the load around at a subcellular level."

"So?"

"So?" Robert leaned back in his chair and scrubbed at his face. "You know what the worst thing is?"

"No."

"Worst thing is that it's against the law to research why." Robert thumped the table with his fist. "It's a god-damned class one felony to even try to figure out what makes it impossible to load a consciousness into a non-clone!"

"What's that got to do with Kathrine?" Gordon asked.

"CDRS happens one in a million when it usually happens, and less than one in several hundred million on a second or third download." Robert leaned forward, staring hard at Gordon. "It happens every single time a consciousness is downloaded into a clone not specific to that consciousness."

"Pete's balls." Gordon whistled. "So, what does any of that do with why you're here in a trailer instead of at your ranch in Colorado?"

"I'm getting there." Robert sipped his bitter brew. "We found a lab down in Raleigh Durham that had the permit to do the research but no funding."

"So, you sold the house?" Gordon looked at the raised carafe and shook his head.

"Sold everything in the house, then I sold the house," Robert put the carafe back on the burner and returned to his chair. "I even sold Lucy."

"Damn, Bobby!" Gordon stared at him.

"Yep." Robert stared off into the distance. "Sold her to the Hall of Fame Museum six months ago."

"Kat loved that car."

"I'd have sold my soul." Robert sat back in his chair.

"How's the research going?"

"We just ran the last test a month and a half ago." Robert scrubbed his face again.

"How bad?" Gordon asked.

"She survived three and a half weeks. Near the end, the hallucinations were so bad she tried to gun me down."

"Now what?"

"Now?" Robert asked. "Now I make salvage runs into the Norfolk and Virginia Beach Dead Zones looking for stuff I can sell to rich assholes."

"Why?" Gordon asked. "You were one of the best-damned gunners in the game. Why not get back behind the wheel?"

"Hell, I tried. Couldn't find a driver I trusted."

"What if I told you there was a new autoduel event?" Gordon leaned forward, elbows on the table.

"I just told you I can't." Robert shook his head. "I'm a wreck without her."

"Hear me out," Gordon said. "It's a cross-country rally race."

"What?"

"You know, a race where you start in one place and drive like hell to be the first to make it to the endpoint somewhere else."

"I know what a rally is," Robert said. "The association approved another Death Rally?"

"I don't know if you've been following the sport much, but attendance and ratings are down, and fans are dwindling."

"How does a Death Rally fix any of that?"

"It's a fusion of old-school autoduelling and rally racing." Gordon grinned. "Except out on the road, anything goes."

"Anything?"

"Anything. Fans are tired of safe duels with drivers winning on points. They want to see twisted metal and blood on the windshield." Gordon said.

"Single seat?"

"Crew of two. The vehicle seats seven." Gordon sat back and grinned.

"What the hell is that?" Robert asked.

"Well, each division is different depending on entrants and sponsorships. The sponsor we have lined up, my company, wants to use the rally to unveil and promote their latest machine."

"I can't work with another driver." Robert shook his head. "And I'm a much better gunner than a driver."

"You used to be something, Bobby." Gordon stared hard at Robert. "Could be again."

"You don't hear so good anymore, do you?" Robert stared at his old buddy. Gordo was clearly working an angle of some sort.

"The sponsor wants you; the association wants you. They figure a legend like you will bring fans back in droves."

"Yeah, nothing like a has-been to bring fans back to the sport." Robert snorted.

"Well, that might be true for most duelists. Not you, though." Gordon said. "Back in the day, you were a bona fide legend."

"Horseshit," Robert said. "I was a pretty good shot and got lucky a time or two."

"If you say so." Gordon pulled a smartphone from his suit coat. He did a quick bit of typing and then slid the device across the table to Robert. "See that?"

Robert picked up the device and looked at the screen. Displayed was a picture of an American Autoduel Association rookie card. The image on the card was a much younger version of himself. The caption read 'Robert Fulton Henry, a.k.a. Bobby Hank the Pale Rider.'

"Okay," Robert said. "You have a picture of my old card. So what?"

"You know what that thing sold for at auction ten days ago?"

"No."

"Twenty-three thousand four hundred fifty-three dollars," Gordon said. "Do you know how many kids had Bobby Hank cards back in the day?"

"All that proves is that I was good then." Robert shook his head. "In case you haven't noticed, I ain't exactly a spring chicken."

"That's part of the appeal," Gordon said. "You're Bobby Hank, the Pale Rider. You survived hundreds of duels. You've never been on the slab, never been downloaded. Do you know how rare that is?"

"Okay, okay." Robert raised his hands in surrender. "Just give me the pitch and quit hand-jobbing my ego, huh."

"The main sponsor is Herolutions. They're partnering with Luxford Drummond Motors and Fire Power Network to sponsor a team for Dead Man's Run."

"Cute name."

"Luxford Drummond is providing eight of their latest machines."

"Wait a minute, Luxford Drummond has always been a luxury brand. Strictly vanity and status." Robert said. "You're telling me they are getting into autoduelling?"

"Sort of." Gordon nodded. "They think people want to travel again, you know, family road trips to see grandma and all that."

"Okay?"

"So, they came up with a van that will let the customer load up the family and drive over the river and through the woods."

"A van?" Robert shook his head. "You want me to ride gunner in a van?"

"It's state of the art. Latest in targeting computers, weapons systems, and armor. The power plant is the latest in magnetohydrodynamic power generation. It has a dedicated gunnery station and an engineer station allowing you to have someone handling power distribution and making repairs on the fly."

"What's the prize?" Robert asked.

"Ten million cash based on place and survivability."

"How does that help me help Kat?" Robert asked. "Even if my team makes it to the end and we're the only survivors, ten million ain't a lot when you start talking restricted research budgets."

"Well, that's where the sponsor comes in." Gordon leaned in now, scenting victory. "Herolutions has agreed to offer Kathrine a spot in their research program. They've been conducting very promising research into consciousness download for the government."

"What?"

"I said Herolutions is— "

"I heard you." Robert leaned in and stared hard at Gordon, measuring him up. "You knew, didn't ya? Here I've been sharing my troubles like we're old pals, and you knew the whole time! You came here looking to leverage Kat's condition."

"I did my homework, Bobby." Gordon patted the air with his hands. "Look, we need a name, a legend to get fans watching again. That's you. Who else has survived as many duels as you have? How many other duelists from our day are still out there mixing it up?"

"Got to be a few," Robert said.

"All right, name one."

"Chip Thompson." Robert held up his right index finger.

"Retired, moved off the grid up in Maine."

"Butcher Bill?"

"He's a commentator for Fire Power. Has his own show and everything."

"Tina Fuentes?"

"Dead."

"Dead?" Robert scrubbed at his face. "How?"

"Didn't have a clone on ice, no consciousness saved to a MMSD," Gordon said. "Got burned alive by the Sons of Vulcan three years back outside of Birmingham."

"How about Steamboat Danny?"

"Got a gig with Blood and Guts," Gordon said.

"The French Bastard?"

"Andre?" Gordon asked. "Runs an autoduel driving school down in Atlanta.

"Rosie and Nate?"

"Settled down in Little Rock," Gordon said. "They got four kids."

"Four?" Robert snorted. "Those two?"

"Hard to believe." Gordon laughed.

"How about Charlotte and Hiram?"

"Black Dragon and Headsman?" Gordon sat back in his chair. "Still in the game when they ain't running down skips or troubleshooting for anyone with the cash to afford them."

"There you go, get them," Robert said.

"They're heels, Bobby. Fire Power wants a Face. Luxford Drummond and Herolutions want a Face." Gordon shook his head. "Besides, you do this, and win, you'll be rolling in product endorsements with Luxford Drummond. They're all set to release a Bobby Hank edition of the Luxford Drummond Quest."

"What about— "

"Look, we can sit here and go through the rest of the roster if you want to." Gordon leaned forward again. "Truth is everyone that fits the bill is either dead, retired, or moved on to safer careers."

"I don't know." Robert stared down at the scratched and chipped tabletop.

"You know what your problem is?" Gordon waited until Robert looked up, and locked eyes.

"You're gonna tell me."

"You got out of the game cause you lost your nerve."

"Bullshit." Robert shook his head.

"You didn't want it anymore. I'll bet you that as soon as it wasn't Kat driving, you started second-guessing your decisions, started missing shots, missing opportunities. Kathrine was wild and dangerous. Hell, you used to be dangerous too."

Robert blinked first. Looked down into his cooling coffee. "It just wasn't the same without her."

"No, Bobby. It's exactly the same." Gordon said. "The game didn't change. You did."

"What the hell would you know about it?" Robert asked.

"Plenty." Gordon gestured at his Israel Sandow suit. "I know the look. I see it in the mirror most mornings."

"After Kathrine got sick I…Other drivers weren't right." Robert stared at his distorted reflection in the stainless tabletop. "You ride with someone long enough you become one person, you know?"

"I know."

"I couldn't focus, couldn't compartmentalize, couldn't take the risks knowing she was dead for good if I got nailed."

"So you started running salvage into the Hampton Roads Dead Zone?" Gordon shook his head. "That place is hundreds of times more dangerous than any autoduel arena."

"Horse shit." Robert pushed his cold coffee away. "Most of those blood-mouth bastards down there can't hit the broad side of a barn. The arena is different. Everyone in there can shoot."

"You let fear win, Bobby," Gordon said. "Fear is a good servant. It helps keep us alive, but as a master, it is utterly useless. Fear rides in everyone's car, Bobby. Question is, does it ride in the back seat or up front where it can choose the radio station?"

"You might have a point," Robert said.

"I know I do," Gordon said. "I'm still trying to get fear out of my own passenger seat."

Sunlight peeked through the armored shutters on the kitchen windows. Robert pushed back from the table. "Okay, I'll think it over."

"Don't take too long." Gordon stood, buttoned his jacket, and handed his cup to Robert.

"When do you need to know?"

"Sooner rather than later." Gordon stepped into the sparsely furnished living room and reached for the door. "First leg ends in Memphis, and you'll have just 72 hours to get there."

"72 hours to Graceland." Robert shook his head and grinned. "I'll be in touch."

Chapter 3

"Had to go and talk trash about the cannibals, didn't you, Rob?" He tromped on the accelerator, mashing it to the floor pan. Ancient electric motors whined in protest, and the old deuce-and-a-half slowed. Behind him, a machine gun chattered and clattered. Bullets struck sparks from his armored door. Several more rounds smacked the armorglass rear window. He glanced down at the multi-function display he'd paid Mabel to install. The power-cell charge was showing around thirty-five percent. More than enough to allow him to pull away when everything was working right. Something was definitely not right.

"Damn." Robert reached up and hit the smoke switch. Clouds of heavy white smoke poured from the nozzles mounted in the rear bumper obscuring his pursuers. "And for my next trick…"

Robert mashed the brake pedal cutting power to the electric motors, locking up all four wheels, and bringing several tons of durasteel, Kevlar, and armorglass to a sudden and complete stop. He stabbed the large red button marked C-WIZ, powering up the salvaged eighth-generation weapon system. He'd had a hell of a time getting the heavy bastard down off the side of the half-sunk carrier. Mabel had grinned for a week after helping him install the radar-guided 20mm Vulcan cannon in the bed of the deuce-and-a-half.

Bikers roared through the smoke screen, passing him on either side. Two more slammed into the armored rear of the old transport with a satisfying thump. The C-WIZ radar chimed with a partial lock.

"Hope this works." Robert pressed the fire button.

The 20mm Vulcan cannon burped out depleted uranium at eighty rounds a second, shredding three bikers and their bikes in less than three seconds before the ammunition tracker showed empty.

"So much for that." He transferred power from the Phalanx C-WIZ back to the drive motors and accelerated through the ground meat and twisted scrap. "We need a bigger magazine."

He emerged through the smoke screen to find two more Blue Blasters sideways in the middle of the highway. Their tattoos gave their exposed skin a bluish cast. They had on little more than their vests and chaps . . . made from human skin, if the stories were to be believed. The human ribs strung into a breastplate lent credibility to those stories. None of which was news to Robert. He'd spent a good many years fighting and avoiding the various cannibal tribes that made the south side of the Hampton Roads Dead Zone uninhabitable for normal folk. What was new was the shiny new anti-tank missile tubes they were pointing in his direction.

"Woah—" Robert hit the trigger paddles on the steering wheel; twin 20mm Vulcan cannons and quad .50 caliber machine guns roared to life, ripping one of the gruesomely armored cannibals from his bike and hammering the Frankenstein's monster of a machine to scrap metal. The other one stayed put, took her time, and sent an anti-tank missile streaking toward him. He felt the detonation slightly ahead of the sound. The deuce-and-a-half shuddered, shrapnel pinging against the armored roof.

"Come on, baby…" He mashed the accelerator pedal to the floor, desperate to coax more speed from the battered vehicle. The speedometer display grudgingly crept up to 46 mph as he limped past the remaining biker.

Robert glanced down at the systems' status display. Power was down to 20%, and his bed-mounted crane flashed red. The threat warning system flashed amber, indicating a device or weapon with active radar. He glanced up at the screens showing the rearview. There, through the thinning cloud of smoke, stood the remaining cannibal. She had another tube on her shoulder.

He shrugged, lifted the red cover off the countermeasures switch, and flipped it up, launching a cloud of crybaby chaff, mylar with micro transmitters in the air behind him. On the screen, he watched the anti-tank missile streak out over the James River and detonate. Robert glanced down at the instrument panel; fifty-one miles per hour; if she had another missile tube, he was in real trouble. The threat warning system remained green and silent. Either she was out of missiles, or it was on the fritz as well. He kept the pedal pressed to the floor, every second bringing him closer to the armored gates of the Monitor Merrimack tunnel and the South Side Ranger garrison located there.

Robert picked up the old CB microphone and checked the channel before squeezing the switch. "Merrimack Station, this is Robert Henry approaching from the south in the deuce-and-a-half. I have unknown number of hostiles in pursuit. They have small arms and anti-tank missiles."

"We have you on approach." The speakers crackled to life. "Your tail is clear. Power down all weapons systems and prepare for inspection."

"Roger, Merrimack Station." Robert eased his foot off the accelerator, letting the old truck slow to a non-threatening ten miles per hour and grinned. He'd made it again.

Robert breathed a sigh of relief when his headlights washed across the weathered sign for the Meadow Lake Estates Mobile Home Park. The winter sun had already set, and the old deuce-and-a-half was lurching and limping. Two of the four wheel motors blinked red on the status diagram; a long series of amber codes scrolled across the top of the display. He eased to a stop at the entrance gate and honked three times.

"Unknown vehicle," the CB radio crackled to life. "Identify yourself."

"For god's sake." Robert keyed the mic, "You damned well know who it is, Pattie. Now open the gate."

"Rules are rules, Mr. Henry." Her slightly nasal voice, amplified by the small radio speaker, grated on Robert's nerves. "The association rules state all vehicles must stop at the gate and be recognized prior to opening."

"Well, I've stopped, and you recognize me," Robert said through gritted teeth. "Now open the damned gate."

"Opening now, Mr. Henry." The armored gate began to rise. "Have a nice day."

"Thanks." He piloted the limping, shuddering machine through the gateway turning south on Vanderbilt Circle toward the back of the trailer park.

"By the way, Mr. Henry," Pattie's nasal voice squawked. "You are in violation of association rule 22.23a. All dwelling colors will be approved by the beautification committee prior to application. Your shutters are not an approved color. If you do not get the proper permissions, I will have— "

"Yeah yeah." Robert clicked the CB radio off. "Put it on my tab."

He limped the deuce-and-a-half up to the sliding double doors of Mabel Holland's shop and powered the battered vehicle down. It was handy living on the lot next door to Mabel's shop. The rent was cheap, and as long as you didn't mind the screech of grinders, the crackle and fizz of the welder, or neopunk at all hours of the day and night, she was a pretty good neighbor. The icing on the cake, as far as Robert was concerned, was that Mae drove Pattie and the rest of the rules-lawyer sheep nutty. Their need for a genius mechanic in the community outweighed their need to enforce the association's rules, and Mae knew it.

Robert climbed down from the cab and walked back to the armored cargo compartment. Fresh durasteel gleamed under the security lights where shrapnel and bullets had scored the paint or punched holes in the flanks of the old transport. The bed-mounted crane was a shambles of torn metal and tangled cable, and a large chunk of metal protruded from the roof. The cargo compartment hatch was bent and distorted, probably from the anti-tank missile. He shook his head and pried the damaged lid open. More work for Mae. He pulled out several packages and tucked them under his arm before slamming the hatch shut and making his way to the partially open doors. Blue-white light strobed from deep within the steel building. The spitting crackle of an arc welder occasionally emerged over the strains of some old-school pop-punk song. It sounded like Sam's The Hero's *Song Without a Chorus.*

"Hey, Mae." Robert banged on the door. The singer was going on about some song without a message when Mabel slid the door open far enough for Robert to enter.

"Rob." She half shouted over the music. She wore grease-stained coveralls with a singed leather apron over the front. The welding helmet's face shield was tipped up revealing an elfin face with a dark smear of grease down the left side. "What brings you around?"

"I got your wheel bearings." He held up one of the packages.

"Oh good." She did something that killed the music before backing away from the opening. "Get in here and shut the door. It's cold."

Robert stepped into the warmth of the shop and rolled the large door closed. He sat the packages down on a nearby workbench. "Got some more of the peanut butter and chocolate-flavored coffee you like."

"Hell yeah!" Mabel pumped her fist, causing the welding helmet to fall over her face.

She removed the helmet and tossed it on the bench next to the bearings before walking to the refrigerator in the far corner.

"Brewski?" She pulled the door lever and retrieved a six-pack of Milwaukee's Best from deep within the antique. When he nodded, she twisted one free from the plastic and tossed it to him. "How was the rest of your haul?"

"Not great." Robert cracked open his beer and took a long pull. "Something's got the eaters all stirred up."

"Eaters." Mabel shuddered. "It's always eaters. Why the hell haven't we eradicated those sons-of-bitches?"

"Hell, Mae," Robert took another drink savoring the yeasty flavor. "We can barely keep people fed and the lights turned on. Reclaiming the south-side just ain't priority for the government right now."

"How's the truck?" Mabel popped the top on one of the red labeled cans.

"Bad shape." He finished his beer and cracked open a second. "Someone's been selling anti-tank hardware to the cannibals."

"What?" She leaned her back against the bench before taking a long pull on her beer.

"Yeah." He nodded. "Radar-guided, shoulder-fired anti-tank missiles. Good thing you installed those chaff buckets."

"What kind of asshole sells radar-guided anti-tank missiles to eaters?" Mabel shuddered. "They worked?"

"Like a dream."

"How about the Phalanx?"

"Worked perfectly. The tracking system locked onto those pointy-toothed assholes well enough to shred them in under three seconds." Robert said. "Needs a bigger magazine, though. I used up all the ammo in about three seconds."

"DU is hard to come by, and those systems were meant to have a much larger magazine. Even with it being an eighth-generation Phalanx, I had to cut enough weight for it to work."

"We could switch to steel-cored lead." Robert took another drink. "Would allow more rounds for the same weight."

"More?" She scrubbed at her neon-orange hair before taking another drink. "You had two hundred and forty!"

"Three seconds of fire support is not a lot when you're being chased by eaters."

"How many were there?"

"Ten or fifteen." He took another drink. "I ditched some of them at the old railroad underpass on Monticello in Norfolk. Shot it out with the rest on the bridge just outside Merrimack Station."

"Why so many?"

"Don't know." Robert shook his head.

"What's with the suit visit this morning?"

"Saw that, did you?"

"I see most everything." She nodded toward a bank of CCTV monitors along one wall of the shop. Each screen showed a different part of Meadow Lake Estates, including the parking area in front of his trailer and the entire area around Mabel's shop and trailer.

"Old pal," he said, "offering me a job."

"What kind of job does a suit need a dead zone scrapper for?" She finished her beer and crushed the can before opening her second.

"Driving."

She sprayed beer out of her mouth and nose. "Like a chauffeur?" She wiped her chin. "I can just see you in one of those monkey suits with the little hat, opening doors, sir-ing and ma'am-ing all the big wigs."

"Not a chauffeur." He laughed. It was good to see Mae snorting and carrying on. The last year or so had been hard, especially without her grandpa Ed around. "Autoduel."

"Stop…You driving in an autoduel?" Mabel didn't just giggle, she cackled. Holding up one hand in mock surrender, she gasped for breath. Pushing back the mop of orange hair Mabel looked up at Robert. "You're serious, aren't you?"

"Yep."

"Like in the arena?" She nodded toward her current project, a small two-seat autodueller. The windshield was a mess of cracked and holed armorglass. The front armor was scorched and scored where a laser had carved a glancing path across the hood.

"Not quite." The grin left Robert's face. Judging from the shape that two-seater was in, the gunner was either dead or very near it in a hospital somewhere. "Cross-country race."

"Like the old Death Rallies?"

"Something like that." Robert finished his beer. "They call it Dead Man's Run."

He'd been thinking over Gordo's offer all day. He needed the money. Salvage paid good but was not without its risks, and the offer to take Kat into their research program meant she would have a fighting chance even if someone managed to punch his ticket.

"You told them to piss off, right?" Mabel asked.

"Told them I would think about it."

"You can't be serious."

"I am."

"Have you looked in a mirror lately?" Mabel grabbed his arm, pulling him toward the deep-sink and mirror in the far corner of the shop. It would have been funny if she hadn't been so serious. He was a solid six feet and two hundred pounds, she was four nine and a hundred pounds soaking wet. He went along anyway.

"Hey— "

"No." She shoved him to stand in front of the mirror. "Look. I mean really look. Does that look like a hard-assed autodueller?"

He looked in the mirror. Some stoop-shouldered old bastard with baggy eyes, worry lines, wild hair, and four months' worth of unkempt beard that was more gray than black looked back at him. She had a point. The guy in that mirror looked like someone's homeless grandpa.

"Fair point." Robert turned and headed for the shop door.

"Wait," Mae said. "I'm sorry, Rob."

"Don't be." He called over his shoulder. Each step felt a little stronger, more confident. "I'll be back in a bit."

"Where you going?"

"Rule One, Mae." He slid the door open and stepped out into the night.

"Always those damned rules." Mabel walked over to the bench and retrieved the neon-pink welding helmet. "Hey Sonya, play Sam's the Hero."

"Shuffling songs by Sam's the Hero."

Crunchy guitar and hammering drums blasted from the speakers. Mabel Holland walked over to the battered car, picked up her welding gun, dropped the helmet mask in place with a practiced nod, and hit the trigger.

Chapter 4

“ “Time for you to go.” Robert stared hard at the old man in the mirror.

He rummaged around in the cupboard beneath the bathroom sink, grunting with satisfaction when he found the clippers. Robert plugged them in and clicked the switch and got busy getting rid of the old bastard in the mirror. When he was finished, Robert swept up the sizable pile of hair and set the shower to heating up before lathering his face and head with menthol shaving cream. By the time he'd scraped the final vestiges of hair from his face and head, the mirror was starting to fog up.

Robert pulled the footlocker from under the bed and brushed years of dust from its top. *Pale Rider* was stenciled in peeling silver script over the top of black block letters that read “HENRY, R.F. A/3-8 CAV.” He let his fingers trail over the faded lettering before lifting the lid. Inside, folded neatly, lay a black racing coverall along with a scarred and battered helmet. The helmet had *Pale Rider* stenciled on the front. Along both sides was the image of a cowled figure on a skeletal horse.

“Old my ass.”

He stood outside of Mabel's shop for the second time today. The howling screech of an angle grinder competed with old-school punk rock. Sex Pistols, if he had to guess. Instead of banging on the door, he slid it open and stepped inside. Sparks fountained from beneath the battered machine. He reached up and hit the power button on the speaker system, killing the music.

"Who the hell is mucking about in my shop?" Mabel rolled from under the car, angle grinder in one hand, pistol in the other.

"Easy." Robert set his helmet on the bench and held up both hands.

"Who the hell—" She squinted through the scarred face shield, sizing him up. When she got to the silver lettering on the racing coverall, she froze. "You're Bobby Hank."

"In the flesh," he said.

"Holy shit, Bobby Hank's in my shop!" She eased the hammer down on the old .45, dropped the grinder, and scrambled to her feet. "I didn't hear you come in. Can I get you a b— "

"Mae…Mae, I was just here."

"What?" She stowed the pistol and pulled off the battered face shield. "When?"

"About an hour ago." He nodded toward the empty beer cans still sitting on the bench. "You called me old."

"Robert?" She held up a hand blocking out the bottom half of his face, focusing on his eyes. "I…the whole time?"

"The whole time." He walked over to the fridge in the far corner of the shop, pulled it open, and retrieved two more beers. He opened both cans with a popping hiss and passed one to Mabel.

"You look just like your card."

"That's how pictures work, Mae." Bobby took a drink of his beer.

"So…you're really going to get back into dueling?"

"I am," he said. "One last race."

"Dead Man's Run?"

"That's the one." He took another swig. "It's a cross-country rally from here to God knows where. First leg ends in Memphis."

"When do you leave?"

"What, no more cracks about my age?" He chuckled.

"That was before I knew who you were," she said. "Hell, you've killed more people than famine."

"God, I hate that line." He looked at the shop floor. "You know some marketing flack came up with that nonsense."

"So, you didn't kill 127 people in sanctioned duels?" She sounded a little crestfallen.

"Not alone." He hopped up to sit on the bench, legs dangling. "Good driving accounts for more than you might imagine."

"Who's gonna drive for you?" she asked. "For that matter, what are you going to drive?"

"The what's been handled by one of the sponsors," he said. "The who? That's a thornier question."

"Not really." She picked up her phone from the bench, swiped open the screen, and opened up the video app before hitting play and passing it to him. "Watch this."

Bobby watched the video. It was a promotional montage. The sort of thing new drivers put together for prospective sponsors. Whoever the driver was, they drove without an ounce of fear and quite a bit of raw ability. He'd ridden shotgun for someone like that once upon a time. "Reminds me of Kat." He handed the phone back to Mae. "Do you know who this is?"

"You're looking at her." Mabel grinned.

"I knew you were trying to break into prime time, but…I don't know."

"What's to know?" she asked.

"A lot." he said. "Just cause your highlight reel reminds me of Kat don't make you her."

"You need a driver. I need a new gunner." She nodded toward the banged-up two-seater on the lift.

"That is not a glowing endorsement." He walked over to the lift and took a closer look. Most of the damage was on the driver's side, and most of that was in the front. The scorched, spattered trail of molten armor that stretched across the hood and terminated in the gunner seat started on the driver's side. "The damage tells me you got guts. It also tells me your gunner is in bad shape."

"No gunner on that run." She shook her head. "Just me. I can't seem to find anyone who can shoot straight when I line up the shot for 'em."

"Sounds like trust issues if you ask me." Bobby looked across the hood at the damaged gunner's seat. "I can't find a driver I trust, and you can't land a gunner that trusts you enough to leave the driving to you and take the shot."

"Come on." She walked around the front of the car to stand in front of Bobby. "With you on the guns and your experience in the arena? We'd be unstoppable."

"You know machines better than anyone I've ever met," he said, turning the idea over in his head. The regular season had just ended, so he would have plenty of time to get comfortable with her, and most of the race was out in the inbetween. This might work.

"So, we're a team?" She looked up at him, trepidation and excitement on her elfin face.

"Yeah," he nodded and stuck out his hand. "We're a team."

"Hey Gordo," Bobby looked across the small kitchen table at his new driver, "That rally, Dead Man's Run, I'm in."

"That's great news, Bobby." Gordon sounded pleased even through the phone's tiny speaker. "We already have a crew picked out—"

"I pick my crew, Gordo."

"Hey, if you got a crew picked out, that's fine by us."

"Got a shit-hot mechanic and a real go-getter for a driver." Bobby gave Mae a thumbs up. "Should be ready to roll by March."

"You don't have till March, Bobby," Gordon said.

"Season opens in March every year."

"Dead Man's Run is a special event," Gordon said. "It starts in three days."

"Three days," Bobby looked at Mae. "That ain't enough time to train. Hell, Gordo, you have any idea how long it takes to train up a tank crew?"

"No."

"A hell of a lot longer than three days." Bobby thumped the table, making dishes jump and clatter. "Christ on a crutch, Gordo. Do you have any idea how long it takes to build the trust you need to have even half a chance at surviving in the arena?"

"Lucky for you, it's a rally race and not an arena duel," Gordon said. "Be in Richmond tomorrow bright and early."

"You just said we have three days," Bobby said.

"You know how these things are done," Gordon sounded bored. "Contracts, the show tour, interviews, photo shoots for the sponsors— "

"Okay, okay," Bobby said. "What time tomorrow?"

"Early enough for makeup. You're the special guest on Morning Fuel with Don Northcraft."

"I hate that guy," Bobby said. "He dueled for one season, then went into commentating like he'd been dueling his whole life."

"Only because you turned down the job," Gordon laughed. "Besides, he's way better at commentating than autoduelling. Be here by 0430, Bobby. Lots to do, lots to do."

Bobby ended the call and tossed his phone on the table. He stared at Mabel. She had that wide-eyed anticipation like a kid on Christmas morning.

"Three days?" Mabel asked. "What happens in three days?"

"Dead Man's Run happens in three days." Bobby shook his head. "I…that's not enough time to prep, to train. If you want to back out, I won't blame you."

"Back out?" Mae leaned across the table. "I'm in. All the way to the end."

"Go pack a bag. We need to be in Richmond by 0430." Bobby stood. "Going to be the guests on Morning Fuel."

"I love that guy," Mae said.

Chapter 5

The past forty-eight hours had been an exhausting whirlwind of activity. When they weren't on the set of one TV show or another for interviews, they were guesting on various and sundry web shows, streaming shows, podcasts, and Clutch-casts. Everyone and their brother wanted to know why. Why now? Why come out of retirement for this unusual autoduel event? Where is Alley Kat? Who is Mabel Holland? Why not update the meat or put another way; aren't you a little old to be making a cross-country run?

When they weren't answering the same ten questions in one studio or another, Bobby and Mae worked well into the early hours of the morning, getting the old deuce-and-a-half in shape for whatever came next. This afternoon's contract signing had revealed a little of what was next. Tomorrow morning they were running deep into the Hampton Roads Dead Zone. When the sun started to set, Bobby had put his tools away, dragged Mabel out from under the dash of the deuce-and-a-half, and led her on a short stroll to a squat brick building half a mile from the shop. *The Spent Casing* was burned into an old hood bolted to the faded red bricks above the entry.

Pushing through the durasteel door, Bobby stood and let the old familiar smell of tobacco smoke, stale beer, and deep-fried algae wash over him. It had been nearly a decade since he'd last set foot in this place. Nearly ten years since he and Kat had pushed through those armored doors for their traditional pre-duel meal. He stood on the small landing at the top of a long narrow flight of stairs and looked down at the bar.

The Casing was nearly full with the usual crowd of drivers, gunners, crew, and the odd looky-loo. The music was loud and old-school. A lot of new faces, mostly new if Bobby was being honest. He'd been out of the game for ten long years, and ten years was an eternity in autoduelling. Today's superstar was tomorrow's worm food. Even with Gold Cross or some other clone insurance, getting slabbed almost always meant a fall to the bottom of the standings. Behind the bar, towel over one shoulder, a Crane Automotive ball cap perched on top of his head, stood Earl "Crash" Crader. Bobby grinned. Earl was as constant as algae and food riots.

Looking past Crash, the grin slid from Bobby's face like the sun sliding behind a cloud. Seated there at the far end of the bar were two faces he'd really hoped he wouldn't see on this run.

"You see those two down at the far end of the bar?" Bobby asked.

"Sure," Mae said. "Looks like Black Dragon and The Headsman. They were at the contract signing today, same as us."

"We steer clear of them," Bobby said.

"Aren't we all on the same team now?"

"Contractually, yes." He nodded. "But that don't mean much. Until we are all seated in L&D's vehicles, we aren't fully on the team, which means they're competition and see us the same. Steer clear."

Bobby led the way down the narrow flight of stairs to the bar proper.

"Hey, Crash," Bobby called over the jukebox. "Gimme two Milwaukees and some menus, will ya."

"Well, if it ain't the Pale Rider himself," Crash said. "I seen you and your new driver on the TV. Wondered when you'd drag your carcass in here."

"You know how it goes."

"Sure," Crash nodded, pulling the handle on the Milwaukee's Best tap and filling two frosted mugs. "Where's Kat?"

"Meat Shakes." He stared down at the gleaming wood of the bar top.

"Shit," Crash set the two mugs down and pulled a pair of laminated menus from under the bar. "I'm sorry."

"Yeah, me too." He scooped up the drinks and passed one to Mabel before picking up the menus and heading for one of the few empty tables near the back of the room.

"What the hell are we doing in this dump?" Mae took the proffered mug and followed.

"This is no dump, kid." Bobby pulled out a wobbly ladder-back chair and sat. "This is the Spent Casing."

"You say so." She drank from her mug and grinned. "This stuff is good in the can, but from the tap? It's fantastic. What are we doing here?"

"Tradition," Bobby said. "Night before the season start, Kat and I come in here and have a burger and a beer."

"Burger?" Mae set her half-empty mug on the tabletop. "You know how expensive real meat is?"

"Yep," Bobby said, "and the cook here makes the best-damned burger you'll ever eat. Steaks too. Besides, who the hell wants to eat flavored algae on what might be the last night of your life?"

"Lots of people eat algae on the last day of their lives," Mae said.

"True." Bobby shrugged. "But they probably didn't know it. If they had…steak."

"What's the point?" Mae sipped at her beer. "I don't think you get to the after, wherever that is, and get judged on your last meal."

"Sure," Bobby drank. "In the grand scheme of things, it don't matter much. Some of these crews have Gold Cross. Some don't. This time tomorrow, the ones that do are going to either be growing new meat at St. Mary's or waking up in new meat. Some will be on their way to Memphis, some will be headed back to home or the shop to patch up their rides and reconsider the dueling life…and some will take their final ride on the funeral pyre with the *Duelists' Lament* to carry them into the after."

"If tomorrow goes badly," Mae leaned over the table. "I don't want any of that last-ride funeral bullshit."

"That won't be a problem for us," Bobby said.

"You telling me that there is no chance we get put on the slab tomorrow?"

"No," Bobby shook his head. "I'm telling you that if we die, by this time tomorrow, Herolutions will have what's left of us loaded up in a cryobag and on the way to their mortality research facility."

"What?" Mae asked. "I'm no hardmode. I don't have meat insurance. I figured on getting some once we win tomorrow's challenge."

"Didn't you read the contract?" Bobby pulled out his phone and pulled up his copy of the sponsorship contract and started scrolling.

"Sure did. Every last word," she said.

"Did you see the words *rights to mortal remains* and *mortality research* in there?"

"Sure," she said.

"That section, this section right here," he tapped the screen with his finger, "is all about what happens to our meat if we die during the run."

"What about the folks with Gold Cross or some other meat insurance?"

"If they got it already?" He scrolled down, looking through the dense legalese until he found the section outlining *mortality insurance*. There was some language about the sponsor having no claim if the deceased had *engaged the services of a company specializing in mortality prevention.*

"Then Herolutions has no claim." He continued scrolling and reading. Looked like the sponsor was only interested in the mortal remains of those without mortality insurance or any religious requirements concerning mortal remains. "If not, part of being sponsored is signing over the rights to our meat."

"What if we get enough prize money on the run and survive long enough that we can set up some insurance?" She asked.

He continued reading. Looked like Herolutions had thought of everything, including purchasing mortality insurance on the road. "Looks like we are good to go if that happens." Bobby finished his beer. "Once the insurer takes the genetic samples, makes the scan, and uploads, Herolutions keeps the meat. We wake up in a meat farm somewhere between here and the finish line."

"Cool." Mae tipped back her beer, finishing it. "Not that I plan on it being us on the slab tomorrow or any other day."

"That's the spirit, kid." He stood and stretched. "I'm gonna get two more beers and figure out where our waitress got off to.

Bobby made his way through the crowd. He hadn't seen the Casing this full since before he and Kat had left the circuit. The usual sorts were pressed around the bar talking loud and drinking fast like this was the last night out they were going to have. Most were young and fresh-faced, looking like they needed permission slips from their mommas to be out this late. Not that you could always tell by looking at folks these days. Gold Cross and the rest of the clone industry made functional immortality a reality for the very wealthy and possible for the moderately successful autoduellist.

Bobby waved at Crash over the heads of a rowdy pair in fresh monocrys armored coats. They had the words *Dog Pound* in jagged script over a glowering bulldog printed right into the armored fabric. He shook his head. The rookies were easy to spot. Fresh gear, rowdy and strutting, they were still trying to sort out what to do with the pre-duel jitters, so they drank too much in hopes of numbing the nagging fear that they were going to die bloody. Crash spotted Bobby and held up two fingers cocking an eyebrow. Bobby nodded. The lanky bartender filled two more frosted mugs and set them on the bar.

"Pardon me, gents." Bobby stepped between the two and scooped up his drinks.

"Watch it, gramps." The one on his left grumbled. He was damned big. From the looks of things, a brooder rather than a shouter. His pal, on the other hand, was grinning from ear to ear.

Bobby turned and headed back to the table, where he could see Mae chatting with the waitress. Not wanting to miss the opportunity to get a burger and onion rings on order, he hurried through the crowd. He made it to the table while the waitress was putting the order pad in her apron.

"Hi, hon— "

"I said watch it, gramps." A catcher's mitt sized hand grasped Bobby's right shoulder. The waitress took several steps away from Bobby and the unknown party. Mae stared up and over his right shoulder with wide eyes.

"Right." Bobby shrugged free of the stranger's grip, set both drinks on the table, and turned to the waitress. "Miss, I'll have the double cheeseburger, lettuce, tomato, pickle, onion, ketchup, and mustard with o-rings on the side."

"Hey." The hand was back. It gripped Bobby's shoulder with crushing force and turned him to face its massive owner. "You really ought to watch who you bump, old man."

"Hey, Mae," Bobby kept his tone conversational, bored. "Remember Rule One?"

"Uh… you got trouble, Bobby." Mae slid back from the table.

"Sure, sure." Bobby looked back at the guy gripping his shoulder. If he had to guess, the fella was easily 6'6" and three hundred pounds. Long hair worn up in that absurd ponytail bun thing that was back in style.

"You need a lesson in manners, old timer," the big man said.

"Hey, my bad." Bobby sized him up.

Like most big men, this guy seemed to be unaware that size alone did not make him immune to the consequences of being an asshole. He stood with his feet too close together, left hand down at his side, leaving that entire side unprotected. His pal had wandered over, and a small crowd started to form.

"How about I buy you and your buddy a round, and we forget the whole thing?"

"How about— "

Bobby grabbed the big man's right thumb and peeled that hand from his shoulder in one smooth motion rotating it out and down. Simultaneously he stepped inside the larger man's reach and delivered a stiff-fingered jab just below the bulging Adam's apple, followed by slamming his knee into the bigger man's groin.

"Rule One, son." Bobby eased the gagging, gasping man onto the floor. "You got to tell folk you're something, then you probably ain't."

"Holy!" Mae bolted up from her seat.

"Just breathe through it." Bobby leaned over the gasping man. "That's it. Breathe. You never been kneed in the stones before?" He looked up at the other half of the Dog Pound. "You, go see Crash at the bar and get some ice for your friend."

By the time the friend returned with a bag of ice and Crash, Bobby had helped the big man into a chair.

"Looks like you boys just learned Rule One." Crash handed the groaning man a bag of ice.

"How many rules do you have?" Mae asked over the top of her beer.

"Hard to say." Crash chuckled. "He does seem to have a rule for nearly every occasion."

"Speaking of," Bobby dragged out his chair and sat. "Looks like it's time for Rule Fifteen; Don't make unnecessary enemies. We'll take two of whatever these boys were drinking and a couple more burgers with all the trimmings."

"Who the hell is this guy?" The big man wheezed.

"This guy?" Crash put a hand on Bobby's shoulder. "This is Bobby Hank, the Pale Rider."

Chapter 6

Three people sat behind a gleaming durasteel desk. The studio lights brightened, shining down on perfection. Perfect hair, perfect tans, a Giuseppe Chen suit worth more than the combined salaries of the entire studio crew, and a Samira Gutierrez dress worth more than any two of Giuseppe Chen's suits combined. The neo-metal anthem of the number-one-rated show on the Fire Power Network, Lock and Load, filled the air. The music faded out, and the hostess of Lock and Load stared straight into the camera, smiling.

"Welcome to Lock and Load. I'm Sasha Goodwin. With me are Butcher Bill and Don Northcraft."

The two men were very different. One was dressed from head to toe in a handmade suit, the cost of which would supply a small family with fresh meat and vegetables for years. The other wore a battered first generation monocrys armored jacket over a faded blue T-shirt. One smiled a perfect smile with gleaming white teeth in a deeply tanned face. The other had a sort of half-smile, making him look slightly bored.

"What do we have in store for our viewers tonight?" she asked.

"Quite possibly the most exciting thing to happen to sports since Crazy Joe Harshman bolted a .50 caliber machine gun to his Chevy!" Don Northcraft, the man in the high-dollar suit, flashed his perfect, signature smile for the camera.

"Dead Man's Run, Sasha." Butcher Bill deadpanned into the camera. Bill was not a fan of Mr. Northcraft, and everyone knew it. That was at least half of the reason most people tuned in to Lock and Load.

"Ooh, I do like the sound of that," Sasha said. "Tell me, Bill, what is this Dead Man's Run?"

"An old school death rally." Bill leaned forward and grinned.

"I've heard of those but never seen one done live. What's it like?" Don asked.

"Well, if you'd stayed in the game longer than one season, you might have gotten in on this one." Bill chuckled.

"Now boys…" Sash said.

"Just bustin' your nuts, Don. It's pretty simple." Bill stood and walked over to a massive holographic map of North America. "The race starts on the same day and time all over the country." Start locations across North America lit up. "When the light goes green, they will race to the first waypoint."

"Where is that first waypoint?" Sasha asked.

"It's different for each group of racers," Bill said.

"What's not different is what happens when they get there." The view cut away from Butcher Bill to Don, now standing in front of a large LED display. "Each waypoint contains a challenge that must be completed in order to discover the next waypoint."

"What sorts of challenges?" Sasha asked.

"The sponsors and the Association have been rather tight-lipped on the matter," Don said. "But here is what we do know. The leg of the race we are covering tonight and every night here on Lock and Load is a run from beautiful

Richmond, Virginia, to the home of the Mississippi blues and the King of Rock and Roll, Memphis, Tennessee."

The view cut away to Butcher Bill. "Who the hell still cares about Elvis and the blues, Don? This is autoduelling. We want burning rubber, twisted metal, and gunfire." At this, the audience erupted into raucous applause.

"Okay…Okay." The camera cut to Sasha and her dazzling smile before returning to Don Northcraft. "You want twisted metal? You want burned rubber and gunfire?" The crowd cheered. "Look no further than the Memphis Pyramid." Don tapped the LED display, and an aerial view of the massive structure appeared on the screen. The audience went silent.

"The Pyramid?" Sasha asked. "That's not a venue sanctioned by the American Autoduel Association."

"Well, Sasha," Don stared into the camera, his face the picture of earnestness and sincerity. "They are not calling it *Dead Man's Run* for nothing."

"Can't argue with pretty boy on this one," Bill said. "The Pyramid is one deadly place. Rumor has it the city of Memphis transformed it into a death maze complete with an entire tribe of cannibal bikers. And get this, they've been using it as a jail for a couple decades. You break the law in Memphis, and you either pay the fine or take your chances in the Pyramid. If the traps don't get you, the eaters will."

"On that gruesome note," The view cut back to Sasha. She gave a little shiver. "Let's have a look at who might be taking their chances in the Memphis Pyramid."

"There are a lot of teams vying for the eight slots with Luxford Drummond Motors," Don said. He and Bill both walked back to the gleaming durasteel desk.

"Most of them are amateurs and don't have much hope of getting out of the arena here in Richmond," Bill said.

"If you were a betting man Bill, who would you say will make it to the Pyramid?"

"Hell, Don, Bobby Hank. Hands down."

"Ooh, that's right." Sasha purred. "The Pale Rider is back. Didn't you interview him this morning?"

"I did." Don's gleaming smile faded.

"Say, didn't he put you on the slab way back when," Bill asked.

"He did," Don said. "Though, if you want to be technical, it was his driver Alley Kat that finished the deed."

"Well, for my money," Sasha interrupted, coming to Don's rescue. "It's team Black Sunshine."

Don grinned, "Didn't they put you on the slab a time or two back in the day, Bill?"

"They don't call Black Sunshine's gunner 'The Headsman' for nothing." Bill returned Don's grin. "Black Dragon and The Headsman have made Gold Cross almost as much money as your pal, The Pale Rider."

"If you're talking strictly arena kills, then you might be right," Sasha said. "Move outside the arena, and those two's bounty hunting and security body count makes Bobby Hank look like a rank amateur."

"Forget the body count for just a moment," Don said. "You both are forgetting that Black Sunshine holds one of the few perfect records in autoduelling. Every time they enter the arena, they win."

Chapter 7

The communication screen flickered to life. "Welcome to the Henrico Autoduel Arena."

The fire-wreathed steering wheel logo of the Fire Power Network faded out, replaced by a leering face, or more accurately, a blank chrome effigy bulging faintly where nose and chin ought to be. The view zoomed out, revealing a lanky figure dressed in an archaic coat and tails, complete with top hat and cane. The outfit might have looked snazzy were it not done in a multitude of garish greens.

"Great," Bobby shook his head. "They brought this asshole back."

"Who?" Mae asked.

"For those who don't know or possibly have forgotten, I am The Dispatcher. From this moment forward, all official communications for the Dead Man's Run will come through me and this channel. Teams, you have ten minutes to complete any final modifications or conduct any final repairs. At the end of that time, we begin."

"Why is the voice all distorted?" She hit the comm display menu button and started to select the diagnostic page.

"It ain't the equipment," Bobby said. "Dispatcher never uses his actual voice."

"Who?"

"The Dispatcher." Bobby ran another check on the weapons and countermeasures systems. All green. "He ran in dueling circles for a while. Kept his identity secret the whole time. Very mysterious. Rumor was he was some big deal BLUD brother come over to AADA to show us how it's really done."

"Was he?" she asked.

"Who knows?" He checked the power allocation display. It oscillated between amber and green. "After a few seasons, one of the older networks, Hot Lead, ran a show called *Road Trip*. This prick was the host. Delivered destinations, narrated challenges along the way, assigned points, and adjudicated disputes. The network stuck with the shtick and kept Dispatcher's identity a complete secret."

"*Road Trip?*" She glanced at the power display and frowned. "Didn't see it."

"Neither did I," he said. "That was Kat's guilty pleasure, shit-ass reality shows."

"And now you're in one." Mae laughed. "Pure irony, that."

"Time to see who's who in the zoo." Bobby flipped on the threat warning system and the external imaging cameras. A series of flat-screen displays Mae had mounted to the dash flashed to life, giving Bobby a 360-degree view of the outside.

"God, how can you stand not seeing out through a window?" She peered through the narrow armored slit to her left.

"I was gunner on a tank crew." Bobby checked the display. "Anti-tank rockets are bad enough when there's three or four inches of durasteel between you and the warhead. Those things cut right through so-called armored glass."

"Hey, look at all those cars." She pointed at the display.

They were starting at the rear of the field, stacked up two by two with the rest of the sponsored dueling teams. Their deuce-and-a-half sat next to a low slung two-seater with brightly colored, skull-faced monkeys painted on the roof and sides. A mishmash of dueling machines stretched out ahead of them for the better part of a quarter mile. Bobby was none too happy about the open call to fill out the field for this event. These *Run What You Brung* things were way too unpredictable for his tastes. This one was no exception, with its wide assortment of vans, two-seaters, pickups, armored motorcycles, and at least one micro-bus with a tank gun mounted on the roof.

"Hey Hank, is that you in the ass ugly deuce-and-a-half?" The CB radio crackled to life.

Bobby picked up the mic and hit the talk button. "Yeah, Hal."

"That has to be the ugliest thing I've ever seen in an arena."

"That's because it was built for salvage, not arena dueling." Bobby chuckled. Of all the people at the contract signing yesterday, he was happiest to see Harvey "Hal" Callahan and his gunner Raymond Russel. They showed up at the Casing last night shortly before he and Mae had finished their meal.

"That why you got a sea-wiz bolted in the bed?" Hal said. "Hell, I figured those things would be too damned heavy for anything short of a tractor-trailer."

"The first and second generation ones are." Bobby looked at Mae and grinned. "But the eighth-generation ones are plenty light. It's the ammo that's heavy and hard to come by."

"Where the hell did you get an eighth-gen sea-wiz?" Ray asked.

"Pulled it off the Eisenhower over in Norfolk."

"Where'd you find a mechanic to get it working?" Hal asked.

"Same place I found my driver," Bobby grinned at Mae.

"You open to a proposal?" Hal asked.

"Might be," Bobby said. "What'd you have in mind?"

"Well, we might be in competition for one of the eight L&D spots. Don't mean we have to kill each other."

"Pretty big starting field," Bobby said. "We'll have plenty of other targets, besides I really don't want to end up with a bunch of wet-behind-the-ears kids watching my ass out there in the inbetween."

"So, we have an accord," Hal asked.

"We do," Bobby said.

"Hey, I see Dog Pound up ahead of us." She pointed at a mud-brown two-seater.

"That's those two numbnuts from last night," Bobby said. "You seemed awfully friendly with the driver. What was his name? Norton?"

"Nate." She jabbed his arm. "His name is Nathan McHenry."

"So, you two know each other?"

"We had a few drinks after you rolled out last night." She looked at Bobby.

"Just drinks?"

"Just drinks." She cocked one eyebrow. "This time. Is that a problem?"

"Not so long as we're all on the same team." He shrugged. "If things change and we have to face off against them?"

"What?" She flushed and looked back out the windshield.

"For the next ten days, I need your head in the game. Guys like Nate Mcnumbnuts are a distraction, and distractions get you dead."

"I hear you." She squinted at the vehicle-packed field stretching out ahead of them. "Hey, that's Black Sunshine up toward the front."

"Good place for them." Bobby brought the targeting computer online.

"What," she asked. "Why?"

"Those two are stone-cold killers, kid," Bobby said. "You keep well ahead or well behind them, you hear me?"

"We're all on the same team, and I didn't come here to lose."

"You didn't come here to die either," Bobby said. "Remember, until we are in a sponsored vehicle, they are competition. Stay clear of them."

"Let's get the navigation up." Mae pressed the NAV button on the master display, bringing a full HUD map to life on her side of the armorglass windshield.

"Welcome to Mapwizard, brought to you by the American Autoduel Association. I am Ada, your guide. Please state your address or approximate destination."

"Mapwizard?" Bobby asked. "Where in the hell did you get a Mapwizard, and why is it in my truck?"

"I skeezed it out of that Cormorant we saw at the contract signing," she said.

"You what?" Bobby half turned in his seat to stare at her. Her grin was practically ear to ear.

"Don't they have that new Executioner anti-theft system?"

"You just stick to shooting things," Mae said. "Let me handle the technical details."

"That system is supposed to reduce car theft and break-ins by ninety percent." Bobby shook his head and grinned.

"The designers didn't account for Mabel Holland with a bag full of tools."

"Please state your dest—desti—destination." Ada's dulcet electronic voice insisted.

"What's wrong with it?"

"Well, the reviews all say Ada can be a little glitchy," Mae said. "Cormorants are usually handled by a professional driver, and those folks usually know the routes in advance, so the Ada wasn't really expected to see serious use."

"Ladies and gentlemen, children of all ages, welcome to Dead Man's Run!" Dispatcher announced. The external sound pickups on the deuce-and-a-half piped in the ragged cheer from the hardcore fans who had braved the cold and rain.

"Show time." Bobby snapped the chin strap on his helmet.

"Dead Man's Run is brought to you by Herolutions in partnership with the Fire Power Network and Luxford-Drummond Automotive. Are you ready for carnage?" The small crowd redoubled their efforts, a few sounding air horns. "Are you ready…"

"Not much of a crowd out there," Mae said.

"Yeah, I hear that's been the case for a couple years now." Bobby pulled up the fire control yoke and locked it in place. The grips felt strangely familiar beneath his grasp. He pulled his hands away and looked closer. "Hey, Mae, where on earth did you find a Dobson Eagle weapons control?"

"A girl has to have some secrets."

"Drivers, activate your machines." The blank chrome oval of the Dispatcher's face filled the comms screen. "You will have ten days to reach Sturgis. Between here and there will be waypoints and waypoint challenges. Each waypoint and challenge will unlock the next. Failure to reach a waypoint or complete a waypoint challenge will result in disqualification from the race. Points will be awarded for kills, machines disabled, and machines destroyed. Points equate to payouts at each waypoint. You may go weapons hot at this time. Remember, premature engagement will result in race termination with extreme prejudice."

"What does that mean?" Mae asked.

"Gunships." Bobby pointed at the display labeled 'ALOFT' in black marker on athletic tape. It showed a 360-degree overhead view. Circling at low altitude were several AH-203 helicopters. "Cheaters get blasted to tiny little bits of burning flesh and shrapnel."

"That's new," she said.

"Naw." Bobby flipped up the red switch cover on the right-hand switch panel, welded to the passenger door, and flipped the switch from OFF to GO BABY GO. "Old school rules."

"This first leg is the Luxford-Drummond 'Run to the Beach.'" Dispatcher's voice had changed from witness protection distortion to the clipped and proper tones of a BBC commentator. "There are eight Luxford Drummond Quests located in sunny Virginia Beach. Ada coordinates are now available."

"Please select your d-d-desss-destination." Ada stammered. The Ada logo in the HUD resolved into a map of Virginia with eight glowing dots in the lower right-hand corner.

"Ada, zoom in on provided coordinates," Mae said.

"To discover the next leg of Dead Man's Run, you must locate, uncrate, and activate one of the eight Quests. You have two minutes before the starting gun. Good luck."

"You focus on getting us there, kid." Bobby grabbed at the holographic HUD and pulled the image to his side of the cab, the gentle glow of the map standing out against the armored plating they'd scabbed over the right side of the deuce-and-a-half's windshield. "I'll get us a route picked out."

"Those are all in the dead zone."

"Dispatcher did say Virginia Beach." Bobby grabbed the holographic map and zoomed in with a spreading motion of his hands. "There we go." He poked the glowing icon furthest south and east.

"That's deep in the dead zone," Mae said.

"That's the idea," Bobby said. "Look, kid, when the gun sounds, you lay back. Let rookies and the amateurs take each other out and for the love of God, stay— "

The starting gun boomed. The coms screen flashed green. "That's cute." Mae mashed the throttle to the floor. The deuce-and-a-half leaped forward. "You handle the shooting. I'll handle the driving."

"This is going to be a long ten days."

Chapter 8

The cracked and pitted surface of the two-lane blacktop cut through a gray tunnel of leafless branches and wild Virginia creeper, a narrow and fading remnant of civilization. Here and there, burned-out houses, collapsed barns, and rusting cars peeked through the overgrowth like grave markers in a forgotten cemetery. The farms soon gave way to towering bald cypress and pools of scum-coated water.

Bobby continually checked the threat warning system along with the other displays. They were deep in the dead zone now and inattention could kill as surely as a bullet. More than one traveler had wound up the main course at a bloodmouth dinner that way.

"Ease up along this straightaway." Bobby squinted at his forward display. The misting rain blurred the image and made it hard to make out any detail more than ten feet in front of them. "The bridge up ahead is probably intact, but I want to check it out in advance."

"Why the hell are we this deep in the boonies?" Mae let up on the throttle, the old deuce-and-a-half slowed to a crawl.

"Because everyone else is taking the old highways to get there. Just like Ada tried to tell us." Bobby patted the dash.

"Ada picks the fastest route given all the variables."

"Right," Bobby released his harness and checked the load on his M310. "Problem is Ada don't have all the variables. Stop here."

"What are you doing?" Mae brought the truck to a stop.

"Checking the bridge," Bobby said.

"What about the eaters?" Mae asked.

"That's why I got Bess here." Bobby patted the smooth black stock of the rifle.

"Right." She shook her head. "Watch your ass out there. I don't want to end up as special guests of the Blue Blasters."

"I'll do my best." Bobby snapped his visor down and popped open the door. "Keep your eyes peeled. Watch the threat warning display. It starts flashing, don't wait. You hit the chaff buckets and get rolling."

"What?" Mae asked. "Why?"

"Remember, some assclown's been selling them anti-tank hardware." Bobby stepped out onto the cracked and crumbling roadway, rifle ready.

"All clear so far," Mae said. She sounded small and frightened over the headset.

Bobby reached up and turned the mic in his helmet to HOT. "Easy, Mae," He jogged to the right side of the road, head swiveling, searching for movement of any kind. Low-hanging clouds and a stiff breeze made him shiver. Typical southern Virginia winter, cold and wet one day, warm and wet the next. "On a day like this, those fools are laying low and staying warm."

"I still don't understand. What would make someone want to eat another person?" she asked.

"Lots of things get real bad, real fast," Bobby slipped forward till he could see the old bridge over the calm waters of the Northwest River. "Back around '47, during the first grain blight, a lot of folks starved, waitin' on the government to save them. Some folks got the hell out of the cities. Others just went hunting."

"No way," she said. "I wouldn't do that. I don't care how hungry I got."

"You ever been hungry, kid?" Bobby squatted down and waited. The old bridge looked good. "I don't mean hungry like you haven't had a meal in a few hours. I mean, boil your boots and eat the leather hungry."

"N-no."

"Well, those folks were past boiling their boots." He scanned the tree line along the far bank. Looking for movement, smoke, any sign that they weren't the only ones out here. "Way I heard it, there weren't a cat, dog, squirrel, or mouse left in the cities. Folks get that kind of hungry, that kind of desperate, they do all manner of crazy shit."

"How do you go from boiling your boots to hunting other people?"

"Well," Bobby said. "I reckon it wasn't a leap from boots to hunting people. My guess is that it started with cooking and eating the recently dead. What would you choose if you had to choose between starving to death or eating Aunt Sally, who just died of starvation?"

"I am not eating another person. I don't care how hungry I get," Mae said.

"That's an easy choice to make when you've got a full belly." He eased back up to standing, his right knee protesting. There were some disadvantages to keeping the same meat for fifty-plus years. He crossed over the road and found another vantage point and settled in to watch the far bank.

"Maybe so," she said. "But what makes 'em still do it? It ain't like there's a shortage of food these days."

"Who knows?" Nothing was moving out there. Just cold, wet, and silent except for the hiss of rain on the river. "I'd heard that the government airdropped a bunch of engineered food into Virginia Beach. Three weeks later, it's all filed down teeth and blue body paint."

"You don't actually buy that conspiracy bull, do you," she asked.

"Not saying I buy the whole story." It was silent, just falling rain on the river. "But like you said, why keep doing it when food is plentiful?"

"Maybe they just hate algae that much?"

"Well, I've fought 'em more than a few times, and there's definitely something not normal about the Blue Blasters." He crossed the road and headed back to the truck.

"How's the bridge?"

"Good to go." Bobby opened the armored door and climbed back into the gunner seat. "Let's roll."

Bobby zoomed in on the giant gorilla in sunglasses and Hawaiian print shirt. Once upon a time, the massive concrete mascot had welcomed swarms of families to Ocean Breeze/Motor World water park and go-cart track. He could still feel excitement seeing the old mascot creep into view. It was a different excitement now. Back then, before the world went to hell, he and his brothers were raucous balls of energy busting at the seams to be the first to ride *The Hurricane*. Now? Now, it was the frisson of adrenal dump knowing that somewhere nearby, men and women in blue body paint and bone armor waited to kill and eat him. Still, he felt a little nostalgic seeing ol' Hugh Mongous even if he had been moved to the middle of the access road and placed on a pyramid of human skulls. The man-eating psychos hadn't stopped there, though. They had mounted skulls and decomposing heads on ol' Hugh all the way to the waist and hung a macabre necklace of heads around his neck.

"I don't like it." Bobby fiddled with the zoom. "Everything is dead quiet out there."

"What is that?" Mae asked.

"That is a statue of a giant gorilla," Bobby said.

"What's all over its legs?"

"Same thing that's on those old flag poles." Bobby pointed. "Heads."

"Holy…"

"There's got to be hundreds of them." Mae breathed. "We need to get out of here. Now!"

"Sure," Bobby said. "Just as soon as we slip in there and pick up our ride."

"It's in there?" Mae asked.

"Sure is." Bobby grabbed the holographic map and pulled outward with both hands zooming in on the glowing dot that was their objective.

"You knew what was here when you chose this one, didn't you?" She flipped up her helmet visor and gave Bobby a hard look. "Didn't. You."

"Yep." Bobby grinned. "This is the heart of Blue Blaster territory, their home base."

"We're gonna sneak into the home of the most notorious cannibal tribe on the east coast?" Mae asked. "No way. You know what happens to me if they catch me?"

"I do," he said.

"Well, I don't want to end up in their breeding pens making little Blue Blasters till I die in childbirth or can't anymore and get eaten."

"Me either." Bobby zoomed out, switched to the 360 view once more.

Still quiet. There was a better than even chance that the Blasters were busy dealing with the hundred or so racers converging on their territory. The other seven race vehicles were scattered from the old Virginia Beach Town Center to the old Oceanfront part of the dead city, all belonging to the Blue Blasters.

"Let's get in there and pick up our ride," Bobby said.

"Why not go for one of the other ones?" Mae asked.

"Giraffes." Bobby checked the C-WIZ system status. If things got hairy, that auto-targeting 20mm gun was their ace in the hole.

"What?"

"Giraffes," he repeated. "They have really long necks. You ever wonder why?"

"Evolution." Mae sat back in her seat.

"Right," Bobby cycled the twin, hood-mounted 20mm Vulcan cannons. He grunted with satisfaction at the whine of the motors and the clatter of the barrels spinning. "Thousands of years of reaching for sustenance that was higher up, further away from the competition, meant they got to eat and continue as a species. The low-hanging fruit isn't always the best choice."

"And those seven other vehicles are low-hanging fruit," she asked.

"She can be taught." Bobby grinned. "Welcome to Rule 13: In a world full of short-necked herbivores, be a giraffe."

"I'd like to be gone before those blue-painted hyenas come back and eat us," she said. "Or do you have a rule for that?"

"Fair point." Bobby stopped cycling through the external camera feeds and took hold of the weapons yoke. "Lay on McDuff."

"Shakespeare." She turned the wheel and drove through the open gate. "First giraffes, now Shakespeare."

Chapter 9

The GPS coordinates led them to the remnants of a parking area on the eastern side of the Shipwreck mini-golf attraction. Old concrete parking bumpers peeked through the dead grass, greenbrier, and trumpet vines like low-lying grave markers. Their objective, a large durasteel cargo container with the Herolutions logo on the side, sat squarely in the midst of the overgrown gravel lot. Scorch marks and pieces of motorbikes littered the ground around the container.

"Looks like there is more to our prize than meets the eye," Bobby said.

"You have got to be shitting me." Mae shook her head.

"What?"

"That is an AP-616 cargo container made by Herolutions," she said.

"Okay?" Bobby zoomed in on the container.

"Do you know what the AP in AP-616 stands for?" Mae continued circling the container.

"No."

"Anti Pirate. Those containers are armored and armed to the teeth."

"So…"

"So?" She let off the accelerator and stared at Bobby. "So, without the security code, that container's AI will do everything, and I mean everything, in its considerable power to kill us."

"So we enter the code and get rolling."

"I don't have the code," she said. "How about you?"

"Nope." Bobby tapped the touch screen on the coms display, bringing it to life. "Let's check in." He selected the Dispatcher's icon and tapped the connect button.

"Congratulations Pale Riders." He was still using the fussy BBC commentator voice. "You have completed stage one of the *Run What You Brung* challenge."

"Great," Bobby said. "How about a security code for this damned container."

"That is stage two. Defeat the container's security system, and the all-new, 2076 Luxford-Drummond Quest is all yours."

"What?" Bobby asked.

"Better hurry." Dispatcher's smug voice admonished. "You do not have an unlimited amount of time. Your hosts will be returning home quite soon, and well, you know what happened to Goldilocks when the three bears found her sleeping in their beds."

"They sent her home with snacks?" Bobby asked.

"Not exactly, Mister Henry."

"That figures." Mae set the brake and unclipped her harness. "You keep those pointy-toothed pricks off me. I'll see to our ride."

"Right." He released his harness and waited until she clambered into the back seat before sliding behind the wheel. "I don't see any doors," Bobby said.

"One of the features," Mae pulled one of several tool bags open. "If you don't have the proximity fob, finding the door is supposed to be next to impossible."

"I bet that makes shipping a bunch of these a real pain in the ass for someone." He transferred all of the weapon's controls over to the steering wheel.

"Here, plug this in." Mae passed a thumb-thick cable over the seat to Bobby.

"Where?"

"Under the com unit, right side. Close to the bottom corner," she said.

Bobby felt around under the front edge of the coms screen until his fingers hit a small round rubber cover. He peeled it back and inserted the round connector. "What's this do?"

"Lets me broadcast RF signals at that container." She connected the other end of the cable to a small cube. She touched something just out of Bobby's sight, and a holographic display and keyboard winked into existence. Mae started typing, her fingers flying across the keys.

"Don't you think they would have thought of that?" he asked.

"Not my first time cracking one of these."

The small tactical display bleeped softly. Bobby glanced down at it. A single contact was rolling up the service road in their direction. "Already?" Bobby glanced up from the tactical display toward the parking area entrance. The low angular nose of a Grenadier Blaze crept into the overgrown parking area.

"Eaters," Mae looked up from her screen.

"No worries, just the competition. Let me get a good angle on these yahoos." He cut the wheel and tromped on the accelerator.

Thirty-inch tires spit gravel, weeds, and dust, slewing the deuce-and-a-half around, bringing the Vulcan cannons and

.50 caliber machine guns to bear. As the targeting reticle settled on the intruder, Bobby stroked both triggers, unleashing a storm of steel-cored lead and depleted uranium on the smaller vehicle. The heavy metal rounds hammered a series of thumb-sized holes through the front wheels and across the hood of the little car. The smaller vehicle reversed out of the line of fire.

"Well, if the three bears didn't know we were here before, they do now," Bobby said. "How's it going back there?"

"Got the door. It's on the north end." Mae switched off the box, unplugged it, and shoved it into the tool bag.

He piloted the truck in a wide circle. He parked just past the northeast corner of the container on a forty-five-degree angle with the nose and the big guns aimed at the narrow entrance to the old parking area.

"Once you dismount, I'll stay stuck to this spot like glue," Bobby said.

"What happens once we start taking fire?"

"Simple," Bobby turned in his seat. "I'll return fire in an accurate and proficient manner. You ready?"

"Ready to break into the most lethal container money can buy, designed to kill anyone without the access code? Or ready to do that while howling cannibals try to kill you and carry me off to their breeding pens?"

"Yep." Bobby nodded.

"Yep." Mae popped the armored passenger door open and stepped out into the wet gray of a coastal Virginia winter's day.

"Do your thing," Bobby said. "I'll do mine."

Mabel stood in front of the glowing, blue-edged seam on the northeast end of the container. A holographic keypad hovered in front of her, the product of cleverly hidden projectors and cameras. That was one of the many features that made the AP-616 container perfect for shipping high-value assets. No physical keypad to plug a computer into and brute-force the code. Mae smiled and pulled her phone out of a zippered pocket. She swiped the screen open, scrolled through her long list of vendor and manufacturer contacts, and selected Herolutions Customer Support.

"Welcome to the Herolutions Customer Care Line." The sultry voice of the customer support AI said. "I am Amy, your automated customer care assistant."

Mae waited while Amy finished her greeting protocol. If you interrupted, the more sophisticated ones got pissy. The whine of 20mm Vulcan cannons spooling was a brief and insufficient warning. The grinding roar rattled her heart in her chest. She dropped into a low crouch and duck-walked over to the right rear wheel of the deuce-and-a-half. Thirty inch puncture-resistant tires on durasteel rims made for excellent cover, especially when you were only 4'9" tall.

"How about a warning next time," Mae shouted into her helmet mic. Her ears were ringing despite the noise-canceling speakers and insulation of her helmet.

"Sorry," Bobby sounded sheepish. "Got some company again."

"Eaters?" Her heart skipped a beat. The only thing that scared her more than cannibals was being trapped alone in the dark.

"Naw," he said. "More would-be competition. How's it going?"

"I'm on the phone with customer support."

"You're what," he asked.

"Please tell me how I can be of service?" Amy finished her greeting protocol.

"Here's hoping this still works." Mae hit the unmute button. "This is technician Holland. ID number 3624368."

Corporate engineers were smart, no doubt about that. The problem with engineers is they thought like engineers instead of mechanics. Every system would eventually wear out, break down, or go on the fritz. It was a universal constant like gravity or missing 10mm sockets. When systems break, mechanics have to physically access the container, and that meant someone somewhere had to either give them an access code or shut down the security system long enough for the mechanic to do their job.

"Identification accepted." Mae grinned.

"I have a malfunctioning unit located at," she swiped over to her map software. "Thirty-six degrees, forty-nine minutes, zero point seven seconds North, seventy-five degrees, fifty-nine minutes, thirty-seven point one seconds West. Can you shut down the external security protocol?"

"I'm sorry, I didn't quite get that. Please repeat your previous statement."

"Shut down the security protocol for the unit located at 36.8164 degrees North, 75.9952 degrees West!" Mae shouted into the mic.

"Please wait while I access that information." Amy's sultry voice dropped off, replaced with the sounds of crashing waves, gentle breezes, and soft electronic Muzak. Mae rolled her eyes.

The Vulcan cannons whined to life, their deafening roar punctuated by the deeper chunk-chug of .50 caliber machine guns. Mae grinned. Helping Grandpa Ed stuff two Vulcan cannons, twin .50s, and four 7.62s into the space formerly occupied by a large diesel engine was still one of her favorite memories.

Bullets splattered and skipped off the durasteel container with a metallic whack, jerking her back to the present. Gravel exploded from either side of the wheel she crouched behind, spraying her with stone fragments and dust.

"Things are starting to get interesting," Bobby said. He sounded pretty calm.

"My records do not show a unit at that location. Warning: your location is considered extremely dangerous." Amy's voice replaced the Muzak. "Please manually enter the unit serial number. The unit serial number can be found on the unit identification tag. The unit identification tag can be found on the top right corner of the unit, above the access door. You will need to utilize the service ladder from your service vehicle and engage fall protection. Do you want a refresher on our fall protection program?"

"Of course." she glanced up at the ID placard. It had to be at least fifteen feet off the ground.

"I'm sorry, I didn't get that," Amy said.

"Wait one damn minute, will you," Mae snapped.

How on earth was she going to get all the way up there in the middle of a gun battle? A hail of bullets spattered and spanged off the container and the deuce-and-a-half in staccato counterpoint to her thoughts. She risked a peek around the sheltering wheel. Several bikes lay on either side of the entrance to the old parking area. The riders' paint-smeared faces, matted hair, and skull helmets peeked over the frames of the downed machines. Fire blossomed from the muzzles of their guns as they fired again. Bullets spanged off of durasteel armor and thumped against the puncture-resistant tires. Mae ducked back behind her covering wheel.

She chinned the talk switch for the ICS radio. "Hey, Bobby?"

"Go."

"I got to get up close to the top of this container," she said.

"What do you need from me?" he asked.

"Take the firefight somewhere else for a bit." She popped open the right rear door and pulled out a hard shell case nearly as big as her.

"You'll be exposed." Bobby looked at her over the seat back.

"Not if you raise enough hell." She slammed the door shut and sprinted around the end of the container, the hard-shell case bumping and dragging in the gravel and the dust.

"I'm gonna start with a little smoke," Bobby hit the big blue button on the countermeasures console. "Give you something to hide in."

Thick white smoke billowed from nozzles in both rear quarter panels and the rear bumper. He mashed the accelerator to the floor and cut the wheel. Thirty-inch wheels spit gravel and dirt, launching the old truck forward. Bobby steered through several ever-widening doughnuts around the container enveloping it and Mae in a dense cloud of white smoke.

"Now, let's take the fight to these assholes."

On the next pass around the container, he steered straight for the parking area entrance, squeezing both trigger paddles. Vulcan cannons and the .50 cals poured out a storm of hot lead, hammering the downed bikes and their riders to smoldering scrap. Bumping over remnants of shattered machines and riders alike, the deuce-and-a-half nosed through the overgrown entrance and out onto the service road that ran through the center of the ruined amusement area.

"Well, shit," Bobby hit the brakes.

To his left, that Grenadier two-seater he'd shot up earlier sat across the service road, effectively blocking the exit. Flames roiled up out of both open doors. Driver and gunner were nowhere in sight.

The right-side armor on the deuce-and-a-half rang like hell's own anvil with the devil himself hammering away. Bobby checked the monitors. More motorbikes blocked the road. No two bikes were the same, and most looked like they'd been cobbled together from scrap metal by third-graders. Each machine had durasteel armor scabbed onto the fronts forming crude shields. Dark circles of gun muzzles in place of the headlights spit fire and lead at him, hammering the right side of the old truck again. Over the top of the armored shields, he could see the riders. Faces painted, hair matted, wearing body armor made of bones, tires, and scrap, they stood and poured fire in his general direction. Not very effective fire, but where there was lead in the air, there was danger.

Bobby looked back to his left. He could probably push the burning car out of the way, but he would be a sitting duck if he got stuck. He looked back at the monitors. One cannibal stood up on the seat of a massive trike and lifted a tube onto his shoulder.

"Time to go." Bobby accelerated across the service road. The deuce-and-a-half rocked and jolted, the oversized wheels clawing up and over some vegetation-obscured obstruction.

He checked the rear monitor. The crowd of cannibals followed, spitting fire from the bike-mounted guns and belching black smoke from their tailpipes. He checked the tactical display. It looked like they'd woken up the whole damned tribe.

"Here's hoping she fixed that power problem." He stabbed at the tactical display with his free hand, trying to assign the pursuing swarm of bikes to the C-WIZ targeting computer. The five-point harness kept him secured despite the jerking and jouncing of the old truck bulling its way through the overgrown fun park, but it did little to stabilize his hand relative to the targeting computer touch screen.

The deuce-and-a-half bounced to a stop, the rear wheels spinning and clawing for traction. Bobby, finally stable for a moment, selected the approaching swarm of bikes as targets before reaching down and hitting the 4x4 button; the front wheels engaged, dragging the big truck up and over whatever obstruction had halted his flight.

A hail of bullets spanged off the armored tailgate and sides of the deuce-and-a-half.

Bobby stroked the engage button for the C-WIZ. The repurposed air-defense weapon burped long and loud. 20mm depleted uranium rounds poured into the cluster of pursuing bikes. On the rear display, red tracers highlighted the stream of death. That skinny bastard on the giant trike was still in pursuit. He could hear the growling roar of the engine in between bursts of C-WIZ fire. The massive motor on the machine belched a thick cloud of coal-black smoke.

"Persistent, aren't you?" He shook his head. Why was it always the angry little guy driving the biggest machine? This one looked like someone had built a trike around the engine of an old-school big rig.

Bobby spun the wheel, piloting the old truck onto a patch of smooth asphalt. He checked the rear display. More Blasters were headed his way, and the big-rig trike was catching up. The pavement curved to the right in a hairpin, back toward the hole he'd torn in the undergrowth and old tire barrier. He disengaged the front wheels, tromped on the accelerator, and cut the wheel hard. The rear wheels broke traction, spinning the deuce-and-a-half in a tight circle to face the swarm of pursuing bikes.

He waited until the targeting computer's lock tone sounded in his headset before stroking both triggers. A shattering combination of 20mm and .50 caliber rounds hammered the advancing swarm, transforming riders and machines into shredded meat and scrap metal.

The threat warning light flashed amber, then red, the RADAR lock tone blatting. Bobby checked the rearview. The little guy on the big-rig trike sat bold as brass with a missile tube on his shoulder.

"Sonofabitch." Bobby shook his head.

A lot of things could be said about the dead zone cannibals; cowardice wasn't one of them. He stroked both triggers again. Too late. The back blast from the shoulder-fired weapon roasted the bike and rider that had taken cover behind the heavily armored trike. The anti-tank missile streaked straight at Bobby.

Chapter 10

Mae balanced precariously atop the collapsible pogo-stick ladder she kept in the lid of the hardshell case. Even with the boost from the ladder, she couldn't quite get eyes on the information placard bonded to the top corner of the AP-616 container. If balancing ten feet off the ground on the top of a collapsible ladder wasn't hairy enough, occasionally stray rounds spanged off the other end of the container, making her flinch and duck. She set her phone to video record before letting go with one hand to reach up and pass the camera lens across the placard.

"Please enter the serial number from the container information placard to proceed," Amy informed her once again.

"I. Am. Working. On. It." Mae growled, bringing the phone back down and checking the image. Finally, a clear view of the placard. She breathed a sigh of relief and climbed back to stable ground.

"Your vocal patterns indicate you are experiencing elevated stress levels, Technician Holland."

Mae collapsed the pogo ladder with quick, efficient snaps. She could hear the staccato, grinding roar of the C-WIZ system working its magic somewhere to her south, followed by a deeper boom. A stray breeze brought her the acrid smell of gun smoke with an undertone of cooking meat.

The distinct grinding rumble of diesel-powered v-twin motors sounded from the direction of the parking area entrance. She peeked around the corner of the container. Three Blue Blasters sat in the overgrown entrance to the lot.

"I'm in very deep shit here. Of course, I sound stressed." It didn't look like they had spotted her yet. That would change if they decided to come on in and have a closer look at things.

Mae chinned the talk switch on her helmet, "I got company back here." She stowed the ladder in the hardshell case lid and turned to the holographic keypad. "Also, why am I smelling pulled pork?"

"Bio-diesel," Bobby said.

"Please enter the serial number of the specific container you are servicing for access to security features." The AI informed her again.

"Alpha Papa tack eight zero zero eight five…" She read off the serial number. The crunching duba-duba of the bikes picked up. Any second, those three bloodmouth bastards were going to come around the corner of the container and find her standing there like the proverbial Christmas goose.

"You mean that stuff they make out of used restaurant grease?" she asked.

"Serial number accepted. Access granted." Mae heard the click-clank of disengaging magnetic locks and the whir of electric servomotors opening the access door. "Would you like access to some breathing techniques to calm your mind and reduce your stress level?"

"Not quite," Bobby said.

"Technician Holland, would you like access to some breathing techniques to calm your mind and reduce your stress level?"

"No," Mae scooped up the hard case and tool bag before slipping inside the open personnel hatch in the AP-616 container. "I would like you to blast those three bloodmouth bastards out there."

"Are you in mortal peril?" Amy asked.

"Depends on your definition of mortal peril." She took a look around the inside of the container. It was much the same as the last one she'd cracked open. An outer armored shell filled with state-of-the-art power systems, weapon systems, computers, and ammunition surrounding a smaller container.

"Bobby, what do you mean not quite?" She asked.

"You see any restaurants around here?"

"So where do they get the oil?" Mae rounded the corner squeezing past conduits and various electrical boxes.

"Think about it."

"You mean they— "

"Yep. Human fat. Apparently good for more than soap."

"I may never eat pork again," she said.

"Technician Holland," Amy interrupted. "Do you have more than one technician in your repair team?"

"No." Mae's heart skipped a beat. "Why?"

"The AP-616 at your location has registered three more people who have entered the container."

"Those are not technicians, and they are definitely not with me." Mae linked the phone to her helmet speakers before zipping it into a pocket on her coverall front. She chinned the helmet mic activating the ICS radio.

"Hey, I got real trouble here," Mae whispered into the mic.

"Sorry," Bobby shouted back over the noise of .50 caliber machine guns firing. "Pretty busy out here. Did you get the door open?"

"Yeah— "

"Shall I reactivate the anti-personnel security protocols?" Amy cut in.

"Are they discriminate?" Mae pulled her Nomad Ordinance Tempest, checking the battery and ammo count on the small needle pistol.

"I do not detect your Herolutions-issued IFF transponder signal," Amy said. "Please activate your transponder to avoid indiscriminate targeting."

"Mae," Bobby asked. "Mabel. Come in."

"Keep your pants on," she whispered. "I've got some company here."

"You're gonna have to handle it," he said. "I got all I can handle."

"Lovely." Mae doused her flashlight and crouched low. Being hunted by bloodmouths scared her worse than anything.

Grandpa Ed had stolen her from those eater bastards a long time ago. He'd told her the story more times than she could count, how he'd been able to get her away. Her momma had died a hero, taking a bunch of them with her. She knew he was trying to give her some sense of her mom, give her something to remember about the woman she'd never met. Unfortunately, he also gave her an abiding fear of bloodmouths, and now here she was, trapped in the dark with three of them.

"Lovely," Mae whispered.

Bobby steered the big deuce-and-a-half into a clumsy bootleg turn, bringing the nose guns to bear on another cluster of bikes. The C-WIZ had run dry some time ago.

"Tell me about it." Bobby stroked the triggers, raking the bikes and riders with armor-piercing rounds.

He'd taken the firefight deeper into the old amusement complex that had once been part water park, part go-cart racing, and part mini-golf. Bobby was operating from memories north of forty years old, and a lot had changed since he had been here with Mom and Dad all those years ago.

For one, there had not been a wall of crushed and burned cars stacked six high and decorated with human skeletons on the other end of the service road where it exited the park onto South Bird Neck Road. Now he sat back to the wall trapped by a semi-circle of scrap-armored bikes.

He was going to have to try and punch through. Bobby checked the ammo counter on the gunnery display. Not good. He was all out of twenty millimeter and only had a few hundred rounds of .50 caliber.

Bobby keyed the ICS radio mic. "Hey, Mae." He mashed the accelerator to the floor. "The new car ready for pickup?"

"Yes and no." Her voice sounded strained.

"Hope it's more yes than no." Bobby stroked the trigger, hammering several more bike-mounted cannibals to scrap metal and hamburger. The remaining bikes raked him with machine gun fire as he punched through the hole. The deuce-and-a-half's smooth acceleration stuttered.

"Sooner would be better." Bobby looked at the status display. The right front drive motor flickered between amber and red, finally settling on red and dragging the deuce-and-a-half into a hard skid.

Mabel checked the load on her pistol and wiped sour vomit from her chin. The load counter showed amber, three shots left. Crouching with her back against the rear bumper of their new ride, she held one nostril closed and blew snot onto the inner container's floor, trying to clear the sick sweet stench of burned hair and flesh. She swallowed hard, forcing her rebellious stomach to settle. The dead eater, the one she'd torched, lay near the inner container's open roll-up door, and the breeze was pushing the smell inside. It smelled like overcooked meat, like the exhaust on their motorbikes.

"Get it together, Mae."

She blew snot from the other nostril and took a tentative breath. The stench was still there but not as bad. Maybe blowing her nose helped. Most likely, her sense of smell was starting to short out.

This entire day felt like one of those good news, bad news jokes. Good news, you're driving for Bobby Hank with sponsors and everything. Bad news, you have to pick up your race vehicle. Good news, you found your ride. Bad news, it's in the heart of bloodmouth central.

She'd managed to sweet-talk Amy the AI into utilizing her phone signal as an IFF transponder. That was good news. The bad? Her battery was down to less than ten percent and dropping fast. The constant transmission was really sucking the power.

They waited somewhere out there, beyond the open roll-up door to the inner container and the open access door to the AP-616. How many, she was unsure. What she was sure of was the fact that they kept throwing people at the container. Their last effort had gotten four past the exterior security measures. Only Amy's warning had saved her from capture. Well, Amy the AI's warning and some quick work with the plasma torch she was using to bypass the interior container's locked personnel door.

She chinned the ICS radio mic. "Where in the hell are you?"

"Headed your way." Bobby didn't sound quite so calm anymore. "How's it going with the new wheels? These are just about finished."

She peeked around the rear of the L&D Quest. The clattering chatter of an old AK sounded. Bullets clanged and sparked inches from her face. Two of the four were still out there using the front corner of the container for cover. She ducked back behind the glittering refractive gold painted van. "I could use some help here. I'm pinned and can't get to the driver's door."

"The Quest has a rear hatch," Bobby said. "Have you tried it?"

"The door has the keypad." Mae crabbed to the opposite corner of the van. She was no gunfighter. This was the first time she had fired her needler at anything other than empty cans and cardboard silhouettes.

"Stay frosty." Mae heard the chunk-chunk roar of the quad .50 caliber machine guns she'd installed on the deuce-and-a-half go silent. "I'm headed your way. Might be best if you had the new ride ready. The deuce is limping pretty bad, and I just used up all the fifty-cal ammo."

"What about the seven six two?" She scooted to the other side of the Quest and peeked around the corner. No wild-eyed eater with an AK. She took a moment to examine the passenger door. It was impossible to tell whether there was a holographic interface at this distance.

"We have a seven six two?" Bobby asked. "It's not on the weapons status display."

"Ford's aching balls," she muttered. "See the page up, page down buttons on the left-hand side of the display?" Mae duck walked over to the passenger door. The AK clattered, more bullets spanged off the Quest's armored hood.

"Damn," Bobby said. "How long have we had those?"

"Couple days." Mae tried to calm her pounding heart and checked the battery on her phone. Three percent. She needed this pointy-toothed goon to expose himself.

"That would have been good to know, I don't know, maybe back in Richmond," Bobby said.

"Technician Holland." Amy's sultry voice sounded in Mae's helmet.

"Yes, Amy." Mae was under the door handle now. The Quest's AI projected a holographic display and keyboard directly in front of her.

"Judging by your conversation with your support team, you are experiencing some distress. How may I assist you?"

"Can you tell me when the intruder taking cover behind the southwest corner of the inner container is exposed?" Mae looked at the holographic display. *Welcome. Please take a moment to register your 2076 Quest.*

"Mae, are you all right?" Bobby asked.

"Kind of busy." She let the needle pistol rest in her lap while she typed furiously. "I'll call back in a bit. Hurry the hell up."

"Intruder is ten percent exposed." AI Amy said. "Would you like to learn about some anti-stress breathing techniques? Herolutions in partnership with Zen-U now offer an entire array of meditation and relaxation classes." The crack and sizzle of laser-ionized air signaled another run on the container.

"No," Mae hit enter on the holographic keyboard before picking up her pistol. The display resolved into a mountain landscape with nine tiny figures trudging along a snow-covered ridge. The landscape and people vanished in a shower of pixels to be replaced with the Luxford-Drummond logo.

Mae reached up and pulled the mechanical door lever. Servomotors whirred, and the door swung out and up like a gull's wing.

"Intruder thirty percent exposed." Mae took the pistol in the two-handed grip Grandpa Ed had taught her and popped up over the hood of the Quest.

The intruder aimed at the van's door rather than the hood. She squeezed the trigger. The needle pistol made a sound like tearing foil. A flurry of tiny tungsten needles struck sparks from the corner of the door and transformed the exposed portion of the intruder into a fine red mist. Mae ducked back down behind the cover of the Quest, and vomited again, her already queasy stomach churning at the sight and coppery smell of fresh spilled blood.

"Intruder neutralized," Amy said in her ear.

Stomach now thoroughly empty, Mae wiped the sour vomit away with the back of a trembling hand and stowed the now empty needler. Standing on shaking legs, she walked around the front of the Quest, opened the driver's door, and flopped, shaking into the plush, memory gel crash seat.

Chapter 11

obby piloted the limping deuce-and-a-half back toward Mae's position. Behind him came the Blue Blasters. Every time he checked the rear display and mirrors the crowd of pursuers had grown. Though they weren't in any particular hurry to get close, not again, at any rate. He'd managed to get the fire from the seized drive motor extinguished in time to hammer the last group with a salvo of rockets from the pods Mae had scabbed onto the rear bumper. Somehow that little prick driving the trike was still back there shouting and shaking that giant meat cleaver, getting another wave worked up for a new run on the deuce-and-a-half.

"This is getting ridiculous."

Bobby checked the weapons display, making sure to scroll all the way to the bottom of the window in case there were any more surprise weapons Mae hadn't mentioned. No luck. All of his rear-facing weapons had run dry.

He reached a four-way intersection of dirt trails. Everything looked the same this deep into the Blue Blasters camp, and he damned sure didn't remember coming this way. Shrugging, Bobby took the path that looked like it went mostly north.

The old truck limped and lurched against the resistance from the dead drive motor. Tree branches slapped and cracked against the armorglass windshield. Bobby checked the systems' status display. The drive indicator showed failure-red for the right-front wheel. The remaining three wheels were marked in cautionary amber. Without the dead motor disengaging, he was going to either run out of battery or end up with another fire, and he'd used up all of his extinguishing agent on the first one.

Bobby hit the ICS talk switch, "Tell me you've got good news."

"Depends on what you mean by good," Mae said. "I got Janice up and running."

"What is it with you and old lady names for vehicles?" He swerved onto a wider fork in the trail.

"I like the way they sound; they're classy," she said. "Now for the bad news, I have an ass-ton of those bloodmouth bastards out there waiting on me."

"How is that a problem?" A hail of lead cracked and spanged off of the back of the truck cab. Bobby checked the rear display and side mirrors. Muzzle flashes winked at him like lethal fireflies. It looked like that little asshole on the trike had organized another attack run.

"According to Amy the AI, they have anti-tank missiles," she said.

"That's a problem,"

The deuce-and-a-half bulled through trumpet-vine covered chain link. Bobby jammed the brake pedal to the floor, bringing the battered truck to a stop. A collection of scrap lumber shanties stretched across what he remembered being a wave pool and splash park, like toadstools after a rain. Women in crude dresses grabbed up half-naked children scattering away from the smoking truck.

"Shit." Bobby hit the reverse button and accelerated back down the narrow trail.

Bare tree branches whipped and scraped down the sides of the old deuce-and-a-half truck. Bullets sparked and spanged from the cab. Switching his focus from the rear display to side mirrors and back, he steered the limping smoking truck straight through the crowd of pursuing bikes.

Mae sat strapped into the driver's seat of the L&D Quest. Its fully suspended smart-gel seat hugged her like a body-sized glove. The systems display reported the magnetohydrodynamic powerplant operating well within optimal parameters. Batteries showed a full charge. She looked at the closed door in front of her. All she had to do was give Amy the word, and that door would retract. On the other side, twenty Blue Blasters waited, armed with anti-tank missiles and armor-piercing heavy weapons. They had given up on getting into the AP-616 after the last bloody effort littered the ground with their burned and bleeding corpses.

It was past time they got the hell out of this place. Mae opened several holodisplays; one to monitor weapons systems, one for operational systems, one for coms, and one for the exterior video feed being piped in by Amy. All those hours spent in VR learning about the Quest were paying off. She checked the tactical display. Bobby was getting close now; the green truck icon she'd assigned to his contact on Janice's radar was 400 yards away and closing.

"Ready to roll." She checked the weapons load out. Nearly every weapon on the Quest showed red, with zeroes in the expendable ammunition magazines. Same with the countermeasures systems. The only thing green on that display page was the Vulcan Gauss cannon. Bobby was not going to be happy about that.

"Okay," Bobby said. "Stick to the plan. I'll rake them on the way by. When that happens, you punch out of there and make for the big monkey."

"Won't they shoot you with those anti-tank missiles?" Mae asked.

"Let's hope you hitting them from behind will jack up their aim," Bobby said.

"Hope?" she asked.

"At this stage, hope's about all I got."

She checked the exterior display. The mob of bloodmouths gathered in the entrance to the overgrown parking area. They had formed a rough double wall with the wide front fairings of their scabbed-on armor. Half faced the container, and half faced the service road. She shook her head. Any armor plating light enough to be used on a motorbike wouldn't be nearly thick enough to withstand the 3mm electromagnetic Vulcan cannon mounted in the nose of the Quest. She grinned. These assholes were in for a real rude awakening.

Mae transferred control of the gauss cannon to the steering wheel, assigning it to the right-side trigger paddle. She watched the tactical display. The timing would have to be just right, or she would end up giving the eaters a shot at both of them. She would have to go when he got to within 200 yards.

"Amy, open the exterior vehicle hatch," Mae said.

The hatch rolled up, leaving Mae with a clear view of the chaos. Grinning, she hit the right-side trigger paddle and held it. The 3mm needle cannon, a Gauss variant on the old 20mm Vulcan cannon, had a cyclical fire rate of 7246 needles per minute at 5500 feet per second. That boiled down to a little over a thousand tungsten rods 3 millimeters in diameter ripping into and through scabbed-on durasteel, motorbike, and rider like the proverbial hot knife through butter, scything down the bone armored cannibals where they stood.

She let off the trigger paddle and selected rough terrain on the suspension control before stepping on the accelerator and hitting the trigger paddles again. Janice leapt free of the AP-616 container like a golden thunderbolt. A steady stream of heavy metal death preceded her, widening the smoking hole through the middle of the Blue Blaster's line.

She steered for the hole, giving them no chance to react to her assault. The smart-gel, suspended seat kept her rock steady while eighteen-inch grippy wheels propelled her over the smoking, blood-drenched wreckage.

"Threat warning. Threat warning." Janice informed Mae in a steamy bedroom voice.

"Why is it always a sexy voice?" Mae tromped the brake, skidding, and made a sliding turn onto the service road.

She checked the rearview display. Bobby was a little more than a hundred yards back and following her in reverse, weaving drunkenly back and forth across the road. Smoke poured out from under the right side of the old truck, and it didn't look like the kind you used for a smokescreen.

"Head for the big monkey," Bobby said.

"You're on fire."

"Yeah," he said. "Lost a wheel drive motor back there, and it won't disengage."

"Missile detected. Countermeasures are unavailable at this time." Janice whispered in Mae's ear.

"Chaff, chaff, chaff!" Bobby shouted.

Mae glanced at the rearview display. Plumes of red-tipped smoke arced up and away from the old deuce-and-a-half, followed by a glittering cloud of crybaby chaff. The crump of the missile detonating amid the cloud of chaff and flare was audible inside the Quest.

"When you get to the giant monkey, hang a right," Bobby said. His voice sounded tight, tense, not the calm professional from earlier.

Mae spared a moment for the tactical display. A swarm of hostile contacts was converging on their position, and it looked like another shield wall of the pointy-toothed assholes blocked their way out.

"We got trouble on both ends."

"Threat warning. Threat warning." The Quest AI whispered.

"Damn," Bobby said. "I'm nearly out of chaff and flares. You'll have to do double duty and cover me when I run dry."

"Bad news," she said. "None of the defenses are active. All I got is the 3mm Gauss cannon in the nose."

"In that case, speed is armor," Bobby said.

"What?" Mae asked.

"Those anti-tank missiles are probably old MK-19s. They have a minimum safe arming distance." The 7.62s chattered again. "When you get the missile warning, punch it and open up with that Gauss cannon, carve yourself a hole. I'll follow up best I can. Just let me know when you see the monkey."

The old deuce-and-a-half was getting harder to steer with each passing second. Bobby's jaw was clenched tight, and his knuckles were white on the wheel. He had managed to get the fire out again on the disabled drive motor, but it was dragging, and he had to constantly steer against the drag, causing him to swerve like a drunk coming off a three-day bender. His erratic driving did make him a harder target. The downside was that it made his fire a lot less accurate, relegating him to spray-and-pray each time he swung the nose of the truck back in line with the motorcycle pack. He kept the rear bumper of the old truck damned near on top of Mae and their new ride so that his chaff and flare envelope would provide some cover from the incoming anti-tank missiles.

The deuce-and-a-half's threat warning system beeped again, notifying him of another RADAR attempting to lock onto the big truck.

"I ever find out who sold these pricks anti-tank missiles," Bobby checked the countermeasures counter. He had one shot left. "I'm going to carve out their liver and feed it to them."

"I can see the Monkey!" Mae's voice was tight with excitement. "They have us blocked in."

The gentle beeping tone of the threat warning was replaced by the strident blatting of the missile warning.

"Punch it." Bobby hit the chaff and flare button and smashed the accelerator to the floor.

Behind him, Mae and the Quest rocketed away. The low-observable coatings and refractive armor, combined with the sudden burst of speed, allowed her to slip past the incoming wave of guided anti-tank missiles before they could arm. By the time they reached him and the deuce-and-a-half, all eleven of the missiles were armed and seeking the blazing heat and massive radar signature the old truck presented.

The chaff cloud, with its crybaby micro-transmitters, created enough radio noise that most of the MK-19s became distracted and wandered off in search of a target. This left three missiles, two of which fixated on the eight-thousand-degree flares and detonated, showering the old truck with shrapnel. The third MK-19, by some miracle of guided weapons technology and the law of averages, streaked past the chattering chaff and the burning flares to strike the still-hot drive motor on the right-front wheel of the old truck. Its shaped charge fired a spear of superheated gasses straight through the burned-out motor, melting it and the wheel to slag and throwing the deuce-and-a-half over onto the driver's side.

Mae kept her finger on the trigger, and her foot mashed to the floor. The storm of 3mm tungsten rods struck the shield wall of cannibals like a thunderbolt. Diesel-powered bikes and blue-painted bodies went down in a tangle of blood, bone, and steel. Superior insulation and soundproofing meant that the entire event happened in near total silence. The destruction outside became a deadly ballet, with Mae's rapid breathing and Janice's soft voice announcing missile launch and ammo count as accompaniment.

The Quest rocketed through the gap carved by the Gauss cannon. Mae felt Janice leave the ground, propelled into the air by acceleration and an impromptu ramp formed by the collapsed shield wall. She came back down to earth in time to brake and drift into the hard right turn out onto the cracked blacktop of General Booth Boulevard.

She checked the rearview display for Bobby and the deuce-and-a-half.

Nothing. Not even bloodmouths.

"Bobby?" Mae radioed. "Bobby, where the hell are you?"

Silence.

Mae hit the brake. Janice stopped hard, her front end diving toward the leaf and twig littered road.

"Hey, Janice," Mae said.

"Hello, Mabel Holland," the AI said. "How can I be of assistance?"

"Show me Dead Man's Run on the Fire Power Network."

"I'm sorry. I cannot do that. You do not have access to that feature."

Mae selected reverse and rolled back. "Bobby…Bobby…damn it…come in, Bobby…."

"I'm a touch busy," Bobby said. Mae could hear the staccato chatter of a rifle over his voice.

"Where are you?" She stopped even with the turn-in and the giant, skull-covered monkey.

The path of her exit was littered with wreckage, both machine and human, though she hardly considered bloodmouths human. To either side of the hole she had carved through the cannibal line, bone-armored men were getting up and picking up their bikes. Further back, she could see a plume of oily black rising into the sky. Looking between the statue's legs, all she could see was a blanket of thick white smoke.

"Trying to get the hell out of here. Where are you?"

"Out on..." Mae looked at the holographic HUD. "General Booth Boulevard."

"Stay put." His voice punctuated by more rifle fire. "I'm coming to you."

"How's the truck?"

"Dead." Mae could see muzzle flashes light up the smoke. The remaining Blue Blasters unslung rifles and moved into the smoke with a series of hand gestures.

"You've got trouble headed your way on foot," she said.

"No worries." The grinding growl of a diesel bike engine revved loud over the radio link. "I got new wheels. Get going. I'll catch up."

"Go where?" She stared at the network of streets, roads, and highways on the HUD.

"Anywhere not here."

"Really?"

"Rule Five: Considered action is better than inaction." The bark of his pistol and the growl of the bike engine nearly drowned out his voice. "Get moving."

"Hey, Janice," Mae accelerated down the empty, leaf-and-twig-covered road. "Take me to Memphis."

Chapter 12

The lights came up, revealing a cozy drawing room. A small fire crackled in the fireplace, its flames reflected in the brass accents and polished surface of the ebony bar. The walls were exposed red brick. The floor? Artfully scarred and well-polished hardwood planks. Two oversized leather chairs faced each other over a black lacquered table set with crystal decanter, ice bucket, and whiskey tumblers. Waist-high shelves lined the walls with leather-bound volumes arranged to suggest casual use. Hanging on the walls were holo-photos from the glory days of autoduelling. Bobby Hank was the focus of several. Occupying one chair, the ever-alluring, always poised, exquisitely made-up Sasha Goodwin.

"Good afternoon, and welcome to Dead Man's Update." Sasha gave the camera her signature half-smile. "This is where we keep you in the know and up to date on the latest developments of Dead Man's Run. This afternoon, my guest is the Vice President of Luxford-Drummond's combat vehicle division, board member of the American Autoduel Association, Chairman of the Mid-Atlantic division of Dead Man's Run, and Autoduel Hall of Famer Gordon Corey."

Sasha flashed a brilliant smile. The camera view switched to encompass her and her guest. He was young, broad-shouldered, and handsome. His blond hair was cut short, neatly combed, and parted on the left. For the price of the suit he was wearing, a family could afford an entry-level Gold Cross package.

"Howdy," Gordon said. He looked like a cover model for a corporate fashion magazine, and sounded like he just came off shift from a coal mine in eastern Tennessee.

"Gordon," Sasha sat back in her chair and crossed her legs. "Dead Man's Run is off to a bloody start. By my count, we already have thirty-eight fatalities. That is thirty more than we saw in the latest autoduel season. Not counting those tragic deaths in Atlanta of course."

"Well, Ms. Goodwin," Gordon leaned over and poured three fingers of the amber liquid into a tumbler.

"Please, call me Sasha."

"Well, Sasha," He sat back and took a measured sip of the liquor before continuing. "When you combine autoduel legends and rank amateurs, a little blood is gonna get spilled."

"Interesting that you would put it that way." She smiled and glanced at her notes. "Most of those fatalities were not at the hands of veteran autoduellists, but at the hands of the Blue Blasters, a notorious cannibal tribe located deep in the Virginia Beach part of the Hampton Roads Dead Zone. Care to elaborate?"

"Sure." Gordon smiled. He was cool and poised. This question was no surprise. "Luxford-Drummond only had eight slots available for the L&D team. That's eight brand-new 2072 Quests. At Luxford-Drummond, we are betting on a Quest not only finishing Dead Man's Run but winning the whole shootin' match."

"What does that have to do with the high casualty rate thus far?"

"Only the very best have any chance at winning this thing, so we figured a test of skill and grit was what we needed to separate the wheat from the chaff…the men from the boys, if you will."

"Men from the boys?" Sasha raised one eyebrow.

"Or women from the girls if that suits." Gordon held up a mollifying hand. "Plenty of damn fine women duelists out there, yourself included."

"So you justify thirty-eight dead duelists and another five critically wounded as part of a…selection process?" She asked. "Most of those casualties were too new or broke to afford access to Gold Cross or any other mortality insurance. Even with Gold Cross, unless they have a body already awaiting download, there won't be enough left for a scan, not after the bloodmouths finish with them."

"They all signed waivers and were fully briefed on the potentialities of this event." Gordon's eyes no longer twinkled with that good-ol-boy humor. "If you want a safe sport, I recommend golf. Fans don't tune in to watch us drive fast, turn left, and score points by shooting out the next car's tires. They tune in to see explosions, twisted metal, and shattered bodies. Check the ratings, sister. Dead Man's Run has already doubled the views of the AADA season championship, and that's just the first few hours."

"Speaking of twisted metal and shattered bodies," Sasha made a swiping gesture to her right, summoning a full holographic viewscreen.

On-screen was a man in a battered monocrys jacket astride a motorcycle that looked like it might have been stolen from the set of the latest Dieselpunk film. The bike was mid-air and perfectly framed between the legs of a giant gorilla statue festooned with skulls and decomposing human heads. The rider was half-turned. pointing a large handgun behind him.

The bright orange and red of the muzzle flash was a perfectly captured blossom of fire. Behind him, emerging from a cloud of smoke, was a pack of riders on similar bikes. Their faces were painted blue and white, and they wore rough leather jackets covered in glistening rib bones. Smaller blossoms of fire adorned the gun muzzles that protruded through armored front fairings.

"What an escape," Sasha said. "It really does look like the Pale Rider is back in the saddle."

"That is classic Hank right there." The good-ol-boy grin was back on Gordon's handsome face. "When the chips are down, he always seems to find a way to come out on top."

"I don't know what was more exciting." Sasha swiped the image away. "His escape from the Blue Blasters' stronghold or leapfrogging in the middle of a rolling gun battle?" The image on the holodisplay changed.

This was a view from above and behind the same man on the same bike. This time he was alongside a sleek Luxford-Drummond Quest; one foot in the open doorway, the other on the seat of the battered bike. He was holding on to the roof with one hand and aiming his pistol at another blue-faced pursuer with the other.

"Guess that depends on your taste," Gordon said. "For my money, that leapfrog maneuver is pretty ballsy. If any of those pointy-toothed bastards had hit that bike at the right time, Hank would have been roadkill."

"Let's switch gears for a moment," Sasha said. The camera switched to a close-up view. "I can understand creating a challenge that separates the wheat from the chaff. I can even get behind bringing the sport back to its roots, cars and crews duking it out on the open road."

"Is there a question in there somewhere?" Gordon asked.

"I'm getting to it." Sasha leaned forward in her seat, well-manicured nails tapping a staccato counterpoint to each word. "Here is what I am having a hard time wrapping my mind around; why allow a BLUD team to compete in an AADA-sanctioned rally?"

"Why not?" Gordon asked. The view switched to a side-by-side view of Sasha and Gordon.

"Why not?" Outrage leaked into her voice. "Because BLUD are unconscionable killers, especially that team."

"Fans are tired of the same old song and dance," Gordon said. "To say the ratings for an AADA series are in the toilet would be an improvement. We got too focused on safety, on protecting the crews."

"That's a bad thing?"

"No." He shook his head. "It's a boring thing. Networks have stopped showing AADA in prime time slots, and streaming views of recent seasons are nonexistent. Viewership is down to the hardcore fans, and even they are watching more CFL than autoduel by a ratio of nearly three to one."

"So you signed a BLUD team to boost the ratings?"

"Yep," Gordon said.

"Well, I hope you can live with yourself." Sasha stopped making any pretense at a dispassionate interview. "What do you have to say to the families of the two teams Black Sunshine shot up getting out of the Henrico arena?"

"Autoduelling is a dangerous sport. Don't come to the dance if you can't pay the piper."

Chapter 13

Route 58 wasn't the only way out of the Hampton Roads Dead Zone, just the fastest if you were headed west. Bobby checked the tactical display and the rearview. No contacts and no signs of pursuit. Hadn't been for at least the last hour, not since they broke free of the Blue Blasters back in the ruins of Virginia Beach. Dumb luck had led them straight into that pack of rookies from Richmond. Between Mae's wheelwork and his gunnery, they carved a path of destruction through the impromptu roadblock and left the bushwhacking rookies and the bloodmouths to sort each other out at the Northwest River bridge.

"You are approaching the fortress town of Emporia." The Quest's AI said. "Be advised, speeding, dueling, and other forms of misconduct within Emporia's walls will be addressed by local law enforcement with extreme prejudice. Please access the AADA Road Atlas and Survival Guide for a more comprehensive description of Emporia and the surrounding environs."

Emporia. It had been a wide spot of sorts, nestled between the larger cities of Suffolk and Franklin. That was before everything went to hell. These days Emporia was the first little bit of civilization a traveler encountered west of the Hampton Roads Dead Zone. It was the last outpost of civilization heading east. Either way, that meant hot food, hot showers, and cold beer. So it was with a sigh of relief

Bobby greeted the little-wall-and-tower icon with the name Emporia under it on the holographic map.

"Thanks, Janice," Mae said.

"You are welcome, Mabel Holland."

"There's a truck stop up ahead," he said. "Pull in there."

"What for," she asked. "We're in the lead."

"A couple reasons," he held up two fingers. "I need to take a leak, I'm hungry, and I need to stretch my legs."

"That's three." She eased the Quest off the highway and through the open gate to Jumpin Joe's Jolt and Go. "I wonder who else made it?"

"Beats me."

"You know what I like?" She pulled into a parking spot near the dining room. A large, bullet-riddled sign proclaiming the virtues of Joe's deep-fried algae burger cast a long shadow in the late afternoon light. "I really like giving up our lead because you have the world's smallest bladder."

"We're in no danger of that." He hit his harness release. "I'd bet a shiny new nickel those other teams had a hell of a time gettin' past the security on those containers, not to mention the Blue Blasters are on the warpath now." He retrieved his matte-black Chrysler .45 from the magnetic holster in the foot well.

"Fine," Mae powered down the Quest and hit her harness release. "Let's go relieve your tiny bladder and get some road food."

"Good. I love the food in this place." Bobby thumbed the open button for his door. The armored door opened on silent servomotors. "Best coffee between Richmond and Greensborough. Think we ought to top off the battery?"

Mae stepped out onto the worn asphalt, freeing herself from her seat. "Nope," she said. "We still have a full charge on the batteries; this new MHD power plant is a modern marvel. We ran Janice wide open from cannibal central all the way through old Suffolk and didn't even dip into the batteries."

"Finally, something breaking our way." Bobby checked the load indicator on the side of the .45 before holstering it. He limped toward the durasteel louvered doors of Jumpin Joe's. Mae followed a couple steps behind.

"Hey," she called. "Why is it you check the load on that pistol every time you get in or out of the vehicle?"

"Old habits, kid." Bobby stepped into the relatively dim interior of the truck stop. The sweet sweet smell of deep-fried algae and fresh coffee washed over him. "The kind of habits you better learn if you're gonna be in this life very long." He glanced meaningfully at Mae's empty hip.

"Damn." She flushed and turned back toward the door.

"Don't sweat it this time." Bobby clapped a fatherly hand on her shoulder. "Emporia's pretty tame. The further along this run we get, though, the rougher things are gonna get. Not everybody tries to kill you in a car. Some folk try to do it out here, face to face. Some'll gun you down from behind. Don't make it easy for 'em."

"Right," Mae said.

Bobby scanned the retail section of Jumpin Joe's Jolt and Go. It was equal parts truck stop, convenience store, and greasy spoon diner. Not much had changed since his last visit.

The same cheap holographic postcards on spinner racks stood at the end of shelves lined with junk billed as must-have comfort items. The ubiquitous Uncle Al's weapons kiosk blared one of many tasteless advertisements for hardware guaranteed to make anyone's ride the most fearsome on the road. The vintage jukebox played Boston's oldie classic *Long Time*.

A short, gray-haired woman in a hot pink polyester shirt stood behind the white Formica and chrome lunch counter, drying and stowing drinking glasses. A thin stream of blue smoke spiraled up from the homemade cigarette in the ashtray to her right.

"Afternoon Edna." Bobby slid onto one of the chrome and red faux-leather stools at the counter.

"Is that you, Robert Henry?" The gray-haired woman set down the last glass. She picked up the cigarette and took a deep drag.

"In the flesh," he said.

"What the hell happened to your beard and hair?" Edna slid two laminated menus across the counter to rest in front of Mae and Bobby before pouring two cups of coffee. "You look like a plucked chicken."

"Decided it was time to be gainfully employed again instead of running salvage." He took a cautious sip of the scalding brew and groaned. "Still the best-damned coffee between Richmond and Greensborough."

"You know you're wearing Bobby Hank's jacket and fire suit?" Edna looked him up and down while she finished off her cigarette.

"Pretty sure I'm wearing his birthday suit." Bobby grinned.

"I had a legend up in my store twice a month for the last seven years, and I never knew it?"

"Would you have given me less shit if you had?" He took a deeper drink of his coffee.

"Nope." Edna leaned over the counter and refilled Bobby's cup. "Probably would have given you more."

"That sounds about right." He chuckled.

"Who's this?" Edna eyed Mae, taking in the grease-stained coveralls, neon-orange pixie cut hair, and clearly second-hand monocrys jacket.

"My new driver, Mabel Holland," Bobby said. "Mabel, this is Edna Jordan, the best damned cook north of Greensborough."

"Flattery'll get you nothing." Edna deftly shook shredded tobacco into a fresh rolling paper, wetted one edge, rolled it singlehanded, and lit it. "Any relation to Ed," she asked through a cloud of smoke.

"He was sort of my grandpa." Mae looked Edna in the eye.

"Damn sorry to hear he passed," Edna said. "He was tougher than woodpecker lips. How'd he go?"

"Stroke." Mae stared at the countertop. "Happened while he was sleeping. I went to wake him up for breakfast and found him."

"No Gold Cross?" Edna took another drag on her cigarette.

"The doc said it was an intracerebral hemorrhage," she shook her head. "Too much damage for a scan to work, and he never got around to having himself uploaded. He didn't trust 'em."

"Well, hell." Edna stubbed out her cigarette and tucked the drag end into her pocket. "You have my condolences. What's got you driving for this old reprobate?"

"He needed a driver," Mae looked back up at Edna. "I needed to get out of Gloucester."

Edna turned to Bobby, "What'll you and the young'un have?"

"Afraid we can't stay around for lunch." Bobby turned to Mae. "How about you handle the road snacks, and I'll order us a couple of Edna's famous deep-fried algae burgers."

Bobby stepped out of the dim interior of Jumping Joe's into the sun-drenched winter afternoon. Squinting against the glare, it took him a moment to see them. They wore black pants and thick winter jackets bulging with protective plates and sporting a gold star. All three held brand-new Swan and Lucas combat shotguns. They were spaced far enough apart that Bobby had to shift his focus to look at them.

"Easy there, boys." Bobby froze half in half out of the door, causing Mae to pull up short.

"Hey, what gives?" Mae stood on tiptoes, trying to see around the armload of grocery bags and Bobby's bulk.

"Hold up." He shifted the sack of groceries to his left hand and eyed the three sheriff's deputies. All three raised their weapons and trained them on Bobby. "Any particular reason you fellas are pointing iron my way."

"Is that him?" The one to Bobby's right asked. He wore a neatly trimmed mustache, and the creases in his pants legs looked sharp enough to shave with.

"Matches the bulletin, Dwight." The middle deputy said. He had shaggy hair. His pants were creased but worn, and his mustache hung down in classic handlebar fashion.

"Who do you think I am?" Bobby asked.

"Don't much matter who we think you are," Dwight said. "You're coming with us."

"Well now," Bobby said. "That all depends on several factors. Chief among them, whether or not I feel like coming along."

"From where I stand, how you *feel* about coming along don't much matter." A voice deep and hollow like the bottom of a coal shaft echoed from inside Jumpin Joe's. Bobby knew that voice. "I reckon whether or not you want to come along might be influenced by knowing I have a Chrysler .45 aimed at your driver's kidneys."

"Virgil," Bobby raised his right-hand shoulder high. "I'd take it as a kindness if you didn't blow a hole in the kid."

"Who the hell are you to be first naming me?" Virgil's voice was flat and menacing, like a high country avalanche.

"Easy Virg. It's me, Rob," Bobby said. "Robert Henry. I roll with the South Side Rangers. We helped you get some women folk back last spring."

"Drop them groceries!" Dwight squeezed the shotgun tight against his shoulder. "Do what the sheriff tells you."

"Whoa there, son." Bobby made eye contact with the anxious deputy. "Calm down."

"If that is you, Rob, what's my wife's name?" Virgil asked.

"Edna," Bobby said. "She still makes the best DFABs between Richmond and Greensborough."

"Lower your weapons, boys." The tight itch between Bobby's shoulder blades eased at the familiar whine-click of a Chrysler .45 hammer being lowered.

"Sir?" Dwight reluctantly lowered his shotgun.

"Look, I have a bulletin to be on the lookout for a vehicle matching this one. Paperwork says you all are in possession of stolen property and are charged with disturbing the peace and endangering the community." Virgil said. "So, how about we move this conversation to my office and have a sit down while we work this out."

"Alright, Virg." Bobby stepped out onto the cracked tarmac in front of Jumpin Joe's. "We'll do it your way. Can we at least put the groceries in the back of the van first?"

"Go ahead." Virgil followed Mae and Bobby out of the truck stop. "Just remember, your hand goes anywhere near iron, I will shoot you plumb full of holes."

Bobby and Mae followed Virgil into the squat, red brick building that housed the Emporia sheriff's office. The smell of stale coffee and reheated food mingling with the subtle scent of gun oil and dust. They were patted down and relieved of weapons and phones before the deputies escorted them through an armored security door to one of three large holding cells.

Bobby noticed how Dwight's hands seemed to rise a little higher than was called for in a friendly pat-down. He saw how those same hands lingered too long when they passed over Mae's hips. And he noticed how Dwight kept staring at his driver in a way that certainly spelled trouble.

"Hey, Dwight," Bobby stepped in between Mae and the deputy, letting her enter the cell ahead of him. "You're new to Virgil's crew, so I'm going to tell you this one time. Keep your hands off my driver."

"That right?" Dwight stepped close to Bobby, towering over the older man by at least six inches.

"That's right." Bobby leaned away from the deputy.

"Or what?" Dwight leaned in, his face inches from Bobby's.

"This," Bobby pivoted at the hips snapping his head forward with the full weight of his upper torso behind it.

The solid bone of his forehead met the bridge of Dwight's nose with a solid crunch. Bobby caught the stunned deputy's shirt, hooked his leg, and eased him to the floor before slipping Dwight's pistol from its holster. He ejected the ammo block, locked the slide back, and tossed the weapon to the deputy with the shaggy hair and worn uniform.

"Hang on to this, will you, Brandon." Bobby backed into the cell and pulled the door closed. "Let Virgil know he hired a creeper while you're at it."

"Dammit," Brandon helped the wounded deputy to his feet. "Why the hell'd you have to go and do that?"

"Same reason I helped get your women folk back from the Blasters." Bobby sat down on one of the molded plastic benches bolted to the back wall of the holding cell. "It needed doing."

Chapter 14

"What in the hell is going on?" Mae stomped over to the molded plastic bench bolted and flopped down for the third or fourth time in the last hour.

She switched between standing at the door and shouting for one of the deputies to let her have a phone call and sitting on the molded plastic bench, brooding.

"Relax." Bobby sat up. "Virgil will be along to let us out in a bit."

"Not after you smeared Deputy Mcgrabass's nose across two counties," she said.

"Should've minded his manners." Bobby scrubbed at the sore spot on his forehead. "First, he's groping the hell out of you, then he's disrespecting his elders. Boy needed a lesson."

"I can handle myself," she said. "Besides, he wasn't feeling my tits. He was feeling my gelform under-boob tool pouches. I could hardly feel a thing."

"You got one of them pouches in your pants?" Bobby asked.

"No." She made a face and shuddered. "He was definitely getting close to the goods down there."

"See," Bobby pulled his ball cap back down over his eyes. "Fella needed a lesson."

"How are you so calm?" Mae sprang up off the bench and stalked to the barred door.

"Not my first time."

"In lockup or assaulting a lawman?" She turned and leaned against the barred door.

"Both."

"What's your friend waiting on?"

"My guess?" Bobby said. "Someone paid him an awful lot of money to slow us down."

"Some friend you got there." Mae let her head thump against the steel bars and looked up at the ceiling.

"I don't blame him." Bobby turned onto his left side, cradling his head in the crook of his arm. "You notice anything about their gear?"

"It all looked older than you?" She looked back at Bobby and grinned.

"Exactly," Bobby said. "Everything Virgil and his boys had was at least twenty years old. Everything except their guns. Those three Swan and Lucases were this year's model with all the bells and whistles."

"Look at you." Mae pushed off the bars. "Regular Colombo."

"That show is total crap," he said. "I can tell you who the killer is within the first ten minutes every time."

"Come on, it's one of the best oldies going. Way better than those 90's reruns everyone raves about."

"If you say so."

"You ready to get out of here?"

"How?" Bobby sat up and straightened the Tate Motors ball cap on his head.

"You notice anything about the ceiling?" Mae reached into her bra. "Take a look and tell me what you see." She pulled a soft gelform pouch from under her right breast. It was flesh toned and gently curved.

"I see pipes, some ventilation ducting, lights, bars--"

"Those pipes," Mae opened the pouch, "are a part of the fire suppression system for this building."

"Most buildings have 'em," Bobby said.

"I'll bet," She pulled two tubes from the flesh-colored pouch and screwed them together. "That if I set off the sprinkler, someone will come running to get us to safety."

"What do you figure on doing when four armed men come to escort us to safety?" Bobby asked.

"That's your department." She slipped the pouch on one hand like a fleshy oven mitt. "Besides, I bet we only get one or maybe two. Your pal is probably sorting out Dwight and his new face."

"Probably," Bobby said. "Still, two-on-one is bad odds. You start trying to take a gun from a lawman, and bad things happen."

"You head-butted an armed lawman in the face." Mae walked to the middle of the cell.

"Different circumstances." He shook his head. "Look, we're racers and duelists, not criminals. Emporia has enough trouble without us getting in a shootout with Virgil and his boys."

"The clock's ticking," she said. "Every minute we're in here, the other teams eat up our lead."

"Some things matter more than winning."

"Bull." She stared hard at Bobby. "Aren't you famous for saying 'winning ain't just a good thing, it's the only thing.'"

"I used to say a lot of stupid shit."

"You are not how I imagined you." She went back to searching the ceiling.

"You've known me for ten years."

"No," She stopped near the back wall of the cell. "I knew old Uncle Rob, the scavenger. You are Bobby Hank."

"They're the same guy."

"Maybe they shouldn't be." She climbed up onto the molded plastic bench. "You ready to bust out of here or what?"

"For the record, this is a bad risk."

"Grandpa Ed used to say, where there's chaos and motion, there's opportunity," she said, grinning.

"He was quoting me."

"I know." She clicked a button at the end of the tube. A jet of white-hot flame emerged from the end. She stood on her tiptoes and aimed the jet at the small electronic eye on the other side of the top bars. Every time the jet passed a bar, it shot sparks and smoke from the beige-painted steel.

The building's fire alarm shrieked its warning a split second before the sprinkler system unleashed a rancid torrent of water, rust orange and stinking. Mae hopped down from the plastic bench, tossing the extinguished micro-lance into the toilet.

"Damn, damn, damn." Bobby stepped to the maglocked cell door and waited. Right on cue, the door banged open. Another of Virgil's deputies bustled into the room. He was young and fresh-faced, probably Mae's age or a little younger. He had his pistol drawn and stayed well away from the cell door as he assessed the situation.

"Stand against the back wall," the deputy ordered.

"What in the hell is going on?" Bobby backed away from the cell door, hands in the air.

"I'm going to unlock this door. Then we're going to get out of here." He stepped to the control panel on the wall.

"Something's on fire somewhere. I don't know what, and I'm not going to have you two die on my watch."

Bobby made eye contact with Mae. She shrugged and grinned. It was contagious. He grinned back and moved to stand in front of the cell door.

The deputy pressed the green button on the door control panel. The mag-locks released, and the heavy door clattered open. Bobby stepped through the opening, hands held shoulder high. Just on the other side of the cell door, he half-turned toward Mae.

"Come on, Mae." He caught her eye and pitched her a wink before turning back toward the deputy. On the next step, Bobby allowed his foot to skid. He collapsed with a groan rolling to his back on the wet concrete clutching at his left leg. "Oh, holy shit. My knee."

"Bobby!" Mae rushed to Bobby's side and knelt down with her back to the deputy. "What's hurt?"

"My knee." He looked from her to the deputy and back again, hoping like hell she was picking up what he was putting down.

"Give me a hand." She called over her shoulder.

"Here, let me see." The deputy rushed to Bobby's side, concern written across his youthful features. He holstered his weapon before kneeling. Mae stood and backed away, making room for the deputy.

"Where are you hurt, sir," the deputy asked.

Bobby looked up and grinned.

"Can't rightly say as I am." Bobby's hand snaked out, grabbed the deputy's shirt front, and pulled him down close. In that moment, Mae plucked the deputy's sidearm from its holster and held it against the back of the young man's head.

"All right," she said. Her hands shook, making the muzzle of the Chrysler .45 wobble and tap against the deputy's head. "You get up and get in the cell."

"Don't try to be a hero here, kid," Bobby said. "Nod real slow if you understand me."

"Sure thing." The young deputy carefully nodded.

"What's your name, son?"

"Vince."

"Vince," Bobby said. "I'm going to let go. When I do, you crawl on into that cell. Don't try and stand up, don't move fast. This water stinks bad enough without adding your blood and brains to the problem. Understand?"

"I do." Vince had closed his eyes and took a deep breath. Tears dropped down on Bobby.

"Good. I'm letting go now." Bobby released Vince's shirt front, ready to grab hold if the kid did anything other than crawl over him into the cell.

Vince did as he was told. He crawled over Bobby on shaky hands and knees through the stinking water and into the cell. As soon as the kid's feet had passed, Bobby rolled smoothly to his feet, stepped to the control panel, and mashed the close button. The cell door rolled into place with a clattering BAM followed by the buzz and clank of the mag-locks re-engaging.

"Good job, Vince." Bobby gestured to Mae. She passed him Vince's gun. He ejected the ammo block and pocketed it before removing the slide and tossing both pieces into the adjacent cell.

"This ain't over," Vince said.

"Look," Bobby said. "This ain't personal. So don't go making it personal."

"A .45 stuck to the back of my head felt pretty personal."

"Yeah, I guess so." Bobby opened the door. "Come on, we need to get going before Virg gets back."

Bobby stepped out of the sheriff's office into the chill brilliance of a Virginia winter afternoon. He turned north, keeping a steady but unhurried pace. Their luck seemed to be holding. Not many folks were out and about at one o'clock in the afternoon.

"Where do you figure they stashed our ride?" Mae asked. She looked like a half-drowned punk rat with her bob-cut orange hair plastered to her head.

"Gee, maybe we could have looked that up if someone hadn't soaked every computer terminal and paper document in hundred-year-old water," Bobby said.

"Who pissed in your algae flakes?"

"You." Bobby rounded on Mae. "You set off the damned fire suppression system for the whole building, jam a pistol in the back of that kid's head all without a single thought to the consequences."

"Consequences?"

"Yes, Mae. Consequences. That kid probably pissed himself back there."

"So."

"So. You make a man that afraid, make him feel that weak and helpless, he's pretty likely to come looking for payback."

"All the more reason to get the hell out of here," she said. "You didn't seem too concerned about consequences when you head-butted Dwight."

"He needed a lesson in manners."

"Oh, I get it. When it's your decision, whatever you do is hunky freakin dory, but I take steps to get us back on the road, and it's impulsive and rash."

"Yep."

"Hypocrite."

"Yep." Bobby turned and headed north again.

When he got to the end of the block, he turned east. A squat single-story building with durasteel shutters and an armored door sat at the end of the street. Chain-link topped with razor wire stretched to the right and left of the building for thirty or forty yards on either side, creating an effective barrier to foot and vehicle traffic. Security cameras were mounted on the front corners of the roof.

Behind the chain-link were four brand new police vehicles complete with 3mm Vulcan Gauss cannons mounted in the hood.

Mae whistled. "Are those what I think they are?"

"Yep," Bobby nodded. "New Luxford-Drummond HP-300Gs. Rocking twin 3-millimeter Vulcan Gauss cannons. I think we know the price for Virgil jamming us up."

"Like I said, some friend you got there," Mae said.

"Emporia is a small town with small town budgets." Bobby headed for the armored entrance door to the squat building. "Those HP-300Gs will go a long way to protecting the town. With the Blue Blasters for neighbors, can you blame him?"

"How the hell are we getting in there?" Mae stared at the armored door. "That thing looks like solid durasteel, and all my tools are locked up in Janice."

"Not to worry." Bobby pulled a green plastic security badge out of his pocket with a small flourish. "While I was teaching Dwight his lesson, I lifted his security badge. Figured it might come in handy."

Bobby waved the badge in front of the small black sensor panel next to the armored door. He grinned at the click-buzz of magnetic bolts retracting then swung the door wide.

"After you, madam." He bowed.

"Don't mind if I do." She stepped through the door. "Damn, it's dark in here."

"Hold up," Bobby reached past her shoulder and flipped on the lights.

"They need to spend some of that money they got for slowing us down on smart lights."

"If I had to choose between smart lights or better weapons . . . " He stopped at the door marked ARMORY, "I'd choose weapons."

"I didn't see Janice in the yard," Mae said.

"Probably in the garage." Bobby waved his purloined security badge in front of the sensor. The buzz and click of magnetic bolts withdrawing sounded.

He pulled the door open, flipped on the light, and stepped inside. The walls were lined with gray metal shelves. A large square table sat in the middle of the room with various weapons repair and modification tools laid out on it. At the other end of the room, pallet after pallet of plastic-wrapped ammunition sat in neat rows near the large roll-up door.

"Boy, I'm glad I got Virg to switch to the .45 caseless a few years back." Bobby walked over to a shelf and started stuffing his pockets with brick after brick of caseless ammo.

"I don't see any ammo for my needler." Mae walked from shelf to shelf.

"Needle gun is a great weapon up close." Bobby finished stuffing his pockets and wandered over to the pallets of ammunition by the door. "Not much good for punching through body armor, though."

"Guess it's time for an upgrade." Mae picked up one of the new Chrysler .45s.

"Jackpot." Bobby stood staring at the pallet closest to the door. "This pallet is all 3mm Gauss rounds."

"Are we out?"

"Pretty near." He pressed the green button on the door control.

The segmented door clattered and rattled open. Off to the right sat four more L&D HP-300Gs. Janice sat in the middle of the bay, nose toward the large roll-up door.

"You know, there are some things that Gordo failed to mention about this race." Bobby grabbed a powered pallet jack and moved a 3mm Gauss ammo pallet into the bay.

"Like what?" Mae asked.

"Not having access to all of the vehicle's weapons systems for a start." He lowered the pallet back to the floor. "Hey Janice, open the back hatch."

"Welcome back, Robert Henry," Janice said. "Back hatch opening now."

"Not much we can do about it now." Mae reached into the rear area and rummaged around until she found her tool bag.

"Yeah, I guess that's what you get when you dance with the devil." Bobby started manhandling crates into the rear cargo area.

"Open the mag access for the 3mm Vulcan cannon, Janice."

"I am sorry, Robert Henry, you are not authorized access to that area at this time."

"What?" Bobby and Mae both asked.

"Access to the forward weapons compartment has not been authorized at this time," Janice said.

"You get started on that," Bobby pointed to Mae's tools. "I'm grabbing another pallet of ammo."

"Right." Mae picked up both tool bags and headed to the front driver's side. "Janice, open the driver's door."

"Good afternoon, Mabel Holland," Janice said. "Opening the driver's door." It swung up, smooth and silent.

"It's high time we got better acquainted." Mae knelt and began feeling around the smooth duraplast panels. "Where did they hide it?"

"Are you referring to my diagnostic access port?" Janice asked.

"Yep." Mae continued to run her hands over the faux-wood finish.

"I am not authorized to provide you with that information."

"I know." She closed her eyes and focused all of her attention on her fingertips. "I bet that means you're not required to stop me from figuring it out either."

She found it directly under the steering wheel, "Bingo." It was a small circle the size of a precrash quarter, disguised as a knot in the faux woodgrain. The perfect edges gave it away.

Mae pressed the knot. Bright blue light briefly outlined a small rectangle centered around the knot. It hinged open, presenting her with the familiar double circle of a sixth generation onboard diagnostic access port.

She reached into the tool bag and, fished out a fist-sized cube with a long cord. She plugged one end of the cord into the cube before sorting through a selection of connectors until she found the one that matched the OBD6 port and plugged it in. With a curt wave, she summoned a holographic display and keyboard from the cube.

"You got that thing sorted out yet?" Bobby rolled the second pallet of ammunition around to the front of the Quest.

"I'm rounding second and headed for third." She grinned at him through the holographic display.

"Lovely," he said. "My driver's getting frisky with the car."

"Looks like someone really didn't want us getting access to our lady friend here." Mae's fingers flashed across the holographic keys. "Best I can do right now is getting that gun compartment opened up." On cue, a line of blue light bisected the vehicle's hood. Both halves retracted smoothly into the right and left quarter panels.

"Let's see what you got going on in here, girlfriend."

Mae stood and leaned over the left quarter panel. The interior of the compartment was neat and orderly, a real improvement over the usual rat's nest of cables and components under the hood of most autoduel vehicles. She reached down, grabbed the top corner of the holo-display, and pulled it up to overlay the compartment. Little identification tags popped into view over each cable, box, and component in the compartment.

"They really went all out."

"Oh?"

"The 3 millimeter Gauss cannon mounted centerline, we already knew about." Mae pointed through the holographic overlay. "We also have side-bearing Gauss shotguns, smoke dispensers, and a recon drone launcher."

"What else do we have?" Bobby lifted a waxed-paper-wrapped brick from the crate. He cut the paper away before sliding the dull brick of tungsten rods into an open slot beneath the rotary barrels of the gun.

"Looks like," Mae swiped through a list on the right side of the holographic display. "A slick dispenser. Radar jamming, rear chaff and flare with the latest in crybaby chaff, a MLRS style mini-missile launcher, and a rear-mounted Gauss shotgun for tailgaters."

"Hot damn." Bobby fed another brick into the receptacle.

"What now?" Mae asked.

"I've fed this thing three crates of rounds, and there's room for a couple more." He loaded another cube. "You were only running on one getting out of the dead zone, and we still had around twenty-five percent to empty."

"About time something went our way." Mae closed down the holographic display. "You finish loading. I'm going to get Janice here ready to roll."

"All done here." Bobby shoved the empty pallet and pallet dolly away from the front of the Quest. "Janice, close the front weapons compartment."

"Please ensure all tools have been removed from the compartment and all personnel are clear." The blue light outlining the compartment flashed three times before the access panels reemerged from the quarter panels and closed, presenting a seamless surface once more.

Bobby pressed the green button on the garage bay door control before jogging to Janice and sliding into his seat. "Let's get the hell out of here before they find another way to jam us up."

"Hey," Mae eased the Quest forward. "Maybe we ought to shoot up the tires on those new vehicles. You know, discourage pursuit."

"We're autoduellists, not vandals." He cinched his harness down tight and pulled on his helmet.

"If you say so." Mae eased out into the vehicle yard.

"On the other hand," Bobby stroked the trigger on the weapons yoke. Sparks showered from the steel gate where the tungsten needles tore it to glowing ribbons. "I wouldn't want Virgil to get the wrong impression."

Mae steered the Quest through the shattered gates out onto the street. "Which way?"

"Turn left here," Bobby said. "Once we get through the gates, head west down 58."

"West it is." Mae made the turn. As they rolled past the Sheriff's office, she noticed the fire department had arrived. Virgil and his four deputies stood on the front steps. Judging from their hand gestures and body language, they were having a heated discussion.

"Looks like we better get a move on," Bobby said. "I don't want Virgil feeling like he's got to give chase, and we got to make up some time."

"Aren't you glad we stopped so you could take a leak?" Mae asked.

Chapter 15

Situated near the junction of 58 and old I-85, South Hill found itself in a unique position. After the dust had settled from two world wars, multiple famines, several plagues, and massive civil unrest, South Hill emerged as a safe haven at the juncture of two major transportation arteries.

The city fathers, recognizing what they had, expanded the walls. Enterprising entrepreneurs set up truck stops, shipping companies, and a shopping district. Earl Habner built an autoduel arena. In the course of several years, South Hill became a major transshipment point for goods flowing north and south along I-85 or east and west along Route 58, and to the delight of the citizens, South Hill became a major stop on the autoduel circuit.

"Incoming communication." The coms screen flashed to life, displaying the leering skull over aces and eights logo of *Dead Man's Run.*

"Good afternoon, Pale Riders." The logo faded out, replaced by The Dispatcher in full evening attire, complete with top hat and a shimmering face covering. "I see that despite your little… run-in with the law, you have made excellent time. Please make your way to the arena and take your place at the starting line."

"Can you believe it?" Mae piloted Janice toward the eastern end of the South Hill arena. "We are going to duel on Fury Field!"

"You ever been here?" Bobby activated the targeting system.

"Nope." She shook her head. "South Hill is prime time."

"Couple things you need to keep in mind." Bobby ran a quick diagnostic on the only weapon he had available to him. "It's one of ten designed and built by Earl Habner."

"He built Fury Field?" She piloted the Quest smoothly through the entrance tunnel and out onto the scarred and pitted blacktop. Mae had heard plenty of tales about the big-time arenas, had watched countless duels fought in them . . . but being in one, on the blacktop, took her breath away. "This place is enormous."

"That feeling you have right now," Bobby turned to his awestruck driver. "The sense that you are a very small fish in a very big pond?"

"Yeah." She said.

"Lock it away." He said. "That shit will get you killed. You are a shark. Everyone else is a minnow. Sharks eat minnows."

"All right." Mae sat up a little straighter in her seat and steered Janice up the curved ramp to the starting line. "Let's do this."

The Pale Riders waited at the starting line. Being the first of the L&D team to arrive meant they started closest to the front of the field. It wasn't long before they were joined by the rest of the Luxford-Drummond race team.

"See those domes?" Bobby pointed through the armorglass windshield.

Fury Field had been designed by Earl Habner using the old cloverleaf on/off ramp where Route 58 and I-85 intersected. Nestled within each of the four turns, a white tower capped with a large saucer-like dome protruded above the level of the track like giant armorcrete mushrooms.

"Yeah," Mae said.

"Those are where the folks with money get to sit and safely "participate" in the duel," he said.

"Participate how?"

"Depends on how much they're willing to spend," Bobby said. There were several things that Bobby knew to a certainty about old Earl. The man was rich, he loved autoduelling, he loved children, and he was nuttier than squirrel turds. "The folk who pay to sit in the towers get to do things to the track based on how much money they spend. Earl hosts an auction before every event."

"Things?" Mae turned to look at Bobby. "What kind of things?"

"Spray lubricant onto the turns, smoke screens, fire bombs," he said. "The more they spend, the further up the lethality ladder it goes. Hell, one race, some rich asshole spent so much money he had access to a 20mm recoilless rifle and a loading crew."

"So, pay attention in the turns," She said. "What do they do with the money?"

"Who?"

"Whoever it is that gets all the money for messing with the duelists."

"That's Earl," Bobby said. "He uses it to fund a children's home."

"Well, at least it goes to a good cause."

"Let me know if you still feel that way after we get out of here."

"Welcome to Fury Field." The Dispatcher was back on the communications screen. The spindly figure stood next to a short, pudgy man wearing a gaudy Hawaiian print shirt. Light gleamed from his balding head. A gray beard, neatly trimmed, framed his chubby cheeks.

"That's Earl Habner," Bobby said.

"This challenge is a race, within a race, within a race. The first three L&D teams to finish seven laps will gain access to all of your Quest's weapons. Fourth and fifth teams to cross the finish line will gain access to three-fourths of your Quest's weapons systems, sixth gets half, seventh a quarter. Last place…" The Dispatcher chuckled, the little man in the gaudy shirt chuckled. "Well, everyone knows what last place gets."

"God, I wish he would shut up," Mae said.

"One small catch…" The Dispatcher gestured with his neon-lit cane at a jumbo display to his right. It flickered to life, showing an overhead view of the arena. A hodgepodge of autoduel vehicles streamed up the entrance ramp behind the Luxford-Drummond teams.

"Damn," Bobby said.

"At the insistence of Mr. Habner," Dispatcher stepped closer to the camera. "And by insistence, I mean gross amounts of money, South Hill and the surrounding localities have assembled their best and brightest amateur duelists. If one of them manages to disable one of you, then you are out of Dead Man's Run, and the local yokel gets ten thousand dollars in prize money, a spot in the upcoming pro season, and the remnants of your--"

"What's up?" Mae asked.

"Racers, you will go on the green light. Good luck."

"I ain't shooting these poor bastards."

"What?" Mae stared at the light tree on her side of the track. The first amber light illuminated. "Why?"

"Most of those cars are barely armored." He said. The second amber light illuminated. "Shooting them with the 3mm Gauss cannon is practically murder."

"Won't they be shooting at us?" The third amber light lit up. Mae adjusted her grip on the steering wheel.

"Yep." He said. "You'll just have to out-drive them."

"Fantastic." The green light illuminated. Mae mashed the accelerator to the floor, sending Janice rocketing off the start line.

"Watch this next turn." Bobby stroked the trigger on the weapon's yoke. Mae turned the wheel in an effort to control the oil-slick-induced skid, causing the stream of three-millimeter tungsten rods to strike sparks from the roadway a scant inch from the spinning tires of Black Sunshine's Quest.

"Why are we shooting at Headsman and Black Dragon?" Mae regained control of the skid just short of the retaining wall and accelerated smoothly into the straightaway toward the next turn.

"Hey, Hank," Headsman said. "Watch where you're shooting." Even over the radio, he sounded like a rockfall.

Bobby hit the foot switch for the radio, "That was no accident, Headsman." He took careful aim and sent another burst of tungsten screaming down the right door panel, striking sparks from the armor and blasting the right-hand mirror to fragments. "Lay off the locals and just run the damned laps."

"Go to hell," came the throaty contralto of Headsman's partner and twin sister Black Dragon. Black Sunshine's Quest headed into the cloverleaf of turn four, spraying tungsten death into the rear end of another poorly armored rig. Mae let Janice drift high into the turn, avoiding the spinning, smoking wreck by inches.

"Half these fools are barely old enough to be in the arena," Bobby said. "None of them can afford Gold Cross."

"If you can't afford the piper, don't get on the dance floor." Black Dragon said. They deftly dodged around another burning wreck and accelerated through the starting line, starting lap number three.

"Would you look at that!" Don Northcraft shouted into his microphone. "Jude, the South Hill Kid, Conroy, just moved up into ninth place."

"This Kid Conroy has been a surprise since the start." Butcher Bill said. "He's disabled three cars and destroyed four more…" Bill left off for a moment holding one hand to his right ear. "This just in; Kid Conroy has three, count them, three confirmed kills. Say, that's three more than you scored in your entire professional career, Don."

"Kid Conroy may have three kills," Don turned to face Butcher Bill. "But chances are he won't be getting many more. He just took a shot at Black Sunshine, and we both know how that usually ends."

"Here we go." Don Northcraft leaned forward in his excitement. "It looks like a group of local boys have teamed up with Jude Conroy, and they are gunning for the trailing car in the Luxford-Drummond Eight."

"On your left, Outlaw." Bobby radioed. The Luxford-Drummond number five car operated by the Iron Outlaws jinked left then right, keeping just out of the crimson tracer stream from an old Hotshot.

"I've had just about enough of this." Hal Callahan, the driver for the Iron Outlaws, called over the L&D channel.

"Is it just me, or are these locals getting better with every lap?" Mae braked hard and swerved to avoid another disabled dueler.

"It ain't just you, sister." Hanna Fields, the driver for Tornado Express, replied. "That yahoo in the Gladiator crippled two of my wheel motors. Sprockets got 'em decoupled before things got too hairy."

"Only two laps to go." Mae cut the wheel and pushed the throttle pedal half the distance to the floor. Janice's rear end started to come around, drifting into turn one and the first leaf of the clover.

"Threat warning, threat warning." Janice's voice remained calm and sultry.

Mae jerked the wheel back straight and smashed the throttle to the floor. The smooth angular motion of the drift became an accelerating skid. Fire and asphalt erupted behind them to their left, then further left in a line of explosions that would have pounded them flat if Mae had continued to drift through the turn. The barrier and the mushroom shape of the Turn One tower accelerated toward them at an alarming rate.

"Woah!" Bobby braced for impact.

"Give me four by four Janice." Mae cut the wheel back to the left and eased off the throttle.

"All-wheel drive engaged." Mae hit the throttle again, steering back into a drifting skid, Janice's bumper scant inches away from the infield barrier.

The small black Gladiator zipped through the turn, pulling ahead of the Pale Riders.

"Son-of-a-bitch." Bobby said.

"Still want to hold off on shooting the locals?" Mae asked.

"The kid has done it." Butcher Bill shook his head in disbelief. "Jude Conroy just knocked the number two Luxford-Drummond car, the Sonic Scorpions, out of the race. I ain't seen driving like this since Jeremy and Kelly Hood!"

"It looks like dreams can still come true in Autoduel America, Bill." Don leaned back in his chair and loosened his tie. "Let's see the replay."

The field was tightly packed. Wrecked and disabled vehicles littered the cloverleaf track forcing the drivers to slow down and bunch up. Jude Conroy rocketed through flames six feet high in the bottom of Turn Three, taking a chance that the oil slick would have burned off enough to give him the traction he needed. His gamble paid off. While the other vehicles slipped and slid through fresh oil sprayed onto the track by the wealthy spectators up in the Turn Three tower, Jude was able to pick up eight places, passing the only two remaining local vehicles still in the race along with six of the new Luxford-Drummond Quests.

In the process of passing through the pack, he bumped the number seven car into an uncontrolled spin that left number two wide open. Fire blossomed from the barrels of his .30 caliber guns like lethal roses. A steady stream of red tracers and exploding rounds stitched a line from bumper to bumper, tearing large chunks free from the wheels on the right side of the Quest. The number seven car wobbled back and forth for a moment before spinning one hundred eighty degrees, rolling up onto its side, and sliding most of the way to the upper wall of the turn. Jude Conroy and his Gladiator erupted from the inferno of Turn Three in third place, right behind the Pale Riders.

"This kid's good." Mae cut the wheel, taking Janice low, slipping the red stream of tracer fire. Exploding rounds blasted chunks from the roadway to her right. Ahead of her, the number six car, driven by the Dog Pound, took the turn high and wide to avoid more fire from behind.

"Too good." Bobby watched the rearview with growing anxiety.

The local kid that had been giving them trouble for six laps had made a serious tactical error in rubbing Black Sunshine into a spin without finishing them off. Black Dragon and the Headsman weren't exactly known for their charitable demeanor. Now Black Sunshine in the number seven L&D car was hot on the local kid's tail. It was only a matter of time before that three-millimeter Gauss cannon shredded the Gladiator and its driver.

"You ever done an Ivan?" Bobby locked the targeting computer on the hood and wheels of the Gladiator behind them.

"I've done my fair share of Rockfords." Mae weaved around another disabled vehicle.

"Not quite the same thing." He said. "I need you to spin this thing around but keep going the way you're going now. I need a clean shot at that kid before Headsman turns him into hamburger."

"I know what an Ivan is," Mae said. "Just never had a reason to try one till now."

"Fair enough." Bobby took a firm grip on the gunnery control yoke. "When I say go, you give me that Ivan."

"Janice?" Mae dodged another burst of .30 caliber fire.

"Yes, Mabel Holland?"

"When I say one, I need you to cut the power to the front left wheel drive motors and reverse the drive on the right-side drive motors."

"Yes, Mabel Holland, on the count of one, reverse the right side drive motors while cutting power to the front left drive motor."

"Good girl." Mae jinked right, dodging more fire from the rear. "When I say two, I need you to give me reverse on all the drive motors."

"Yes, Mabel Holland, reverse on all drive motors on the count of two."

"Ready when you are."

"Did you see that?" Don Northcraft shook Butcher Bill's arm in unbridled excitement.

"Of course I saw it, Don." Bill's grin stretched from ear to ear. "We just witnessed one of the all-time slickest maneuvers I have ever had the privilege of seeing."

"We just watched a rookie pull a Crazy Ivan."

"No, Don," Bill looked straight into the camera. "We just witnessed autoduel history being made right before our very eyes. What Mabel Holland, the driver of the Luxford-Drummond number eight car, just did was give Bobby Hank the window he needed to take down three cars at once, stealing the kills from Black Sunshine and ensuring all of the L&D team vehicles finished the race."

"How is that autoduel history?" Don asked.

"It's the first time that Black Sunshine has entered an arena, BLUD or AADA, and not finished first. Mabel Holland and Bobby Hank just ended a fifteen-year winning streak."

"Well, you can't win 'em all." Don sat back in his swivel chair with a big toothy smile.

"No, you can't." Bill agreed. "What a race. And the subscribers got to see it from inside any one of the L&D cars as it happened, unscripted and raw."

"Let's take a look at the standings before we go to Sasha." Don turned and swiped a holodisplay into being on his right side. "First place by mere inches is the Dog Pound in the number six car--"

"Talk about a photo finish." Bill brought up a holodisplay on his side of the desk. On it was the top-down view of the finish line. The video advanced frame by frame showing the Dog Pound Quest crossing over the finish line just ahead of Black Sunshine.

"Second place is Black Sunshine in the number seven car— "

"You know what they call second place, Don?" Bill asked.

"What, Bill?" Don pitched the setup back Bill's way with a single arched eyebrow.

"The first loser." Bill looked straight into the camera and gave the viewers his very best wolf grin. "Tonight, Black Dragon and the Headsman are the first losers."

"Easy, Bill." Don stared at Butcher Bill, unease clear on his well-tanned and blemish-free face. "Trash-talking Black Sunshine can come at a high price."

"Life comes at a high price, Don." Bill gestured to the large display behind them showing an overhead shot of the South Hill arena. The track was littered with disabled and destroyed cars. Rescue crews were on the scene pulling the wounded and the dead from shattered machines.

Chapter 16

"Which way?" Mae asked.

They'd jammed three tables together in the back of Papa G's, a ramshackle hole in the wall that operated as Papadopoulos's Gyro and Gyros. A repair facility and Greek restaurant owned and operated by retired D5 champion George Papadopoulos. Old-school duelists had adopted it as a place for a meal and quiet drink back when Bobby was a young man.

Bobby looked around the table at the faces of the assembled Luxford-Drummond team. Most of it anyway. Sonic Scorpion's driver and gunner were still in the hospital getting patched up, and Black Sunshine had yet to show. The usual collection of oddballs and hardasses that gravitated to autoduelling; they all looked so very young. Not that looks were anything to go on. Gold Cross made age a hard thing to gauge. Then again, only he, Black Sunshine, and the Iron Outlaws were from the old days. He looked down at his hands; the first wrinkles and age spots had arrived somewhere between Poughkeepsie and today. He took a deep breath and let it out. When had he gotten old?

"West," He looked back up at the assembled drivers and gunners.

"Great," Mae rocked her chair back on two legs and leaned against the wall. "You still remember which direction Memphis is. How are we getting there?"

"I'm partial to 58." He traced Route 58 west along the southern border of Virginia.

"You must be partial to being kidnapped by hill folk as well." Tornado Express's driver, Hanna Fields said.

"We're heavily armed and rolling six deep," he said.

"When did this switch to we, Hank?" Black Dragon shouldered between Nate McHenry and Hanna.

"When Dispatcher announced Knoxville as our next waypoint," Bobby said.

"That's funny," Black Dragon shook her head. "I seem to recall you shooting at us just this afternoon."

"I shot near you, not at you," Bobby said. "You think I missed at that range?"

"You stole three kills and cost us first place."

"I didn't do that to rob you," Bobby shook his head. "I did that to save those kids' lives. Most of the fatalities out there were because of you two BLUD holes."

"If you can't pay the piper," Headsman loomed behind Black Dragon, his head inches from the low ceiling. "Don't get on the dance floor."

"I bet you two like to beat up little kids and take their candy." Mae rocked forward in her chair and stood up next to Bobby.

"Quiet, honey," Black Dragon stared at Mae. "Grownups are talking."

"Is that a fact?" Mae asked. "We'll see how grown you are after I kick your ass."

"Best get your pet on a leash." Black Dragon's hand fell to the worn grip of the pistol slung around her narrow hips. Drivers and gunners alike stepped away from Black Sunshine and The Pale Riders.

"Whoa," Bobby grabbed Mae's wrist, pinning her hand to the table. "We ain't going down that road."

"What's the matter, Hank?" Headsman asked. "Lose your nerve?"

"I ain't here to measure dicks with either of you," Bobby said. "I'm here to figure out how to get us into Knoxville in one piece. Last I checked, getting in and out of Knoxville takes a large, well-armed convoy."

"That's still true," Rita Tambour said. She rode as gunner for team Skull Monkey, and based on her earlier performance, she wasn't someone Bobby wanted gunning for him. "We ran escort on a convoy into Knoxville last winter. Lost three cars and fifteen people, and that was just on the way in."

"That's funny," Headsman said. "We were just through there on our way to this little soirée; didn't have a bit of trouble."

"That a fact?" Bobby asked.

"Breezed right through." Black Dragon moved her hand away from her pistol.

"How'd you manage that little miracle?" Bobby asked.

"What's that little rule you're always going on about?" Black Dragon pulled a chair out and sat. "If you have to tell folks your something, then you are not. Guess those big bad outlaws around Knoxville just know when they're outmatched."

"I bet they are watching this race, same as everyone else." Hanna sat back down in her hastily vacated chair. "I bet they won't give two shits who any of us are."

"Which brings us back to the question at hand, which way?" Hal asked.

"We are rolling south." Black Dragon said. "I-85 to I-40. I-40 all the way to Knoxville. Any of you kids that don't want to get taken by hill folk can follow us."

"Route 58's the better bet," Bobby said. "Multiple ways through the mountains. Only one way over the mountains on I-40, and it passes through Asheville."

"What's wrong with Asheville?" Curt Bulow asked. He drove for Rolling Thunder. As far as Bobby could tell, Curt was solidly middle of the pack as drivers went.

"Asheville's Mayor," Bobby said.

"Been through there a couple times." Audrey Mendoza said. She was the driver half of team Skull Monkey. According to Mae, they were in their third season as a team. It looked like they were fully embracing the hottie-duelist shtick, in tight pants and low-cut shirts. "Not a lick of trouble."

"You probably weren't driving brand-new machines either," Bobby said. "Mayor Parkinson's got a thing for levying a tax on anyone who even smells like money, and sister, we reek of it."

"Sounds like a sponsor problem." Headsman pulled out the chair next to Black Dragon and sat.

"Tax might be too generous of a term." Bobby waved down a waitress. "If she's been having bandit trouble, you can count on a term of service as part of the price of passage."

"That sounds suspiciously like being taken by hill folk," Hanna said.

"Let's do this," Hal said. "Half of us go south and cross over the mountains at Asheville, and the other half run west and cross at Bristol."

"Works for us," Black Dragon said.

"Let's make it interesting." Mae stared across the table at Black Dragon. "Last ones to Knoxville buy the beer."

"That's mildly interesting." Black Dragon kicked back in her chair and rested her feet on the table. She was wearing black, knee-length riding boots polished to a high shine. "How about the losing team buys the beer and polishes the winner's boots."

"Deal." Mae looked down at the scuffed and stained leather of her square-toed safety boots. "I drink Milwaukee's Best. Their classic brew made with barley, malt, and hops; not that fermented algae piss."

"I'll take a bottle of Asphalt Angels aged ten years," Nate said.

"You throwing in with them?" Bobby nodded toward Black Dragon and Headsman.

"I ain't had either one of them throat punch me or knee me in the junk." Chris McHenry said.

"Look, kid. You have bad manners, and it may or may not catch up with you." Bobby shrugged. "Turns out it caught up with you. You follow these two hyenas around long enough; you'll end up with worse than a punch in the face."

"What's that supposed to mean?" Black Dragon stared hard at Bobby, her right hand creeping toward the table edge.

"Don't." Bobby shook his head. His left hand was already under the table. "I ain't no wet-behind-the-ears kid. You try consequences with me, and Gold Cross will be rebooting you and your sasquatch partner."

"Maybe." She paused, her hand still visible on the tabletop. "Maybe not. You still haven't explained what you mean."

"What I mean is young kids like him," Bobby nodded toward Chris, "been in the game since breakfast. He doesn't know how to spot a backstabbing jackal just yet."

"Seems to me you're the one doing the backstabbing." Headsman rumbled. "Taking shots at us, stealing our kills, knocking us out of first."

"If you can't afford to pay the piper..." Bobby slowly stood. He locked eyes with Black Dragon and eased the hammer on his Chrysler .45 down before slipping it back into the holster on his right hip. "Come on, Mae; it's a long way to Knoxville."

Back on the road, the Pale Riders drove lead for the westbound convoy, followed by Iron Outlaws, Tornado Express, and the Skull Monkeys. They were headed straight into the setting sun with more than a fair number of miles to put in the rearview before they hit Knoxville. Bobby had replaced Mae at the wheel so she could get some time on the weapons controls and get some much-needed shuteye. They'd been running hard since she agreed to be his driver back in Gloucester.

"I could have taken that skinny bitch." Mae swiped into the navigation page and entered Knoxville as a destination.

"If your hand had gone anywhere but where I pinned it, you'd've been dead before you hit the floor." Bobby squinted into the glare and wondered for the millionth time whether or not Kat would have made the same decision.

"She's that fast?" Mae asked

"Yeah, kid," Bobby said. "Probably faster. Word around the campfire is that meat suit she's in is optimized for maximum physical performance. Increased reflexes, maxed out adrenals. Probably just a rumor started by sore losers. I bet you wouldn't have even cleared leather before she shot you dead and me into the bargain."

"Pale Rider, this is Tornado Express."

Bobby hit the foot switch, "Go ahead, this is Pale Rider."

"AADA Road Atlas says Route 58 runs straight through ungoverned territory. Won't even let Ray select it as a possible route."

"The route you have selected has a safety rating of 2 on the AADA Road Atlas and Survival Guide Sixth Edition safety scale. Please select another route, Mabel Holland."

Bobby hit his foot switch, "we're getting the same over here." He looked at Mae and grinned. "Shut down the navigation. We'll have to do this old school."

"Okay," She swiped the navigation from her part of the holodisplay. "What exactly do you mean by old school?"

"Can you reach my go bag there behind the seat?"

She reached behind the gunner seat and pulled a battered olive drab pack up into her lap. "Got it."

"Should be several maps in that top pocket; pull out the one with two strips of tape on it."

"You weren't joking when you said old school." She pulled a stack of battered and creased maps from the pack. "How old are these things?"

"Used 'em back in '38 on the way into and out of Texas," he said.

"Gulf or Bust, right?" She thumbed through the stack till she hit the one with the two strips of folded-over ordinance tape on it.

"That's what the bigwigs up in DC were calling it," he said.

"What did you call it?" She pulled the map open and gawked at hundreds of handwritten notes in the margins, symbols, and hand-drawn routes marked in different colors.

"A shit show," he said. "The big wigs were all about us showing them boys in the oil states just how the hog eats it with our new, electric-powered tanks. Turns out that once you get very far away from your logistical tail, you can't operate. The boys with turbojet tank engines could go further on a tank of fuel than we could on full batteries."

"So what are we supposed to do?" Hal was back on the radio.

Bobby hit his foot switch. "Mae is going to send you some images. It's a map of southwestern Virginia, southeastern Kentucky, and northeastern Tennessee. Your route is marked in red if any of you get cut off from us or if we have to split up."

"Roger." Hal radioed.

"Copy." Both Audrey and Rita chimed in.

"We need to get a move on." Bobby radioed. "Unless things have changed very much, they button up Bugg's Island at sundown."

The gates were closed. Bobby scratched his head and looked at his watch. The old battered timepiece showed 1740 on the dial. The last rays of the setting sun struck fire from the sky and glinted on the barrels of the 20mm Vulcan cannons and dismounted 120mm guns trained on the road. The large LED marquee read CLOSED TO ALL TRAFFIC. TUNE RADIO TO AM 730 FOR FURTHER INFORMATION. TUNE CB RADIO TO 27.490MHZ FOR CONTACT WITH GATE CONTROL.

"Hey, Janice," Bobby said. "Turn on the AM radio and tune it to AM 730."

The mild background hiss of AM radio filled the space between the words, "...CLOSED TILL FURTHER NOTICE. THIS MESSAGE REPEATS. THIS IS A RED FIVE ALERT. AS OF 1625, BUGG'S ISLAND, RIVERDALE STATION, AND CLARKSVILLE ARE CLOSED TO ALL INCOMING OR OUTBOUND TRAFFIC AND WILL REMAIN CLOSED UNTIL FURTHER NOTICE. THIS MESSAGE— "

"Janice, turn off the AM receiver," Bobby said. He hit the foot switch, "Everyone switch over to VHF 30.6 for team coms 'til further notice." He swiped open the coms display, selected VHF 30.6, and assigned it to the left trigger paddle on the steering wheel before tuning the CB radio to 27.490. A strong sense of unease crawled up his spine and set up shop in the back of his head. Times like this made him miss Kat. She'd already be awake and running comms for him.

"Hey," Bobby gave Mae's shoulder a shake. "Wake up."

"What time is it?" She sat up, rubbing the sleep from her eyes.

"1740." He held up the watch for her to see.

"What the hell? I just got to sleep."

"Bugg's Island is closed." He said.

"What?" She squinted bleary-eyed at the armorcrete walls and durasteel gates.

He hit the foot switch, "Bugg's Island control; this is the lead car in a four-car convoy requesting entry."

"We see you." Bugg's Island radioed back. "The road is closed to all inbound and outbound traffic at this time."

"Find us a way around." Bobby pulled the map out of the center console and dropped it in Mae's lap. He clicked the foot switch, "Any particular reason?"

"None we're discussing with you." Control said.

"Looks like we might be able to get over the river on Highway 360." She squinted at the notes on the map.

"We're just passing through." He radioed back. "Probably not," He leaned over and looked at the map. "The bridge over the Staunton River on 360 got destroyed back in '39 or 40 when the ARF tried to assassinate Virginia's governor."

"Not through here." Bugg's Island Control replied.

"We are enroute to Knoxville using Route 58. Please advise." Bobby radioed.

"We advise you to get the hell off of our doorstep." Bugg's Island Control said.

"Next place you got marked is Watkins Bridge." Mae jabbed a spot on the map further north.

"Look we— "

"We don't want you or your kind anywhere near here. So I advise you to turn those vehicles around and go before we turn them into burning wreckage."

"Threat warning," Janice said.

Mae called up the warning and countermeasures display on her holoscreen. "They just painted us with laser targeting."

"Watkins Bridge it is. Get a route sorted out and send it to the rest of the team." Bobby clicked the transmit paddle on the steering wheel, "Let's roll, folks. I think we've worn out our welcome."

"Pale Rider, Tornado Express." Hanna's voice came in over the VHF. "What's the plan?"

"Roger Bugg's Island Control. We are leaving now." Bobby said. He clicked the left wheel paddle. "Did y'all catch any of that?"

"Enough," Audrey said. "We heading south?"

"Nope." Bobby powered Janice through a tight U-turn and headed back the way they came. "Stand by. Mae will send you the new route."

"You know," Rita's nasal twang sounded in Bobby's ear. "South is looking better by the minute."

Bobby toggled the VHF over to hot mic. "Someone wants us to go south," he said. "That's reason enough for me to keep rolling west."

"I tend to agree," Hal said. "First, Black Sunshine pushes for us to roll in that direction. Now this?"

"We had a saying in the Army," Bobby said. "Once is happenstance, twice is coincidence, and three times is enemy action."

"So weird coincidence?" Mae asked.

"You know what I learned dealing with corporations?" Bobby asked.

"There's no such thing as coincidences?" Audrey said.

"Yep."

"You know they're watching right now, listening to everything we say and do," Hal said.

"Kind of my point," Bobby said.

"I got us a route picked out." Mae jabbed at the battered plastifilm map with one grease-stained finger.

Bobby eased Janice to a stop, leaned over, and looked at the route she'd outlined in red grease pencil. It stayed well away from the river and avoided the major bridges and known settlements until Watkins Bridge. He put Janice in park, hit the door latch and harness release before stepping out onto the crumbling blacktop of Route 58.

"Come on, Mae, I need to stretch my legs." Bobby pulled off his helmet, tossed it onto the driver seat, and made eye contact with Mae, nodding toward the brush and trees encroaching on the old highway.

"Right," She hit her seat and door release. "Me too."

One by one, the other vehicles rolled up to a stop behind the Pale Rider's Quest. Doors hinged up like silent armored wings. The drivers and gunners for Iron Outlaws, Skull Monkeys, and the Tornado Express stood up out of their Quests, tossed their helmets back inside, and walked over to where Mae and Bobby stood.

"What up?" Hal asked

"Team meeting." Bobby nodded skyward. "Private like." He turned and headed into the darkness beneath the trees.

"Gotcha." Hal nodded and stepped off the road behind Bobby Hank.

Bobby walked about thirty or forty yards into the trees picking his way through the thorny vines and underbrush, only stopping when he found space where the vines and smaller plants had been choked out by a heavy carpet of pine needles and a thick canopy of branches overhead. He stood still and listened for the quiet, tell-tale buzz of camera drones. They were there but up above the treetops. It looked like the dense web of pine boughs was keeping the AI-controlled drones from descending close enough to see or record them.

"What's with the secret meeting?" Rolling Thunder's gunner, Teddy Sould, asked.

"Don't want Big Brother," he nodded skyward, "to know what we're doing next."

"Pretty sure that's part of the deal," Rita said.

"Sure," Bobby said. "What ain't, is them knowing our route. The deal was we run the race; they set the conditions, set up the challenges, and adjudicate the results. This ain't no damned reality show where they make *production decisions* to amp up the tension."

"You think they're doing that?" Hal asked.

"I can't say for sure." Bobby shook his head. "What we got right now could be coincidence, or it could be the network trying to up the tension to bring more viewers to the race."

"Odd they would lock us out and then threaten to gun us down," Ray said.

"Maybe the network or Herolutions or some other sponsor paid them to shut us out," Mae said.

"Maybe they're having legit problems," Audrey said. "That radio message sounded righteous to me."

"Problem is we don't know," Bobby said. "Here's the deal, I ain't the boss of any of you. If you want to roll south and catch up with the others, you can. If not, Mae will send you the route."

"You got a way to encrypt it?" Audrey asked.

"Like it matters." Hal pointed up. "They'll be on us as soon as we start to move."

"Don't mean we want them to know in advance where we're headed." Mae pulled the map from inside her coat. "How about everyone just take a picture of the route right now?"

"Let's do that," Bobby said. "Next, we need to get on the web and find out what the hell is going on; whoever rides shotgun handles research and recon, so put your best tech brain in that seat. Mae, that means I drive, you search."

"Works for me." Mae nodded.

"Questions?" Bobby looked around the circle. "Anyone want to try their luck catching up with the others?" Bobby waited. "All right then. We head for Watkins Bridge, cross the Staunton River there, then back south to catch 58 in South Boston. From there, we follow 58 to Bristol. If we're lucky, we can come at Knoxville from the north while the other three teams are coming at it from the south. Might be we split the bandit's attention and get into Knoxville clean."

He looked around the circle again, their faces pale smears in the deep shadows beneath the trees. Damned if he wanted to be in this position again. The first time this happened, they pinned a medal on him and called him a hero; the last time it happened, he'd lost ten years watching Kat die ugly over and over. He had that twisting feeling in his gut that it was going to be much more like the latter.

"All right then." Bobby turned on his heel and headed back through the thickening night toward the road.

Chapter 17

Bobby watched the miles roll under Janice's hood. They were making pretty good time, Clarksville notwithstanding. The detour to Watkins Bridge had been slow going, even with Janice in rough terrain mode. Even her AI-controlled, independent, smart suspension could only do so much to overcome roads that hadn't seen a maintenance crew since the early forties. Hell, he mused. Most of the route Mae had chosen probably hadn't seen an automobile, let alone a road crew, since the early forties. Fortunately, Highway 301 was in better shape on the far side of the river. He glanced over at Mae. She sat cross-legged in the gunner seat with her holocomputer running five displays and a keyboard.

"Any progress?" he asked.

"Some." She looked up from the display in front of her. "Looks like some kind of bandit attack on Riverdale Station."

"That's not good." He reached over and activated the tactical tracking display. Janice appeared as a green icon inside a blue circle on the topographical map. Behind at forty-yard intervals were three more miniature Luxford-Drummond Quests in red, yellow, and gold.

"Why not?" She asked.

"Because we're headed right for Riverdale Station."

"Didn't that emergency message we picked up back at Clarksville say something about Riverdale being closed?" she asked.

"Yep," Bobby said.

"Then why are we trying to get there?" She reached into the left-hand holodisplay, pulled out a wiggling pixilated octopus-looking thing, and tossed it onto the scrolling data stream.

"Because that's the best place left to cross the Dan River till you get to Danville proper."

"What's wrong with crossing at Danville?" She asked.

"You ever hear of the Tyrant of Danville?" He asked.

"No."

"What the hell did Ed teach you all those years?

"Mainly mathematics, machines, computers, and guns." She looked up at Bobby through a holodisplay and grinned. "He tried philosophy and poetry, but it didn't stick."

"Short version then," Bobby checked the tactical display; still only L&D cars on the radar. "Danville was taken over by a gang during the food riots. That gang was run by a real piece of work named Dalton Rigby."

"Wait a minute," she said. "I have heard of this guy. Ran a crew called Rigby's Roughnecks, right?"

"That's right." Bobby nodded. "While starving people were busy burning and looting in most of the big cities, Rigby organized a militia and shut down the mobs in Danville before they could get started. Then he recruited the mob and led a series of raids into North Carolina, gathering resources. By the time anyone knew what was happening, Rigby controlled everything from Roanoke to South Boston."

"So he's the tyrant of Danville?"

"The Tyrant is a former United States Army colonel who was sent to handle Rigby," Bobby said. "Colonel Parker led a mixed division of mechanized infantry and tanks into

Rigby's little kingdom. When the dust settled, Rigby was dead, and Parker had decided he was in charge of Danville."

"How's that bad for us?"

"The Colonel, like the Mayor of Asheville, levies a tax on everyone and everything that passes through his city."

"Let me guess," Mae said. "Autoduelists are often retained for a term of service rather than accepting cold hard cash?"

"Bingo." Bobby checked the tactical display. Just the four of them. "And we don't have the time to linger as one of Colonel Parker's guests."

"I got something here." She held up a hand to her earpiece. "You may want to pull over and watch this before we get any closer to Riverdale Station."

Bobby slowed to a stop. "Put it on so everyone can see."

Mae had managed to work her way into the observation post cameras Riverdale Station had posted around in the ruins of South Boston and on the wall of Riverdale Station proper. On the screen, the sun was still up but well on its way to setting. He recognized the rhythmic clatter of multibladed helicopters before they roared into frame and set down in a cloud of dust and debris in an old parking lot. They were massive MH-72s, six of them. Judging by the stylized Vanguard stenciled on the back two-thirds of the massive teardrop-shaped fuel tanks and the large red horse head painted on the front third, they belonged to Vanguard Heavy Lift. Somebody with very deep pockets had paid to have these boys to deliver something out here in the ruins of South Boston.

Aircrew in sage green flight suits and red aviator helmets unloaded three oversized steel pallets. The pallets were loaded down with ratty-looking motorcycles. Bobby's stomach dropped. Those looked like the same bikes the Blue Blasters rode. At the same time, more green-suited crewmen unloaded similar pallets. Instead of bikes, these pallets were loaded down with people. Bobby used the holodisplay to zoom in on one. Those people were covered in tattoos and blue paint. What little clothing they wore was bone-studded leather vests and chaps.

"You seeing this, Hal," Bobby asked.

"Yeah."

"Looks like Blue Blasters," Mae said.

"That's because it is." Bobby started to zoom out, then froze in horror. As the crewmen from the second bird made their way up the ramp, several blue-faced savages leaped up and rushed up the ramp into the aircraft. The rest was over in less than a minute. Leather and bone armored men were jumping to their feet and storming into still-turning aircraft. The last bird in line started to take off. At twenty feet above the ground, it began to yaw and pitch wildly before arrowing down into the next helicopter in line. The spinning rotors collided, transforming both massive helicopters into spinning flopping meat grinders. The sporadic pop of small arms fire could be heard over two helicopters beating themselves to burning pieces.

"Son-of-a-bitch." Bobby said.

"It's not over." Mae pointed at the display where several crewmen ran across the bridge toward Riverdale Station. Behind them, the four remaining helicopters lifted smoothly into the air, pivoted to face Riverdale Station, and opened fire with their chin-mounted 20mm Vulcan cannon. The view from Riverdale Station's walls turned to static.

"That was roughly three hours ago," Bobby said. "About the same time, we were getting turned away at Clarksville's gates."

"Now check this out." Mae switched the holovideo to a new camera.

Judging from the view, this camera was positioned somewhere high up in the rubble of South Boston. Wreckage from the two stricken helicopters smoldered and burned. A small knot of survivors limped toward the camera. Behind them, a small group of bone-armored cannibals gave a chase. The pursuit looked half-hearted to Bobby.

If those pointy-toothed bastards really wanted your blood, they would keep coming till you ran out of ammo, or they overran your position. In the background, the remaining Blue Blasters were mounting up on their bikes and riding off into the ruins of South Boston. Overhead four MH-72 helicopters roared off in the same direction, their formation a textbook V.

"What do you make of that?" Audrey asked.

"Looks to me like some pilots escaped," Ray said.

"Just the ones on the ground," Bobby scrubbed at his face.

"You think those eater bastards learned to fly a helicopter that fast?" Hannah asked.

"No, but I'm pretty sure they learned how to access the onboard AI that fast," Bobby said.

"Don't those have biometric security measures?" Mae asked.

"I imagine so," Bobby said. "Bloodmouths ain't exactly squeamish; all you need is a thumb and an eye to unlock the AI. Voice commands should get you where you're going after that."

"You mean…"

"Yeah, the Blue Blasters just got themselves four heavy-lift gunships," Ray said.

"Are we going in there?" Mae asked.

"Can you leave six people to the eaters?"

"No." She shook her head. "Not even Black Dragon."

"I'm not sure she counts as people, but I take your meaning."

"Do you think they're still alive?"

"Hard to say." He shrugged. "They were alive four hours ago. It'll take us another half hour to get there."

Partially collapsed buildings protruded into the sky like hands digging out of a grave. The fire that lit up the horizon backlit those protruding remnants giving them an eerie cast. For a city that had burned as many times as South Boston, it was a wonder that there was much of anything left to burn. But here it was on fire again.

Bobby had spent a few minutes making calls until he reached the ops manager for Vanguard Heavy lift. Ten minutes later, he had the UHF SATCOM frequency for the crew's rescue radios. He assigned the UHF transmitter to the left paddle switch on the steering wheel and made sure his VHF transmitter was still set on HOT MIC so the rest of the team could hear. He clicked the left-hand paddle on the wheel, "Vanguard, Pale Rider."

"Go, Pale Rider." The transmission was filled with static and electronic noise, and it sounded like the person on the other end was whispering.

"What is your status?"

"Two in critical condition. Two wounded. One dead."

"What is your location?"

"We're holed up in a burned-out shell three hundred yards or so northwest of the crash site. We are secure for now but will need a medivac ASAP."

"Roger," Bobby said. "Do you have a location on the other four aircraft?"

"No," Vanguard said. "They circled about for a bit before heading northeast."

"What about hostiles on motorbike?"

"Pretty much everywhere," Vanguard said. "I think they are trying to figure out where we went to ground."

"On our way. We are in a gold van. Don't shoot."

Bobby eased the Quest down main street and checked the tactical display. Something was definitely off. Maybe it was the amount of ground clutter; maybe they were being jammed. Either way, the display was damned confusing. It kept adding and removing contacts. Half a second earlier, there had been four contacts due north. Now just Janice and the three other Quests.

"Tornado Express, Skull Monkey, drop back a half mile and hold," Bobby said. "You're our reserve if this thing goes tits up. Iron Outlaw you hold here. Your QRF on this one."

"What's QRF?" Mae checked the targeting computer.

"Quick Reaction Force." Bobby checked tactical again. The four contacts to the north were moving straight south in their direction. "We get overwhelmed, cut off, or any number of bad things, Outlaw will come running."

"And if he gets in trouble?" she asked.

"Skull Monkeys and Tornado Express'll ride to the rescue," he said.

"And if they get in trouble?" She looked at Bobby and grinned.

"Then we switch to plan B," he said.

"What's plan B?" Hannah asked.

"Shoot anything that ain't us and run like hell," Hal said.

"If this does go all to hell," Bobby said, "head for Knoxville the best way you can. We'll meet up there."

"Vanguard, I'm pretty sure those four birds are inbound," Bobby said. "It's hard to tell, something is interfering with my tactical data."

"The birds have active jamming," Vanguard said. "Plays holy hell with coms and tactical sensors."

"Lovely," Ray said.

"I'm switching the team channel back to the stomp mic." Bobby looked at Mae. "Hey kid, you ready for this?"

"I'm scared shitless." Her hands flexed, gripping and releasing the weapons yoke.

"Good," Bobby said. "Fear keeps you alive."

"You're afraid?" she asked.

"Every damn day, kid." He checked the tactical display. Those four contacts were inbound and moving fast. "Just not of dying."

"Threat warning, missile detected," Janice said, her voice steady.

"Again?" Bobby threw the Quest into a skid, sliding around the burned-out remains of South Boston city hall. "Get us some countermeasures."

"I'm working on it." Mae's fingers flew over the holographic keyboard. "When Luxford-Drummond locks you out of something, they don't screw around."

"We need an angle on these birds," Bobby said.

"Tell me about it." Mae swiped the display closed and took hold of the weapons yoke once again.

"What are you doing?" Bobby looked at her, then back to the road; he cranked the wheel, sending them into another drifting turn. "We need countermeasures. You know, chaff, jamming, tinfoil, and a flare gun. Something."

One of the MH-72s roared straight at them, its belly less than ten feet off the ground, the 20mm Vulcan cannon spitting fire. Bobby swerved. He felt the car shudder and skid, spinning into the burned-out shell of a building. He cut the wheel and mashed the accelerator to the floor.

Nothing happened. No tires spun, nothing even whined.

"Hey, Bobby," Mae looked at him, panic in her eyes. "We need to go, now. There are a lot more headed our way."

"I'm trying." He mashed the accelerator again. "No power to the wheels at all."

"Pale Rider," Hal called. "You need to be moving. All four birds are swinging around for another run on you."

"No shit, Hal," Bobby grumbled through gritted teeth. "Mae, a little of that mechanic magic wouldn't hurt."

"Janice, damage report." Mae opened the maintenance holodisplay. The drive train showed red.

"The main power feed to the drive motors has been disconnected or severed, Mabel Holland."

"Fan-damn-tastic." She unclipped her harness and started crawling into the rear of the Quest.

"What the hell are you doing?" Bobby asked.

"Looking to see if I can reconnect the power feed to the drive motors." She called over her shoulder. "Maybe you could hold those sky cannibals off for a few moments?"

"Sure. I'll just take my rifle out there and see about knocking down a heavy lift gunship."

"Anything would be better than this." She pulled tools out of the hardshell case, lifted a spool of monowire, and froze. "Hey, do we have a flare gun?" she asked.

"Sure. In the emergency kit." He selected the 40mm grenade launcher and slaved it to the right trigger paddle on the steering wheel.

"Threat warning. Airborne adversary approaching from the east. ETA three minutes."

Bobby mashed the stomp switch, "Outlaw, Monkey, Tornado."

"Go, Pale Rider."

"Change of plans. We are dead stick. Mae is working on it. We will hold their attention. You make the rescue run. Tune UHF radios to 243.0 MHz to communicate with the pilots."

"That sounds like a bad plan to me," Audrey said.

"If you got a better one, I'm all ears," Bobby said. "Otherwise, get moving."

"Roger," Hal said.

"Wait until they are mid-run on us, then you go like hell for this location." Bobby marked the location of the pilots.

"Airborne adversary approaching from the east. ETA two minutes."

Bobby watched the four aircraft approach in a standard diamond attack formation on the tactical display. The readout showed the distance between the massive MH-72 helicopters at precisely 55 feet with no deviation.

"Hey, some good news," Bobby said. "Those clever bastards have accessed the combat AI to make attack runs."

"How is that good news?" Mae pulled a flare gun out of the emergency kit, broke it open, and passed the end of the monowire braid down through the barrel before fusing it to the side of a flare with molibond adhesive.

"Combat AIs are very rudimentary, highly predictable, and don't have access to onboard weapons," Bobby said. "Basically, they exist to help rookie pilots make attack runs. Give the crew a rock-solid platform to fire from." He grabbed and dragged the weapons control display from Mae's side of the van over to his. The primary problem was that the engineers at Luxford-Drummond had not designed the Quest with assault by air assets in mind.

"So?" Mae eased the flare into the open breach of the pistol, careful to keep the monowire from binding in the barrel. She slipped the spool over a long flathead screwdriver and passed the scratch-built contraption to Bobby.

"So," he took the flare gun, screwdriver, and spool of monowire. "They are going to run a standard ten and ten profile. Ten feet off the ground at ten knots forward airspeed to give the gunners plenty of time on target. What am I going to do with this?"

"Fire that up into their rotor blades," she said.

"What?"

"Helicopters are fragile machines." She peeled back the aramid and rubber floor matting and pried open the access panel to the main power feed that ran from the MHD generator to the drive motors. "If the big fan on top stops turning, it falls out of the sky."

"This tiny wire is going to stop a spinning rotor head that weighs thousands of pounds?" He asked.

"That tiny wire is made of thousands of strands of durasteel, one molecule thick, braided together for a tensile strength of eighty thousand pounds." She pulled the severed end of the primary drive power feed cable up and stared at it. "That gets wrapped up in the rotor blades; it will cut them to pieces."

"Airborne adversary approaching from the east. ETA thirty seconds."

The plan popped into his head, fully formed like a thunderbolt from God. "Janice, give me maximum elevation on the 40mm grenade launcher. Use high explosive grenades and set them for detonation at 22 feet elevation. Fire on my verbal command." Bobby unlatched his seatbelt and slid over the console into the gunner seat before popping open the passenger door.

"Yes, Robert Henry. It is not recommended to open the personnel doors during combat operations."

"What are you doing?" Mae asked.

"You focus on getting us moving." Bobby stepped out into the fire-lit night, closed the gunner's door, and crouched against the armored skin of the Quest.

The approaching roar of four MH-72s drowned out everything. The four aircraft slowed to ten knots forward airspeed. Their chin-mounted Vulcan cannons spat more fire. 20mm rounds chewed a line of destruction into the road and rubble around the Quest. More than a couple of rounds hammered the Quest's side and roof like steel-cored hail making Bobby's scrotum tighten as he squeezed tight to the opposite side of the Quest.

He waited until he could see the blur of rotor blades from the lead aircraft passing overhead. "Now, Janice." The steady thump of the grenade launcher firing was barely audible over the sound of 20mm Vulcan cannons firing. "Here goes nothing." He pointed the flare gun straight up, slid the spool of monowire onto the screwdriver, and jammed it handle first into the rubble before pulling the trigger.

The flare rocketed into the air, pulling the hair-thin monofilament wire behind it like a gossamer strand of spider web. At the same moment, high explosive grenades started exploding in and around the left-hand helicopter in the formation. It had turned to keep the nose and roaring gun trained on Janice. The shrapnel from the steady barrage of high explosive grenades wreaked terrible havoc on the helicopter's rotor, sending it spinning and careening into the ground. The rear MH-72's rotor blades caught the wire and pulled it singing from the spool. Bobby popped the gunner door open and dived back inside, pulling it closed behind him.

"That's two less sky cannibals," he said. "How are you coming with the drive problem?"

"Good enough," she called. "Several rounds punched through the very light armor on the belly and played holy hell with the drive power feed cable."

"You fix it?" He slid back behind the steering wheel.

"Sort of." She closed the access cover and flopped the aramid and rubber mat back on top of it. "You should have power to the rear drive motors at the very least. I had to steal wire from a less critical system to repair the power feed."

"Which one?" He asked.

"Would you believe there are powered locator beacons on here, and they are transmitting, or were. I figured locator beacons were less critical than drive motors."

He cut the wheels and hit the accelerator. Janice rolled into motion once again. "You are a marvel, Mabel Holland."

"Don't get too excited," she said. "That wire was never meant for the load we're putting on it."

"Outlaw," Bobby called. "How's the extraction going?"

"Shitty," Hal said. Bobby could hear the high-pitched ripping foil sound of a 3mm Gauss gun firing in the background. "We just rolled to the location you sent, and you know what was there?"

"Cannibals on bikes?" Mae cycled through a weapons status check. The 40mm grenade launcher was empty.

"Lots of 'em," Rita said.

"I was on coms with Vanguard 21." Bobby shook his head in disbelief.

"So were we," Hal said.

"I'm beginning to think we've seriously underestimated those pricks," Hal said.

"What's your status?" Bobby checked the tactical display. The three icons that represented known friendlies were on the far side of the river side by side. On the other side, the Pale Rider's side, a large cluster of hostile red icons were regrouping.

"We got across the bridge and are holding." Ray radioed. "Tornado Express hurt them pretty bad on that last run. Looks like they are gearing up for another."

"I think it's probably time for plan B," Bobby said.

"We shoot everything that moves and run like hell?" Audrey asked.

"Not quite." Bobby chuckled. "We downed two of those birds. The other two ain't been back yet, so either we scared them off, or they're running low on power. I don't want to wait around and find out. When they make the next run, we'll roll up behind them. Catch 'em between us and shred 'em."

"Damn straight," Audrey said.

"Here they come," Hal radioed.

"Here we go." Bobby accelerated down the fire-lit remnants of South Boston's main street.

They gathered near the burning remnant of Riverdale Station. Bodies and bikes were stacked chest high in some spots where the Blue Blasters had made their final run. Trapped between the Pale Riders and the other three Quests, the bone-armored savages hadn't stood a chance. The 3mm Gauss cannons and anti-personnel mines built into the front bumpers of the Quests had shot the motorbike-mounted cannibals to rags.

Janice had stalled halfway onto the bridge, and only Mae's quick work got them back in action.

"I think it's time," Bobby said.

"Time for what?" Raymond asked.

"Time we split up," Bobby said. "Our ride needs significant repair. No way we can keep up."

"Not so sure I like that idea," Hal said.

"I don't like it either. In our current shape, we're dead weight, and this is a race," Bobby said.

"He's not wrong," Audrey leaned back against the hood of the Skull Monkey's Quest.

"Look, I know a place where I can get some repairs handled. The guy who runs it don't much like company or strangers." Bobby leaned against Janice's hood. "Y'all head south. Take your chances with Asheville. We'll catch up."

"All right." Hal stuck out his hand. "But I still don't like it."

"See you in Knoxville." Bobby shook Hal's hand.

Chapter 18

"Time to wake up." Bobby gave Mae a gentle shake.

"Wha...what's going on." She pawed for the weapons yoke.

"Easy," Bobby said. "No emergency. We're here is all."

"Oh, okay." She sat up and scrubbed the sleep from her eyes. "Where exactly is here?"

"A wide spot in the road used to be called Wheeler," he said. "How's our girl?"

"Let's have a look-see." Mae swiped the holodisplay over to the vehicle diagnostic page. "The MHD power plant is still offline, and the batteries are at forty percent; we have no grenades and only half a mag of 3mm gauss left. The rest of the weapons are still off-limits. Same for the entire countermeasures suite."

"How about tracking and cameras?" Bobby pulled the Quest into the remains of a gas station. Thorny vines and ivy hung down from the gas pump awning. The building was completely taken over by Virginia Creeper and green briars. If he squinted just right, he could still make out the sign that read PATTY'S NEIGHBORHOOD FOOD MARKET. Not that he needed to squint. He'd spent a lot of afternoons peddling here from Granny's house just up the holler. He spent every summer there until he was sixteen, and every afternoon she sent him for two packs of Kools and a two-liter of Diet Coke.

"I robbed the wiring from the tracking system, the cameras, the internet router and receiver, and the onboard microphones." She shook her head. "Hell, I damn near pulled wiring from the countermeasures systems since we can't use 'em."

"I'm glad you didn't." He eased the Quest up under the overgrown pump awning. Janice's hood parted the creeper and vines like a thorny green curtain. Once they were fully beneath the awning, Bobby shut her down.

"What are we doing here?" Mae asked.

"Waiting on an old friend." Bobby pulled the Chrysler .45 out of its holster, ejected the magazine, and locked back the slide before placing it on the dash.

"Why you doing that?" Mae turned on her helmet's headlamp.

"This old friend isn't fond of visitors, so I'm making sure there are no misunderstandings." Bobby reached behind Mae's seat, unzipped his go bag, and rummaged around in it for a moment before pulling out a battered OD green radio that looked like a prop from a war movie.

"What's with the antique?" she asked. "We have UHF, VHF, CB, SATCOM, and I think maybe ULF radio, and you want to use that thing?"

He extended the antenna, clicked it on, and hit the talk button. "Warthog, this is Armadillo two six. Armadillo two six calling Warthog. Over."

"What the hell are you doing?" she asked.

"We need a place to lay low, patch Janice up, get us access to all of her features, not just the ones our corporate overlords allow us to have," Bobby said. "This is the best place I know to do it."

"Unless we got a couple days to sit here in the gas station time forgot and let me tinker, it ain't happening." She scrubbed at her face. "Maybe, if I am very lucky, I can get chaff and flare online and the rest of the weapons."

"What if you had access to a real shop and an off-the-grid version of Uncle Al's?"

"And this old buddy of yours has that?" she asked.

"That and more," he said.

"And he's going to just let us into his super-secret shop?"

"We served together back in '38, '39," Bobby said. "He'll help." He pressed the talk button on the radio again. "Warthog, this is Armadillo two six. Armadillo two six calling Warthog. I am at extraction point Papa November Foxtrot Mike. I repeat extraction point Papa November Foxtrot Mike. No hostiles present at this time. Requesting extraction. Warthog, this is Armadillo two six at extraction point Papa November Foxtrot Mike requesting extraction."

He sat and listened to the hiss and pop of static on the old handset.

"So," Mae pulled her purloined .45 and needler from their holsters, ejected the magazines, and laid them on the dash next to Bobby's. "Who's this old friend?"

"I told you we served together back in the day," he said, taking off his helmet and leaning back in his seat. "We made a push into Texas, and when things turned bad, we had to retreat. They were so sure of their victory that they didn't plan for failure. The president was swapping generals faster than underwear, turned the whole thing into a real shit-show. Some outfits broke and ran while others stood and fought."

"What did your outfit do?" she asked.

"We stood and fought," he answered. "When it became clear no one was coming for us, what was left of the 8th Cavalry, Alpha Company-- the armadillos -- linked up with our mechanized infantry, Bravo Company, and fought our way from the hills of Texas all the way to Arkansas's border."

"Was Warthog part of your unit?" Mae asked.

"Yeah he— "

"Armadillo two six," The old radio crackled to life. "This is Den Mother."

"Go Mother," Bobby said.

"We have you at extraction point, Papa November Foxtrot Mike." Den Mother said. "The sun was out earlier, but it looks like rain later."

Bobby grinned. "So long, and thanks for all the fish."

"What?" Mae asked. "Shouldn't you say something about an umbrella?"

"Not unless I want to get hit with a rocket mortar or whatever else Warthog has up his sleeve." Bobby shook his head. "The system we worked out way back when has a number of possible opening sentences. Each of those sentences has an acceptable range of responses that have absolutely no correlation with the original sentence. Today is Saturday. They mentioned the weather; weather plus Saturday equals a Douglas Adams reference."

"I didn't really study history much," Mae said. "Was he one of the Boston Tea Party guys?"

"What— "

"Copy Armadillo. We have an extraction team enroute. ETA one five mikes," Den Mother said. "Hope you brought a towel."

"Copy Mother. I brought two." He clicked the old radio off and stuffed it in his go bag.

"Okay." The woman behind Bobby said. "Take off the bags."

Bobby ever so cautiously reached up and pulled the stinking burlap sack from his head. He felt the barrel of the woman's pistol digging into his spine, so he was careful to keep his hands in view, shoulder high. He studied his surroundings, squinting and blinking. The walls were made of corrugated tin, and the roof was at least 20 feet high, with bare lightbulbs fixed every so often along the rafters. To one side of the room, wood rounds were stacked neatly from floor to ceiling. On the other side, wooden crates with MREs printed on them in stark black lettering lined the wall. A familiar smell filled Bobby's senses - dust, axle grease, freshly cut wood - it smelled like home.

Bobby scrubbed at his head with both hands. Partially to clear the little bits of whatever had been in the burlap sack from his face and head, partially to try and get rid of the odor.

"What the hell did you have in that bag?" Mae asked. "It smells like a skunk got it on with a potato in there."

"You're not far off, miss," a deep voice said from behind them.

It wasn't a deep gravelly rumble like some men have. No. This voice was smooth like Kentucky bourbon, rich like fresh cream. Bobby recognized the soft Virginia mountain drawl and grinned. "What's with all the theatrics, Hog?"

"You can never be too sure," Hog said. "Especially in my line of work."

"Fair enough," Bobby said. "We good to turn around?"

"Depends," Hog said. "Who's your partner? She doesn't look nor sound like Kathrine."

"New driver," Bobby said. "Kat's been back on the slab for more than a year now."

"Shit," Hog said. "Y'all can go on ahead and turn around. Sorry for the precaution. You gave the code for company Henry, not friends."

"Mother said towel," Bobby and Mae turned around. "Towel is the word for number in your party."

"Yep," Hog nodded. "And the response if you brought along properly vetted friends is the number in your party and the word beach. Just the number means unvetted company."

"What would have happened if he'd said 'bath'?" Mae turned to look at Bobby.

"Well, miss," Hog nodded and grinned. "You'd be sleeping off a sizeable dose of horse tranquilizer right about now."

"Good job, Bobby." She punched him in the arm, hard. "You nearly got me tranqed."

"Be glad he didn't use *dish towel*." The woman holstered her pistol.

Hog led them out of what he called the woodshed, across the wide graveled yard to an even bigger building roofed and sided in corrugated tin. It looked like the black and white pictures she'd seen in Grandpa Ed's old photo albums. Her opinion of the structure changed immediately upon stepping through the battered wooden plank door.

If the outside looked like a barn from the olden days, the inside looked like Q's shop straight out of the latest Bond movie. The floor was white-painted concrete, the walls were covered in sound-deadening panels, and the lights overhead were bright white LEDs that lit up the entire space. Along one wall sat a series of fabrication machines, including several Pyro Maker 10k 3d Printers. On a bench along the back wall were multiple holocomputer cubes. The underside of that same bench was filled with drawer after drawer labeled in clear block letter stencils. And glory of glories, three Ironclad Goliath lifts sat well-spaced from each other and the tool bench.

"Bobby," Mae said, her voice a little husky. "I think I'm in love."

"I have that effect on the ladies." Hog chuckled. "Will this suit your needs?"

"I'd say so." Mae walked toward the tool bench. "Are those Mirage AT-3500 computers?"

"Probably," Hog said. "I've never been much of a mechanic; my talents lie elsewhere."

"You have any of the same crew as last time I was through the holler?" Bobby asked.

"Sure," Hog said. "Mel and Eric are out picking up your ride. You won't know the rest of the crew. They're all newer additions."

"How long till they get here with Janice?" Mae eyed the eclectic collection of couches and chairs in the far corner of the shop. Her eyes were gritty with too little sleep, and her head was pounding from the stench of the head bags.

"A half hour at the very least." Hog checked his watch. "That's the next window in the satellite coverage, and Tonys got to make sure it's clean before bringing it all the way into the holler."

"What exactly is going on here?" Mae turned and looked at Hog, really looked this time. He was a short man, not much taller than her. His beard and hair were both cut short and neat. His face was young, not much older than her if she had to guess unless you counted the eyes. His eyes told a very different story.

"Best not ask too many questions," Bobby said.

"I have enemies in high places," Hog said. "High places with deep pockets. How about you go have a sit-down and wait for my crew to roll your ride in here; then you can get started setting it to rights."

Mae stared at Hog for a moment, "Any port in a storm, I guess." She turned on her heel and walked toward the lounge area.

"Oh, I like her, Henry." She heard Hog say as she passed out of earshot.

Bobby watched Mae pull her floppy ballcap out of her hip pocket and put it on before flopping down on the threadbare couch.

"Let's you and I take a walk while Miss Holland waits on your ride." Hog turned and walked toward a smaller door between two work benches along the left-hand wall of the shop. "You know she kind of reminds me of Lizzie Hood."

Bobby shrugged, turned, and followed Hog into the cold early morning darkness. He followed Hog along a familiar, well-worn path down one side of a brush and boulder-choked ravine and up the other side to a small house set on a flat spot carved out of the side of Hog's Holler before he or Hog's grandparents were a twinkle. The porch railing looked new, as did the planks of the front steps. A single bulb burned bright, illuminating the front porch. An open-topped box held a sizeable supply of split wood, and a galvanized bucket half full of coal sat next to the wood box.

"Still living in Mamaw's old house," Bobby said.

"Yeah," Hog kicked the toe of each booted foot against the edge of the plank steps before stepping up onto the covered porch. "Ain't much to look at, but it's mine."

"Looks like you've done a fair bit of work to the place." Bobby followed suit, kicking the toes of his boots against the porch steps to knock off any dirt before climbing the four steps to the porch proper.

"A man should take care of what's his." Hog turned the knob and pushed the door open. "Come on in."

Bobby stepped through the door into the small mudroom. Horseshoes had been welded together and nailed to the wall to make coat hooks with pegs above that for hats, just like he remembered. He sat on the bench and pulled off his boots before opening the second door and stepping into the dining room / kitchen. A fire was going in the old cast iron stove, and a coffeepot was percolating away on the top of it. He walked to the old chrome and Formica table, pulled out one of the ladder-backed chairs, and sat.

"You ain't changed a thing, Hog," Bobby said.

"Oh, there've been a few changes." Hog pulled two mugs from the cupboard and carried them to the table. "For example, I pulled out the gas-burning cook stove and put in an old wood burner like Mamaw had when we were little."

"Why go backward like that?" Bobby asked.

"Natural gas might be easy to get in the big cities." Hog used a floral print potholder to grasp the handle of the coffee pot and poured for both of them. "Here in the holler, not so much. So I switched back to wood and coal. Wood's abundant, and I reopened that little doghole mine of Papaw's, so I got access to a solid coal seam."

"How did you solve the electricity problem?" Bobby blew on his coffee before taking a cautious sip.

"Sorry, Henry," Hog shook his head. "A man's got to have some secrets."

"Fair enough." Bobby took another drink. "This is good. Where the hell did you get this?"

"Also a secret," Hog said.

"You didn't bring me out here just to wow me with coffee and secrets," Bobby said. "So, how about we get to it."

"I've been watching Dead Man's Run," Hog said.

"And?"

"I saw that stunt you pulled getting out of the cannibal camp."

"Saw that, did you?"

"According to the ratings, half the damned country saw it," Hog said. "Ain't you getting a little long in the tooth to be pulling that sort of thing out of your ass? At least in that meat suit. I thought you had Gold Cross."

"I used it up."

"On what? That meat you're wearing is the body you got when you mustered out of the army," Hog said.

"Kat," Bobby said. "She got sick not long after we were through here last."

"Sick?" Hog refilled his cup. "What kind of sick do you get that Gold Cross can't fix?"

"CDRS," Bobby said.

"Okay, that's bad." Hog set his cup down. "You could have come here."

"Unless you got a clone research facility tucked away around here, I couldn't," Bobby said. When Hog didn't respond Bobby leaned forward and sat his cup on the yellow Formica. "Do you?"

"Well, The Mountain provides," Hog said.

"You still running with those knuckleheads?" Bobby asked.

"They might have been knuckleheads twenty years ago." Hog shook his head. "But those knuckleheads are why we ain't under the thumb of any corporation or the government."

"For now." Bobby finished his cup and held it out for a refill. "Anyway, we started with Gold Cross, and when that failed, we started trying other places. The last one was a mostly off-the-books research project near Gloucester. Been living in a trailer out that way for the last ten years or so. The last treatment failed, and I was working on scratching together enough cash to try again when this deal fell into my lap."

"Let me guess, they needed a legend, a star, to bring fans back to the sport."

"Yep," Bobby said. "Gordo came to recruit me."

"Gordon Corey?" Hog asked. "I'm telling you, that guy is no good."

"Naw, Gordo's good to go," Bobby said. "We go way back. Hell, we came up together on the dueling circuit."

"I'm telling you, that oily bastard is nothing but trouble."

"You say that about everyone in a suit and tie, Hog."

"But I mean it about him." Hog stared Bobby in the eye and shook his head. "Tell me this. If Gordon is such a pal, why'd didn't he offer to help his old pal out and get Kat into some big time corporate research program for the shakes?"

"He's VP of Luxford-Drummond's Combat Vehicles division. You know those corporate types never give you something for nothing."

"So which is it, Henry?" Hog stood up from the table, walked to the stove, and opened the door. "He your old pal, or is he a Company Man?" Bobby could hear the capital letters.

"Can't he be both?"

"Not for long." Hog opened the heavy cast-iron stove door with the door dog, crouched, and prodded the fire with a poker before adding a couple more billets of wood. "Time'll come, if it hasn't already, Gordon'll have to choose between you and the corporation. My money is on the corporation."

"Like you don't have an angle here." Bobby snorted.

"Of course, I got an angle." Hog closed the stove door with a clang and hung the door dog on a nail. "Difference is, I'm upfront about it."

"What's this little stop-off gonna cost me?" Bobby asked.

"This?" Hog gestured with his cup. "Nothing. I owe you a hell of a lot more than some repair work on your ride."

"You don't owe me nothin." Bobby shook his head.

"You save a man's life, that's got to count for something," Hog said.

"We saved each other's lives, Hog," Bobby said. "Hell, we'd have never made it to Little Rock if it weren't for you."

"How about we call it even after this," Hog said. "Next favor you owe me."

Bobby strapped into Janice's driver's seat. Mae was already snoring in the gunner's seat. Frost coated everything in a gossamer layer of white, transforming the creeper-covered pump awning of the old gas station and food mart into a glittering fairy wonderland.

"Your girl and my crew found a fair bit of unpleasantness." Hog leaned on the rear frame of the driver's door. "Five separate tracking beacons, cutoff switches programmed for every system on the car, and an explosive device tucked up under that new MHD powerplant. Looks like your boy Gordon made his choice."

"Maybe," Bobby ran a series of pre-start diagnostics. "Maybe not. Either way, I'm going to have some questions for him."

"Look, you can just quit the whole damn thing. Stay here." Hog said. "I sent those tracking beacons five different directions about two hours ago."

"I can't."

"Why not?"

"Two reasons." Bobby held up two gloved fingers. "I gave my word to Luxford-Drummond I would drive their vehicle in this race. Two, they have Kat's MMSD, so even if I was inclined to break my word, and I'm not, they have the only copy of Kathrine as a hostage."

Hog took off his hat and scratched at his shaggy head. "What if they didn't?"

"What?" Bobby asked. "Have her hostage?"

"Yeah. What if they didn't have her as leverage?"

"I'd feel a whole lot better about this whole thing," Bobby said. "I still gave them my word."

"You don't feel that rigging your vehicle to blow up by remote control might change things?"

"I gave my word, and I won't go back on it without some explanation."

"You're a dinosaur," Hog said. "Man of honor in a den of vipers."

"Not for nothing," Bobby shrugged and pressed the START/ACTIVATE button. "I do love being back in the game."

"Maybe so, but you're helping those bastards stay in power." Hog shook his head. "Bread and circuses. They're gettin' rich off of poor men's dreams."

"What do poor men dream about, Hog?" Bobby asked.

"That's easy." Hog stepped back from the open gull-wing door. "They dream of being you."

Bobby pressed the button to close his door. He watched Hog walk back to the rollback tow truck and climb in the passenger seat. Maybe Hog was right. Maybe he was a dinosaur. Bobby shook his head. A man had to stand for something, had to have a code. Without it, nothing made sense. He put Janice in drive and headed west.

"Hey, Janice." he said. "Play me some music."

"Sure thing, Bobby," Janice said. "Anything in particular?"

"Bobby?"

"Mae made some adjustments to my programming, she removed the corporate stick from my ass."

"Okay," Bobby shook his head and chuckled. "Just shuffle up the stuff I like."

"Very well."

The mournful, haunting notes of Alice in Chains' oldie *Rooster* crept from the speakers into his ears, wrapping him in melancholy and nostalgia.

"Good one, Janice." He mashed the accelerator to the floor. With any luck, they'd be in Knoxville before ten.

Chapter 19

"Approaching Knoxville," Janice said. "Distance 27.7 miles, estimated time of arrival zero nine-thirty."

"Thanks Janice." Mae said from the driver's seat.

Her voice was still sultry and silk smooth but without that stilted quality. She sounded more real to Bobby now. Maybe it was because Mae and the Butcher Holler crew unlocked the complete functionality of the computer and AI. Maybe it was because they removed all the Luxford-Drummond safety protocols designed to help a suburban mom safely navigate from home to football practice and back.

At any rate, she had stopped refusing to give them usable routes through areas deemed unsafe or ungoverned. That didn't stop her from providing a steady stream of cautions, warnings, and notes from the AADA Road Atlas and Survival Guide Sixth Edition.

"The Atlas states: The roads around Knoxville are rated extremely dangerous. The AADA does not advise travel to any location with a rating of Extremely Dangerous."

"Thanks, Janice." Bobby yawned, sat up, and stretched. He rubbed his sleep-gummed eyes and squinted at the sunlit landscape. His tongue felt like some leathery alien creature clinging to the roof of his mouth. "How long was I out?"

"You passed out before I got back in the car at that Jumpin Joes in Jellico." She handed him a large disposable travel mug. "Guess you senior citizens need your rest."

"Thanks." He grimaced, took the cup, and pulled the tab at the bottom, activating the reheating element.

Bobby swiped open the tactical display while he waited for the Jumpin Joe's Jolt and Go cup to work its magic. The display showed the wrinkled contours of the Cumberland Mountains descending down to the Powell River and the Norris Dam on their left. Nothing moved within the reach of Janice's radar or her Orbitlink augmented systems.

"I got the cameras working before pulling out of Jellico." She looked at Bobby and raised one eyebrow.

"Anything from the network or the sponsor?" He asked.

"As a matter of fact, we had a call from Sasha Goodwin looking to get the exclusive scoop on what happened after we went dark. And we got a call from your pal at Luxford-Drummond."

"Gordo?"

"Sounds like a good ol' boy, wears a fancy suit, and looks like a golden god?" she asked.

"That's Gordo, and he's three times your age." Bobby took a drink of his coffee and grimaced.

"He might be in his seventies, but that meat he's wearing looks like a very recent twenty-five," she said. "What's the matter? Not enough cream and sugar for you, gramps?"

"No." Bobby shook his head. "Reheated truck stop coffee tastes like Satan's asshole."

"Incoming call from Gordon Corey, Mae."

"Put it on Bobby's screen," she said.

"On screen."

"Glad you're finally awake, sunshine." Gordon's hair was mussed, his tie hung loose around his unbuttoned collar, and his suit jacket was nowhere in evidence.

"Looks like you slept in your suit, Gordo." Bobby took another drink of lousy coffee.

"You look worse, Hank." Gordon scrubbed at his face. "Mind filling me in on what in the actual hell happened there in South Boston?"

"Mae didn't tell you?"

"She said you took some rounds through the bottom of the Quest, that they severed most of your power couplings."

"That about sums it up." Bobby nodded. "She got us enough power to fight— "

"I saw the footage from the other three Quests."

"Then you know what happened," Bobby said. "We limped north and west till we found a place to hole up and get Janice back in action."

"Then why in the hell," Gordon leaned closer to the camera pickup, "does tracking have you in Pennsylvania, Ohio, Maryland, West Virginia, and Georgia!"

"Hey, don't get pissy with me," Bobby said. "If your engineers had sense god gave geese, they'd have armored the belly of these things. How in the hell do you get your power feed taken out by ricochets?"

"They weren't designed to take on gunships." Gordon sat back in his chair.

"No shit, Gordo." Bobby deadpanned. "Tell me, how exactly did a bunch of Blue Blasters end up with four MH-72s?"

"Well, that's— "

"And while you're at it, what in the hell were they doing in South Boston, Virginia?"

"You really want to know?"

"Yeah, Gordon." Bobby's voice had gone flat. "How about you tell me."

"We, the network and sponsors, ran a viewer poll after the challenge at South Hill. Fans and viewers overwhelmingly supported another face-off with the Blue Blasters. Vanguard Heavy Lift offered to sponsor the event, so we made it happen. The ratings were off the charts."

"Did your plan happen to account for the bloodmouths having a higher metabolic rate and shaking off whatever you used to sedate them?"

"How— "

"Did your plan have a contingency for containing those psychotic bastards if they got loose or somehow captured those aircraft?"

"We didn't think they could fly one if they did capture it."

"You have got to be the dumbest sonofabitch I ever met." Bobby thumped his armrest. "They are psychotic savages, not idiots. They can handle AIs same as anybody else!"

"MH-72s— "

"Have biometric security to prevent theft?" Bobby finished. "Blue Blasters probably killed the crew, cut off their thumbs, cut out their eyes, and accessed the AI that way. And if the crew was very lucky, it happened in that order."

"That's bad."

"Bad?" Mae shouted. "You turned bloodmouths loose beyond the containment perimeter. And now they have two heavily armed helicopters, that is so much worse than bad."

"Look, it wasn't my call," Gordon said.

"You don't seem too broken up about it," Bobby said.

"I didn't call to debate morality, Hank," Gordon said. "I called to congratulate you on surviving a bad situation and to pass on a message from the sponsors and the network."

"Best hop to it then, Company Man," Bobby said.

"You are being compensated to run this race on camera, the whole race. See to it that you do."

"Well, Gordo," Bobby leaned in close to the camera pickup. "I tell ya what. You tell your pals at corporate to stop screwing with the race for ratings and stop *producing* the show, and I'll do my best to keep the cameras rolling. Janice, end call."

"Call ended." Gordon's face vanished from the coms display. "Incoming call. Shall I put it on screen?"

"Sure," Bobby said.

The Dispatcher leaned against a steel and wood desk, his silver-gold suit sparkling in the light. His face was a distorted blur cycling through an infinite selection of features. On his right, an old corkboard towered with a map of Tennessee, Mississippi, and Alabama pinned to it.

"Welcome back to the race, Pale Riders, and welcome to the Knoxville challenge." He still used that fussy Oxford accent.

"The siege of Birmingham is in its third consecutive year." A glowing tower and wall icon appeared on the map. "Ammunition and medical supplies are in high demand and short supply thanks to the persistent efforts of an outlaw gang called the Vulcans."

The map and corkboard dissolved into a life-sized rendering of a heavily armored motorcycle being ridden by a figure covered head to toe in durasteel armor, not unlike a medieval knight.

"You and the rest of the Luxford-Drummond team are to deliver seven trucks loaded with ammunition and medical supplies through these ruffians' stranglehold on that jewel of the south. Proceed to Big Bill's Dine and Dash to rendezvous with your team and your mission."

Bobby pushed the door of Big Bill's open and stepped into the dining area. The gargantuan man behind the register grunted in greeting without looking up. A grease-spattered apron the size of a circus tent hung over the counter, and a cigar thicker than two of Bobby's fingers smoldered in an ashtray carved out of an old piston. The smell of hot grease, fried algae, and coffee mingling with cigar smoke made the unfamiliar place feel like home.

"Why do truck stops always smell like bad coffee and stale smoke?" Mae pushed past Bobby. "Where is everyone?"

He scanned the room, searching for the rest of the Luxford-Drummond team. "Hey Bill, you get a bunch of newcomers through here?"

"Name's Tyrone." The big man tapped the name tag pinned to the apron with a sausage-thick finger without looking up from the creased and battered paperback.

"Great, Tyrone. Have you seen a bunch of new faces come in here?" Bobby asked.

"In the back." Tyrone slid a white and yellow receipt across the counter before picking up the cigar and taking a big drag, still reading his book. "Said an old fart, and an orange-haired kid would be in to pay the tab."

"That's me." Bobby took the receipt and jammed it in his pocket. "We're gonna need two coffees, algae and eggs if you got em, and whatever the lady wants."

Tyrone set down the plastifilm news sheet, scooped up the apron, and pulled the top strap over his head. "No eggs but plenty of scrambled Memphis Red."

"Two plates of that, then." As algae went, the Memphis Red was his favorite. Bobby rounded the end of the counter and stepped through a set of batwing doors.

The Luxford-Drummond team sat around another group of pushed-together tables. The remnants of breakfast littered the table below a shimmering holographic map of Tennessee and Alabama.

"Look what the cat dragged in." Hal stood and made for Bobby.

"Glad to see you made it all right." Bobby clasped Hal's hand.

"Hardly any trouble at all til we caught up with the rest of the team," Hal said.

"Bandit pricks had them penned down in a ravine about ten miles out." Sprockets chuckled. "We had the whole thing on tactical, so we swung around to the south and hit 'em in the flank. Rolled 'em right on up."

"From there, it was a running gunfight all the way to Big Bill's gates," Nate said. "You should've seen it. Headsman killed three bandits on his own, no car, just him; he just walked down the middle of the— "

"Point is," Black Dragon rolled her eyes. "You are the last ones to show; make sure you pay Tyrone on your way out."

"That's right," Chris smirked.

"I got the tab right here." Bobby patted his pocket. "Tyrone made sure."

"Well, now that the gang's all here, we can get going on the mission brief." Headsman turned back to the holomap.

"Where's the truck drivers?" Mae walked in, holding two cups of coffee. Tyrone loomed behind her, carrying two plates piled high with steaming red algae. Bobby pointed to a couple open spots between Black Dragon and Hal at the table. Even Hal didn't want to sit within arm's reach of her.

"They got the trucks loaded and staged, then hauled ass," Hannah said. "Heard they were destined for Birmingham and quit. Every last one."

"As I was saying," Headsman swiped open a side panel showing team names. "We will depart in staggered order. One person from each team will have to drive one of the delivery trucks. Dog Pound, you take the lead with Iron Outlaw and Tornado Express following up. Skull— "

"Hold up." Bobby poured a liberal helping of ketchup and *Shellback Beau's Habanero Hoedown* over his algae.

"Yes?" Headsman stared at Bobby.

"You figure it's smart to put the pups," Bobby nodded toward Nate and Chris, "no offense, on point?"

"Who are you calling pup? Chris pushed back from the table and stood up.

"Calm down." Bobby took a bite of his food and groaned. "You two are both green as grass. It don't make— "

"Green?" The big man let his hand settle on the grips of the pistol slung low on his right hip. Black Dragon and Hal both pushed away from the Pale Riders. Mae glanced from Bobby to Chris back to Bobby and followed Hal out of the line of fire.

"How many convoys you ever run point on?" Bobby cut a piece of algae-free and swiped it through a pool of hot sauce before eating it. "Two, six, ten?"

"None." The big gunner looked confused.

"Right." Bobby shoved another bite in and washed it down with a gulp of coffee. "Show of hands, who here has ever run point on a convoy escort?"

He looked around the table. Hal from Iron Outlaws had his hand up, as did both of the Skull Monkeys, Hannah, and of course, Black Sunshine.

"Back to my original point," Bobby leaned forward and stared at Headsman chewing another mouthful of algae.

"Either pull iron or sit down." Black Dragon said. "You look ridiculous."

Once Chris sat back down, Bobby pushed for a plan that didn't rely on the greenest crew running point. He didn't like being spread so thin. What they should be doing was rolling in a tighter formation so that they could provide maximum coverage and deliver maximum firepower if a threat emerged. Instead, they were rolling in a long line spread out at half-mile intervals. It was dumb, but after the shitshow in

New Boston, nearly everyone was listening to Black Sunshine.

Bobby stood at the counter, counting out bills to Tyrone. Between breakfast this morning and the drinks from the previous evening, it had nearly wiped out his roll. The rest of the Luxford-Drummond team filed past the register and out to the compound to look at the delivery vehicles.

He was ready for it, watching for it out of the corner of his eye. When Chris tried to shoulder-check him, Bobby slid smoothly back, caught the kid's arm and neck in an iron grip, and shoved him up against the counter before pulling Chris's pistol from its drop holster and pressing the barrel against the back of the larger man's head.

"I ain't looking to hurt you, so knock it off." He growled in the kid's ear. "You keep carrying water for Headsman and Black Dragon; you're gonna end up dead."

"Jesus." Chris croaked.

"I'm going to let go," Bobby said. "You are going to turn around nice and slow. Then you're going to hear what I have to say. Understand?"

"Y-y-yeah."

Bobby let go and took three steps back. The giant gunner turned around slow and easy, his shaking hands held shoulder high. A dark stain spread down the front of his pants.

"Have a seat." Bobby nodded toward one of the chrome and red leather stools at the counter. When the larger man had sat, Bobby slid onto another stool keeping one between him and the shaking gunner. "First time anyone ever got the drop on you like that?"

"Yeah."

"It does make the butthole pucker." Bobby nodded. "Like I said, I ain't looking to hurt you. But you keep making runs at me, and it's gonna happen. Understand."

"Yeah."

"Good." Bobby ejected the magazine, removed the slide, and slid all three pieces across the counter to Tyrone. "Here's some advice for free. Don't be someone else's fool. If Black Dragon or Headsman wants to try consequences with me, they can step up. Stop letting those two yank your chain before it gets you killed. Understand."

"Uh-huh."

"Okay, I'm going to go on outside and see how Mae is coming with our truck. You sit here, gather your thoughts, have a drink on me and some fresh pants. Do not come through that door for at least three minutes, or I'll think you didn't take me seriously." Bobby laid the rest of the bills on the counter. "When you come out, you tell your friends whatever story you like about our conversation; I'll back you up."

"Thanks, I think."

"Sure thing, kid, just trying to do you a solid." Bobby stood up from the counter. "Tyrone, hang on to that iron til I'm out the door, will ya?" He waited until Tyrone had slid the weapon, slide, and magazine from the counter before turning and walking to the door.

Bobby followed the sounds of Sam's the Hero and a constant stream of cursing to a battered old M-212 Moose. He pulled open the gunner side door to find Mae's combat-booted feet protruding onto the seat. The rest of her was buried to the waist underneath the dash of the old military transport. Wires were strung into the gunner's footwell and up onto the gunner's seat.

"Hey, Nate," one small hand groped around on the driver's seat. "Pass me the blue micro-fuser, will ya?"

"Here you go." Nate grabbed something from the tool bag on the seat and put it in her hand. Bobby did a double take; across the floorboard of the Moose, he saw Nathan McHenry staring at him.

"Not that one, the blue one, numb nuts." She tossed the offending tool back up onto the driver's seat. "Hey, the blue one. You do know which color blue is, don't you?" Not getting an answer, she flailed and kicked free of the old truck's dash and sat up. "Did you bump your—Oh hey, Rob."

"Hey Mae, what's with the spaghetti factory?" He nodded toward the colorful rat's nest.

"This weapons control system must have been designed by two blindfolded drunks throwing darts at a list of routing options and features." She grabbed a blue-handled micro-fuser from her bag. "This one, Nate, these are the blue ones."

"Hey, Nate." He nodded toward the tongue-tied driver before looking at Mae and raising one eyebrow. She gave him a half grin before diving back under the dash.

"Have you seen Chris?" Nate shuffled his feet and looked down at the ground.

"Still inside." Bobby climbed up on the running board to get a better look at the truck's control interface and instrument display.

"Uh, right. Are you good to go here, Mae?" Nate asked.

"Yeah," she called from deep in the dash. "Thanks for the assist."

"I'd better be going." Nate turned and walked away, shaking his head.

"So, Nate McHenry?" Bobby hit a series of tabs on the dash before pulling the entire top section free. He set the carbon-fiber and aramid composite panel aside and looked down through the tangle of wires and electronics at Mae.

"What about him?" She asked.

"Seems like he might have been assisting with more than this." He surveyed the multi-function display configuration behind the dash. "Looks like we got stuck with a Charlie model here."

"What of it?" she asked.

"As I recall, the Charlies were a step up over the Bravo," he said. "Better weapons load out, improved threat warning system, first-generation auto-pilot AI, some countermeasures, and better-armored cockpit."

"Yeah, but they added all those new features and didn't bother improving the power supply." She wormed her way from under the dash. "And that is not what I was asking about. What about Nate's assistance?"

"I didn't know you two were— "

"What of it?"

"Just making an observation." Bobby held up his hands in mock surrender. "Didn't think you dated drivers is all."

"Not that it's any of your business, but yeah, off and on for the past year or so." She started winding up the tangled wires into neat bundles, securing them with cable ties before shoving them into the tool bag. "Someone recommended me to him for some upgrades on his car."

"Seems like he got more than a performance upgrade," he said.

"Keep giving me shit, and you're gonna get the boot in ass upgrade." She tossed the rest of the tools in the bag.

"Hey, your love life is your business." His grin grew wider. "I just find puppy love so…cute." He barely dodged the roll of electrical tape she was putting in the tool bag.

"One more of those, and I'll molibond your lips shut while you sleep, old man." She chuckled.

"Okay, okay." He picked up the dash access and slid it back into place with a loud snap. "What's the deal?"

"Aside from being designed by blind drunks and having been maintained by a bunch of meth-cranked hyenas, I've got her about as good as she's gonna get."

"Meaning?"

"The power supply is still inadequate for the demands on the system. You can either accelerate or fire the laser but not both. Same goes for the laser and nearly any other system."

"I don't recall the Moose Cs having a laser."

"They don't, hence the meth-cranked hyena comment." She hit a switch. The front compartment of the old transport opened upward like groaning, rusted gullwings.

"Someone added a laser?" He climbed out of the battered truck and walked to the front for a better look.

"Yep." Mae leaned out of the open truck door and pointed. "Some drug-addled lunatic installed a Mantis mark IV."

"Christ." Bobby stared at the massive weapon. "Those are supposed to be anti-tank weapons for fortifications."

"If you really want to vaporize something, point the truck in that direction and fire. Of course, without improving the suspension, adding gyro stabilization, or installing the targeting computer, you're basically just spraying and praying."

"Is the turret functional?" he asked.

"It's about the only thing that they didn't modify." She ducked back inside the truck. "Stand clear. It closes kind of sudden."

"Clear." The two open halves slammed shut with a loud clang. Servo motors whirred and pulled the halves down, latching them in place. "You trusted that to not crush you while you worked on it?"

"Hell no." She reappeared, leaning on the open door and the front slope of the windshield frame. "Nate installed the mechanical locks on those hood servos before I went crawling up in there."

"Some girlfriend you are," Bobby said. "Putting the boy in harm's way like that."

"He offered," she shrugged. "Who am I to stand in the way of chivalry?"

"So the turret does work?"

"Sure does," she nodded. "And I slaved the gunnery controls over to the steering wheel so I can shoot and drive."

"Whoa, whoa, whoa," Bobby walked around to the open driver's door. "You ain't driving that wreck into a firefight."

"Why not?" she asked. "And you'd better not give me any of the it's too dangerous bullshit."

"You ever been behind the wheel of anything bigger than Janice?"

"Your deuce-and-a-half."

"Deuce-and-a-half don't count."

"Then no."

"I have." Bobby shrugged. "Between the two of us you're the better driver. I would rather have you covering my six from Janice than the other way around. I got a funny feeling about this one."

"Fine." She grabbed the tool bag and tossed it to Bobby. "You drive the rolling deathtrap."

"Glad that's settled." He sat the tool bag on the ground. "Anything else I need to know before we get rolling?"

"Like I said, the power system can't handle the laser and anything else." She hopped down out of the truck. "That includes the steering servos. You fire that thing, and you are coasting until everything comes back online."

"So don't fire the laser unless I really need— "

"Don't fire it at all." She picked up the tool bag. "I don't know what will come back online or if anything will come back online. It's not like I've test fired the thing."

"Roger." Bobby climbed up in the truck. "Weapon of last resort."

"I installed a software upgrade to connect the turret to your helmet HUD. Where you look, it points. The turret has a limited elevation and depression distance."

"That is a huge improvement." He hit the power button and watched as the gauges came to life and the multi-function displays started through their startup tests. "They always promised we'd get that feature, but it never materialized."

"Last but not least." Mae looked up and grinned. "I installed autopilot software."

"These trucks don't have the computer space for a proper autopilot," Bobby said.

"I added an after-market holocomp with ST 3.4."

"You what?"

"That's what I was doing under the dash. Tyrone gave me a good deal on a used holocomp from the pawn shop."

"You installed Sleepy Trucker."

"Sure," she said. "It's the best thing Macworth has for these sorts of after-market upgrades."

"The damned things are psychotic." Bobby shook his head. "Had a real problem with taking the wheel even when the driver was alert and in control."

"That was 2.7.3." She shook her head. "They fixed that bug in the 3.4."

"So I can just turn on Sleepy Trucker and take a nap?"

"If you need to let go of the controls, Sleepy Trucker can keep this bucket of rust on the road till you get back."

"Lovely." Bobby hopped down out of the M-212C. "Let me get my gear swapped over before we get rolling."

"PHONE CALL FOR BOBBY HANK." The compound loudspeaker blared. "PHONE CALL FOR BOBBY HANK."

"Who in the hell knows I'm here to call me?"

"Someone who doesn't have your cell number?" Mae said.

Chapter 20

Bobby didn't see the ambush start. He heard it. The team channel on the radio exploded in a chaotic jumble of shouts and weapons fire before dissolving into static. He checked the rearview. A column of black smoke climbed into the sky.

"You hearing this, Mae?" He reached for his tactical display to zoom out and see what was happening behind them.

He'd argued for keeping the seven trucks together where they could use the quad .50 caliber turrets to cover the roadsides and use three Quests on lead and four on chase to handle any trouble from either end. Eventually, it came to a vote. Black Sunshine won ten to four with the Pale Riders and Iron Outlaws in opposition.

"I'm on it." She eased off the accelerator and slid to the left, letting Bobby pull ahead. "I got Outlaw on VHF. He says Skull Monkeys hit some kind of roadside bomb. Their truck is wrecked. Hal is turning around and running an extraction with Audrey."

"I got nothing on tactical." He scanned the road ahead.

Empty. Just the cracked blacktop of I-75 and the encroaching wall of vegetation down either side. Tight. Constricted. The perfect place for an ambush.

"I got something," Mae said.

He glanced back at the tactical display. Five contacts appeared at their six, where there had been nothing a moment before. He checked the driver's side mirror. Three large cycles were being pushed upright on the roadside. He glanced at the right-hand mirror. Two more were already up and moving between Mae and the Iron Outlaw truck.

"You got company, Mae."

"I see them." The Quest started to slow.

"Don't drop back," Bobby called. "Stay tight on my bumper until we know what's ahead."

"Pale Ri— " the transmission broke off, then picked back up. "This…ack…hine escort. Pick—"

"Say again," Bobby called. "Your transmission is broken and unreadable." He pushed the truck up to 50. "Outlaw Cargo, do you see those five tangos back there?"

"Five?" Raymond said. "I got seven between me and Mae and nine or ten more coming up from behind."

"Let's do something about that," Bobby said. "You close up on me. Mae, drop back and handle the ones behind Ray."

"All right." The Quest skidded into a bootleg turn. Armored cycles went down in a shower of sparks, 3mm tungsten rods turning them into scrap metal and shredded meat. Bobby watched Mae zip past Outlaw cargo on the right, straight into the teeth of the advancing pack of cycles.

He checked the tac display. There were so many contacts at the twelve-o-clock position the dated display could only shade that direction a pulsing crimson. Bobby craned his neck to try and get a glimpse as he crested the rise.

"Look sharp, Outlaw," Bobby said. "We got incoming."

Bobby crested the rise. "Christ…"

A wave of armored bikes came down the far side of the next valley, rolling three wide.

"Grab your nuts, Outlaw," he said. "This is gonna suck."

Bobby targeted the lead element and opened up with the turret. At this distance, he didn't expect to hit much. He was more interested in convincing them he was desperate. Sparks flew from heavy front armor. The bikes accelerated into his fire, closing the distance. Whoever was in charge of this outfit understood the value of reducing time under fire.

"Here's something you turds didn't expect." He reached down and lifted a bright orange switch cover, and flipped the switch labeled BFL to ON. His HUD range showed 372 yards. The lead bikes started up the slope toward him.

"Ray," Bobby radioed. "I'm about to slow way down. When I do, put the hammer down and punch through to Birmingham. I'll draw these asshats in and keep them busy until Mae and the rest show up."

"Roger."

Bobby selected Laser on the master display and assigned it to the right-hand trigger paddle on the steering wheel. The lead element of the gang was sixty yards and closing.

Mae scanned the rearview. Two bikes down. She smashed the accelerator to the floor, rocketing past the Iron Outlaw truck, Janice's speedometer spooling up toward 100. Clear of the double trailer transport, she cut over to the middle of the highway and opened up with the 3mm Gauss cannon, taking the incoming pack head-on. She smashed into the lead bike.

Rider and machine tumbled up and over the hood and roof. The durasteel armor shrugged off nearly half a ton of meat, armor, and machine. She tore through the small pack leaving a trail of shattered machinery and flesh in her wake. The few that survived continued in pursuit of the trucks and their precious cargo.

"Janice," Mae said. "Increase range on tactical display to ten miles."

"Increasing range displayed on tactical to ten miles. You'll lose resolution due to the limitations of radar combined with the nature of the surrounding topography. Additionally, I detect active jamming. This will reduce resolution and accuracy."

The tactical display blinked, showing Janice at the center of a ten-mile circle. Outside a one-mile radius, everything was a jumble of static laid over a three-dimensional rendering of the surrounding terrain.

A line of ridges ran along the west side of the highway, with a lesser series to the east containing the route in a narrow valley descending towards Birmingham. The static resolved into a mass of amber contacts to the north before dissolving back into static.

"Janice, what are all of those contacts to the north," Mae asked.

"Unknown," Janice said. "Terrain and electromagnetic interference are making identifying anything beyond a one-mile radius uncertain."

"How uncertain?"

"Beyond one mile up to three miles, I can provide resolution with approximately 80% certainty. Between three and six miles, the probability of certainty drops to sixty-three percent. Between six and the ten-mile limit you've requested probability of certainty drops to forty-eight percent."

"Use your best guess."

"Luxford-Drummond is not responsible for best guess analysis. Please acknowledge your acceptance of this condition to proceed."

"When I get some time, we are going to dig all of that corporate bullshit out of your programming, sister."

"Do you accept the stated condition?"

"Yes." Mae groaned.

"Updating tactical display resolution to reflect best estimate interpretation of information."

The display resolved from static and intermittent contacts into a computer-rendered view of the area from a top-down perspective. The mess to her north resolved into a computer-generated view of five trucks and six Quests formed up in a single large column, with the five trucks running in a staggered formation so that each truck covered the empty space of the one in front. Two Quests ran about one hundred yards ahead while three more Quests brought up the rear. Janice had labeled the rear Quests Iron Outlaw, Tornado Express, Rolling Thunder, and Skull Monkey. The lead Quests were marked Black Sunshine and Dog Pound. It looked like Hal had made the extraction, and the convoy was back on track.

To her south, Bobby and Raymond were side by side, surrounded by a growing swarm of motorcycles, climbing the next rise and losing speed. A trail of destroyed bikes littered the road behind them.

Mae cut the wheel, powered through another bootleg turn, and floored the accelerator sending the Quest rocketing back in Bobby and Ray's direction.

Bobby hit the right-hand trigger paddle at fifty yards. He held the left down, hammering the oncoming bikes with the steel-cored .50 rounds. This particular band of bandit assholes had solved the problem of armor-piercing rounds by armoring themselves and their machines in durasteel plating, making them look like medieval knights mounted on horses of iron and chrome. It didn't do much for the kinetic energy delivered by a steady stream of steel-cored lead moving at nearly 3500 feet per second. The M-212C went completely dead. The instruments, both multi-function displays, the radio, and acceleration all vanished as a blue beam of coherent light eighteen inches in diameter tore through the oncoming motorcycles, vaporizing armor, setting both machine and rider alight, and melting the blacktop of the rising road before winking out, leaving Bobby at the helm of ten tons of inert durasteel, rubber, and glass.

He'd managed to get the old truck up to sixty-five miles per hour or so before he fired the laser, which meant he and it had become a kinetic missile weighing more than 20,000 pounds. The bikers not instantly incinerated by the laser blast or hammered from their armored machines by the veritable river of lead pouring from both M-212Cs' turret, flowed around the two trucks. The rest fell beneath the heavy transport's wheels, armored man and machine transformed into mangled steel and oozing jelly.

He watched Raymond accelerate through the river of bikes into the space created by the laser blast and disappear over the hill. Outnumbered, no radio, no steering, no weapons, Bobby grinned. He engaged the mechanical steering lock and grabbed his carbine before shoving open the hatch and climbing up into the armored cupola of the quad-barreled turret. It was time to show these assholes a thing or two.

Mae saw Bobby's truck stalled on the hill. Bandits in durasteel armor sheltered behind their bikes, firing at the transport's cupola.

"Janice, focus display on the rear of Pale Rider Cargo."

"You got it." A smaller holodisplay window opened center windshield, focused on the rear of the M-212C. Her stomach dropped, five heavily-armored bandits were climbing up the cargo net attached to the back of the old truck. The road was strewn with casualties. At least two more hung half-in-half-out of the turret cupola. She switched coms back to the helmet-mounted ICS radio and clicked the transmit button on the steering wheel. "You still alive in there?"

"I'm a touch busy," Bobby said over the ping and whine of bullets striking armor.

"You're about to be a whole lot busier." She said. "You've got five coming up the back side of your cargo."

"Good to know." She watched him pop up, aim and fire. One of the bandits on the ground flopped flat, feet kicking. "Any chance you could give me a hand with the ones on the ground?"

"Sure thing." She selected the mini-missile launcher, highlighted an area to the left of Bobby's truck, and fired.

The hatch hummed open. The Quest shuddered as a salvo of mini-missiles rippled free from their launch tubes, arcing high into the air before streaking back to explode in an anti-personnel air burst one meter off the ground. A storm of tungsten and durasteel shrapnel scythed into the exposed bandits.

"Hot damn, girl." Bobby laughed. "That certainly evened things out."

"Switching to composite imaging."

The holodisplay switched from smoke-filled footage to composite imaging. White radiance marked burning machines and riders. Orange-highlighted figures retreated to the deep ditches on either side of the road, dragging their wounded away from the stalled truck.

Five orange-highlighted figures had made it to the top of the load, netted down on the flatbed of the truck, and were low crawling toward the cupola and Bobby.

"You still have incoming across the top of the cargo," Mae radioed.

"How long before this rusty bucket of bolts will power back up?" Mae watched Bobby outlined in blue, pop up and fire two bursts into the advancing bandits.

"Depends." She gently accelerated down the hill, swinging to the right for a better view of that side of the truck. "Did enemy fire cripple the truck?"

"No." He popped up and sent another burst into the advancing bandits. That one did it. The remaining Vulcans rolled off the cargo, preferring the fifteen-foot drop to the smoking asphalt over the withering fire coming from the turret cupola.

"You fired the laser then?" She triggered the 3mm Gauss cannon. Tungsten rods tore down the transport's right side, forcing the remaining bandits to low crawl away from their machines into the ditch.

"Yep." He popped up and fired three more aimed shots into the right-hand ditch, only dropping down when return fire started striking sparks around him.

"It should be ready for restart any second now," she said. "Do you need me to hop in and get the start sequence initiated again?"

"Can I do that while you hold these bastards off?" Bobby popped back up, sending a burst into the left-hand ditch. Another Vulcan rose to his feet, clutching his chest before rolling backward out of sight.

"Probably." She steered Janice down the right-hand side of the truck. Nothing moved in the targeting display or on tactical. The ones sheltering in the ditches were hunkered down and not moving. "All you need to do is hit the start button again. You should be good to go if the capacitors have enough charge to get your drive motors spooling."

Bobby shoved two dead Vulcans out of the turret cupola before pulling open the hatch and sliding back into the cab. He scanned the dash. Sure enough, the gauges were working again, and the start button glowed blue. He slid behind the steering wheel and hit the power button. The battered transport's multi-function displays hummed to life running through their startup checks.

"How we looking on tactical?" Bobby asked.

"Bad guys got their heads down for now," she said.

"Don't believe it for a second." He hit the accelerator powering the heavy rig up the slope. It occasionally jostled and bumped as it rolled over the corpses of men and machines. "Where the hell is everyone else?"

"Hard to tell on this side of the ridge," Mae said. "Janice's best guess had them moving in our direction with five transports bracketed by two Quests up front and four in the rear about a minute and a half ago."

"Let's have a look." Bobby selected the tactical page.

The thirty-year-old radar showed a clear road ahead with multiple contacts in the ditch on either side of the road behind them. He zoomed out to the ten-mile max on the dated equipment. The display showed Outlaw Cargo a little over four miles ahead of them. Behind them, ten enemy contacts. He reconnected his helmet to the truck's radio, selected the team channel, and hit the foot switch.

"How's things back there?" He called.

"Tou—go there fo— to go—"Bobby thumped the wheel in frustration. He switched back to ICS.

"Still jamming us." He said. "These Vulcan pricks are a hell of a lot better equipped than we were led to believe in the mission brief."

"Do we turn back and link up with the rest of the team?" Mae asked.

"We need to catch up to Outlaw Cargo," Bobby said. "The way we are now is an engraved invite to defeat in detail."

"What?"

"We're in three groups. One big hard-to-handle group and two much smaller, much more manageable groups. Which one would you try to hit?"

"The smaller ones," she said.

"That's what we call defeat in detail. Break an enemy into smaller bite-sized bits and roll them up one by one." He checked the laser's status on the weapons page of the MFD. It showed amber with a small lightning bolt through the icon. Still charging the capacitors. "So we need to link up with Outlaw Cargo to make us a much tougher bite to chew."

"I see." He clicked the foot switch, "Outlaw Cargo, this is Pale Rider Cargo. What's your status?"

"Smooth sailing. So far," Outlaw Cargo said. "Glad to see you got clear."

"We're too vulnerable spread out like this," Bobby said. "Can you slow up a bit? We're coming to you."

"Roger, I'll cut her back to 35," Outlaw Cargo said. "Give you time to catch up."

Chapter 21

The Birmingham Guard met them a mile outside the city. Three years of constant hit-and-run warfare with the Vulcans had left them nervy and on edge. Bobby couldn't blame them, not if that ambush was anywhere near the level of trouble they dealt with daily. He noticed how not one of the escorts relaxed until the massive iron gates of Birmingham closed behind his truck and Ray's tandem trailer.

They rolled into the logistics compound like conquering heroes. Forklifts and work crews were already working to unload and distribute the badly needed supplies before he could get his rig shut down. Bobby shoved the door of the truck open.

A worker dressed in grease-stained coveralls eyed the bullet-scarred skin of the transport truck. "Looks like you had one hell of a fight."

"It wasn't pretty." Bobby slung his carbine and climbed down from the truck.

"Still, you came out better than the rest of your convoy," the man said.

"What?" Bobby turned back to the man.

"Easy, Mister Hank." The man held up his hands. "All I was sayin' is that y'all came out better than the rest of your outfit."

"What's that mean?"

"You ain't heard?" the man asked.

"No."

"Hell, it's all over DuelTube."

"Show me."

The man pulled a phone from his coverall pocket and swiped open a small holographic display. It showed a top-down view of the convoy. A truck was jack-knifed with the trailer tipped over and resting on the back half of one of the Quests, which lay on its side. Two other trucks and four more Luxford-Drummond vehicles were laagered up around the wreck. Armored bikes with armored riders made circling passes on either end of the position. Tracer rounds filled the air in a confusing crisscross of light and death.

"What are we looking at?" Mae sauntered up, a large grin on her face. Raymond followed several steps behind her.

"Looks like we got bamboozled." Bobby pointed to the holodisplay. The video was a thirty-second loop.

"Son of a bitch." Ray grabbed the phone out of the kid's hand.

The warehouse crew cheered and whistled. Bobby looked up to see another transport roll in. It was the Wolverine rig dragging three trailers in tandem. Headsman leaned out of the driver's window, his windshield an impenetrable mass of cracked and spider-webbed armorglass. A bullet-scarred and scorched Quest rolled into the compound behind it. Bobby turned back to Ray and Mae. They were sprinting toward Janice.

"Thanks." He patted the worker on the shoulder and ran to catch up.

Mae had already strapped in. Ray had slid open the right side door and was climbing in. Bobby slid into the gunner seat and started strapping in.

"This is gonna be hairy." Bobby brought up the weapons display and swiped it to his right-hand side before bringing up tactical and targeting.

"Tell me about it." Ray slid the door shut and started strapping into the middle row of seats.

"Incoming call from The Dispatcher," Janice said.

"Put it on screen." Bobby swiped the targeting display front and center before adjusting the weapons yoke and starting system tests on all the weapons and countermeasure systems.

The comm display resolved to show The Dispatcher. He wore a glittering crimson and plum-purple suit and leaned on a chrome cane. "Congratulations on completing the Birmingham— "

"Don't have time for your bullshit," Bobby growled.

"In point of fact, Mister Henry, you do." Dispatcher leaned into the camera, the shimmering silver and gold face cover shifting to solid black. "You are, under no circumstances, to return to the route. Once you've crossed the finish line, your participation in this leg is complete."

"Nope." Mae hit the button, closing her door.

"As per the contract you signed, there is no going back once a leg is complete. Each team will make it as they can or not."

"They're cut off and in a nasty firefight." Bobby checked the load on the 3mm Gauss cannon. The indicator showed a green eighty percent of max. "We don't help; they might not get out at all."

"Not your problem, Pale Rider." Dispatch said. "The race *is* called Dead Man's Run."

"And if we roll out anyway?" Ray asked.

"Forfeiture of points, pay, and position for this challenge and a start penalty for tomorrow's race to Memphis." Dispatch twirled the chromed cane before pointing to each of the stated consequences as they materialized in the air next to him in large red letters. "Need I remind you of a little phone call you received, *Mister Henry?*"

"No." Bobby gritted his teeth and stowed the weapons control yoke. "Stand down, Mae. They'll have to make it on their own steam."

"What the hell is this circus freak talking about?" Ray leaned forward between Bobby and Mae.

"Yeah, *Mister Henry.*" Mae stared hard at Bobby.

"Nothing I can talk about," he said.

"Well done." Dispatcher's mask had returned to a shimmering mix of silver and gold.

"They are dying out there!" Mae called up a holographic keyboard and typed. A moment later, the center part of the windshield resolved into a top-down view of the same firefight they had seen on the video. Two people were pinned down, using the wreck for cover. Armored bandits lined both ditches, more circled about and charged from both sides of the wreck like motorcycle-mounted Mongols.

"Autoduelling is an inherently perilous undertaking, *Miss Holland.*" The Dispatcher leaned on his cane; each word slow, deliberate, condescension dripping from them like raw sewage.

On the holodisplay, a wave of bikes charged the northern side of the lager pouring fire into the cab and trailer of the wrecked truck. With the bandits at a hundred feet, the truck's turret opened up, glowing green tracers a bright finger of destruction. Thumb-thick rounds of steel-cored lead tore through the bandits emptying bike seats but doing little to slow their charge. At twenty feet, the lone Quest on that side of the lager cut his wheels and launched a countercharge. A storm of 3mm tungsten rods backed by several tons of armored machine shredded the lead bikes and riders.

"Bobby," Mae stared at him. Looked at him the way that Kat had outside Poughkeepsie. The same way Arlo had in the Texas hills when the order came to pull out. To leave the beleaguered 403rd mechanized infantry to die. "They can't last much longer." Then and now overlapping in a surreal bit of synchronicity, Arlo and Mae's voices blending together in his head.

"Mae, you heard…" He couldn't handle that look. Never could, really. The look that said they were watching someone turn out to be so much less than they had hoped. That look of disappointment. "You know what," he unstowed the weapon's yoke. "To hell with it. Let's go."

Mae tore out of the logistics compound and headed north in a cloud of tire smoke and flying road grit.

"Where are you going?" Dispatcher asked.

"Back out," Bobby said.

"The consequences for leaving Birmingham are not insignificant, *Mister Henry.*"

Bobby glanced over at Mae. She had a hard set to her eyes; she looked at him and flashed her teeth in a fierce grin. "So are the consequences for staying. Best you stop talking. We got work to do."

"Very well." Dispatcher's facemask had become a deep black. "The outcome for this disobedience rests squarely upon your shoulders." The coms screen switched back to the skull over Aces and Eights logo for the race. Bobby shuddered.

"What the hell does that mean?" Mae stopped the Quest.

"Means they are holding Kat's MMSD hostage against my good behavior." He gripped the weapons yoke hard, his knuckles turning white. "I play nice, toe the corporate line; they help cure her CDRS."

"Christ, Bobby," Ray said. "What do we do?"

"What Kat would have done." He scrubbed at his face, trying to rub the stress and fatigue away.

"What's that?" Mae looked at him. She still wore that wild-assed grin.

"Let's go be heroes."

Working from the engineering console in the back, Ray had reconfigured the tactical display using real-time camera feeds from the network drones circling like voyeuristic vultures.

The situation at the lager had become desperate. The four Luxford-Drummond vehicles and the trucks had been repositioned to protect the wreck. At some point, the trucks must have run out of ammo. The drivers were hunkered down behind the vehicles returning fire with their personal firearms.

Wonder of wonders, as far as Bobby was concerned, the stocky gunner had managed to turn one of the drones into a repeater for the Viperlink lasercom system and establish a link with the other half of the Iron Outlaws.

"Hal," Bobby called, using the laser com to bore through the electronic jamming and interference to establish a link with the Iron Outlaw driver. "What's the situation?"

"Better now that we got coms again," Hal shouted. "How'd you manage that?"

"The drones filming your increasingly inevitable demise use Viperlink, same as the Quests," Raymond said.

"Less inevitable if we got anything to say about it," Bobby said. "Now, what is the situation?"

"Somewhere between TARFU and FUBAR."

"Who's in the wreck?"

"McHenry," Hal said.

"How bad's he hurt?" Bobby looked over at Mae. Her face was pale, and her lips clamped shut in a bloodless line.

"Haven't got inside to find out," Hal said. "Between fighting off the bandits and the jammed doors, we just don't know."

"Cut the damned thing open," Mae shouted.

"Need a torch, a plasma cutter, or shaped charges."

"How much longer can you hold?" Bobby checked the composite tactical display. The bandits were retreating.

"Not too much longer," Audrey said. "I'm low on ammo for all of the Quest weapons."

"Same here." Rolling Thunder's gunner said.

"We'll be there in…" Bobby checked the tactical display for distance to the wreck. They were ten miles out.

"Eight minutes." Mae mashed the accelerator to the floor. Janice leaped forward, her speedometer quickly spooling up past one hundred miles per hour.

"Eight minutes is an eternity in a gunfight." Bobby selected the area north of the wreck and preassigned it as target Alpha. "Hope they can hold out for that long." He selected a section of road just south of the lager and designated it as target Bravo. "Janice, when I give the order, I want a salvo from the MMLS-15 on targets Alpha and Bravo set for air burst, altitude of one and a half meters."

"Standing by to deliver mini-missile salvos on target areas Alpha and Bravo."

"When we get there, we're coming in hot." Bobby selected the ditches along either side of the road and designated them targets Charlie and Delta before selecting the only rockets that would be left in the mag, high explosive incendiary. "I'll radio a thirty-second warning. When I do, get small. Pass the word."

"Roger Pale Rider," Hal said.

"You got something in your bag of tricks that will work to cut open Dog Pound's ride?" Bobby asked.

"Yeah." Mae jerked a thumb over her right shoulder. "Got a CyberTek Inferno in the hard case back there."

"Okay, here's how we do this…"

Bobby hit the radio foot switch, "Thirty seconds." He started a thirty-second countdown on the tactical display.

The Quest approached the crest of the incline at a blistering speed. "Janice," he said when the countdown reached zero. "Execute pre-registered fire order."

"Firing on all predesignated targets." Thirty mini-missiles rippled from the Quest's tubes.

Janice crested the rise giving Bobby and Mae their first real view of the situation. The wrecked truck's trailer was burning. A horde of armored bandits circled on either side of the lager, pouring fire into the beleaguered defenders. The rocket salvos detonated amid both groups of bandits. High-explosive-propelled durasteel shrapnel blasted man and machine to scrap and ground meat. The second set of salvos dropped HEI missiles along both ditches. What high explosives and shrapnel failed to shred the incendiary set alight, transforming both sides of the highway into a live-action Hieronymus Bosch painting.

"All teams, get ready to roll." Bobby triggered the smoke dispensers, laying down a thick, white curtain.

Mae turned the headlong charge into a powered slide ending with Janice facing the western ditch. Bobby popped his door up, hit the release on his harness, grabbed his small med kit, his rifle, and stepped out of the Quest into the smoke-filled hellscape. Ray followed suit, slipping through the sliding side door, combat rifle ready, the CyberTek Inferno with its attendant gas bottle slung in straps on his back.

Bobby chinned the helmet mic, "We're clear, Mae. Go to work." He put one hand on Raymond's shoulder and waited until Mae sped off, laying down an obfuscating cloud of smoke. "This is Pale Rider actual; hold your fire on the south side. We're moving toward the wreck."

"Welcome to the party, Hank," Hannah said.

"Moving." Bobby gave Raymond a tap on the shoulder. They moved through the smoke-filled hellscape. The ground was littered with dead and dying bandits. Some of the bike fuel tanks had ruptured and ignited, sending sooty black columns of smoke into the air.

"What the hell is that smell?" Raymond passed between the number four and the number one Quests.

"Burning biodiesel." Bobby followed him through the gap in the lager.

"I thought that stuff was supposed to smell like fried food." Ray picked up the pace once he had passed into the lager running for the wreck.

"It does." Bobby gave Audrey a wave as he passed into the lager. "Just depends on what you call food. I think I know where those bloodmouth pricks have been getting their anti-tank hardware."

The wreck looked way worse at ground level. An explosion had torn ragged, fist-sized holes in the belly of the Dog Pound Quest and flipped it onto the roof. Judging from the final location of the big rig, sideways across the road with the trailer tipped over and resting on the wrecked Quest, the McHenry brothers had been rolling much too close to one another. Easy meat for a remote-detonated IED. Mae was undoubtedly right about Luxford-Drummond skimping on the belly armor. Those holes did not bode well for anybody on the inside. Chris McHenry sat back to the damaged racer, hands bloody, holding a wad of fabric against his stomach.

"Hey, kid." Bobby crouched down next to the wounded gunner. Ray leaned his rifle against the scorched belly of Dog Pound's racer and went to work.

Chris's eyes fluttered open, "'sup, Bobby."

"Let me see what you got under there." Bobby moved Chris's hand, blood pumped from the hole. "I'm gonna need to see your back, kid."

"I…I don't swing that way." Chris groaned and turned. Bobby could see where the bullet had passed through the kid.

"That's a good sign." Bobby pulled vibro-shears from his kit and set to cutting away the wounded gunner's armored coverall.

"What is?" Chris asked.

"The bullet passed through." Bobby pulled the fabric back, giving him a clear view of the wound and space to work.

"That's a good sign?"

"No, you still being with it enough to crack jokes. That's a good sign." Bobby said.

"So I'm not dying?" Chris asked.

"Not if I got anything to say about it."

Mae skirted the wreck on the eastern edge of the highway. While Raymond and Bobby were cutting Nate out of that wreck, her job was to shut down whatever kept jamming up the coms and sensors.

Given how effectively these turds had spoofed Janice's sensors, they had to have an awful lot of gear packed into something mobile, a van or a truck and trailer. Whatever it was, it had to be close. And it had to be undercover.

According to Bobby, the odds were good that the asshole coordinating the ambush would be holed up with all that gear. He called it a cee-two element. She wasn't sure what the hell that meant, but she sure as hell was going to find it and burn it down.

"Where would I hide if I were in something big, soft, and full of valuable equipment?" She scanned the composite map Janice had aggregated using imagery from the camera drones.

A cloverleaf on and off-ramp area about two miles further north with a number of overgrown pre-crash buildings clustered around it looked likely. She highlighted the large cluster to the right. "Janice, can we take a better look at that area right there?"

"Sure thing, Mae." The image expanded until it filled the screen. The ground and most of the structures were covered in kudzu and trumpet vine, including a high awning.

"Betcha Warthog ain't the only one to use something like that as a hidey-hole. Janice, give me real-time imagery of that area." She checked her tactical display. If it was to be believed, the bandits had pulled back into the trees away from the highway and the lager. There were more than she had counted on, and it looked like they were regrouping.

She chinned the ICS mic, "I think I found where they are hiding that cee-two thing you were talking about."

"Good," Bobby said. "Can you get to it?"

"I think so," she said. "By the way, the bandits are regrouping for another attack run."

"Roger. You hit their Command and Control. Hopefully, the resulting chaos will buy us enough time to get the hell out of here."

"You get to Nate yet?" She accelerated toward the cloverleaf a couple miles to her north.

"Just about…" He trailed off. "You need to be prepared for— "

"For what?" She swallowed hard against the knot in her throat, blinking back stinging tears. "He's been trapped in there for a solid half hour. I damned well know. Okay? I know. Just don'—"

"We'll get him out." Bobby's voice sounded strained in her headset.

"Thank you."

She drove on in silence. Nate was most likely dead. She knew that. The name of the race was called Dead Man's Run, after all. Mae blinked away the tears. This was why she had a rule against attachments. This is what she got for breaking that rule. Attachment left you vulnerable and weak.

"Hey, kid," he said.

"Yeah?"

"Watch your ass out there. We can't come get you if it all goes to hell."

Bobby Hank had patched up the wound in Chris's side before the shit hit the fan again. He had the big bastard's arm slung over one shoulder and was pulling the wounded gunner to his feet when the rounds came cracking into the lager with that flat whack of projectiles breaking the sound barrier.

"Taking fire here." Bobby shoved Chris back to the ground and dropped to one knee. "Anybody got eyes on the source?"

"The trees on my side." Sprockets called.

"Seems more like spray and pray than aimed fire," Hal said.

"Well, whoever they're praying to must be half inclined to help out." Bobby dropped the rifle, letting it hang from the sling. "Hey, big boy. Gonna need some help here." He pulled Chris back upright. The larger man groaned and pushed Bobby away.

"I'll get it." Chris struggled to his feet. Bobby slung one meaty arm across his shoulders, and together the two staggered to the rear of a Quest.

"Hey!" Bobby banged on the vehicle's rear hatch with his rifle butt. "Open up. I ain't carrying this big bastard back to Birmingham."

"Keep your pants on, old man." Audrey radioed.

The rear hatch swung open. Bobby spun Chris around and sat him in the Quest's cargo area. "Well, this is nice," Rita squatted down, grabbed the big man under his arms, and started dragging him further into the vehicle. "I was just telling Aud how much I wanted to drag Chris into the back of a van. God, he's heavy."

"You ain't kidding." Bobby lifted Chris's legs. More rounds cracked and spanged.

"Get in here," she said.

"Got to watch Ray's back." He slammed the door closed and made the crouching run back to the wreck.

"I got McHenry," Raymond yelled from inside the wrecked Quest.

"How bad?" Bobby asked.

"As bad as it gets, Hank."

"Son of a bitch." Bobby leaned against the belly of the wrecked Quest. "Can you get him out of there?"

"Already on it." Ray backed through the hole dragging the crash seat with the kid still strapped in.

"We just needed the kid," Bobby said. More rounds cracked overhead. There had to be some kind of service road nearby for them to keep getting reinforcements like this.

"Was easier to cut the seat free." Ray crouched low. "Besides, we need a seat for the pyre. The one he died in was available, so why not?"

"Well, you always were a traditionalist." Bobby grabbed one end of the seat, trying and failing to ignore the wreckage that had been Nathan McHenry. He nodded toward the rear of Skull Monkey's ride. "Let's get the hell out of here before those bastards make another run."

"Mabel." The radio crackled in her ear.

She knew. That one word, her name, said everything. The knot in her chest threatened to come undone and drown her in a choking flood.

"He's dead, isn't he?" She checked her speed. Eighty-five. The cloverleaf was coming up fast.

"Yeah."

"Get going." She powered into the curve, picking up speed, relying on Janice's traction control and suspension to keep her on the road. "I'll catch up."

"That's a bad idea," he said.

"What?"

"Trying to take them all on your own." She could hear the rising chatter of automatic weapons fire over his radio. "Just hit that cee-two element and get back here."

"I'll take it under advisement." She rocketed out of the exit and onto the service road, only slowing a bit before powering into a drift that lined the nose of the Quest up with the vine and kudzu-covered awning.

She saw camouflage netting hanging over a large hole cut into the thick overgrowth. Men in durasteel armor ran out from under that growth toward the road. The muzzles of their guns flashed in some ineffable code. She kept Janice in a slide, kept the nose and the 3mm Gauss auto-cannon pointed right at them and the awning.

That rising grief met something else growing in her chest. Something hot and tight. A white-hot spark of anger met the rising tide of grief and ignited into something new. Fury. She mashed both trigger paddles on the steering wheel, unleashing a torrent of hypersonic tungsten darts.

Chapter 22

The set held three richly upholstered chairs. Three crystal tumblers rested on the black lacquered table, each with three fingers of amber liquid. The facets of those very expensive, square-cut tumblers caught and multiplied the firelight. The dim and cozy lighting implied an intimate conversation between old friends. The mood? Somber. Sasha Goodwin, Don Northcraft, and Butcher Bill, each dressed for a funeral, were seated in those exquisitely upholstered chairs. The lights brightened, and the camera zoomed in on Sasha. She took a sip from her tumbler before turning to the camera.

"Welcome to Dead Man's Update. Tonight, we come to you with heavy hearts. The mid-Atlantic division of Dead Man's Run has had its first fatality." She turned to the two men on her left. "With me are autoduel legends Butcher Bill and Don Northcraft." Bill lifted his glass in silent greeting. Don smiled his million-dollar smile.

"Tonight, we say goodbye to rising talent Nathan McHenry," Sasha said.

"That's not all we're saying goodbye to." Don leaned forward and picked up his glass. "It looks like we might be saying goodbye to Bobby Hank or at least the prospect of Bobby Hank making a real autoduel comeback."

"What?" Bill stared at Don Northcraft like the man has just proclaimed that down is up. "You've got to be joking."

"How?" Don sat back and sipped very expensive whiskey from the equally expensive tumbler.

"After the rescue that the Pale Riders pulled off, you think the Referee is going to DQ them?" Bill snorted. "Aside from Bobby, the Ref is one of the only duelists to retire in his original meat. If anyone respects the actions taken by Hank, Holland, and Outlaw gunner Raymond Russel, it's the Ref."

"That remains to be seen." Don took another sip. "At the very least, there will be penalties."

"You know something, Northcraft?" Bill said. "You're an asshole.

"Why?" Don looked genuinely confused at Bill's hostility.

"A driver is dead." Bill thumped the arm of his chair. "And all you care about is seeing the Pale Riders punished?"

"Nothing Gold Cross can't sort out." Don leaned back in his chair and crossed his right leg over his left.

"Not every driver has Northcraft money, you pampered nitwit." Bill leaned forward and set his glass on the table. "McHenry is dead. Not just on the slab waiting for Gold Cross to grow him a new meat tractor, but real death dead. You rich assholes really piss me off."

"Boys," Sasha said, her tone bringing the temperature in the room back down to something more cordial. "Mister McHenry is dead. But he did not die at the hands of a fellow duelist in the arena, did he?"

"No." Bill and Don both shook their heads. Bill picked up his glass once more.

"Nathan McHenry died at the hands of well-armed, well-coordinated bandits." She leaned back in the chair. "To your point, Don, had Bobby Hank, Mabel Holland, and Raymond Russell not made that rescue run, it is possible that we would be holding memorial services for a lot more of the Luxford-Drummond team."

"You got that right." Bill grinned and took another sip from his glass.

"The real issue here is not drivers and gunners dying in the arena. It is the danger and lawlessness that plagues the land in between our cities and fortified towns…."

"And we have to ask how safe is it outside the cities?"

Chapter 23

The sun, sinking low, painted the western skyline with a burning brush. Brilliant oranges and vibrant reds smeared the horizon as though the gods of autoduelling signaled their pleasure with the day's sacrifice of blood and steel.

Bobby stood next to the empty flatbeds. All the ammo and supplies spirited away while he paced and worried, stopping long enough to climb into one cab or another, grab a radio mic, and try to contact Mae. He'd paced till his left knee ached before stopping to make another fruitless call. Truth be told, he should have swapped into a fresh meat-suit years ago. Bobby shook his head. No sense in dwelling on would've and should've. Where was Mae? He climbed into the cab of the old army transport, left knee throbbing with the effort, picked up the CB handset, and keyed the mic.

"Mae? Where the hell are you?"

"Keep your pants on, Bobby." Her voice crackled in his ear. It sounded thin and static-laden, but it was there.

"Hot damn girl!" He thumped the dash. "Where the hell have you been?"

"Taking care of business." She sounded tired, wrung out.

"You okay?"

"I'm fine," she said. "I took out their cee-two location and killed every last one I could find."

"How's Janice?"

"Besides continuously trying to connect me to a grief counselor?"

"Yeah."

"She's a little banged up," Mae said. "Nothing I can't fix if we have a facility to work with."

"How far out?"

"Just rolled through the main gate. Be there in a minute."

Bobby clambered out of the battered truck and limped toward the compound's armored gate. She was so much like Kathrine had been before Poughkeepsie; wild and dangerous, convinced of her own immortality, furious at the impudence of death stealing from her. Truth was, death was neither impudent nor capricious. The reaper lurked around every corner, taking everyone eventually. She got a taste of that reality today. It was a hard lesson, and only the first of many if she stayed on the burning road that was the life of an autoduellist.

Seemed like yesterday he and Ed Holland were sitting on Ed's porch, whiskey in hand, watching the sun set across the Ware River while a seventeen-year-old version of Mae tore ass out of the trailer court test driving her first completed project. Ed had asked him to look after the kid when he was gone. Bobby laughed. He was still hopeful of finding a cure for Kathrine's condition in those days. Ed had been right. That girl had a temper and a wild streak a mile wide.

The crunch of tires on the grit and debris of the compound brought Bobby back to now. Their ride was covered in scorch marks and lead smears. The back armor glass window was mostly gone, no antennas protruded from the roof anymore, and the left rear wheel was more rim than tire.

The driver's door swung up, and Mae stepped out of the battered machine. She held the helmet under one arm. Her hair hung limp and sweat-soaked like a worn-out flag. She looked to be in one piece if you didn't count the thousand-yard stare.

"You look like shit." He ran forward and wrapped her in a fierce embrace.

"Me." Her voice was raw and raspy. "You're limping like you took one through the leg."

"Did you get him out?" she asked.

"Yeah." Bobby nodded.

"Where is he?"

"Are you sure you're— "

"Where?"

"Easy." He stepped back. "I'll take you."

They stood around the pyre. Thirteen drivers and gunners all staring at the fourteenth strapped in his seat atop a pyre of cut wood, busted pallets, used tires, and old magnesium wheels. Each held a glass of amber liquid. Each stood silent, lost in their musings on mortality and what might come next. When the Birmingham police and CDF (Citizens Defense Force) found out how Nate had died, they took to the socials. Within the first half hour, they had raised enough money to pay for Gold Cross to send a scanner team out and get a clone started. That's when they discovered that he was a Hardmode.

His family belonged to one of several fundamentalist groups who believed cloning, clones, and consciousness transfer to be an affront to the almighty. They called themselves the Sanctified Community of the One and Only Life. Most everyone else called them crazy. Not because they chose to only live once but because they also made that choice for their kids. Rumor had it they made sure they could only live once by injecting a nano-virus that made uploading their consciousness impossible.

"Goodbye, Nate." Hal stepped forward, drained his glass, and set it next to the full glass at the dead driver's feet. "You drove fast, shot straight, and died behind the wheel. We should all be so lucky." He turned and walked into the growing night. Passing between Chris and Mae, he clapped each on the shoulder before walking on.

"Sorry, we didn't get you out sooner." Raymond drained his glass and set it next to Hal's. "Goodbye, kid." He turned and followed Hal, giving Chris and Mae a similar pat on his way by.

One by one, the other drivers and gunners stepped forward and said their goodbyes. Passing between Mae and Chris on their way back to the bar. Finally, only the Pale Riders, Black Sunshine, and Chris remained.

"Goodbye, kid." Black Dragon tossed off her drink and threw the glass side arm into the pyre. "Some of us are lucky, some ain't." She turned on her heel and strode past Bobby. He put a hand on her arm, stopping her short.

"You knew that kid was hardmode, and you left him out there to die."

"Well, Hank." She looked down at his hand and then back up into his eyes. "You know what they say. If you can't pay the piper…" She shrugged off his hand and walked away.

"Sorry, kid." Headsman swallowed the whiskey. He stepped forward and gently set the empty glass at the foot of Nate's blood-stained seat before turning and passing between Mae and Chris on his way into the gathering night.

"Goodbye, Nate," Bobby raised his glass in salute. "You died with your boots on." He sat the glass next to Headsman's and stepped back to stand beside Mae.

"Goodbye." Mae drank her whiskey in one swallow, then hurled the glass to shatter amongst the piled wood. "I got the bastards that got you. Hope that's some comfort."

"I guess it's time to roll." Chris tossed back his drink before setting the glass next to the others. He pulled an emergency flare from his coat pocket, lit it, and tossed it onto the pyre.

Bobby watched as flames roared around Nathan McHenry's body. Tradition was the dead man or woman's partner stood vigil till the pyre had burned down to nothing but smoking ashes. Chris had a long night ahead of him. "If you want to finish what you and Nate started, come find us in the morning," Bobby said. "I'll see you in a while, Mae." He turned and limped his way back toward the bar.

Bobby felt the presence of someone else before he saw them. Just that sense of no longer being alone in a space. He transferred the welding gun to his left hand before dropping his right to the pistol strapped to his side.

"Easy, Hank." The voice was muffled and sounded like it was coming from the end of a long hallway. Even filtered by the welding helmet's hearing protection and noise cancellation, he would have recognized Black Dragon's voice. Especially tonight.

"You two…" He hung the welding gun from Janice's rear bumper and lifted the protective helmet. Bobby leaned against the cooling durasteel plate he'd welded into the gaping hole where the Armorglass window had been. Black Dragon and Headsman stood at the end of the repair bay. Neither one of them had hands anywhere near a weapon.

"Just stopped in to say hello." Black Dragon leaned against the large tool chest. For once, she was missing her signature smirk. She looked a little bit worn about the edges.

"Brought this along by way of an apology." Headsman held up a bottle with a diagonal red label.

"That is one hell of an apology." Bobby eyed the bottle. "What's a bottle of precrash scotch go for these days?"

"Depends on where you're at." Headsman walked into the repair bay. "In New York City, a bottle like this went for eighty-five at auction last month."

"Eighty-five hundred for a bottle of scotch." Bobby shook his head. Granted, he hadn't seen a bottle of scotch in some time. One of the many things he'd had to live without since Poughkeepsie.

"Eighty-five thousand." Black Dragon's smirk was back.

"Got to say," Bobby pulled the helmet from his head and set it on the nearby workbench. "You are about the last two folk I want to see or talk to right now."

"Like I said," Headsman gestured to the bottle. "Apology."

"You two assholes left that kid and the rest of the team to die out there," Bobby said.

"No." Black Dragon pulled out a stool and sat. "We finished the job."

"You know," Bobby picked up the apology, turned it over in his hands and watched the amber liquid shift, "Nate and Chris thought you two were the real deal."

"This is no game, Hank." Headsman shook his head. "Not out there."

"Hell," Bobby sat the bottle beside the welding helmet on the workbench. "Chris was starting to walk and talk like you assholes. They trusted you, though you had their back."

"Never trust anyone that ain't in the seat next to you." Black Dragon stood up. "You know that, Hank. Some of us learn that lesson sooner than others."

"They teach you that in some BLUD douchebag academy?" Bobby asked.

"That's part of your problem." She walked deeper into the bay, trailing one gloved hand along the bench top. "You and the rest of those association pussies. You still think your rules and safety precautions somehow make you superior. They don't. They make you soft. They make you weak."

"Then why the apology?" Bobby asked.

"It was his idea." She turned on her heel and strutted out of the bay. "See you on the road, Hank."

"The pair on you." Headsman pushed himself up to sit on the bench, booted feet still touching the dusty concrete.

"What?"

"I bet you need a dump truck to haul 'em around." Headsman chuckled and shook his head. "You told Dispatcher to pound sand, which, by the way, is not a safe move. Then you tear ass back into that ambush. No clue what was really going on, no good recon, coms down, tactical sensors jammed, and you and that wild-assed driver of yours decide you're the motherloving cavalry."

"I wasn't leaving Mae to make that run alone," Bobby said.

"Hell, after seeing the video feed, she should've joined BLUD," Headsman said. "Not that any of that will matter after tomorrow."

"What's tomorrow?" Bobby asked.

"You didn't get the brief on the next leg?" Headsman asked. "Check your messages."

"I've been busy." Bobby nodded toward the cooling patch. "What's the word?"

"Tomorrow night, we run the Pyramid. Elimination challenge. Only one team is moving on to the next leg of the race." Headsman patted the top of the bottle. "Hence the apology."

"What exactly are you apologizing for?" Bobby asked.

"Killing a legend." Headsman hopped down from the bench and walked out of the bay, hands shoved deep in the pockets of his armored jacket.

Chapter 24

“**G**ood morning, and welcome to Morning Jolt.” The camera zoomed in tight on Donald Roland Northcraft. His hair was well barbered, not one hair out of place. He smiled his million-dollar smile, sitting in one of two large, comfortable-looking chairs separated by a square chrome and glass table. On the table were two large steaming mugs. “I, as always, am your host Don Northcraft. Today is day three of Dead Man's Run. Only two days have elapsed, and the Luxford-Drummond team is down to six vehicles. One lost to rising star Jude Conroy, the other to a well-orchestrated ambush by the Vulcans. Ladies and gentlemen, help me welcome our first guest to the stage, Gordon Corey!” The music rose, a throbbing neo-metal anthem. Out onto the stage walked the duelist turned company man.

“Good morning, Gordon.” Don stood and shook hands with the tall executive. Like every exec, Gordon looked young until you looked at the eyes. The eyes almost always gave it away. While Gold Cross could provide perpetual physical youth, there was little they could do for the worn and weary soul that inhabited their product, and for those who knew where to look, Gordon Corey was clearly worn.

“Mornin, Don.” Gordon took a seat in the other chair.

“Let's get right into it, shall we,” Don said.

“Sure.” Gordon nodded. The makeup did little to conceal just how tired he looked.

"Yesterday, the Luxford-Drummond team lost another vehicle and a driver, and had Bobby Hank not gone back out, quite possibly several more." Don took a drink of coffee and let that land on Gordon.

"Is there a question?" Gordon picked up his cup and took a cautious sip.

"Why did the AADA commission penalize The Pale Riders and Iron Outlaws for making that run?"

"It's in the rules of the run, Don." Gordon leaned back in the chair and rolled his eyes. And with good reason. Gordon had given the same answer on no less than twenty-five interviews in the last twenty-four hours. "Once a leg is complete, teams are restricted to the finish location 'til the next day's start."

"And you don't think an exception could be made in this instance?" Don leaned forward.

"Well, Don," Gordon says. "Late last night, Mr. Varaday, in his capacity as Referee for Dead Man's Run, not only made an exception, he awarded the Pale Riders and Iron Outlaws a cash bonus for their role in extracting the rest of the Luxford-Drummond team from the ambush."

"What does Luxford-Drummond have to say on the subject?" Don grinned like he always did when he thought he'd pulled off a particularly pointed question.

"Very little." Gordon took a longer drink. "We provided the vehicles and sponsored all parts and repairs for the duration of Dead Man's Run. Our only interest is in seeing a Quest not only finish the run, but win. We want housewives and families around the country to see that the Luxford-Drummond Quest is the best vehicle you could own to get from one place to the next."

"So you have no opinion on the conduct of Black Sunshine or the Pale Riders?"

"Officially, we do not."

"How about unofficially?" Don arched one perfectly plucked eyebrow.

"Well, I'll say this," Gordon set the cup down, leaned forward, and gave Don Northcraft a steely stare. "What we witnessed yesterday is just Bobby Hank getting back in the saddle. Black Sunshine would do well to keep that in mind."

Don's eyes flickered away from Gordon's face for an instant, distracted by the voice in his ear calling for a commercial break. He glanced down at the holographic cue card on the back of his massive coffee mug to check the name of the first segment's sponsor.

"Well, that's quite the unofficial opinion," Don said. "Let's take a break and pay some bills. This morning's talk was sponsored by Goodyear Coffee. When we return, we will discuss what is in store for the remaining L&D teams in Memphis."

Chapter 25

obby yawned and tried to rub the grit from his eyes. They'd poured over Janice all night, welding and soldering, making her roadworthy once again. Gone was the sleek polished machine that had rolled off the Luxford-Drummond assembly line. In its place sat a steely mount that was battered but not broken, ready for another day on the road.

While he had labored to patch up the damaged rear end, Mae had spent the evening inside, restoring damaged radar and radio wire runs, and mounting three new boxes under the dash. To Bobby, they looked like a smaller, newer version of the holocomputer she used to run diagnostics and build programs.

"Coffee?" With a loud snap, Mae latched the hardshell toolkit and slid it in through the left side door.

"About a gallon of it if you can round some up." He powered up Janice's combat systems and started running checks.

"You know Janice can run those." She climbed into the passenger area of the Quest. "And, as an aside, you could have just patched the hole where the back Armorglass was instead of welding the entire rear hatch shut and scabbing tank armor wafers over the whole damn rear and halfway up the sides."

"Rule 8: Never trust your system checks to someone else even and especially if it's an AI. Rule 12: If you have the horsepower to spare, there is no such thing as too much armor."

"Didn't we sign a contract that stipulates we would only perform L&D-approved repairs and modifications for the duration of the run?" Mae grunted, struggling to shift the heavy tool kit between the two mid-row bucket seats.

"You're one to talk." Bobby held up a wrist-thick bundle of cables ending in an octopus of sensor pads and electrodes.

"That won't be visible." She shoved the hardshell kit onto the cargo plate formed by the folded-up rear seat and started strapping it down. "And after yesterday, I figured we might need some insurance."

"It looks like an octopus orgy with an MMSD induction net." He sorted through the tangle of electrodes and neural induction connectors.

"Maybe so," She crawled back through the middle seats and out the side door. "But this scab job looks like you taught a troupe of chimps to weld and turned them loose."

"What does this thing even do?" He dropped the mass of induction connectors and electrodes back between the two seats.

"Like I said," she gestured toward where one of several camera drones hovered above the Quest. "Insurance."

"Right." He went back to the six holodisplays he had open. "At some point, I'm going to need you to explain exactly what that means."

"A girl's gotta have some secrets." She turned and headed for the greasy spoon diner across the street.

"Don't forget that coffee," he called.

"Did you say coffee?" Chris slid the right side door open and tossed a duffel between the mid-row seats.

"Yep," Bobby said. "If you hurry, you can catch up and get your order in."

"Okay." Chris slid the door shut with a bang.

Bobby returned to his checks. Somewhere in the cold dark hours of early morning, the big gunner had wandered into the Pale Rider's repair bay, dropped his duffel and weapons on the workbench, and set to helping make Janice roadworthy. He wasn't as sharp a mechanic as Mae, but he was handy enough, and it didn't hurt to have his muscle on hand when it came time to weld those armored wafers in place. The first hour or so, he hadn't said two words. He just picked up what Bobby needed picked up and was there with whatever tool Bobby needed next. Eventually, Chris'd started talking. Small things at first, growing up with Nate, life on a farm near the HRDZ, and how they ended up joining Dead Man's Run. By dawn, he'd taken to calling Bobby "boss." When Bobby tried to dissuade him, the big gunner just shrugged. After the third or fourth time, Bobby stopped trying. Some folks just need someone to follow, he guessed.

"Good morning, Runners." Dispatcher leered from the coms display, his face mask shimmering silver. The rest of his outfit looked like an accident in a paint factory. "Welcome to day three of Dead Man's Run. As you know, today's start will be staggered based on the overall standings thus far...."

"Why?" Mae thumped the wheel with her fist. "Why do we got to be strapped in and ready to roll if we can't start for another couple of hours?"

"It's the way of the world." Bobby shrugged. "You swim upstream, and the bureaucrats find a way to punish you with the rules."

They rolled out of Birmingham three hours behind Black Sunshine and two hours behind the Skull Monkeys and Rolling Thunder. Rain had rolled in overnight. It came down soft and steady, turning the day wet and gray, like all of Alabama was mourning the loss of Nathan McHenry.

Tornado Express ran point on their little convoy with the Iron Outlaws in the middle and the Pale Riders running tail-end-Charlie. Bobby grinned and sipped his coffee. It had felt real good to hear both Tornado Express and Iron Outlaw tell Dispatcher to get bent when their start time had come up. He checked his tactical display. Tornado Express was two miles ahead of the Iron Outlaws. Mae kept the tail end of the Outlaws' Quest just inside the visual range.

"Y'all really didn't have to wait around on us." Bobby radioed.

"Safety in numbers," Hal said. "That ambush yesterday was a professional operation. We were too spread out."

"It's like the sumbitches knew we were coming." Sprockets said.

"I imagine outlaws and bandits watch Dead Man's Run, same as anyone else." Bobby watched the mix of green vines and gray of leafless winter roll by.

"I thought the cameras were on a two-hour delay," Raymond said.

"That would be more than enough to—"

"We got something up here." Sprockets broke in.

"Something covers a lot of territory." Bobby checked his tactical display. Nothing moving except them.

"Smoke, Hank, we got a big plume of smoke up ahead."

"Hold." Bobby returned the coffee cup to the cup holder and rechecked the tac display. They were roughly three miles behind the Tornado Express Quest. "We'll be there in four minutes."

"I can do it in two," Mae said.

They arrived at Tornado Express's position in a spray of rainwater. The tactical display still showed nothing more than the three Quests on the radar. The rain had gone from soft and steady to a sporadic drizzle, and Bobby could see the clouds thinning further west. He looked around the circle of drivers and gunners. Not precisely the crew he'd have picked for this run. Hal and Raymond were veteran duelists, Chris was willing but still green as grass. Hannah and Sprockets weren't as green as Chris and Nate had been, and the run from the HRDZ to here had rubbed a little tough on them. He looked over Hal's shoulder at the thick black cloud clawing its way into the sky. Trees and the rolling Alabama countryside conspired to hide the location and distance from view.

"What's the play?" Hal asked.

"Road's not all that wide out here." Bobby looked around. Between decades of decline and the Vulcans' years-long rampage around Birmingham, the road crews hadn't been this way in a long time. New growth of oak, maple, pecan, and pine had crept right up to the edges of the roadway, and with them came a cornucopia of briers, vines, and brambles squeezing the once broad highway into two narrowing strips of faded blacktop. "Can't see shit, and we really need to see."

"I tried a thermal, but without recon drones, aircraft, or a satellite view, all I got is cold trees, cold road, and a rising plume of heat where that smoke is," Raymond said.

"Let's put a drone up and see what's what," Hannah said.

"Don't have any," Bobby said. "Outlaws?"

"Nope." Raymond shook his head.

"We had a group of fans airdrop some to us after yesterday's disaster." Sprockets leaned back on the hood of the Tornado Express Quest. "Sent us a whole case."

"You guys get stuff from fans?" Mae stared at Hannah.

"Sure," she shrugged. "Don't you?"

"Not recon drones," Bobby said. "Laminated armor plating and the like, sure."

"Maybe you need to engage with your fans more." Sprockets walked to the side door of the Tornado Express Quest and disappeared inside.

"That was always Kat's thing." Bobby shrugged.

"Who the hell has time for Clutch posts?" Mae asked. "I can barely keep up with not dying and keeping Janice here roadworthy."

"Holy – you seeing this?" Sprockets' voice was a tense whisper in Bobby's helmet speakers.

"Yeah," Bobby said.

On the holodisplay, the burned-out remains of two Luxford-Drummond Quests sat nose to nose across the highway. Hanging from the sides, spikes driven through hands, feet, and shoulders were the naked remains of the Skull Monkeys and Rolling Thunder. From the look of things, they had all died hard. The rain had returned with a vengeance. The driving downpour had all but extinguished the remains of the fires that had gutted both vehicles.

"Holy shit." Chris leaned forward between the seats and pointed. "Is that— "

"Uh-huh," Bobby said.

"Why?" Mae asked.

"Someone is sending us a message," Hal said.

"What kind of message is this?" Hannah asked.

"At a guess— "

"Missile warning, Missile warning."

Bobby thumbed the countermeasures button on reflex sending flares and crybaby chaff bursting from the sides and top of Janice. In the Outlaws' Quest, Raymond had been a half second behind deploying their countermeasures. The crybaby chaff from both vehicles caused the incoming missiles to explode early, showering them with a rattling rain of shrapnel.

"Look alive, Sprockets." Bobby looked at his tactical display, searching for the source of the incoming rounds.

The noise and static from the settling chaff cloud had turned the display into a confusing mess. The only thing that was clear to Bobby was the ground around them.

The burned-out vehicles blocked the road ahead. A gaping hole where the bridge had been ensured they weren't going that direction, even if they could bypass the gruesome roadblock. On both sides of the highway, trees masked near vertical walls where the roadbed had been cut through the Alabama sandstone. They were trapped, hemmed in on both sides. To the right was a semi-gentle slope covered in a growth of trees too thick to pass between and too large to drive over. Whoever set this ambush knew their trade.

Mae accelerated backward away from the burned-out Quests. Tornado Express followed suit.

"Chris, you get your big ass strapped back in and take over countermeasures." Bobby highlighted the gently sloping area on the tactical display. "Janice, designate this as target area Alpha and share with Outlaws and Tornado Express."

"Area designated and shared," Janice said.

"Hal, Sprockets, hit that area with a salvo of HE rockets. We need to cut a route out of here." Bobby said.

"What's wrong with the road?" Sprockets asked.

"I'm betting they cut the bridge behind us," Bobby said. "It's what I would do."

The road between Janice and the Tornado Express Quest erupted in a fountain of asphalt and dirt. A half second later, the world vanished in a roar of detonating explosives and fountaining earth. Bobby watched earth and sky trade places several times with the stomach churning rapidity of a violent roll-over. They came to a stop, right side up, staring through rain streaked mud at a landscape of craters and rubble.

"Janice, damage report." He glanced over at Mae. She sat there shaking her head, blood dripping from her chin. "Mae, you good?"

"I bit my lip," she said. "What the hell was that?"

"Artillery barrage. Get moving." He explained. "Chris, you okay back there?"

"Depends on what you mean."

"All systems are fully operational." Janice reported.

"Mae!" Bobby rapped the side of her helmet. "Roll. Now."

"Right." She cut the wheel hard right and stepped on the accelerator. Nothing. Tires spun, and the Quest rocked a bit but otherwise sat still.

"Chris?" Bobby checked the tactical display. Mostly static with clear contacts for Iron Outlaws and Tornado Express.

"I'm good." He sounded strained. "Right arm is hard down. I'm pretty sure it's busted."

"Can you handle countermeasures and threat assessment?" Bobby asked.

"Sure."

"Good. Get a screen open back there and dig out the source of that attack before they get reloaded and another on the way."

"We ain't moving," Mae said.

"Feels like we're high-centered on something." Bobby checked his mirror; it was a crushed and mangled mass of durasteel and reflective armorglass. He hit the stomp switch for the radio. "Hal, Ray, Hannah, Sprockets, do you copy?"

Mae hit the accelerator. Motors whined, and tires spun. Janice rocked slightly with the torque.

"Hey, Bobby," Chris said. "I think they're running a Bollix. I can't get anything but fuzz and mush on tactical.

"We have to get moving." He hit the harness release and the door latch. "If they get reloaded before we move, we're dead ducks."

"What are you going to do?" Mae asked.

"Two things." He pulled his carbine free of its mount and checked the load. "Unless this was a preregistered target, they, whoever the hell they are, have a spotter out there calling in fire. If I can get to the spotter, then the next round of fire will be a lot less accurate."

"What's the second thing?" she asked.

"We need to get the hell off of whatever we're stuck on. I'll take a look and see what I can do."

"We won't be able to talk to you out there," Chris said. "Bollix jams everything."

"Let me worry about that."

"Sure thing, boss," Chris said.

Bobby stepped out into the pouring rain. He kept in a low crouch and looked around their position. The highway had been blasted into a moonscape of asphalt and mud. Neither Iron Outlaws nor Tornado Express's Quests were visible. He ducked down and took a look underneath their ride. During the crazy rollover, Janice had come to rest atop a sideways chunk of road, balanced nearly perfectly with the front wheels hanging in the air. Their rear wheels sat stone dead against the broken asphalt while the others spun forward, then backward, as Mae tried to rock the vehicle enough to gain traction.

He stood on his tiptoes and hit the door latch, catching it before it could hinge open.

"The rear wheels are dead." He looked through the gap at Mae. She nodded and started to unhook her harness.

"I got it," Chris called.

Bobby shoved the door closed again and moved out into the rain-soaked afternoon, keeping low, moving from shell crater to shell crater. He pulled up behind a spot where an exploding artillery round had heaved a ten-foot piece of asphalt road vertical and scanned the surrounding area. The horizon was close. The road passed through a wide cut in the sandstone and clay of the Alabama hills, essentially placing them in a ten-foot deep, hundred-yard-wide gully. Trees, vines, and brush choked the edges of the cut, providing enough cover for a platoon.

Behind him, he heard tires spin on pavement. Bobby turned to see all four of Janice's wheels spinning. The rear ones caught and pulled the Quest backward off the obstruction and onto the southern shoulder of the highway. He waved at them. Gave a thumbs up and pointed. Mae flashed the headlights in acknowledgment before picking her way west.

Bobby turned back to the northern side of the road. "What I wouldn't give for a pair of binoculars."

He raised the rifle to his shoulder and scanned the top of the cut. Nothing. Just bare gray limbs against a gray sky. Maybe they used the roadway between the two bridges as a preregistered target. No observer needed.

He broke cover, moving north toward the edge of the highway. Then again, they needed some way to know when their quarry was deep in the trap. Whoever it was, they clearly weren't using an autoloader. Otherwise, the barrage would have kept going. No. That damned observer was up there, waiting to call more fire and death down on Bobby and his people.

"Not if I got anything to say about it." He broke cover again, sprinting for the trees.

Mae picked her way north and west along the southern shoulder. Growing up, she'd heard of artillery and had watched more than her fair share of war movies with Grandpa Ed. The fountains of dirt and red-orange flash on the screen didn't do justice to the reality of having massive amounts of high explosives detonate within feet of your vehicle. The volume alone was overwhelming. Her ears still rang, and her head felt like a hive of wasps hatching behind her eyes.

"Any luck on cutting through the Bollix?" She steered around another crater.

"Got a big bunch of nothing on that front," Chris said. "Too bad we can't figure out direction and distance."

"The purpose of the device is to prevent radar from providing that information," she said.

"Won't it jam them as well?" Chris called up a keyboard, wincing as the motion jostled the broken arm.

"Yep." She nodded. "They would need a laser com to communicate once they powered up the Bollix. Which means, if that observer is out there waiting to hit us again, they have to have a direct line of sight with whatever was shelling us."

Chapter 26

obby leaned against a tree, sucking in great gulps of air. Ten years of hospitals and salvage jobs had not left him in full fighting form. It had taken him much longer to scale that rock face than he thought it would. That was one of the downsides of running around in sixty-year-old meat. Another downside, everything hurt. His right knee throbbed in counterpoint to his left shoulder and both elbows.

"I'm too damned old for this." He shook his head, stood up, and started working his way north.

The second rock face came as a surprise. It was completely masked by a much older and more mature growth of hardwood and evergreens planted by the precrash road crews.

"Pale Rider, this is Pale Rider Actual." He tested his ICS radio. The hiss and crackle of jammed coms was the only response.

That was good news, in a way. The Bollix would keep whoever was directing fire from using radio coms. Of course, if they had a laser com, all bets were off. They would need a direct line of sight with the artillery battery if they were using a laser com. Bobby looked up through a network of bare branches at the low clouds and falling rain. What were the odds the observer was up a tree? What he really needed was a topo map of the area and a link to some counter-battery elements. What he had was a jammed ICS radio linked to an up-armed and armored all-terrain minivan.

It was the smell of weed that gave the observer away. That sticky stench, like someone was molesting a skunk with a hot poker, led Bobby straight to the observer's perch. Bobby eased up through the vine-choked woods 'til he could see where someone had driven thumb-thick spikes into the tree trunk to form a crude ladder.

That same someone had left their ride leaned up against another tree, the Bollix strapped to the rear fairing with its sizable battery pack. A thick power cable ran along the ground and up the tree with the spikes. Bobby grinned. Whoever it was, they were as sloppy as they were inexperienced. Using a tree as an observation post was fine if you brought someone to watch your back. This clown was out here solo.

"Hey, Shep."

Bobby froze. The observer was male and a heavy smoker judging by his raspy voice.

"Quit dicking around and get firing again. You missed at least two, and they're on the move."

Bobby eased away from the observation post until he had a good angle on the upper branches of the pine.

"Keep your pants on, K-Dog," Shep said. His voice was a gravelly rasp.

Bobby shook his head. The damned fool wasn't even bothering with an earpiece for his comms. Definitely not pros.

"Where they gonna go?"

"You know who's down there?" Bobby worked around the OP in a clockwise circle, quiet and careful.

"Six dead racers and a bunch of expensive scrap?" Shep asked. "Too bad we got to smash them. I'd definitely like some alone time with that orange-haired driver."

"Come on, man," K-Dog said. "You hogged up all the time with the other two. We had to nail 'em up before I got a turn."

Bobby found K-Dog perched near the top of the tree. The shiny buckles on his boots gave him away.

"RHIP K-Dog."

"You know that's Bobby Hank down there."

"So?" Shep asked.

"So, that is one bad dude." Bobby grinned and took aim just above the dinner plate-sized belt buckle. "He's the whole reason we're out here instead of back at the clubhouse."

"Just keep that Bollix going and let me know if they find a way out of the box."

"Fine."

Bobby waited. He breathed in and let the breath out nice and slow, his finger taking up the slack in the trigger.

"Just hurry. I'm feeling kind of exposed out here like this."

Breath fully exhaled, in that moment of stillness between inhale and exhale, Bobby squeezed the trigger sending three rounds of 5.56 ripping through K-Dog's gut.

Bobby sprinted to the base of the tree and started climbing. The angle of the shot should have sent rounds up into the lungs and heart. He couldn't take the chance that the bastard was still breathing and might get off a call for help, might let the assholes on the other end of that radio know things were not going according to plan.

"You think he's okay?" Mae asked.

She had navigated the jumbled and broken moonscape that had once been I-22/ Highway 78 and could see the remnants of the bridge where the Skull Monkeys and Rolling Thunder vehicles had been staged. Now there was only torn-up asphalt and mud to mark where they had been. Someone had taken the time to spike all four racers to their vehicles' sides before lighting them on fire. Mae shuddered.

She found the Iron Outlaws tucked into a crater nose down behind torn-up chunks of roadway the size of tractor-trailers. That meant the mass of twisted metal and burning plastic was all that remained of Tornado Express. Mae choked back the rising panic and directed the laser com at the Outlaw's Quest.

"Hal, Ray…You okay in there?"

"Good enough," Hal said. "You?"

"Took a rollover. Chris patched us up enough to get rolling again."

"Where's Hank?" Ray asked.

"He took his rifle and went looking for a spotter," she said.

"Sounds about right," Hal said. "The man is pathologically addicted to doing things the hard way."

"I ain't heard nothin' for a minute," Mae said. "You think he's all right?"

"If anyone is okay out there, it's him," Chris said. He'd climbed into the gunner's seat and was scanning the tactical display.

"Careful, McHenry," Mae said. "I think you're becoming a fan."

"He saved my ass." Chris looked up from the tactical display. "I didn't give him one good reason, but he walked into the middle of that gunfight and carried me out again."

"Incoming communication from an unidentified source," Janice said.

"Let's hear it," Mae said.

"Pale Rider." Bobby's voice was sharp and clear, like he was sitting in the seat next to her.

"Bobby!" She looked at Chris. He shrugged and grinned. "I read you loud and clear."

"Good, get a line of sight on the other vehicles and use the laser com. We're in deep here, but I have an idea."

"Way ahead of you." She put the laser com on HOT MIC. "We got Outlaw on laser com…Hannah and Sprocket… They took a direct hit from whatever the hell that was."

"The kids told us what you're up to, Hank," Hal said. "You're a little old to be doing sneak-n-peeks in a monsoon."

"And you're some spring chicken?" Bobby snorted. "I killed the spotter. Turns out he brought along the Bollix that's wrecking our RADAR and comms."

"So shut it down," Chris said.

"I do that, and the four, two-hundred mike mike artillery pieces they have will be able to hammer us with RADAR-directed fire."

"Holy…" Ray said.

"Where'd they get four 200mm guns?"

"Beats me," Bobby said. "They haven't had them long, and they're way under-crewed. You ever watch five guys try to handle loading a 200mm?"

"No." Hal snorted.

"Why's that funny?" Mae looked at Chris. He shrugged.

"Cause 200mm guns typically have a crew of twenty to handle the loading," Ray said. "The shells are massive and heavy as hell. Handloading requires hydraulic lifting equipment. Not to mention, early models didn't handle moisture and dirt all that well."

"That's about the long and short of it," Bobby said.

"What's the play?" Mae asked.

"See that tree-covered slope to the northwest, the one I designated as target area Alpha?"

"Yep." She was looking dead at it. "Janice ain't navigating that. Too thick."

"Right." He said. "Chris, Ray hit that area with some HE missiles— "

"Like using a daisy cutter to clear an LZ." Raymond cut in. "Yeah, I think we can make that work."

"Set the warheads to detonate at just above ground height and lay the salvo down so it makes a line between where you are and the old service road on the other side of that hill."

"You're gonna have to kill the Bollix for that to work," Chris said. "I can't even see the terrain clearly right now, and the warheads all use RADAR for proximity fusing."

"True," Bobby said.

"If you kill the Bollix, they'll know something's up." Mae eyed the slope. It was gentle enough. The engineers at Luxford-Drummond had done a decent job designing a vehicle that could handle the poorly maintained roads. Off-roading through torn earth and blasted forest was not quite what they had in mind. "We'll be sitting ducks slogging up and over that hill. Without the Bollix, they can't miss."

"I'm not going to give them a chance to shoot," Bobby said.

Bobby finished strapping the Bollix device to the back of the bike. He was breathing hard, and his knee was on fire. The battery pack weighed a solid eighty pounds, and the device itself wasn't very light either. Lucky for him, K-Dog had been a sloppy, lazy asshole and had left the battery pack strapped to the bike.

The undermanned gun crews were still struggling to load the massive guns last he'd looked. Bobby grinned; these dumb bastards wouldn't know what hit them. He stepped onto the bike and held the cold start button down, letting the glow plugs work their magic before hitting the start button and cranking the diesel-powered machine to life. The smell of pork grease made Bobby's stomach turn. After this run, it would be a long time before he ate pork again. He rolled the throttle back and took off toward the guns, the knobby rear wheel of the bike spraying a rooster tail of pine needles and dirt into the air.

Mark Shepherd, known as Shep to his Vulcan brothers and sisters, wasn't known for his patience. Hell on wheels in a gunfight, hard-drinking, fast-riding, and ruthless with his enemies? Yes.

Patient? No.

It was his own fault. The crew who delivered the four 200mm howitzers last night were adamant that they have a crew of twenty per gun. He'd figured fifteen or so Vulcans properly motivated could handle loading the four guns. He'd figured wrong. Truth be told, Shep hadn't figured anything would survive that barrage. He'd seen every movie ever made about the Gulf or Bust campaign. In each and every movie, the big guns destroyed everything they hit.

He paced to the furthest gun on the line where ten Vulcans, wet to the waist in red clay mud, struggled to bring the heavy shells from the ammo trailer to the open breach of the massive gun.

"What the hell is taking you clowns so long?" he growled.

"These shells are heavy as hell even with the powered loaders." T-Money shoved again with the other Vulcans. The loader's wheels spun, spattering the straining men with more red clay. "And the rain ain't helping us."

"Hurry it up, you look like a bunch of monkeys humpin' a football."

The grinding growl of a diesel dirt bike sounded over the power loader's whine and the men's grunts and curses. Shep looked up to see one of his scout bikes flying down the hill straight at them.

He lifted the radio and hit the transmit button. "K-Dog, what the fu— "

Fire blossomed from the dual-mounted 5.56 machine guns on the front of the scout bike. Shep dropped the radio and dove for cover. With no warning beyond Shep's dive for cover and the crack of 5.56 rounds breaking the sound barrier around them, the Vulcans struggling to load the big gun had no chance. The man in the scuffed and battered monocrys jacket rode straight through the middle of them. Twin machine guns and the barking .45 in his hand dealt death wherever the stranger went.

Bobby rolled back the throttle, planted one leg, and kicked the bike around in a mud-churning turn showering the wounded behind him in red clay and the men down the gun line with lead. Once the knobby tread of the rear wheel grabbed traction, he tore off east along the gun line. Ahead of him, Vulcans dove for cover and weapons. Bobby grinned, his teeth skinned back in the age-old smile of predators, maximum teeth revealed, letting the prey know they were next.

He reached the end of the gun line and spun the bike's rear around in another mud-churning skid before coming to a halt behind one of the ammo trailers.

Bobby reached back, toggled the Bollix off, and chinned the ICS mic. "Go now. Don't let up til you hear from me."

Fire blossomed in his leg. It buckled, sending him to the ground with the bike on top. Several Vulcans had recovered from his attack run and were returning fire. "Not good." He grunted. He dragged himself free of the bike and half scooted, half scrambled behind one of the stabilization legs of the easternmost gun. The flat crack of high-velocity lead let him know they were less than pleased with his stunt.

Bobby looked down at the injured leg. Blood pumped from the wound. It felt numb, like "the bullet hit the bone" numb. Not good. He reached up, unzipped the right vertical pocket on the old armored jacket, and snatched out a packet of clotting agent. He ripped the top open with his teeth and dumped the whole thing on the wound before wrapping an auto-compression bandage around the leg and pulling the rip tab. Pain, searing hot, burned up his leg from the clotting agent and the pressure of the bandage clamping down on the wound. The squelch of feet in mud was the only warning he had. Bobby rolled to his right, up under the support, brought the .45 to bear, and unloaded the entire magazine into the legs of the approaching Vulcans.

Still grinning, Bobby reloaded, and belly crawled through the mud beneath the big gun. He emerged covered in mud like a revenant from the grave. The three Vulcans that had taken cover behind the next gun in line stared at the mud-smeared apparition. Bobby almost felt bad for them until he remembered the charred bodies spiked to the sides of still-burning vehicles. The old emptiness he'd been holding back washed over him. He shot all three dead before they could raise their weapons.

Shortly after the radios and RADAR had started working again, a massive explosion to the northeast shot a roiling cloud of fire into the sky and shook what leaves remained from nearby trees.

"Bobby, come in." Mae radioed again for what felt like the hundredth time.

Navigating the shattered trees and churned mud of the hillside had been easier than she'd anticipated. Getting back to the highway took a little longer.

"Pale Rider calling Pale Rider Actual." She radioed again.

"Come on, kid," Hal said. "We're still in range."

"No." She shook her head and stared at Chris.

"I got nothing on tactical," he said.

"Is it sensitive enough to pick up a single person on foot?" she asked.

"I've reset the filters so that anything bigger than a badger would show up."

"Bullshit." She grabbed the binoculars from the center console, hit her door latch, and stepped out onto the rain-drenched blacktop.

She heard something. The hiss and patter of falling rain nearly drowned it out, but it was there fading in and out, the clattering growl of a diesel-powered bike. Mae climbed up onto Janice's roof and raised the binoculars. There, coming over the hill, was a small bike. The gusting wind brought the grinding growl of its diesel engine to her in fits and starts.

"Recheck your filters!" She stomped on Janice's roof. A large grin grew on her face. The figure on the bike had no helmet and was covered head to toe in orange-red mud.

Hal stepped out of the Outlaw Quest and walked back to stand next to Mae's open door. The figure skidded to a stop and grinned, his teeth flashing white through a mask of mud and soot.

"We should probably get moving." Bobby stepped off the bike and let it hit the road. He favored his left leg as he limped to the gunner's door and hit the latch. "There's a chance enough of them are still alive and able to get one of those guns up and running."

"You look like hell." Hal pulled Bobby into a rough hug, slapping him on the back.

"It looks worse than it feels." Bobby looked down at Chris. "You good to handle gunner for a while?"

"I think so." Chris stared up at Bobby's muddy face.

"Good. I need to see to this leg and maybe take a nap."

"I told you he'd make it." Mae hopped down from Janice's roof and climbed back into her seat.

Chapter 27

The road was empty to the limits of Janice's sensor suite. Bobby swiped the tac display to a small square and shoved it into the bottom right side of the windshield. Iron Outlaw had been out of range for more than a half hour. Hal figured the Vulcans' reach didn't extend into Mississippi, and even if it did, the pounding they'd taken over the last couple of days probably had them licking their wounds and regrouping. Bobby figured Hal had figured right, so when Janice's power system started acting squirrelly, he'd sent Hal on toward Memphis.

The Pale Riders were running a very distant third in the standings, mainly by virtue of not being dead. The Iron Outlaws were a very tight second behind Black Sunshine. A solid second-place finish would keep them in the running. Not that standings mattered much in an elimination challenge. Three crews would enter the Pyramid. One would leave.

Bobby leaned back, pulled his ball cap down low, and closed his eyes. Getting shelled, scaling two rock faces and a tree, getting shot, and nearly killed by a 200mm ammo trailer exploding really took the starch out of a fella. Hal was right; he was getting too old to pull stunts like that.

"You all right over there, old timer?" Chris asked.

"Sure, kid," Bobby said. "You just focus on keeping Janice here on the road. When we get to Memphis, I'll buy you a lollypop."

"Is he always like this?" Chris called back to Mae.

"No," Mae popped up from between the middle row of seats. She had the power run tunnel open and wires strewn about in a chromatic rat's nest. "Sometimes he's actually funny."

"You get that power fluctuation sorted out yet?" Bobby lifted the hat and turned in the seat to look at her.

"Pretty sure," she lifted up a black box about the size of Bobby's head, "this is the source of the problem."

"What is it?" he asked.

Chris glanced in the rearview mirror, "Looks like a power conditioner."

"Yep." Mae slammed it down on the deck between the seats once, twice, three times before diving back into the tunnel.

"Loose circuit card?" Bobby turned back around in his seat and pulled the ball cap back down over his eyes.

"Hope so."

"Wake me up if anything interesting happens."

"Do other cars on the road count?" Chris asked. "Cause four just popped up on tactical."

"Yes." Bobby sat up and swiped the tactical display into full view.

The display showed four contacts. Janice tagged three of them in the pale blue of an unknown contact. The sensor data identified them as Omega 68s. The fourth contact was marked with the bright green of a known friendly and labeled Black Sunshine.

Black Sunshine was nine miles out, on the same side of the highway as they were and coming straight at them. One of the Omega 68s was closing in from the rear while another kept pace in the opposite lane. The third Omega kept pace with Black Sunshine. They were boxed in, and the box was shrinking.

"Get strapped in back there." Bobby designated the two Omegas behind them as Bandit One and Two. Bandit One being the Omega on their side of the road. He redesignated Black Sunshine as hostile and marked the third Omega as Bandit Three.

"No can do." she said. "We need full power if it's a fight."

"Four-on-one is bad odds. I was looking to run."

"Three on two," Chris said.

"No." Bobby shook his head. "Your pals out there are coming to finish us off."

"What?" Chris looked at Bobby then back at the road. "Why?"

"Probably because someone paid them an awful lot of money."

"But we're all one team," Chris's voice heavy with disbelief.

"Yes and no." Bobby ran an ammo and countermeasures check. They still had three loads of chaff and four of flare. The missile magazines were dry. The 3mm Gauss cannon was at seventy percent. The side and rear-mounted Gauss shotguns were fully loaded, as was the mine dropper.

"We can switch to battery and run for a while," Mae said. "But if it comes to a fight, the Gauss weapons eat up a lot of power, and so do the jammers. Right now, I can give you enough power to run wide open and fight for about thirty minutes, or I can give you enough to run and gun indefinitely, but we won't have enough power to utilize Janice to her full potential."

"What does that mean?" Bobby looked in the rearview mirror.

"You'll have the 3mm up front for short bursts, no extended firing." Mae crawled out of the power run tunnel. "If you run jammers, radar, and weapons, top speed is going to be about ninety or so."

"That's fast enough if we can break contact." Bobby glanced at the map. They were passing around the northern edge of the Tupelo Dead Zone. Tupelo wasn't much more than mounds of vine-choked rubble since the Scuz Squad had bombarded it with Willie Pete a few years back. Lots of ground clutter.

"They are going to take us heads up and try to kill us in one pass. Headsman won't be likely to miss, and Black Dragon ain't going to flinch, so don't try to beat her at chicken."

"What do I do?" Chris looked at Bobby, then back at the tac display and the rapidly closing bandits.

"Show 'em our ass."

"What?"

"You want me to drive?" Mae called.

"No," Bobby said. "You keep working. Chris is about to learn how to pull a reverse J."

"I know how to do a reverse J," Chris said. "Just because I was Nate's gunner don't mean I can't drive."

"My bad, Turbo." Bobby grinned. "When I say now, you give me a reverse J. That'll put the most armor between us and Black Sunshine and give me the best shot at Bandit One."

"What do I do after that?"

"Pull another J before we get to the next exit and get off the highway. The ground clutter combined with our jammer should help to even the odds." Bobby selected Bandit One as the primary target on the tactical display. "Janice, please disable our IFF transponder once the shooting starts. I don't want Black Sunshine to find us that easily.

"Yes, Bobby, I will disable the IFF so we can hide from those bitch ass— "

"Whoa," Bobby and Chris stared at each other.

"Like the personality upgrade, I gave our girl?" Mae giggled.

"When did that happen?"

"Warthog's boys hooked me up with the software. Just didn't patch it in till last night while I was installing some of the other goodies we picked up there."

"What else did he hook us up with?" Bobby asked

"Well…we did swap that dinky rear-mounted Gauss shotgun for a proper chase weapon."

"What did they install?" Bobby looked in the rearview mirror. She was snapping the armored deck plating back in place.

"A 30mm Gauss gun." She giggled. "It sucks power like a ten-dollar hooker, but there ain't much that can stand up to a thumb-thick, four-inch long chunk of tungsten moving 9400 feet per second."

"Son-of-a-bitch." Bobby grinned back at Mae. She looked like some demented techno-pixie, with her grease-stained face peeking through the sweat-damp mop of bright orange.

"Do we have full power?" Chris asked.

"It's a qualified yes." She wiped the grease from her face and hands. "We really need to replace the connector for the power conditioner and add a shock mount, so it stops rattling the circuit cards loose."

"Qualified how?" Bobby turned back to the tactical display.

"I bypassed the power conditioner and hardwired the transformer-rectifier directly into the distribution hub." She snapped the hardshell case closed and strapped it down. "It's dirty, but we got max power as long as we don't do any more rollovers or get banged around too much."

Bobby checked the tac display. Black Sunshine and Bandit Three were a mile out and closing fast. Bandits One and Two were two miles back and closing.

"Slow down." Bobby assigned the 3mm Vulcan-G to his right trigger, then assigned the 30mm Gauss gun to his left trigger and rechecked the controls for chaff and flare. "I want Bandit One close enough to kiss when you hit that reverse J."

"You're the boss." Chris let off the throttle, bringing their speed down to around thirty-five. The matte-black Omega rocketed up on them.

"Here, Bobby." Mae passed him one of the factory helmets that came with the Quest. "Better this than nothing."

"Thanks." Bobby strapped the helmet on. He checked the rearview. Mae was strapped into the left-center seat. "Ready?" he asked.

"Ready," Mae said. She sounded tense.

"Ready." Chris snapped his helmet visor down.

"Chris, in three, tw—"The driver's side mirror vanished in a cloud of molten armorglass and durasteel. "Now, Chris, go now!"

Bobby gripped the weapon's yoke tight and watched Chris crank the wheel, sending Janice into a skid.

"Actively jamming now," Mae called.

Chris tapped the brakes and cut the wheel, snapping the front of the Quest around hard. He stabbed the reverse button before mashing the accelerator pedal to the floor.

Bobby watched a strip of armor boil off across the right-hand quarter panel and across the hood, spattering the armorglass windshield with molten durasteel. As soon as the targeting reticle in his HUD flashed green, he hit his right-hand trigger and sent a stream of 3mm tungsten darts straight into the hood and windshield of Bandit One. The sleek black Omega spun sideways, putting fresh armor between the driver and Bobby's murderous fire.

"What was that?" Chris stared at the rearview screen and steered straight for Black Sunshine.

"X-ray laser." Bobby let off the trigger to conserve ammo. Black Sunshine raked them with a full salvo. 3mm tungsten rods struck the scabbed-on armored wafers sounding like hell's own speed metal drummer.

"Threat – missile warning." Janice chirped.

"Crybaby away." Mae coughed. The concussion of multiple missiles shook them.

The rear target reticle cycled from yellow to red. Bobby stroked the left-hand trigger, sending a thumb-sized tungsten rod into the hood of the Black Sunshine vehicle at nearly 10,000 feet per second. The force of the impact vaporized armor and caused the other Quest to stand on its nose briefly before slamming back to earth.

Chris whipped Janice around the smoking ruin of Black Sunshine's Quest, flicked the wheel powering through a proper J turn, and accelerated around the offramp.

"We got to break visual contact and get to cover." Bobby checked the rearview mirror. Daylight streamed through several holes in the rear hatch, and something was smoldering, sending up tendrils of smoke. "Mae, see if you can bump up the power on our jammer. And get that fire out." He checked the tactical screen. Black Sunshine and Bandit One were moving slowly toward the exit. Bandits Two and Three had made it to the same exit on the opposite side of the highway and were gaining on them.

"Right." She sounded strained.

"You good?" He risked a glance over his shoulder. He could see her working on something in the countermeasures holodisplay.

"Good enough…" The sound of a CO2 extinguisher drowned out the rest of her words.

"Missile warning. Missile warning." Janice broke in.

Bobby checked the nav screen. "Take this next ramp going west, then take the southbound ramp after that."

"On it." Nearby explosions rocked them. Chris slalomed around several burned-out wrecks. Fire blossomed just off the front bumper, showering them with chunks of asphalt and gravel.

"That was close." Bobby checked the chaff counter. It hadn't moved. "Maybe use chaff on the next one, Mae."

"Sure—" She coughed.

"You don't sound so good." Bobby checked the rearview. Her head lolled with the motion of Chris drifting through the tight three-sixty of the next exit. "Janice, can you give me vitals on Mabel Holland?"

"Transferring weapons and countermeasure controls to you, Kid." He swiped the entire gunner station holographic overlay across to Chris and hit his harness release. "Left trigger is rear guns, right trigger is front gun. The mine dropper and shotguns are unassigned, but Janice can handle those on voice command. Same with chaff and flare. Break contact and get us out of sight."

"Right." Chris looked at Bobby, looked in the rearview. "Is she— "

"Not yet." He climbed through the gap and into the middle compartment.

Daylight shined through the side door where the laser had penetrated the thinner armor. Smoke swirled and danced in a thin blue-white haze. He grabbed the trauma kit off the back of the driver's seat and ripped open the Velcro closures, letting it unroll.

"Do we have bio-metrics, Janice?"

"Yes, I can monitor body temperature, blood pressure, pulse— "

"Good. Give me her pulse and BP. Keep giving it to me until I tell you to stop."

"Yes, Bobby. Pulse is 62. BP is 90 over 60."

"Janice, give me full cabin lights."

"Full cabin lights. Pulse 60. BP 88 over 57."

Bobby got his first good look at Mae. Her protective jacket and coverall were charred. The laser's heat had fused suit and flesh on her left side in a mass of charred fabric and scorched meat. He'd seen wounds like this before. Lasers were nasty weapons to get hit with. They left horrible burns behind cooking and cauterizing frail flesh. That didn't account for the dropping blood pressure. She had a bleeder somewhere. He did a quick feel and found her front, wet with blood. The Quest swerved right then left, flinging Bobby against the smoldering left-hand door.

"Son of a bitch." Bobby crawled back to Mae. "A little warning would be nice."

"Sorry." Chris glanced a question at him in the rearview mirror. He shook his head and went back to assessing Mae.

Bobby hit the release tabs and pulled the monocrys jacket open. She'd been hit low on her left side, blood leaked through three holes in her coverall, soaking the fabric. He grabbed vibro-scissors from the trauma kit and started cutting.

"You…" she coughed. "Are a little too old to be taking my clothes off."

"You aren't exactly my type either." He cut away her undershirt, exposing the wounds.

"Pulse 55. Blood pressure 79 over 58."

"Too young, and as a rule, I don't date drivers." He grabbed the red adrenaline injector and ripped the plastic packaging free with his teeth. "How's the pain?"

"Bad." She coughed again, spattering her visor with carmine droplets. "Get the…insurance."

"What?" He jammed the auto-injector against the bare skin of her thigh.

"Gahh!" Her head snapped back against the seat, arms and legs stiff.

"Pulse 75. Blood pressure 95 over 63."

"I think we've lost them," Chris said.

"Good." Bobby tossed the auto-injector aside. "Shut down to batteries."

"Shouldn't we shut it all the way down?"

"We do that," Bobby looked up a Chris in the mirror. "We're sitting ducks."

"Right," Chris said. "Janice, shut down to battery."

"Recent upgrades to my systems require more power than the current battery configuration can support."

"I know." Bobby dumped clotting powder onto the bleeding wounds before wrapping the pressure dressing around her stomach. "Shut down to battery power now."

"Shutting down. Switching to power conservation mode. Battery currently at one hundred percent."

The cabin lights winked out, and the subtle hum of Janice quieted into the silence of spooling down fan motors and the pop-ting of cooling metal. Sunlight streamed in through the holes in the back hatch and the burned-through gash in the side door.

"Chris, keep an eye on tactical. Nothing active, just thermals and the seismograph. Ain't nobody around but us. Good chance we'll feel them coming."

Bobby flipped up the face plate on his helmet and activated the map lights mounted on the front. The bleeding had stopped. Now for that god-awful burn.

"Get…damned insurance…" Mae dragged her helmet free and let it fall to the deck with a clunk. She reached for the wrist-thick cable with its mass of electrodes and induction pickups Velcroed to the rear of the driver's seat.

"Blood pressure 80 over 58."

"What the hell are you doing?" Bobby pulled the can of BurnFoam from the trauma kit.

The worst thing about burns in the field was the inability to protect them or immobilize the area so that proper medic types could treat them in a facility. BurnFoam was the answer to that problem. It immobilized, anesthetized, and coated the wound in a hard, sterile shell, sealing it up tight for the docs on the other end to handle. He lifted her arm and hosed her entire right side. The sharp smell of antiseptic filled the cabin while green mush coated her from armpit to hip.

"Ahh, that…that's better." Mae coughed again; cherry red droplets spattered Bobby's face and helmet. "Shit, that still hurts." She dropped the balled-up mass of smaller cables and wires into her lap, fumbling one-handed with the Velcro straps. She coughed again, longer and harder, spraying the cables and Bobby with blood.

"Mae." He put his hand under her chin and lifted her head. "What. Are. You. Doing?" Blood stained her chin and ran down her front.

"In—insurance." She coughed. "Warthog's— crew— MM—S—D."

"This," Bobby held up the ball of cables. "This is an MMSD?"

Mae nodded. She plucked weakly at the Velcro strips holding the mass together.

"Where the hell did you get a MMSD?" Chris asked.

"Long story." Bobby ripped the straps away.

The mass flopped open a nightmare octopus of cables surrounding a fist-sized central cup covered in tiny needles. Dead center, a single large spike peeked through. He looked up into her blood-smeared face. "Now what?"

"We got company," Chris said. "Seismograph has three contacts at three-quarters of a mile."

"On my—" Mae's head lolled. Her breath came in short sharp gasps. "—head."

"What about this?" He held the center of the mass close to her face and tapped the tip of the large needle.

"Deep—probe." She coughed up more blood. "—in back—base—skull."

"Shit."

"Hurry— "She gagged and heaved. Blood and vomit splashed them both.

"Blood pressure 60 over 35. Pulse 40."

"Okay." He slapped the contraption onto her sagging head and placed the large cup against the base of her skull.

The thing came to life. Cables adjusted and tightened, pulling the entire net of sensors, electrodes, and probes tight against her hair. Mae's head snapped up, her eyes wide and rolling.

"Blood pressure 40 over 20."

"Oh—" She moaned through clenched teeth, "it hurts, it hurts, Bobby, it hurts." Her back arched. Heels drumming against the armored deck, she clutched his arm.

"Scanning now." The display and instrument lights winked out.

"We just lost everything," Chris called.

"A little busy," Bobby growled.

Tendons stood out in her neck, the moan of pain crescendoing into clenched jaw grunts of agony.

"She's not going to make it, is she? "

"No." Bobby stared at Chris in the rearview mirror. "Get us back online. They find us like this, and we're all dead meat."

Chapter 28

Chris McHenry stared into the rearview mirror. It sounded like Mae was dying and dying hard. Bobby stared back at him, face and helmet spattered with blood. It wasn't the hard-nosed gunner and legend staring at him now. Just some old man, blood-spattered and helpless. Maybe that was who had been there all along. None of that mattered. Not now. What did matter was getting Janice up and running. If those bastards found them like this, then nothing would matter.

He looked down at the center console. Like the Dog Pound Quest, Janice had an access cover release button between the center console and the dash. Chris hit the release button and lifted the cover.

"Okay," Chris looked at the double row of switches and the single red button labeled start. "Here's hoping the start battery is separate from the main power system."

He flipped the toggle switch labeled MASTER POWER to the ON position. The next switch was the Magnetohydrodynamic Generator Auxiliary Power Generator switch. He clicked it to ON. "Once I hit start, we'll pop up on their tac screens, boss."

"Good," Bobby said. His voice was hard and flat.

Chris looked into the rearview. Mae wasn't making those awful noises anymore. She'd gone limp, fallen forward into the Bobby's arms. He looked at Chris in the mirror. The helpless, broken old man was gone. In his place sat the flat-eyed killer Chris had glimpsed in the diner . . . Bobby Hank, the Pale Rider.

Bobby climbed into the gunner's seat. For the first time in a long time, he felt it. A quiet ember nearly extinguished by time and trouble. Mabel was a good kid, and she'd died hard. The people who did that were out there right now searching for them. Looking to spill his blood, Chris's blood. Some of those people should have been on their side, standing with them. Instead, Black Dragon and Headsman stood against them, looking to kill them.

"Start her up," Bobby said.

Chris reached into the switch well and pressed the red button. The hydraulic motor shrieked to life, powered by three thousand pounds per square inch of hydraulic fluid released from the start accumulators. The generator on the end of that motor hummed to life. When the button labeled MHD ST glowed blue, Chris hit it. Immediately the subtle thrum of the magnetohydrodynamic generator resonated through Janice. Holographic displays flashed into existence.

The tac display winked back on. Bandits Two and Three passed to their east on the remnants of a wide street moving south. Black Sunshine sat on an overpass a mile and a half to the north. Bobby pulled up the system status display. They still had the 3mm Vulcan-g and the 30mm cannon functional. Countermeasures were no longer operational, and the jammer was dead as well.

"Can you try to get our countermeasures back in action?" Bobby asked.

"I can drive, or I can mechanic."

"I'll drive." Bobby hit his harness release. "You just keep us running long enough to kill these sonsabitches."

"You got it." Chris hit his harness release and crawled through the gap into the rear of the Quest.

"Threat warning. Threat warning."

"Time to go." Bobby mashed the accelerator to the floor.

Wheels churned, and the Pale Rider Quest burst from its hiding place in a cloud of gravel and ash. He glanced at the tactical display. Bandits Two and Three angled toward them. Bobby's lips skinned back in the old predator's grin. Those Omegas were dead fast on a smooth road. Down here in the burned-out remains of Tupelo, Janice had the advantage of mobility with all-wheel drive, AI-controlled suspension, and eighteen inches of ground clearance. She was no rock climber, but Janice could damn-sure handle the rough terrain better than those low-slung death machines.

"Janice, give me off-road mode," Bobby said.

"Off-road mode engaged."

He cut the wheel and powered south across an overgrown parking lot that once belonged to *Fred's Super Dollar*, according to the rusty sign peeking through a thin covering of vines. The street behind them erupted in gouts of asphalt and fire. Bobby picked a low spot in the ashen rubble and accelerated toward it, angling away from Bandit Two and toward Bandit Three.

"Threat warning. Threat warning."

Janice powered up and over a low mound. Bobby cut the wheel hard again and accelerated. Without chaff and flare, smoke dispensers, or the jammer, their only defense against the missiles was speed and unpredictability. They bounced free of the collapsed building and onto the remnants of a wide street. He steered Janice south and floored it, rocketing away, building the distance between them and Black Sunshine's position on the overpass.

"Could you hold us steady for thirty seconds," Chris said.

"I do that, and Headsman will cram a missile up our ass." Bobby watched the tactical display. Bandit Three followed them. Bandit Two was angling to cut them off. "We must have damaged Sunshine's targeting system."

"What makes you say that?" Chris asked.

"Headsman keeps missing." Bobby aimed straight for Bandit Two across another overgrown parking lot where kudzu had crawled up over cars and rubble. "No radar lock."

"That's good," Chris said. "Cause the jammer and countermeasures runs are completely fried. That laser melted the whole thing into one big bundle. I couldn't fix this with two good hands, and I only have the one."

"Not good." Bobby checked the tac display. Bandit Two had stopped moving. "Got you." He pressed the accelerator, sending Janice up and over another mound of vine and sapling-covered brick.

The sleek black Omega 68 sat broadside to them, nose slightly elevated thanks to some creeper-covered debris. Smoke poured from the churning rear wheels. Janice's hood came down to line up with the side of the high-centered car. Bobby stroked the right-hand trigger on the steering wheel, sending a storm of hyper-accelerated tungsten ripping through the thinly armored door.

He switched the VHF to the frequency they had been using for the Luxford-Drummond team. "Hey Headsman, Black Dragon, you got your ears on?"

"We can hear you, Hank." Black Dragon said. "What do you want?"

"I just smoked one of your boys." Bobby reversed back down behind the mound of rubble. He turned south, keeping the low mounds of overgrown brick between them and Bandit Three.

"That's the name of the game," Headsman said. "Hazard pay for hazardous jobs."

"I don't know what you paid these fools, but it's too much; you might want to get a refund." Bandit Three was moving away from the Pale Riders, sticking to the broader streets where ruin and mother nature had not yet begun their reclamation.

"Not my money, honey." Black Dragon said. "See you in Memphis." The contact marked Black Sunshine accelerated northwest away from the Tupelo Dead Zone toward Memphis.

"What does that mean?" Chris asked.

"Like I thought, someone hired them to come for us." Bobby jounced onto the same broad stretch of road as Bandit Three. "Someone, not them." He skidded to a stop. Bandit Three accelerated toward them.

"What are you doing?" Chris asked.

"Getting answers." Bobby floored the accelerator. "You should strap in."

"They have a laser, Bobby." The big gunner's voice went up a half-octave.

"I know."

"You don't go heads up with another car when they have a laser."

"No." Bobby grinned into the rearview mirror. "You don't go heads up with a car when they have a Gauss cannon. Lasers are great for knife fights. This is a gunfight."

"They're both guns!"

"Quiet, boy." Bobby sped toward the Omega.

It was visible now, a black smudge silhouetted against the plume of dust and ash kicked up by its passing. The other driver would want to be sure. How they handled the ambush and subsequent hunt told Bobby they were new to this sort of fight. Rookies make rookie mistakes, like relying on the targeting computer to tell them when to shoot. Targeting computers were a great aid to skill, but they were no replacement.

He waited, finger poised on the trigger watching the range. The numbers dropped so fast that only the far left digit could be tracked, and it was ticking down at an increasing rate. The Omega's laser could kill them at half a mile on straight, smooth ground. Out here in the inbetween where road crews hadn't been seen in decades, where war and mother nature turned once smooth thoroughfares into cracked and cratered ruin, that laser wouldn't hit anything with any duration at more than fifty yards. His 3mm Vulcan-G, on the other hand, with its AI-assisted gyro stabilization? Well, it was deadly at a significantly greater distance.

Bobby caressed the trigger at two-hundred yards, sending a stream of tungsten into the hood and cockpit of the oncoming Omega. The Omega's laser burned grit and ash from Janice's hood. The anti-laser coating did its job and spread the laser's energy. Bobby kept the trigger down and powered into a skid, keeping the heavy metal storm on target. Bandit Three ripped by, front wheels turned toward Janice in an ill-conceived effort to keep the laser on target. It began a skid that turned into a roll. The sleek black car tumbled over and over before resting on its roof. Bobby smashed the brake, bringing Janice to a stop. He hit the harness release and stepped out into the settling dust and ash.

"Chris, pass me that cutter, will ya."

"S—sure." Chris slid the side door open. "Where is it?"

"Hardshell case." Bobby leaned across the pale-faced kid. He popped open the case and pulled out Mae's portable cutter and a handful of the thumb-thick cable ties before grabbing the open medkit.

"What are you doing?" Chris released his harness.

"Like I said." Bobby turned and limped toward the upside-down Omega. "Getting answers."

Mae's industrial cutter zipped through the Omega's armor like the proverbial hot knife through butter. Bobby stepped back and let the door hit the ground, sending a cloud of ash into the air. The driver hung upside down, still strapped into his seat. Tungsten rounds had turned his leg into a mangled mess of meat and bone below the knee. Bobby looped a thumb-thick cable tie around the shattered leg and yanked on it until the bleeding slowed to a drip.

The major bleeder attended to, Bobby turned to the man's torso. The hired gun's armored jacket had proved no more effective at stopping 3mm tungsten rounds than Mae's had. Bobby unzipped the man's jacket, cut away the blood-soaked layers of clothes, and doused the wounds with clotting powder.

"Why are you patching him up?" Chris's boots crunched on the grit and ash of the road.

"Can't ask a dead man questions." Bobby pulled the wounded man's helmet free. No head wounds.

His original assessment of the driver being a rookie wasn't too far off. He was young. Close-cropped hair and ink for Oklahoma Airborne Rangers on the neck told the rest of the tale. Probably had gotten out of the Oil States army and got picked up to work freelance security for one company or another. Bobby reached across the unconscious driver and fished the pistol from its holster. Moving fast, he cable-tied the driver's hands to the wrecked Omega's steering wheel before grabbing a red plastic-wrapped syringe from the medkit.

"Time to wake up, asshole." He tore the packaging away with his teeth and slammed the thick auto-injector against the unconscious man's chest.

It hummed, pumping adrenaline straight into the dangling man's heart. The unconscious driver's eyes snapped open. He inhaled in pain and surprise, then coughed violently. His arms jerked, stopping hard against the cable ties binding him to the steering wheel.

"What the—" The driver coughed and looked around, taking in the state of his vehicle before coming face to face with Bobby crouched down in the dust and ashes. "Damn…that hurts…"

"Hope your Gold Cross is paid up," Bobby said. "What's your name?"

"Should've known better than to go head to head like that," the man said.

"You got a name?"

"Sure…Conner."

"Who sent you, Conner?"

"What?" His eyes fluttered shut.

"Who sent you?" Bobby dug his fingers into the meat of the mangled leg. Pain brought Conner back around.

"Like I'm telling — "A fit of coughing cut him off, spraying the steering wheel and windshield with blood.

"Those legs are ruined, and you've been gut shot." Bobby felt around inside Conner's jacket. He grunted with satisfaction and came out with a thick envelope. "From the weight of this envelope, someone just paid you a lot of cash to drive all the way out here and try to kill me and my crew."

"I— "

"Don't talk." Bobby pulled the combat knife from its scabbard on his belt. "This can go one of a few ways. I can take your thumb and an eyeball and go see some folks I know. They'll be able to tell me everything there is to know about you in less time than it will take me to remove your thumb and eye. Hell, you might even still be alive by the time I get there. Especially if I keep the tourniquet on your leg. You ever see a man die of a gut wound?"

"Yeah." Conner nodded and swallowed.

"Bobby," Chris put a hand on his shoulder. "What are you doing."

"Getting answers." Bobby brushed the hand from his shoulder and stood up. "No shame if you ain't got the stomach. Conner here's a dead man, no matter what. The only question is, does he die several hours from now in agony, or do I loosen the tourniquet and let him bleed out quick?"

"This," Chris gestured at the wrecked Omega and the dying driver. "This is not who I thought you were."

"I know." Bobby nodded and crouched down face-to-face with Conner. "This ain't who I thought I was anymore, either. Turns out I was wrong."

Chapter 29

Bobby drove north in silence. Chris hadn't said two words since Tupelo. The kid either stared out the window at the parade of leafless branches or at the tactical display. This was not going to work if they were going to survive tonight's Pyramid Death Match.

"What's eating you?"

"You killed that man."

"That fella killed himself." Bobby shook his head. "The second he took that envelope full of cash and came hunting us, he was a dead man. He just didn't know it."

"You just cut the tourniquet and let him bleed out."

"He told us what he could," Bobby said. He thought about the thumb he'd wrapped in plastic and sandwiched between two emergency ice packs. "I kept my word."

"Did you have to torture him first?" Chris asked. His voice was rough with emotion. "You're Bobby Hank. You're one of the good guys."

Bobby brought Janice to an easy stop.

"Look, Chris. Good guys, bad guys. That's just part of what we tell ourselves so we can sleep at night."

"But you came back for me and Nate and— "

"You're trying to reconcile the man who pulled your ass out of that ambush with the monster willing to torture another person for information."

"Yeah." Chris nodded.

"They're the same." Bobby scrubbed at his face. He felt Mae's blood flaking and peeling away. "The problem is, I was too busy trying to be the good guy when I should have been busy being the monster. I forgot rule one. I was trying to tell myself I was the good guy, the hero, the legendary Bobby Hank. I was so busy selling myself a line of shit that I got Mae killed."

"You said rule one was *if you got to tell folks you're something, then you ain't.*"

"That's what I mean," Bobby said. "I'm a killer. I'm good at it. Whenever I try to be someone else, the people I love get hurt. Today that was Mae."

"So you just cut—"

"I did what I said I would." Bobby shrugged. "He was going to die either way, and as much as I hated him in the moment for what he did to Mae, for coming after my blood. I couldn't let him die screaming and begging for a drink of water or his momma."

It happened to everyone if they stayed in the game. The fire of combat burned away the thin varnish of civility, revealing the savagery and violence lurking just beneath the surface. It happened to Bobby decades ago in a war remembered by old men, history books, and movies. Today was Chris's day. Today Chris met the dark part of Robert Fulton Henry. Today the kid met Bobby Hank. Too bad that man had been dormant behind the veneer. Maybe Mae wouldn't have died kicking and choking.

He pushed through the door of the private call booth in the back of Smokey's Blacktop Bistro. The smell of old fry grease and fresh coffee made his stomach growl. It had been a long day. Two ambushes. A dead driver. Bobby sat on the stool, leaned back against the door, and let his eyes sag shut. Damned if he wasn't tired. He shook his head. No time for self-pity or self-reflection, for that matter. They needed to get back on the road. He peeled several small bills off the dead hitters' cash roll and fed them into the slot.

Bobby waited while the old-school LED display flashed to life and ran through the advertisements. First one was an ad for Dead Man's Run with an image of him on that cannibal bike with the giant gorilla in the background. Bobby shook his head. The ad switched over to a top-down view of a glass pyramid. Superimposed over the pyramid were images of him, Headsman, Black Dragon, Hal, and Raymond, and the caption read *Showdown at the Pyramid.*

"Come on." Bobby groaned. After cycling through several more ads, including one for Smokey's Blacktop Bistro and their latest upgrade, a full MMSD suite complete with financing, and a free consultation with a Gold Cross representative, the menu screen popped up.

"Finally." He punched in the number Arlo had given him and waited.

"How do you get to Carnegie Hall?" A tall thin man stared out of the screen at Bobby. High forehead starting to go bald, black hair swept back in a style out of fashion before electricity had been invented and wearing a light brown vest over a white shirt with a white ruffled cravat at his neck. Looked like Arlo was still running the same old sign and countersign gag. Usually, talking to "Salieri" made him chuckle a bit. Not today.

"Rock me, Amadeus," Bobby said.

"I figured you'd be calling."

"Cut the cloak and dagger bullshit," Bobby said. "I need that favor."

"I saw." The face and form on the screen dissolved in a flurry of pixels; Arlo's bearded face replaced Salieri's. From the look of it, he was in a truck stop booth as well. "Did she get uploaded in time?"

"What do you mean, you saw?"

"You ain't seen," Arlo asked.

"Seen what?"

"You are all over. Every channel, every streaming service, everybody who's anybody on Clutch. All talking about Bobby Hank. They've been running Mae's death over and over, or at least all the way up to when your cabin cameras shut down."

"Yeah, that tracks." Bobby leaned back against the booth door. "I think she got uploaded in time. What the hell was that contraption?"

"Homemade MMSD," Arlo said.

"Damn thing made her last moments hell."

"We're working on that." Arlo nodded. "Regular MMSDs take several hours to scan and upload a consciousness. This one does it in less than two minutes. That big-assed needle penetrates the skull and sends a couple thousand microfilaments direct into the brain. Direct connection makes for faster upload."

"So that favor…"

"I do this, Henry, I help you out, you owe me one."

"Name your price." Bobby leaned forward. "I just came into a substantial sum of cash."

"Not how this works." Arlo shook his head. "You owe me one. Maybe I collect; maybe I don't. You just have to roll them dice."

"Fine, I owe you," Bobby said. "One more thing. Get Kat out of Herolutions hands."

"That's a tall order." Arlo tipped the faded green trucker hat back and scratched his head. "I get that done, you owe me big. And I *will* collect."

"Done."

"You sure, Henry?" Arlo asked. "Getting Kat out is gonna put you in my pocket. Deep in my pocket. I ain't running no charity here. We got mouths to feed and a war to run."

"I'm sure."

"I got your word?" Arlo leaned close to the camera.

"Yeah, Arlo. You have my word." Bobby said. "You get Kat out and take care of Mae. I owe you big."

"Good enough." Arlo clapped his hands together. "Here's what you're going to do…"

Chapter 30

The wheels of civilization along the eastern seaboard ground to a halt. From New York City to Miami, from D.C. to Memphis, people stopped whatever they were doing and found their way to a screen. Fire Power Network was billing it as the greatest grudge match in the history of autoduelling. That it didn't start for several more hours did not matter.

On loading docks, shop floors, and job sites, work stopped while people clustered around phones and tablets. In homes, rich and poor alike settled in with their algae snacks to watch the Dead Man's Run. Bars and restaurants, truck stops, and even nail salons all tuned into one show - *Lock and Load*. And in the streets, people crowded around displays in store windows, trying to catch a glimpse of the action.

The set was different. No giant chromed desk. No bright lights. Just the three hosts in three oversized chairs styled to subtly remind the viewer of a crash seat. The sound was different. Instead of the driving metal anthem of *Lock and Load*, a solo electric guitar played a high and haunting melody. An earlier generation called it *Amazing Grace*. The viewers all knew it as *Duelist's Lament*. The lights came up. The camera zoomed in on the tastefully dressed, perfectly coiffured Don Northcraft.

"We are here to pay our respects to the fallen." Don's tone was serious. No million-dollar smile. "Tonight, we say farewell to the brave men and women claimed by Dead Man's Run. Won't you join us?" The music volume swelled.

The solo guitar was joined by rolling drums. The camera pulled back to encompass the three hosts and a massive curved display behind them. On the display was a picture of two young men. Though one was head and shoulders taller than the other, the family resemblance was unmistakable. They were leaning against the hood of a Luxford-Drummond Quest.

"Nathan McHenry." The screen cycled through several images of the shorter man, showing him in the usual candid slide show, clowning around in a garage, grinning and holding an amateur autoduel trophy, posing with girls in a nightclub.

"Audrey Mendoza" The images on the screen dissolved to be replaced with pictures of two young women sitting on the hood of a vintage Indra GT.

"Rita Tambour. Hannah Fields, Oliver 'Sprockets' Utley…"

It took Don a couple of minutes to finish his reading of the names. The last name he read was Mabel Holland's. The guitar and drums faded.

"We expected to lose a crew here and there to the dangers of the run." Don turned to Sasha. "But we didn't expect to lose over half in the first three days."

"Well, you know the saying, Don," Bill said. "If you can't afford to pay the piper…"

"Don't get on the dance floor." Sasha finished. "It would seem this piper charges a very high fee."

"No." Bill shook his head. "The price is the same it's always been. Sometimes the dance speeds up, is all."

"It does look like one team has decided to step off the dance floor." Don swiveled his chair so that he could see the display. Two duelist profiles flashed on the screen, Harvey 'Hal' Callahan and Raymond Russel. "The Iron Outlaws have withdrawn from Dead Man's Run. They declined to comment on their decision."

"That leaves us with just two teams for tonight's event." Sasha swiveled her chair, looking past Butcher Bill to the display.

Now, the heavy metal anthem of *Lock and Load* swelled. Flames raced across the display. When they dissipated, the giant screen was divided down the middle with four duelist profiles on display. Black Dragon and Headsman on the left, Bobby Hank and Chris McHenry on the right.

"After today's events, after Black Sunshine's unexpected betrayal in Tupelo, Black Sunshine and the Pale Rider face the Memphis Pyramid." Don swiveled back toward the camera; his million-dollar smile firmly in place.

"You mean *face-off* in the Memphis Pyramid." The view zoomed in tight on Butcher Bill.

"You don't think they will set aside their differences to survive the Pyramid?" Don asked. The view split into thirds bringing all three hosts on screen. Don on the left, Butcher Bill on the right, leaving Sasha in the middle.

"First off, Don, it's an elimination challenge." Bill shook his head. "Second, anyone with half a brain knows Black Sunshine killed Mabel Holland."

"And Bobby Hank will be out for blood," Sasha said.

"Even in the Pyramid?" Don arched one perfect eyebrow.

"Especially in the Pyramid," Bill said.

"The Pyramid is unlike any arena in the country," Don said. "A proper death maze. Traps on every level. Spiked pits, poison gas chambers, hologram-disguised pits of burning oil, and let's not forget the residents."

"That's right. The Mayor of Memphis," Sasha nodded; viewers all over the southeast could practically see the capital letters. "She transported an entire population of cannibals into the Pyramid and gave them the blueprints."

"Who are you two telling?" Bill shook his head. "I was drinking in a Beale Street bar when The Mayor moved those bloodmouth assholes in. Called it her solution to crime and entertainment. She dumped a busload of prisoners in there the very next day. Told them if they could reach the top alive, their debt to society was paid, and they were free to go."

"Did any of them make it?" Don asked.

"Not a one." Bill grinned. "They were showing the highlight reels for weeks."

"And you don't think that being locked in the Pyramid will foster some cooperation between Bobby Hank and Black Sunshine?" Don asked.

"No." Bill shook his head. "Headsman and Black Dragon took a run at Hank. Killed his driver."

"An event that has been known to occur in the arena." Sasha steepled her fingers together.

"Mabel Holland didn't die in the arena," Bill said. "She was killed in an ambush. Killed by a crew that was supposed to be on her team. There's a code out there on the road, in the inbetween. You watch the back of the folks you're with. Black Sunshine broke that code. To a man like Bobby Hank, that matters. You could put all the cannibals in the world in the Pyramid, and it won't stop Hank from settling the account."

"Odds makers have 32 to 1 against either team leaving the Pyramid if they don't work together."

"The bookies ain't never stepped foot into an arena against Bobby Hank." Bill leaned back in his chair and smiled. "He spent the last ten or twelve years running salvage in Norfolk and Virginia Beach. Cannibals ain't new to Hank. He's smart, and he's experienced. My money is on him."

"My money is on Black Dragon and Headsman." Don looked at Bill and flashed his signature smile. "The Pyramid is their home turf, and I have it on excellent authority that they are both honorary members of the people dwelling there. My source tells me they even consumed human flesh as part of the adoption rite."

"On that note," the view returned to a single screen focused on Sasha. "We have to take a break."

Flames rushed across the screen leaving behind the *Lock and Load* logo, then rushed back across the screen. The show's anthem swelled and faded, replaced by the iconic four-tone jingle for Herolutions.

Chapter 31

"We made it." Bobby shook Chris awake. Highway 22 became Highway 78 just north and west of the precrash town of Byhalia, Mississippi. The change was stark, like someone had drawn a line and decided that civilization and order reigned supreme on one side while chaos and ruin owned the other.

South of I-269, bandits, potholes, burned-out wrecks, and kudzu were the order of the day. North of the I-269 overpass, well-armed Memphis PD vehicles patrolled in pairs while road crews and their armed overwatch kept the pavement smooth and the greenery at bay.

"Incoming message," Janice said. "Shall I put it on screen?"

"Who is it?" Bobby asked.

"The Dispatcher. He seems annoyed that I will not allow him to simply come on screen."

"Put him on."

"Welcome to Memphis." The Dispatcher leered from the communication's display. "Memphis is known for several things; Elvis, the blues, and the Pyramid. Should you survive the latter, then perhaps you will get to experience the former. Who can tell?"

Bobby and Chris exchanged eye rolls.

"The Memphis Challenge, which was intended to be a team race, has been altered in response to public demand. The magnitude of support for an old-school death match was so great that we had no choice but to heed the people's call. Two cars enter, only one car leaves. Although it will not be in either of your present vehicles. No, no, no. That simply will not do at all."

Bobby leaned over and hit the mute button. "I am getting really tired of this prick."

"— a test of skill. Muscle and bone wrapped in howling steel. Both teams will be issued matching Hotshots. You will have three hours to modify and or upgrade your rides. Consider this challenge a test of skill in the arena and in the garage. Most unfortunate, you must make do without the inimitable Miss Holland. Truly tragic. Two local repair facilities have been made available to you. What is available has been dictated and funded by the fans. Follow the GPS to your facility. The modification portion of the challenge begins at 2100 sharp. Don't be late." The communications display blanked to the L&D logo.

Bobby reached over to the center console and flipped up the cover on a small panel Mae had added. He flipped the PRIVACY switch to the ON position before turning to Chris. "If you want out, now's the time."

"Why in the hell would I want out?" Chris stared at Bobby.

"Seems you might not be cut out for what comes next."

"How's that?" Chris asked.

"You've been butt-hurt over how I handled that hitter."

"You..." Chris shook his head. "If you'd cut that door loose and shot him, I would've understood that. What you did..."

"Like I told you before. Them fellas were dead and didn't know it. I needed information."

"So you—"

"Did what I had to do." Bobby watched buildings grow closer together. He slowed for the increasing traffic flow. "Odds are this is going to get a whole lot worse before it gets better. If it gets better."

"Worse?"

"From here on in, it's gonna get bloody. Squeezing a dying man for intel is gonna feel like a fun summer day by comparison."

"In," Chris said. "Black Dragon and Headsman left me and Nate as a distraction so they could get away. They killed Mae and tried to kill us."

"Only one of us is driving out of that Pyramid," Bobby said. "Those two are stone-cold killers. They won't moralize, debate, or hesitate. We can't either. You good with that?"

"I got no trouble killing in the arena." Chris nodded. "You killed those men in cold blood."

"You do it enough times, it's all in cold blood." Bobby shrugged. "Okay, now, for the second reason, I want you out."

"I just told you I'm in."

"Hear me out first." Bobby turned off the highway, following the highlighted GPS route. "I'm about to do some things that puts us on the wrong side of some serious people. There's no way they believe you weren't involved if you don't leave now."

"What are we doing?" Chris asked.

"For starters, we're stealing Mae's corpse."

"How is it stealing?" Chris glanced over his shoulder toward the cargo area where they had zipped Mae's remains into a Cryobag for preservation.

"Cause the contract states that all bodies go to Herolutions in the event of our death."

"What about Nate?"

"Different story. He was a Hardmode." Bobby shrugged. "Religious exemption clause. Herolutions has full property rights to our corpses postmortem. Their way of making sure we stick to the non-resurrection clause in the contract."

"So even if Nate hadn't been a hardmode, all those people chipping in for a Gold Cross wouldn't have mattered?"

"Pretty much." Bobby nodded. "Didn't you read your contract?"

"Johnny said it was all standard, boring, boilerplate, whatever that means."

"Who's Johnny?" Bobby asked.

"Our attorney," Chris said.

"And he didn't bother to explain any of the contract?"

"Just told us it was all standard stuff. Boring legal mumbo-jumbo were his exact words."

"Where'd you find this guy?"

"He has billboards all over Richmond."

"Wait a minute..." Bobby stared at the big gunner. "You two pups hired Johnny B?"

"Yeah," Chris said.

"Dresses like a peacock pimp?"

"Yeah."

"Tell me you didn't sign him as your agent." Bobby ran his hands over three days' worth of stubble.

"Well, Nate figured since we were big time now, we were gonna need one."

"Fan-damn-tastic." Bobby shook his head.

"What?"

"Never mind," Bobby said. "One problem at a time."

"Sure," Chris shrugged. "So why are we stealing Mae's body?"

"I'm getting her in the hands of some friends who are not friends of big corporations. That plus my refusal to play ball in Birmingham plus another favor those friends are working on will seriously piss off Herolutions and possibly Luxford-Drummond." Bobby rolled to a stop outside a closed garage door. "And those boys play for keeps."

"Is that who paid for those hitters?" Chris asked.

"Good chance that's the case," Bobby said. "It would take pretty deep pockets to put a team in three Omega 68s and even deeper pockets to put Black Sunshine on the hit."

"Count me in."

"If you're in," Bobby stared hard at Chris. "You're all the way in."

"Then I'm all the way in." Chris locked eyes with Bobby. "What's the plan?"

The Pyramid loomed large across the eastern sky, a modern-day monolith from a different age, its black armorglass shedding rain in ribbons of liquid silver. Bobby stood just inside the garage bay door, listening to the hiss of rain on pavement, watching the lightning dance.

"Certainly does look evil." Hal stood next to Bobby, wiping grease from his hands.

"Have to admit," Bobby turned away from the open shop door. "It's a mite imposing."

When he and Chris rolled into the repair facility Hal and Ray were waiting, packed bags at their feet, slung weapons on their shoulders. Without a word, they'd helped Bobby and Chris unload the four cryo-bags before getting to work putting Janice back to rights.

Bobby checked his watch. Nearly 2100 hours. The race official would be there any minute to start the clock. Fatigue dragged at his mind, scratched at his eyes every time he blinked. The white-hot fury that burned in his guts back in Tupelo had guttered out, replaced by a cold gnawing ache that could only be filled by gun smoke and death.

"You and Ray should take the kid and get going." Bobby pulled a fat envelope from his blood-stained jacket. "No need for you to be a part of this."

"Horse shit, Hank." Hal pushed the envelope away. "You're gonna need a support crew for this run, and you're gonna need a driver."

"I've run these sorts of things solo before." Bobby held up the envelope again. "Give this to Chris and go. It's more than enough cash to start over anywhere he wants."

"No." Hal pushed the envelope aside. "You've never run the Pyramid. And no one has ever survived a solo death match against Black Dragon and Headsman."

"That's only because I've been busy."

"It's suicide." Hal shook his head. "You know as well as I do if the vehicles are evenly matched, it comes down to crew skill. One head ain't enough. You'll have to handle driving and shooting. Dragon will outdrive you while you're trying to shoot, and Headsman will outgun you while you're trying to drive…suicide."

"Maybe that's what has to happen." He looked at the four bright blue bags. They were still fully inflated, their holographic displays showing a stable 34 degrees.

"What?" Hal asked.

"Maybe this is how it ends for me."

"Bullshit." Hal snorted. "You might be buying that 'over the hill' nonsense. I ain't. You just got yourself a belly full of regret. That's all."

"I got Mae killed back there, in Tupelo," Bobby said.

"No." Hal shook his head. "Mae got herself killed back there. She strapped into that seat and took the same chances as the rest of us."

"No." Bobby turned back to the open door. "Those were paid hitters, and it sure wasn't Black Sunshine paying the bill."

"Who you figure is paying the bills?"

"Maybe Luxford-Drummond, maybe someone bigger." Bobby shrugged. "Either way, I want the kid out. And I want y'all out. Mae didn't get killed in the arena, taking the risks she signed up to take. She got killed out there on the road 'cause someone paid those assholes to kill me. She was collateral damage. Just like Kat."

"And that's all your fault?" Hal asked. "The great Bobby Hank is responsible for every bad thing that happens around him?"

"Hal— "

"Maybe she was collateral damage. Maybe her dying out there on the road was your fault. Maybe your wife developing

CDRS is your fault too. Hell, maybe the last damned grain blight was your doing. Or maybe, just maybe, everyone makes their choices and takes their chances." Hal jammed the rag in his back pocket. "Maybe Mae was riding with you because she believed in you. Same as Kathrine. Same as us and same as that man over there." Hal pointed at Chris's hulking form, hunched over and backlit with the searing blue light of the welder.

"Hal," Bobby leaned in close. "After tonight, whoever is after me will be after you too. You stick around, and they'll believe you're in on it no matter what you tell them."

"In on what?" Hal asked.

"For starters," Bobby put a hand on Hal's shoulder. "Bringing Mae back."

"How is that going to piss off whoever is gunning for you?"

"One, it's a contract violation. Two, you noticed how everyone who's died on this run is permanently dead?" Bobby asked.

"Nate was a hardmode." Hal said.

"Right, so no reboot for him," Bobby nodded. "The Skull Monkeys and Rolling Thunder dead and their bodies torched."

"They rolled out on their own," Hal said. "Sons of Vulcan were waiting on them. Spiked to your ride and burned is standard Vulcan vengeance killing. Sends a message, I'm told."

"Maybe so, but they're still permanently dead," Bobby said. "Tornado Express took a direct hit from that artillery— "

"That was just plumb bad luck." Hal shook his head. "Could have happened to any of us."

"Sure, them taking a direct hit like that." Bobby nodded. "But every last one of them is permadead, all out there on the road, between the cities. I bet none of them have Gold Cross or a backup stored away waiting for their untimely demise."

"Okay…"

"Mae has a backup," Bobby said.

"How?"

"You know how we dropped out of sight for a while after South Boston?"

"Yeah," Hal said. "You said you holed up in some farmer's barn and did the repairs."

"We weren't in some farmer's barn." Bobby shook his head. "We were in an FMS repair facility."

"Shit," Hal stepped back. "You're tied up with those assholes?"

"I am now." Bobby shrugged.

"Still don't explain how Mae's got a backup stored away."

"From what I can tell, Mae and the FMS crew installed some kind of MMSD. She used it to upload. It drained the entire battery charge to do it. But I'm pretty sure I have Mae stored in this." Bobby pulled a metal cube out of his coat.

Hal whistled, "That's impossible." He lifted the cube, hefting it and turning it from side to side. "This holds all of her?"

"Best I can tell." Bobby nodded. "Hell of a lot smaller than the current models."

"What are you going to do with it?" Hal returned the cube to Bobby.

"Get it to some folks that will grow her a new body."

"Don't they need her original meat for that to work?" Hal asked.

"Different crew is coming to pick that up." Bobby tucked the cube back inside his armored jacket.

"Why not pick up the meat and the mind at the same time?"

"Don't know." Bobby shrugged. "My instructions are to drop this at a particular place at a particular time. Someone else is handling the body. Standard FMS practice, I'm told."

"Man, I just can't wrap my head around you stooging for those terrorist pricks," Hal said.

"I don't know that they are," Bobby said.

"What?"

"I don't know that they're terrorist pricks." Bobby turned back to the rain-drenched evening.

"For God's sake, Hank," Hal said. "They destroyed Pine Creek. Burned it to the ground!"

"How many women and kids did they hurt?"

"What?"

"Women and kids," Bobby turned back to the shop. "How many women and kids got hurt in that attack?"

"I…I can't rightly say."

"I can't either, but since no one was raising hell about it, I bet it's none." Bobby shook his head. "That's the point. All we know is what the corporations and the government tell us, and in case you ain't noticed, the corporations seem to have a lot more pull than they used to."

"So you're turning revolutionary now?"

"No." Bobby turned up his collar and pulled his battered hat down low. "I'm just trying to make a couple things right, and for now, today, that means getting in bed with Free Mountain. Hell, I've already been in bed with the devil."

"How you gonna do that and prep your ride for tonight?"

"Well," Bobby turned back to the shop. "Chris was going to handle the mods and upgrades while I take a little walk."

"How about this?" Hal said. "How about Ray and I sign on as support crew for team Pale Rider. We'll take your winnings and some of ours and bet on you in the showdown. You win, we'll take the winnings and pick up a proper support vehicle. Anything else you win after that, we get half."

"After tonight, we're going to be up against whoever tried to kill us. They're gonna know we know, and they're gonna come for us," Bobby looked at Hal, then at Chris and Raymond. Chis had his welding helmet up, laughing. "All of us."

Hal grinned, "Hell, Hank, they already came for all of us. How do figure the Sons of Vulcan got their hands on four 200mm artillery pieces?"

The officials for Dead Man's Run arrived in a convoy of slick firepower. A brand new Luxford-Drummond Cormorant, three large vans, and a tow truck rolled to a stop in the hissing rain. Crew in body armor and coveralls sporting Dead Man's Run logos disgorged from two vans and set to work unstrapping and unloading the machine on the flatbed. The crew from the third van unloaded a stretcher and headed for the cryobags laid out along the south side of the shop.

"Let's see what Santa brought us." Hal and Bobby turned to watch the corporate crew push the low-slung machine into the bay.

"Evening." A good-natured voice called.

"Evening," Bobby turned to watch Gordon Corey enter the repair bay.

No coveralls or body armor for him. Gordon wore another charcoal gray suit, probably a Salvatore Giovanni if Bobby had to guess. Gordo had always been something of a dandy. The only concession made to weather or environment was an equally well-suited and booted assistant carrying an umbrella to keep Gordon dry on his trip from the sedan to the shop. The assistant paid the icy rain that soaked him no more mind than Gordon paid the umbrella.

"You run out of company asses to kiss?" Hal asked.

"Nice to see you again, Harvey Callahan," Gordon said. "Seems you're still harder to kill than a Poughkeepsie cockroach."

"I'll take that as a compliment." Hal chuckled and stepped forward to shake Gordon's hand. "How's life as a sell-out?"

"Safe." Gordon watched the Dead Man's Run crew remove the cover. "Often boring, but safe."

"What did you bring us?" Bobby asked.

"A classic."

"It's a goddamn relic." Ray stood staring at the unveiled machine.

"You want us to run the Pyramid in that?" Bobby stared at the low-slung fastback.

"What the hell did you do, rob a museum?" Hal asked.

"What's the big deal?" Chris pulled off the welding helmet and started walking around the Hotshot.

"Side armor is real thin on these things," Hal said.

"Maybe," Chris ran one hand along the sleek slope of the hood. "But this baby won the first two Division 15 Championships."

"In case you ain't noticed, things have changed significantly since then." Hal walked to the rear of the Hotshot and squatted to look underneath. "It still has the rear flame throwers. You really did rob a museum."

"Not exactly." Gordon watched his crew continue to unload several crates from the vans and the back of the flatbed. "Back in '60, Drummond was one of the first to mass produce arena ready cars. The Hotshot was one of those models. When Luxford Automotive merged with Drummond to form Luxford-Drummond, they acquired an entire warehouse full of unsold stock, including this beauty and several others like it."

"So this thing has been in a warehouse for sixteen years?" Bobby stepped to the gunner's door, pulled it open, and looked inside.

It had been some time since he'd seen the inside of a Hotshot, and this was an early example. No targeting computer, no AI, no tactical displays, no radar. Just four wheels, an oversized powerplant, four flamethrowers, and two machine guns. It still had that new car smell all these years later.

"It has."

"Does it run?" Chris opened the driver's door.

"We took her and seven more out on the L&D test track back in August." Gordon slapped the hood. "She works just fine."

"So what are the actual terms of the challenge?" Bobby sat down in the passenger seat.

"Death Maze Elimination," Gordon said. "The goal of this challenge has always been to winnow down the L&D eight pack to just one team. The winner of the Pyramid will go on to make the next leg of the race to Chicago. Now that we are down to just two teams, this will be a Death Maze Death Match."

"You are one heartless bastard," Ray said.

"Hey, you boys knew the score when you signed on." Gordon shrugged. "Besides, y'all have put up a spectacular performance. Ratings are through the roof. There won't be a single screen in the country tuned to anywhere but Dead Man's Run. Hell, the pay-per-views for tonight's event have earned more than the last five autoduel seasons combined."

"Fine by me." Bobby got out of the Hotshot. "What are the terms of the match? And don't give me that showman horseshit that the Dispatcher likes to sling. I want the real terms."

"Sure. Just one small thing first." Gordon looked at Ray and Hal. "All non-participants have to go. This is a privileged conversation."

"Suck it, buttshark," Hal said.

"Gordon," Bobby closed the Hotshot's door and grinned. "I'd like you to meet my newly signed support crew."

"You boys sure?" Gordon asked.

"Why the hell wouldn't we be?" Hal walked around the Hotshot to stand next to Bobby.

"From here on in, things get serious," Gordon said. "The run from here to Chicago is gonna be Fox and Hounds. Between the sponsors and fan crowdfunding, they have enough cash to charge up every bounty hunter, hitter, and bandit from here to Canada to be hounds. They've had weeks to make the trip. Support crew is just another term for leverage."

"We ain't your average support crew." Ray walked around the rear of the Hotshot to stand on Bobby's other side.

"Fair enough." Gordon turned to the very wet assistant with the umbrella. "Kelly, please append Iron Outlaw's contract to reflect their conversion from active race team to support crew for team Pale Rider and update the liability release forms to reflect their acceptance of risk for leg two of Dead Man's Run."

"Right away." Kelly handed the umbrella to Gordon before making a sharp about-face and returning to the armored sedan.

"Here are the terms." Gordon turned and walked to a stool and sat. "Death Maze Death Match. Both teams have three hours to modify their vehicles with the provided material. You will load up and drive to the starting line at the end of those three hours. Black Sunshine gets a thirty-minute head start since they were the first to arrive in Memphis. Victory conditions are simple. Be the only car to roll out of the exit."

"Why not kill them both now and get it over with?" Hal shook his head. "The Pyramid's Black Dragon and Headsman's home turf."

"That has been taken into account," Gordon said. "Do you accept the terms?"

"We do." Bobby stuck out his hand.

Chapter 32

Winter in Memphis is a varied and bipolar season. Some days are achingly clear. Some are gray and wet. Most days, wet or dry, it's bitter cold. Occasionally the weather turns warm and mild, like spring come early. Bobby had been in Memphis a time or two in the winter. Not once had he caught a mild day. Today was no exception.

Bobby turned up the collar of his jacket and stepped onto the sidewalk. On one hand, the weather would make it hard for the cameras to follow him. On the other hand, he would be cold and wet long before he reached the address Arlo had given him.

He turned west on Union, put his head down, and picked up the pace. Mae's death sat on him like a hundred-pound bag of cement, not quite crushing but much more than he was prepared to carry at this stage of life. Turning left on 4th Street, he heard Beale long before he saw it through the pelting rain. Muted drum and bass rhythms pointed the way as surely as any neon sign.

Stepping onto Beale, he paused. Time can change a lot of things. Time allied with famine, plague, and societal collapse had changed nearly everything. Everything except Beale Street. Some places just seem to go on no matter what; Duval Street in Key West, Bourbon Street in New Orleans, and Beale Street in Memphis. Different buildings, different weather, different cultures, same place. The world may have ended, but people still wanted something to eat, something to drink, and to see someone naked, and not necessarily in that order.

Bobby walked with his head up and his coat clear of his gun. Beale Street was not the place to look like an easy target. The early hour and wet weather conspired to drive most people inside or at least close to the various bars, brothels, and sludge pits that lined both sides of Beale from 4th Street to Riverside Drive. A rainbow of flashing neon and high-resolution holograms beckoned, promising cheap booze and reasonably priced company. Bobby shook his head and kept walking, ignoring several half-hearted come-ons from brothel doors. He found his destination sandwiched between a Graceland Tabernacle of the Risen King and B.B. King's Blues Club.

Bobby stood beneath the flickering neon sign that switched from the silhouette of a woman performing an improbable act on a pole to that of a man in the same position. He rechecked the address before pulling the durasteel and armorglass door open.

Standing in the tiny entry were two women. Their low-cut tops and skin-tight pants said fun. The well-worn grips of their weapons said trouble. Bobby stood still and waited for them to make the first move.

"Cover's fifty, weapons are peace bonded, or you can piss off elsewhere." The one on the left said. She was at least two inches taller than Bobby, and that didn't count her lime green liberty spiked hair.

"Fair." Bobby raised his hands. "I'm here to see a man about a train."

"Train station's on the north side of town."

"This train don't have a station, and the conductor only takes you one way."

"Get those hands all the way up." The one on the right let the barrel of her weapon drift into line with his head. She was also tall but sported a clean-shaven head, the swirling tattoos making it look like one of those Mexican Day of the Dead skulls.

"Sure thing." He raised both hands high like he was trying to touch the ceiling. Spikes stepped forward with a small hand-held device and passed it over him. It gave out a series of chirps and bleeps.

"He's clean." She stepped back.

"Follow me." Baldy lifted her weapon away from Bobby's face, turned and pulled the heavy door open, and stepped through.

A blast of hot air and heavy bass washed over him, smelling of perfumed sweat, stale beer, and fried algae. He followed his escort through the club, the pounding house music a near physical presence beating and throbbing against him. On stage, a heavily muscled man and a leggy woman coated in sweat and oil kept the mixed crowd's rapt attention with their rhythmic gyrations around the gleaming poles at either end of the narrow, neon-lit platform. Scantily clad waitstaff swayed through the crowd, keeping everyone well supplied with strong drink and unfulfilled promises of other delights just out of reach.

His guide passed around the end of the bar and pulled open another heavily armored door gesturing with her shotgun for him to proceed. Bobby quirked an eyebrow at her.

"This is my stop." She gestured down the black-carpeted stairs to a polished wooden door. "Down there, through that door. The conductor is behind the door at the end of the hall. You're on camera, so don't go snooping. Folks on this train like their privacy. You follow?"

"I follow." Bobby stepped through. The door closed with an echoing bang and the buzzing click of a magnetic lock reactivating.

Ears ringing in the sudden silence, Bobby descended, his boots making little sound on the deep pile carpet. The door at the bottom was either some dark wood or had been stained dark. It looked like someone had stolen it from an old-time movie about prohibition, with a brass knob and large back plate polished to a high shine. Bobby turned the knob and pulled. The weight of the door dispelled any illusion of another time and place. No matter how you dressed it up, armored doors were heavy.

Stepping through the door, he could have sworn he'd stepped into one of those old movies. Dark doors punctuated the bare-brick walls, each gleaming with polished brass knobs and placards inscribed with numbers and names in heavy calligraphy. Bobby focused on the door at the end of the hall and made for it, the *tok* of his boot heels on the mint-green tile nearly loud enough to drown the sounds of passion, pain, and occasional laughter that bled through those doors. Not his business.

The door at the end of the hall was solid durasteel with no effort at disguising it. It had been polished to the point Bobby could see a distorted version of himself reaching for the knob. Even with dim lights and a weak reflection, the face looking back at him looked like hell. He had three days' worth of graying stubble, and the bags under his eyes looked large enough to hold a change of clothes. Old, tired, and worn out is what that face said to the world.

"Fix your face, Hank." He turned the knob.

The click-buzz of a mag-lock releasing echoed down the bricks and tile. He pulled the door open and stepped into another tight entry, this one devoid of guards and cased from floor to ceiling in polished durasteel. Same for the ceiling. The floor tile matched the hallway and sloped to a brass screen-covered drain.

"Close the door behind you, sir," a voice said. "The inner door cannot open unless the outer door is closed and locked."

"All right." Bobby let the polished door swing closed. The click-buzz of a mag-lock engaging was loud in the small space, making the hair on the back of his neck stand up. This was a kill box. "Now what?"

"This way, sir," said the voice. A rectangle outlined in blue-white light appeared opposite the door. It slid back an inch or so before sliding left into the wall revealing stark white tile and polished steel walls.

"You don't want me to leave my weapons?"

"Sir, you are at present a guest, and guests are allowed to retain their personal effects and weapons. Should your status as guest be revoked," the voice said, "no weapon you could carry here would be enough to cause undue trouble."

"Where the hell is Hank?" Hal asked.

"He did say he was walking to the drop spot." Chris checked his watch. It read ten-twenty, right on time. Hal had been asking that question every twenty minutes for the past hour.

"He also said it was just over on Beale," Hal popped up from under the right-hand side of the Hotshot, wiping his hands on a rag. "Between B.B. King's and one of those Graceland Tabernacles."

"Elvis freaks are something else," Raymond said. His feet were still the only thing Chris or Hal had seen of the Outlaw gunner for the last hour.

"How's the mine dropper coming?" Chris walked over to Ray's feet and squatted down.

"Just hooked up the mag feed to the dropper." Ray rolled out from under the rear of the vintage dueling machine. "You think Hank's in trouble."

"Hell, Ray." Hal walked to a nearby open crate and fished out a test magazine. "I know he's in trouble. The question is— "

"What's the question?"

Chris jumped and turned at Bobby's gruff voice coming from the open shop door.

"Bobby." Chris ran to him. "You look like hell."

"Feel like it." Bobby put an arm around the big man's shoulders and limped into the shop, leaving a bloody boot print every other step.

"The question was whether or not you needed help." Hal jogged over to Janice's open side door and pulled out the medkit.

"Clearly, we have an answer." Ray swept aside tools and discarded packaging on the nearby workbench. "Let's get him up here so we can take a look."

"I'm good," Bobby said.

"You're bleeding." Chris guided Bobby to the bench.

The old man looked bad. He was gray-faced and sweating. His breath came in short, shallow gasps. Chris was no doc, but this looked a lot like what the training courses called shock.

"Okay, kid." Ray ducked under the wounded man's other arm. "Hook his leg with your free hand and lift when I say lift."

Chris did as the older man said, the two forming a human chair. "Lift," Ray nodded, and they both lifted Bobby onto the bench and laid him flat using an empty cardboard as a pillow.

"Get the coat open." Hal unrolled the medkit. "We need to find the bleed."

"It's not as bad as it looks," Bobby said. "Most of the blood's not mine."

"Where you hit?" Hal asked.

"Lower left— just above the belt," Bobby panted. Hal pulled the armored jacket open.

Chris leaned over to see. A hole about as big around as his index finger leaked blood where Bobby said it would be. The old man's pants and shirt were soaked with blood.

"That's a lot of blood." Chris stepped back, his stomach churning.

"Easy, kid." Ray shoved a work light into his hand. "Hold this so Hal and I can see to patch Hank up."

Chris took the proffered light, pointing the bright beam at the bleeding hole. "Is he going to be okay?" He watched Hal roll the wounded man onto his side and check his back before rolling him flat again.

Hal looked at Chris and Ray. "The bullet's still in there."

"Does that mean you're going to operate?" Chris asked.

He was new to handling bullet wounds. He'd been wounded a couple times in the arena back in Virginia, but both times medics had treated him. Sure, he'd watched the first aid and combat medicine vids when he and Nate decided to make a run at becoming pros. They'd even taken a class put on by the Southside Rangers with a pretty lifelike dummy. None of it was like this.

"No." Hal shook his head. "He ain't pumpin' blood out through that hole, and it don't stink like shit, so I figure we leave it alone till we can get him to a doc."

"No doc." Bobby shook his head. "Pyramid first."

"Can you drive?" Chris looked from Hal to Bobby and back to Hal. "Can he drive like this?"

"He's a stubborn sumbitch. But even Hank here ain't driving like this." Hal shook his head.

"Y—you," Bobby grabbed Chris's arm. The old man's grip was still like a vise. "You drive."

"He's going to need some blood to replace what he's lost." Hal unscrewed the cap on a tube of quickseal and squirted the neon green goop over the leaking wound. It began to bubble and fizz.

"Get a pressure bandage on it, keep the seal in place…" Bobby hissed, teeth clenched against the pain. The fizzing stopped. A rubbery green shell now covered the hole.

"You're ten pounds of crazy in a three-pound sack." Ray shook his head. "You have at least one bullet rattling around in your guts, and you want to just slap a bandage on it, top off and get back in the seat."

"Got to," Bobby said. "I drop out, Mae stays dead, and the company will keep Kat."

"What?" Hal asked.

"Herolutions." Bobby swallowed. "They got their hands on Kat's MMSD. They say they have a program that could cure her CDRS. They said they would help her if I played ball and made a comeback. If I refused, they promised to keep downloading her and studying her death and send me the video."

"You didn't try to go after them on your own?" Ray pulled a length of IV tubing from the medkit, a small bag of dark blue fluid, and two sterile IV needles. He cut the tubing into two lengths and affixed a sterile needle to each one.

"They didn't open with the or else bit," Bobby said. "We got any quikblood?"

"No." Ray dragged a stool over next to the workbench and sat. "Gonna have to do this old school. Person to person infusion."

"We don't even know his blood type." Chris looked from Raymond to Bobby. "What's your blood type?"

"B positive." Bobby grinned.

"Funny." Chris shook his head. Lying on a bench, a hole in his guts, and he was cracking jokes.

"His type doesn't matter all that much." Raymond affixed one of the modified tubes to the blue bag before handing the bag to Chris. "This stuff makes any blood compatible with any other blood. When this was new, they said you could take a transfusion from a goat." He handed the end with the needle to Hal.

"So your blood mixed with this blue goop will be compatible with Bobby's?" Chris stared down at the bag. It had two chambers, ribbed tubes, two small petcock-looking valves, and a pull tab.

"That's the idea." Hal rolled up Raymond's sleeve and swabbed the inside of his elbow.

"And Hal can do IVs?"

"Been a few years, but yeah." Hal looked at Chris. "Now stop talking. I need to concentrate."

Chris had at least ten or fifteen more questions swirling around in his head. He clamped his lips closed and watched instead. He was a tough guy. Growing up on a farm that borders the HRDZ made sure of that. He'd shot his first cannibal at twelve. He'd been the fourth of seven and had watched cancer take his Papaw a few years back. Some kind of treatment-resistant strain, the doctors had said. Either way, he was no stranger to pain and death. But these three old men were something else.

Chapter 33

Bobby gingerly lowered himself into the gunner seat of the vintage dueling machine. He gave the sour-faced man in white coveralls with a clipboard and holographic stopwatch a thumbs up and a grin. They'd made it with at least three minutes to spare.

"Little something for the road." Hal passed him a duffel with spare magazines for his carbine and .45. "I know how much you love staying strapped in."

"Doubt I'll be getting out for this one." Bobby tucked the duffel under his legs. It was heavier than a bag of spare mags ought to be. He shifted the top layer of carbine magazines and saw another bag held closed with Velcro straps. He looked back up at Hal, cocked one eyebrow, and reached for the seat harness.

"Hank," Hal leaned into the car and helped him pull the shoulder straps into place. "You've gotten out of the car on nearly every challenge. I don't expect this'll be any different." Hal glanced meaningfully at the bag, then back at Bobby and gave him a wink.

"He's not wrong." Chris finished clicking into the restraint. "Man, I miss that suspended seat rig in the Quest."

"Yeah," Raymond leaned in through the driver's door and checked the old-school harness. "Really makes a difference when you're trying to focus on the road and deal with impacts and bad terrain."

"Time is up." The official in white said. The holographic timer flashed three red zeros. "We will now inspect the vehicle for compliance." A team of men and women in white coveralls with clipboards approached the Hotshot.

"Listen," Ray gave Chris's harness straps a tug. "Black Dragon and Headsman want you to think they're going to try for the quick kill early in the duel…."

"Bastards are going to wait till we get snagged in some trap or get stuck in with the bloodmouths." Bobby checked the carbine's magazine before locking it into the mount. "Then they'll hit us. When they do, it will be hard, fast, and with everything they got."

"And they got a lot." Hal nodded toward the bag of spare magazines. "I checked the Clutch feed. They put up several million dollars of their own money."

"I follow Sandy Decker on there," Ray said. "She posted a video for the 'sick ass build' she was doing for Black Sunshine. Pretty sure I saw an empty crate for a Bluestar 105mm."

"How the hell are we going to go up against that?" Chris said.

"My advice," Ray patted Chris's shoulder and grinned. "Don't get hit." The old gunner stepped back from the car and closed the door.

"Start time." The race official called.

"All right kids, don't do anything I wouldn't do." Hal closed the gunner's door and stepped away from the Hotshot."

"Easy." Bobby looked at Chris. "Black Dragon and Headsman bleed just like everyone else. They'll die same as everyone else."

Bobby watched the massive entry gate for the Pyramid compound roll back. Down here on the ground, it was bigger than it looked on the screen. Way bigger. He looked over at Chris. The big man still gripped the steering wheel like a drowning man hanging on to a scrap of driftwood.

"You plan on driving this thing or strangling it to death?" Bobby asked.

"What?" Chris's head snapped around.

"You squeeze that wheel any tighter, you'll leave permanent finger grooves." Bobby nodded toward Chris's white knuckles.

"Oh…" He let go of the wheel for a moment, flexing his hands.

"Don't sweat it." Bobby took hold of the weapons control yoke. Some fans had paid to have a Dobson Eagle drone dropped. Hal or maybe Ray had installed it along with a brand new FCX-20 tactical computer. He cycled through the settings menu to the controls page using the middle thumb controls. He assigned the two linked machine guns in the front to the right trigger, the right flamethrower to the right thumb button, and the left flamethrower to the left thumb button. The rear machine gun had been assigned to the left trigger, and the mine dropper had been wired directly into a foot pedal on the left side of the gunner's foot well.

"You aren't nervous?" Chris looked over at Bobby.

"Nervous?" Bobby did a quick inventory of the duffel Hal had given him and gave the smaller bag a closer inspection. Looked like Hal had rigged up some kind of satchel charge. "Not really. I've been around this particular block so many times I've worn grooves in the pavement."

"You ain't worried about Black Dragon and Headsman waiting somewhere in there?" Chris nodded toward the massive structure peeking through the opening gate. "Black Dragon said they pay the Mayor to let them run the Pyramid just for practice."

"Black Dragon says a lot of stuff." Bobby pulled the spare magazines from the duffel and stowed them in the pockets of his armored jacket.

"Pale Rider, Iron Outlaw." Hal's voice broke in. Static hissed and popped in the background giving Hal that old-school CB radio sound. "Radio Check from pit two. Radio Check from pit two."

Bobby switched the radio to HOT MIC, "Got you loud and clear, Hal."

"Same," Chris said.

"Still crapping your pants, Chris?"

"A little." Chris looked at Bobby and gave him WTF hands.

"Good." Hal chuckled.

"How is feeling like this good?"

"Fear's a tool." Bobby said, "A little bit keeps you alive, keeps you from doing foolish things. Too much leaves you paralyzed."

"Aren't you afraid?"

"Yep." Bobby nodded. "Afraid of failing, afraid of what happens if we don't win, afraid of letting Kathrine, Mabel, and you down."

"That's what you're afraid of?" Chis looked through the open gate. Fire shot into the sky from massive bonfires scattered between the walls and the black glass of the pyramid. People danced around those fires, leaping and cavorting, the firelight briefly illuminating painted skin.

"And spiders." Bobby gave a shiver.

"Spiders?" Chris laughed.

"I really hate spiders."

They sat at Gate Four. The Pyramid had eight such gates; four led down to the subterranean levels. Gate Four had a distinctly downward slope.

"Weapons hot." Bobby lifted the spring-loaded red cover on the WPN SLCT switch and clicked it to the ON position.

"Roger. Good luck." Hal radioed.

"Looks dark in there." Chris stared straight ahead, eyes fixed on the traffic light above the durasteel grid blocking their path. The light was still red.

"Yeah," Bobby said. "My bet is the lighting is controlled by the bloodmouths that live here."

"NVGs?"

"Not yet." Bobby cycled through the light amplification on his helmet. Night vision was something of a misnomer. For it to work, there needed to be some sort of light, even if it was infrared. Hal and Raymond had mounted IR emitters around the Hotshot, but combat damage would render them increasingly ineffective. Better to start with plain old white floodlights and switch to night vision if they had to. Odds were the lighting would get better. Otherwise, no show for the subscribers, and this show was sold out.

"Yellow." Chris's voice broke through Bobby's reverie.

"Ready?" The gate slid left into the wall.

"Yep."

"Still freaked out?"

"A little."

"Remember, this is a duel, not a race. Only one of us is driving out of here tonight." Bobby looked at Chris and grinned. "Let's make sure it's us."

The light turned green. Bright white lights snapped on, illuminating the narrow tunnel leading beneath the Pyramid. Black scorch marks marred the glossy white paint on the walls, and several layers of burned rubber tire tracks stretched off into the maze.

"Glad we didn't go for the NVGs?" Bobby checked the small tactical readout mounted to the center dash. Some prince of a supporter had ponied up a third-generation Ironsight TMD-20. It used radio, lasers, and sonar to generate a reasonably accurate 3D image of the immediate surroundings.

"Yeah." Chris glanced at the tactical display. "How'd you know?"

"Lucky guess," Bobby said. "Let's get rolling."

"Right." Chris eased the Hotshot forward into the tunnel. The gate with its wrist-thick durasteel bars rolled shut behind them.

Down, down, down they went. The walls continued to scroll up as their platform descended. Bobby counted eight different floors before they came to a stop. A red-lit open tunnel not much wider or taller than their Hotshot stretched off to the right. A digital counter was spooling down from thirty on the wall in front of them.

"How the hell are we supposed to get in there?" Chris asked.

"Hold the brake, cut the wheel, and get those tires spinning," Bobby said. "Pretty sure we don't want to be in here when that counter hits zero."

"This is going to be really tight." Chris followed Bobby's instructions. Smoke rolled up from the spinning rear tires reducing visibility to feet. Once the rear wheels really broke loose, he cut the wheel. The rear end of the Hotshot slung around, pointing them at the smoke-hazed opening. He released the brake, rear wheels spinning, they began to roll forward. Chris hit the red AWD button on the steering wheel. The front wheels engaged, snapping the small car forward into the narrow, red-lit tunnel.

"Brake, brake, brake!" Bobby shouted. The tunnel made a hard left turn, the wall to their front a mass of gleaming spikes.

"Shit." Chris cut the wheel and powered into a wheel-spinning drifting turn.

Bobby cringed away from the door anticipating durasteel spikes puncturing the thin side armor at any moment. When that didn't happen, he opened his eyes. The tunnel wall was less than an inch from the gunner side mirror and flying by.

"Damn, kid." Bobby laughed. "I didn't know you could do that."

"Me either," Chris said.

"How long have we been down here?" Chris checked the rear and side view mirrors.

The big guy had been doing that a lot since their narrow escape from the previous level. Being constantly ambushed tended to have that effect. The Pyramid dwellers had come out of holes in the walls riding small single-seat machines, lightly armored, and armed with .50s if the noise and fresh holes in the right side armor were any indication. It seemed like the little bastards were around every turn. Repeated use of the side-mounted flame throwers and a couple of well-timed dropped mines had finally discouraged that sort of behavior.

"Fifteen, maybe twenty minutes." Bobby kept a close eye on the tactical screen. No threats or unknown contacts on the Ironsight. Not that it was a lot of help in the claustrophobic tunnels. Even with the distance tolerances set to the lowest possible resolution, there was little to no warning. The sound of rounds on armor was the first and only sign of trouble. Worse, everything down here was low and tight. If they had to bail out, he was going to have to find a way to break through armorglass from the inside since the walls were much too close to allow the doors to open.

"Already feels like forever."

"Time moves funny in a fight." Bobby scanned left to right. "The lull between attacks feels like an eternity. Then, when things heat back up, an hour feels like thirty seconds."

"Tunnel exit ahead." Chris rechecked the rearview.

"All right, we play it just like the last one." Bobby eyed the opening. Flickering red-orange lit it like a narrow gateway into hell. "Keep us in motion. A moving target is a hard target."

"Right." Chris steered them through the narrow tunnel opening out onto flat concrete. "Is that another one of your rules?"

It was a cavernous space, the ceiling lost overhead in a layer of haze and smoke from scattered fires. Near the middle loomed a large and amorphous mound.

"No." Bobby shook his head. "But it ought to be."

"What is that?" Chris turned left, keeping their distance from the mound and the armorcrete walls.

"Can't tell at this distance." Bobby checked the Ironsight. It had identified no less than thirty contacts as unknown, clustered on the far side of the mound.

"I think it's some kind of scrap heap." Chris slowed the Hotshot to an easy ten miles per hour.

"Glad you could make it, Hank." The radio flattened Black Dragon's voice, but it was definitely her.

"Does she always have to sound so damned smug?" Chris mashed the accelerator to the floor and cut the wheel, sending the Hotshot fishtailing away from the wall.

"Easy, cowboy."

"That you, Dragon?" Hal broke in.

The light in the space grew brighter bit by bit. Bobby could see the mound clearly now. It was less a scrap heap and more of a monument to the defeated. Scorched paint, torn and punctured metal, and spider-webbed glass formed a flat-topped ziggurat of dead cars fifty feet high. Jets of fire shot from pipes built into the corners, and smaller fires in tire rim braziers ignited, illuminating white shining steps leading to the top. At the foot of the steps squatted the other Hotshot, firelight reflecting from the glossy hood.

"Who else could it be?" she asked.

"Hard to tell. You corporate skanks all sound the same on the radio."

"Walk soft, old man." Even flattened by the radio, there was no mistaking the gentle menace of Headsman's voice.

"Hold up." Bobby put a hand on Chris's arm. "Looks like they want to palaver a bit before we set to killing one another."

"What?" Chris hit the brakes bringing the Hotshot to a skidding stop.

"What do you want?" Bobby glanced back down at the tactical display. More contacts were streaming into the cavernous space from all directions. Several of those low-slung gun carts zipped past. One driver, their vehicle covered in soot, shot him the bird on the way by.

"What do I want, Hank?" A figure in shining black stepped out of the driver's door of the other Hotshot. "I want what the viewers want. I want what our sponsors want and what tens of thousands of fans clamor for." She walked across the ash and grit-littered concrete, hips swaying. "I want what my employer demands." She stopped outside Bobby's side window and rapped her gloved knuckles against the armorglass. Bobby hit the button lowering the window.

"You going to get to the point or talk me to death?" he asked.

"I want," She squatted down, bright green eyes staring at him from deep inside her helmet.

Her visor was up. He could pull iron now and kill her dead. He'd never have a better chance. Bobby could see Chris staring at her, at him. He let his right hand fall into his lap, a scant inch from the well-worn butt of his .45.

"A showdown. Just us and you. No support, no interference from bystanders. How did you so quaintly put it…ah yes…I want to try consequences with you and your puppy there."

"Shoot the bitch." Hal's voice crackled in their headsets.

Bobby looked at Chris. The kid's knuckles were white against the gloss black of the steering wheel. He was staring at Black Dragon, eyes wide in his pale round face. He glanced at the tactical display. There had to be over two hundred contacts on the screen. Out on the floor, those little gun carts had formed a large circle around the perimeter. The armored fronts of their machines formed an unbroken wall of durasteel. He looked back at the kid.

"No, Hal." Bobby shook his head and put his hand back on the weapons yoke. "That's not who I am." He stared straight into Chris's wide eyes a moment longer and grinned before turning back to the slinky, green-eyed menace crouched at his window. "We accept. Terms?"

"The usual." she said.

"If we win, are your pals out there going to have a go at us?" Bobby nodded toward the platform and the circle.

"Probably not." She shrugged. "Hard to tell what they'll do sometimes, but a proper duel held in the circle? They'll honor the terms."

"We have an accord." Bobby stuck his hand out the window. "Duel to the death. Winners keep the salvage, losers are on the menu."

"Deal." She gripped his hand. They sat there for a moment, two predators frozen in time, her bright green eyes locked on his pale gray ones. He grinned. She smirked, let go of his hand, spun on one heel, and raised her right fist into the air, thumb up. The arena erupted in a cacophony of shouts and honking horns.

"Is it me, or does she have even more sway in her hips?" Bobby watched her strut back to her car.

"You just agreed to a showdown with one of the deadliest autoduellists alive, and that's what you notice?" Chris asked. "Her hips!"

"Got to take time to smell the roses, kid." Bobby looked back at Chris. "Black Dragon is a lot of things, and most of them bad, but she is beautiful."

"I can still hear you." Black Dragon's voice crackled in their ears.

Chapter 34

The Pale Rider Hotshot sat in a ring of fire. The blue flames had started taller than the roof of the car. Now they were only bumper high. Chris squeezed the steering wheel, looked at Bobby, then back at the flames. The old man looked calm, bored.

How?

Butterflies danced in his stomach. Cold sweat ran down his neck. How was Bobby so calm? When those flames guttered out, he was going to have to out-drive Black Dragon.

How did he get into such a mess? He'd watched or read everything there was about Black Dragon and Headsman. Until that challenge at South Hill, they had been undefeated in the arena, and they held the record in bounties for the number of fugitives tracked down and reward money collected. Getting to roll with them from Richmond to Birmingham had been a dream come true. On the road fighting cannibals and bandits, racing across the inbetween, he could hardly contain himself that first day. They'd even offered to take him and Nate under their wing, show them the ropes. Now here he was, waiting to go heads up with them.

"Whatcha thinkin'?" Bobby's calm voice broke his reverie.

"What?" Chris looked at the old man.

"What's going on in your head right now?"

"Just trying to figure out how I got here." he said.

"Same as me. One damned thing after another."

"This was going to be our big break," Chris shook his head. "We were rolling with Black Sunshine."

"Those guys have always been assholes," Bobby said.

"We didn't know." Chris stared at the flames out his side window. They were down to about a foot and a half now. "None of the biographies, movies, comics, news, net shows, or Clutch feeds even came close to the truth about those two. None of it."

"It's all bullshit," Bobby said. "It's all made up to keep folks entertained. Especially these days. Everyone talks about this or that brand, your brand, my brand. Black Dragon and Headsman have an image they work real hard to maintain. It all goes back to rule one. You got to spend that much time and money telling the world you *are* something, then you probably are *not*."

"So they aren't as good as the hype says they are?"

"I didn't say that." Bobby shook his head. "Make no mistake, those two are stone-faced killers. They are probably the best crew to ever sit their asses in dueling seats."

"Better than you?"

"Probably." Bobby nodded.

"Great."

"That don't mean I ain't gonna kill the both of them for what they did."

"How?" Chris stared at the dying flames. They were less than half a foot. Any minute now.

"Don't come at them heads up," Bobby said. "If they really did mount a Bluestar 105, then Headsman will blow our lights out in a head-to-head pass."

"No head-to-head pass." Chris nodded. "What else?"

"Don't give them a clean shot at our sides. Hotshots have paper sides."

"Right. No head-to-head, don't let them get a clean shot at the doors. So basically, don't let them get a good shot at us at all." This was beginning to feel hopeless. They were outmatched and outgunned. Bobby was admitting it.

"Pretty much." The old man shrugged.

"Won't they be doing the same?"

"Yep." Bobby nodded.

"So we're screwed." Chris let his head rest against the seat-back.

"Maybe not. They brought in Sandy Decker. She's known for big firepower and thick armor in small packages. Hotshots didn't roll off the factory floor with as much horsepower as they really should have. Adding heavy weapons and more armor is going to slow them down. Now Sandy has a trick or two to bump up the powerplant's performance, but I doubt even she could do a full powerplant swap in three hours."

"So we'll have a speed advantage?" The flames were guttering now. Nearly gone out. Chris picked his line around the platform of wrecked machines in the center of the arena.

"Well, speed and this." Bobby patted the duffel bag between his feet.

"What's in there?" The last of the flames flickered and died. Chris accelerated out of the charred circle aiming just a little left of the platform's corner.

"A surprise."

"She's on our tail, Chris!" Bobby watched Black Sunshine's Hotshot fishtail out of a drift from behind the central platform and accelerate in their direction. Red blossoms flashed from the left and right fenders where the headlights used to be. Steel-cored lead beat a lethal tattoo across their rear armor.

"I hadn't noticed." The big man pushed the accelerator to the floor. The Pale Rider Hotshot accelerated smooth as silk, easily opening the distance.

Bobby was partially right about the modifications that Sandy Decker had been able to make in the allotted three hours. She did manage to shoehorn a Bluestar 105 in Black Sunshine's ride. She'd also managed to boost the horsepower enough to compensate for the increased weight of the big gun and some upgraded armor. The Ironsight display showed the Black Sunshine car gaining on them.

"We're in it now, kid." Bobby checked the rearview mirror. His side mirror had been sheared off by a close miss with that damned 105mm gun. Chris had gotten him a couple clear shots at both sides of the other car. Their .50 caliber machine guns hadn't even come close to penetrating the driver or gunner doors. They had punched a couple of holes in the right quarter panel.

"If we stay out in the open, they'll eventually get us. We need to break contact and set up an ambush. Think you can pull off a 'Crazy Ivan'?"

"Didn't you say not to go head to head with Black Dragon?" Chris looked at Bobby then back to the arena ahead of them.

"Yeah." Bobby checked the mine dropper count. They still had a couple left from the run into the Pyramid. "We can't stay out of reach forever. Eventually, they'll get lucky, or we'll make a mistake, and it'll be all over. We need to be unpredictable."

"How is going heads up," Chris juked left. The muzzle of Black Sunshine's big gun flashed, and a 105mm projectile blasted a smoking hole in the circle of Pyramid denizens. "Going to help with that?"

"We need to break contact." Bobby selected fire mines and waited with his thumb over the button. Chris powered into a drifting turn near the north end of the circle.

Black Sunshine, anticipating which way Chris would break, cut inside their turn, raking the side of their Hotshot with heavy machine gun fire. The steel-cored rounds stitched a line of holes in Bobby's door, missing him by scant inches, blasting the tactical display and half the dash to smoking splinters.

"Holy shit!" Chris floored the accelerator pulling away from the murderous fire. "You okay?"

Bobby did a quick check, "I'm good. No more holes than what I started with." He looked at the ruins of the dash. Blue-white smoke rose from somewhere deep inside. He was still holding part of the weapons control. It was no longer connected to the Hotshot. "Ironsight's trash, so is the weapons yoke."

"Now what?" Chris steered for the corner of the scrap ziggurat.

"Now we kill them." Bobby dropped the remains of the weapons yoke and pulled open the bag at his feet.

Sweeping aside the spare magazines, he pulled out a black satchel. It was fat and heavy. The burned metal and hot powdered-sugar odor of fresh solder and GMX-45 explosive wafted up. He peeled open the Velcro closure at one end, exposing a small control pad. Hal certainly knew his business when it came to crafting explosive devices. This one felt like there were at least ten pounds of GMX-45 backed by a thick durasteel plate to direct the blast.

"We can't shoot back." Chris cut the turn at the corner of the massive scrap platform, nearly clipping his mirror. Heavy machine gun fire cracked and spanged across the rear of the Hotshot before the corner of the ziggurat hid them from Headsman's fire.

"Sure we can." Bobby flipped the switch on the satchel charge to on, pocketed the detonator, and pulled the carbine from its keeper. "Keep close to the platform. When you clear the next corner, we're gonna pull a Josie Special."

"What?" Chris looked at Bobby, then back out through cracked armorglass.

"Something Kat and I cooked up a long time ago. You clear that corner and start cutting doughnuts."

"Why?"

"I'm getting out, and I need some concealment." Bobby checked the load on the carbine.

"You're insane."

"Weapons yoke's busted." He released the racing harness and slipped the carbine sling over his head. "You want to die running from these pricks or fighting them?"

"So doughnuts?"

"Yeah, big and slow. Lots of smoke from the tires. Don't blow 'em out. Just roast the hell out of them."

"You got it." Chris nodded. He looked over at Bobby and grinned. "Hope this works."

"If it don't, we're going to be the main course at Black Dragon and Headsman's celebration feast."

"That's comforting." Chris shook his head.

Black Sunshine's Hotshot slid into view behind them. The heavier car took a little bit longer to recover forward momentum from the slide. Fire blossomed from heavy machine guns. Steel-cored rounds blasted sparks from the concrete and the scrap platform behind the Pale Riders. He powered into another drifting turn, keeping close to the burned and twisted metal of the platform.

"Next turn good for you?"

"Good enough." Bobby gripped the door handle.

He checked the rearview. The kid was no Kat or Mae, but he knew his way around the steering wheel. Even with a gimp arm he was holding his own against Black Dragon. Black Sunshine's Hotshot slid around the turn, still taking a half a second longer than Chris to recover from the skid. It was a testament to Black Dragon's driving that she could keep them in sight at all, given the clear disparity in weight. There was a big muzzle flash. The anti-tank round blasted another hole in the platform, showering the Pale Rider Hotshot with slag and shrapnel. Headsman was getting closer and closer. Next turn or the one after, he was going to land a solid hit.

Bobby shifted his attention to the front. Chris was already powering into the drift that would let them clear the next corner. He watched the bullet-riddled scrap zip past, their entire car sliding now. Chris flicked the steering wheel left, controlling the drift, then snapped it straight and accelerated. Bobby waited for his moment. The timing had to be just right. If he stepped out too soon and the Hotshot still carried too much angular motion, he would tumble. Or he would step out with no concealing smoke, and Headsman would shoot him to rags. Wait too long, and Headsman would damned sure put one of those 105mm rounds through the door, blasting Chris and him to mush.

Bobby looked at Chris. The kid was fully in the zone. Hands loose on the wheel, confident and calm, he eased the Hotshot into a slide, breaking traction before giving it full acceleration. The wheels began to spin, and the Pale Rider Hotshot's rear end came around bleeding speed in a wide circle, a thin cloud of smoke forming around them.

"That's it, Chris. Burn 'em up!" Bobby pulled on the door handle, taking up all of the slack in the mechanism. "When I step out, you take off in a nice straight line."

"Got it." Chris pushed the accelerator closer to the floor.

Bobby checked their rear. Black Sunshine's Hotshot slid into view. Fire blossomed once more from the hood-mounted machine guns. Chris had the rear wheels spinning freely now, smoke rolled up from them in a thick, noxious cloud. All forward momentum gone, the Pale Riders' Hotshot pivoted in near-perfect circles.

"This is my stop." Bobby pulled the door handle and stepped out into the howling, smoke-filled chaos. Pain, hot and throbbing from the gunshot wound in his side, threatened to steal his breath. The knee stiff from sitting and weak from abuse collapsed.

He shrugged and waited. No sense in trying to run. They were coming to him. Out here, without the soundproofing of the Hotshot, the chatter of heavy machine gun fire, and the squalling howl of tires burning rubber was deafening.

Black Sunshine's Hotshot flashed toward them on silent wheels, pouring a steady stream of amor-piercing rounds into the smoke. Chris powered through another doughnut and rocketed away. Black Dragon steered her car into line behind Chris. Bobby armed the satchel charge and whipped it, sidearm, out into the path of the speeding car and hunkered down.

The Bluestar 105's boom and the crack of the shaped charge detonating came so close together Bobby couldn't tell which one happened first. Fire blossomed beneath the front of Black Sunshine's Hotshot, sending it into a rolling tumble. The explosion must have been first because the anti-tank round detonated high up against the thick armorglass of the Pyramid. Bobby forced the traitor knee to hold and stood. He limped toward Black Sunshine's Hotshot, rifle ready. The car had come to rest right side up, the interior masked by swirling smoke. Bobby approached the driver's door, trying to see into the wrecked machine.

Peering through the driver's window, he saw Black Dragon. A fragment of the dash or maybe the floorboard protruded from between her helmet and the top of her armored jacket. Bobby limped around the rear of Black Sunshine's car to the gunner's door. Headsman was still alive. The lanky gunner pawed ineffectually at his harness release.

Bobby tried the door handle on a whim. By some miracle of design, it worked. Though it did require a bit of yanking to open. Probably the force of the explosion or the rollover had tweaked the frame. Chris had returned by the time he'd peeled Headsman's door open.

Bobby squatted down where he could look at Headsman. The lanky man had given up on releasing his harness or pulling his gun. Instead, he fumbled for his helmet's chinstrap with broken fingers. Bobby reached in, unsnapped the strap on the pistol, and tossed it onto the ground behind him before unstrapping and removing Headsman's helmet. He could see now why the gunner couldn't release the harness. He was pinned in place by a hydraulic strut for the Bluestar 105. The other end somewhere in the dash.

"He dead?" Chris's feet crunched on the grit of the arena floor.

"Not yet, pup." Headsman coughed, spraying carmine droplets into the air. "Soon enough though."

"What about her?"

"She's dead." Bobby looked back over his shoulder at Chris. The big man wasn't looking at him or the remains of Black Sunshine. He had his pistol up and was turning in a slow circle like he was trying to cover the entire arena. Bobby looked past Chris. A crowd was forming. They kept a ways back, but no one there seemed much impressed by the big gunner or his weapon.

"Relax, pup." Headsman chuckled. "It's just the tribe come to take their due. Looks like Dragon and I are the guests of honor in a little while."

"Lower your gun. If they wanted us dead, we'd be cooling on a hook by now." Bobby turned back to Headsman. "Someone paid you to hit us in Tupelo."

"That didn't sound like a question." Headsman let his head lean back against the seat.

"It's pretty plain you and Dragon got paid to take a run at us." Bobby reached into his coat, pulled out a flask, unscrewed the cap, and handed it to the stricken gunner. "Who?"

"Client name is confidential—but they have pockets deep enough to afford us and that team of heroes you— put down—" Headsman coughed again and spat blood into the floor. "Pockets deep enough to outfit them in Omega 68s."

"That a fact?" Bobby took the flask back and drank before passing it back to Headsman. The burn of the liquor in his stomach did little to drive off the chill racing up his spine. He'd said, heroes. Those hitters had all been clean-cut and clean-shaven. They'd all had that fresh out-of-the-army look or the look of big-time corporate security. That had to mean the main sponsor had paid good money to take him, Mae, and Chris out of the picture.

"It is." Headsman took a long pull on the flask before handing it back. "Best get on with it."

"Reckon so." Bobby screwed the cap back on the flask and put it back in the inner pocket of his coat. He retrieved Headsman's pistol from where he'd tossed it and checked the weapon. The load status lights on the grip were green. "Looks like you're all set. I don't much care for these needlers, though. No stopping power." He put the weapon in Headsman's lap before standing and taking a couple steps back.

"For what—for what it's worth," Headsman coughed and looked over at Bobby. "I really liked that driver of yours. She had sand." He reached for the needler.

Headsman was still greasy fast, even with a gun support through his guts. Not fast enough.

Chapter 35

"Coffee," Bobby looked up at the waitress, "black, three eggs over easy, two slices of green algae toast."

"Sure thing, honey." Her pen scratched out his order on the pale green pad. The thick-set woman turned to Chris and smiled. "How about you, sugar?"

"Coffee." Chris stared at Bobby over the laminated menu. The brown squirrel of the Memphis Big Bill's Dine and Dash grinned at him like some mad messenger. "Four eggs and the country-fried algae steak. With the gravy."

"You got it." She collected the menus in hands the size of dinner plates and headed for the kitchen window, a little more swing in her hips than when she arrived if Bobby was any judge.

"Seems Darleen there has taken a shine to you." Bobby chuckled. "Too bad we got to get on the road. You might have had yourself a right good time."

"Shut it." Chris stared down at the faux wood grain of the tabletop.

"Sure thing." Bobby leaned back, giving Darleen space to deposit two steaming cups of coffee, two glasses of ice water, and a small bowl full of half-and-half pods.

"Y'all need anything else?" She stared at Chris for a long moment.

Perhaps the big man felt her gaze boring into the back of his head, or maybe the silence. Either way, he looked up. "N—no thank you, ma'am."

"I knew it." Darleen turned to Bobby. "You're Bobby Hank, and that makes this Chris McHenry. I saw the whole thing live last night, or well, early this morning, actually. We all sat right over there and watched it. The whole truck stop shut down! What a fight."

"Well—" Chris stammered.

"You really can drive." She pulled her order pad back out of the dark brown apron with its cheeky squirrel logo on the pocket and slid it onto the table. "Would you mind signing my pad?"

"Well, sure." Bobby reached for the pad.

"Not you, honey." She pushed the pad in front of Chris. "I want his autograph. Anyone who can out-drive Black Dragon? They gonna be famous."

"Looks like rule one is still alive and well." Bobby sat back and watched his red-faced driver sign Darleen's pad.

Once she'd put the pad back in her apron pocket and strutted off to the counter to check on their food, Chris looked across the table. "Now what?"

"Now?" Bobby looked back. "We get Mae's backup to Arlo and run the next leg of this race. Hal called while you were sleeping. He and Ray made a mint bettin' on us last night. They already picked up a proper support rig. A rolling shop in a big rig."

"So we're still doing this?"

"Bet your ass we are." Bobby took a drink of coffee. "Someone went to a lot of trouble and expense to stop us, so they ain't gonna stop just because we quit. At least out there on the road, we can fight back, figure out what the hell is really going on."

"What is going on?"

"I don't rightly know yet." Bobby shook his head. "But I'm gonna find out. When I do, someone will have to answer for an awful lot."

We hope that you enjoyed this title and look forward to many more to come in the Car Warriors: Autoduel Chronicles. Please, leave us a review! Reviews matter to all of our authors.

And don't forget to check out the latest edition of **Car Wars**

http://www.sjgames.com/car-wars/

Or the other amazing titles from
Steve Jackson Games

http://www.sjgames.com

Take a look at some of our other award-winning series at https://threeravenspublishing.com/series-universes/

Visit us at https://www.threeravenspublishing.com and sign up for our newsletter for the latest and greatest news on upcoming titles and events.

Other series and titles you might enjoy.

DECLAN FINN
DECLAN FINN
DECLAN FINN
DECLAN FINN
Demons are Forever
LOVE AT FIRST BITE TWO
Honor at STAKE
LOVE AT FIRST BITE ONE
Live & Let Bite
LOVE AT FIRST BITE THREE
Good to the Last Drop
LOVE AT FIRST BITE FOUR
The Dragon Award Nominated Series
FREE on Kindle Unlimited!

AVAILABLE ON
AMAZON
JOINT TASK FORCE
13
HOLDING THE LINE
BETWEEN HEAVEN AND HELL
13

MYSTERY,
MAGIC &
MAYHEM
WITH A TWIST
OF ROMANCE
J.F. POSTHUMUS
ON AMAZON
FIND ME
B.E.N.T.
BIOLOGIC
ENHANCED
NASCENT
TALENT

THE RAVEN
AND
THE CROW
MICHAEL K. FALCIANI
FIND ME
ON AMAZON

STARFLIGHT

IT CAME FROM THE
TRAILER PARK

3R
Three Ravens
Publishing
Are you looking for fun, new fiction?
The Written Word Will Never Be The Same…
https://www.threeravenspublishing.com
Veteran Owned and Operated

You can also keep up to date with our latest release announcements on <u>Scifi.radio</u> and get some of the best fandom programing on the planet.

Scifi for your Wifi

Spare Parts Emporium
and Towing
Henry's
Garage
EST.
For all of your Rare
& Spare Parts Needs

SILLY LADY
PEPPER
COMPANY

FELLHAVEN
Restaurant & Tavern

www.ingramcontent.com/pod-product-compliance
Lightning Source LLC
Chambersburg PA
CBHW060732190726
48285CB00001B/168